CAPTURING YOU

WRIGHT HEROES OF MAINE
BOOK 6

ROBIN PATCHEN

Copyright © 2025 by Robin Patchen

All rights reserved.

No part of this book may be reproduced in any form or by any electronic or mechanical means, including information storage and retrieval systems, without written permission from the author, except for the use of brief quotations in a book review.

Published in Austin, TX.

Cover by Lynnette Bonner

Paperback ISBN: 978-1-950029-59-4

Large Print ISBN: 978-1-950029-60-0

Hard Cover ISBN: 978-1-950029-61-7

Library of Congress Control Number: 2025908783

CHAPTER ONE

She was finally going to get the perfect shot.

In the gray light of pre-dawn, Brooklynn Wright shifted on the jagged rocks, scraping her belly through her thin shirt. At least it was low tide. Otherwise, she'd not just be cold, but wet.

She snapped a few photos with her Nikon, adjusted the small tripod, and snapped a few more.

Excitement bubbled inside her. Just four minutes until sunrise.

She could see it in her mind's eye. The rising sun shining through a wave as it crested and rolled. Behind it, the gleaming rocky headland north of the small bay that gave Shadow Cove its name.

Catching the wave and the sunlight at the perfect moment. That was the challenge. So much depended on her success. Her gallery, her very livelihood.

One more minute till sunrise.

She snapped photos as the eastern sky turned from midnight blue to indigo. Clouds she hadn't seen in the darkness added richness to the view as light shone around them in deep red and coral and orange.

Finally, finally, the sun clawed back darkness with its perfect radiance.

Birds quieted as if to mark the moment. Even the ever-present breeze seemed to still.

Beautiful.

Brooklynn snapped, snapped. Catching waves and sunlight. Sunlight and waves.

But sunlight *through* waves? She didn't know, didn't stop to absorb what she'd captured. Just kept snapping.

A low hum rumbled beneath the sound of the incoming tide. A boat engine. She prayed it wouldn't ruin her shot. She had a minute, maybe less, to get this.

Her father thought she was flighty, and...whatever. It didn't matter. But he didn't know this part of her. None of her family understood the single-minded focus it took to catch nature's fleeting moments of beauty.

If this photograph came out the way she thought it would, if it won the prestigious Arthur Whitmore award, her sisters would congratulate her, her mother would sing her praises. And her father would pat her on the head—metaphorically, if not physically—like a cute little puppy.

Or maybe, just this once, he'd be proud of her.

The engine was getting closer.

Ignore it. Focus.

Snap, snap, snap.

Too soon, the sun was above the horizon, bathing Brooklynn and the Maine coastline in its warm light. She removed her camera from the tripod and flipped through the photos.

Decent. Good. Maybe great, but...

She gasped. Enlarged the tiny image.

Sunlight streamed through a cresting wave. No ugly

seaweed inside, just clear blue. Behind it, the indescribable beauty of a new day. To one side, a seagull diving for breakfast. To the other, the rocky shoreline.

She'd done it. She'd finally gotten a photograph that could final for the most prestigious photography award in northern New England.

Just that would put her little gallery on the map. And if she won the cash prize...

She could survive past the tourist season—and prove that she *could* make a living doing what she loved.

Prove to her father that she mattered.

A shout carried on the breeze, the words lost in the roar of the surf.

Who in the world...?

Brooklynn stood, brushed sand off her jeans, and shoved her camera and tripod into her small leather backpack.

The boat had come from the north, but it hadn't moved into view. Where had it gone?

If Brooklynn were smart, she'd hightail it out of there before she got caught trespassing.

But curiosity had her climbing to the top of the rocky cliff. She slipped between the few trees separating this edge of the outcropping from the other and peered inland down the narrow waterway and through the trees to an old, dilapidated dock.

Sure enough, a fishing boat bumped against the rotting wood. Two men carried a box onto the dock. By the way they strained, the box was heavy. They set it on a dolly, and someone else pushed it toward an army-green Polaris just inside the tree line.

A fourth man was returning with an empty dolly.

Meanwhile, a fifth watched the operation from the edge of a small beach.

Maybe the new owners of the Victorian mansion built on

the hill above the cove were having something delivered? Though...why on a boat? The house had a driveway. Also, the path where the Polaris was parked led not toward the house but away from it, through the thick woods to who-knew-where.

She took out her camera and zoomed in on the men, the boat, the vehicle, and the boxes. Snapping photographs for no good reason except... Well, she was a photographer. It was what she did.

A weird acidy feeling filled her stomach, but she ignored the distraction. Something was wrong, something...

"Hey!"

The man's shout was too close.

The ones moving boxes turned toward her.

Shoving her camera into her bag, she scanned the beach below the headland where she stood.

A figure was climbing, barely more than a shadow.

A quick glance back at the dock...

The men were running toward the headland. Toward *her*.

She had no idea what was happening, but...

Run!

She scrambled across the top of the headland and started making her way down the other side, angling toward the rocky beach, toward the path to the road where she'd left her Bronco.

A man shouted behind her.

"Cut her off. Close her in."

"Don't let her get away."

Where could she go? On one side, the cold sea.

On the other, men determined to...what? Capture her? Harm her?

Kill her?

She couldn't risk the road.

If she could make it around the headland on the northern edge of Shadow Cove, maybe she could flag someone down.

There'd be people in town. There were always people walking the beach.

But that would mean running across jagged rocks. She'd be exposed. They'd see her.

They'd catch her.

Their voices were growing louder. Behind her. In front of her. Above her.

She stopped halfway to the bottom and pressed against the rocky cliff wall. Could she hide here? For now, but the sunlight was creeping toward her. She'd be exposed any second.

She was trapped.

A hand gripped her arm and yanked her back into darkness.

She gasped, fear clogging her throat.

The man—it had to be a man—held her around her middle, her back to his front. He curled around her body, imprisoning her.

He covered her mouth, not that she could scream past the fear.

He was speaking, low, insistent. She couldn't decipher his words over the chaos of her terror.

She fought to escape, but he was strong, so much stronger.

"Stop struggling." His whisper was vehement.

Those words registered.

"They'll hear you. Stop."

They. Who were *they*? Who was *he*?

"Trust me, please." His words were barely audible.

She stilled. Fighting was useless. *Think.*

"These rocks are like a megaphone." The warning came out in a soothing cadence, no doubt intended to calm her. "If you make noise, they'll hear you. If we're quiet, they'll go away."

She had no idea where she was. Somehow, she'd been transported from the cliff to this...darkness.

She shouldn't trust the stranger who'd grabbed her, but if not for him, she'd have been caught.

"I'm trying to help you." His words were even, unhurried. "Trust me. Please."

Trust him?

She couldn't even see him.

But now that her eyes had adjusted to the darkness, she made out rugged stone walls, a low ceiling.

The man was backed against the wall, his body pressed against hers. In the smallness of the space, she understood why.

"You're not going to yell?" he asked.

She shook her head.

His hand lifted from her mouth.

"Who are—?"

"Sh. Sh. They're close."

How did he...?

"I swear, she was right here."

Brooklynn startled at the voice, which sounded only inches away.

Her captor pressed his fingers to her lips again, the hold surprisingly gentle, a reminder more than a demand to keep quiet.

"She's gotta be here," another man said, then shouted, "Anything?"

From farther away, "She's gone."

A curse.

"Don't just stand there. Find her."

Rocks skittered nearby. Then silence.

It stretched for seconds, minutes.

Brooklynn should've been overwhelmed with terror. When she'd run for her life, she'd never been so terrified. But here, in the darkness with this stranger, she felt secure.

Protected.

Which made no sense at all.

"Are you okay?" The man's whisper warmed her ear, his breath brushing the hair at her nape and sending goosebumps across her flesh.

Was she? Aside from the psychotic break evidenced in her strange attraction to a man whose face she hadn't seen?

Maybe she'd gone crazy. Maybe she'd dreamed the whole thing.

Was she still in her warm bed, conjuring all of this in her imagination? She'd always been the most creative of the Wright sisters.

At this point, that option seemed entirely plausible.

But the arms around her weren't blankets and sheets. The man's warm breath wasn't heat from a furnace.

If it was a dream, this was the most vivid she'd ever had.

"I'm gonna move my hand," her dream-savior said. "Don't scream. I can get us out of here, but if you make any noise, you'll get us both killed."

"Killed?" He'd spoken her fear as if he had no doubt. "Who were those—?"

"Not now. Keep your head down. The ceiling is low." He placed his hands on her hips and moved her gently away, then slipped in front of her. "Stay right behind me. Grab my shirt if you need to."

Why could he talk but she couldn't?

A question she wouldn't ask right now, considering that he obviously knew what he was doing. Of course, he might be leading her to a different kind of captivity. Or death.

Lord, protect me.

Because she couldn't fight more than one bad guy at a time.

She hoped and prayed this was a good guy as she gripped the back of the stranger's T-shirt and followed him into the darkness.

CHAPTER TWO

He'd been so close.

Forbes Ballentine led the intruder through the cave that had been hidden from strangers for generations. As soon as he'd seen the boat motoring into the private inlet, he'd set out to witness the goings-on in person. The video feed from cameras he'd had installed all around the mansion never gave him enough information.

Forbes needed to know exactly who they were and what they were doing—and how it related to the murders of his parents and his sister.

All of which he might have discovered if not for the woman who'd ruined his plans.

He'd assumed the trespassers were dangerous, as dangerous as the smugglers almost a quarter century before had been. This morning, the way they'd chased this stranger after she'd witnessed their activities confirmed his fears.

The first round of smugglers had been ruthless. He guessed this latest round was no less so. If he hadn't been there, they'd probably have killed her.

One more senseless murder he could've prevented.

At least this time, he'd acted, even though in the acting, he'd ducked right back into hiding.

Having this stranger in his arms had done something wonky to his brain. Or, more to the point, his body. She curved in all the right places, smelling of salty air and coconut shampoo and...

And that line of thinking needed to stop. Now.

Regardless how perfect she'd felt against him, she'd ruined what would probably be his best opportunity to find the people who'd murdered his family.

Nothing else mattered.

Nothing else would *ever* matter.

The tiny sliver of light that'd cut through the darkness at the mouth of the cave was long gone. The space, narrow enough that his shoulders bumped the walls on both sides, was darker than the darkest night, with no stars or moon to lead the way. It'd been chilly outside. In here, it was cool, but in a different way, as if the coldness had settled in millennia past and no warmth would ever reach it.

To Forbes, everything about it felt familiar. It was amazing how much he remembered, considering the years since he'd been here last. He didn't need light to know where he was going. He bent to keep from bashing his head on the low ceiling and felt his way forward.

Maybe it would've been kinder to illuminate the path for his frightened trespasser, but he wasn't feeling particularly kind at the moment.

"Ouch." She stumbled, bumping into his backside.

"Quiet." He winced at his own demanding tone.

"I'm fine." She matched his vehement whisper with one of her own. "Thanks for asking."

He felt his lips tick up at the corners, an odd sensation. When was the last time he'd smiled?

They reached the end of the natural cave lined with rough

walls that elbowed out to jab and scrape unsuspecting victims and moved into the passageway that had smoother walls and a higher ceiling. This extension of the sea-carved cave was man-made.

Forbes had once believed it'd been carved out for him and Rosie. When he was young and innocent and thought the world was a beautiful place filled with adventure, this cave had been the scene of countless games of hide-and-seek and treasure hunts and pirates.

He was wiser now.

He'd learned that danger lurked beneath the surface of the most beautiful spots.

Ahead of him, black turned to variations of dark and shadow.

He turned a corner, bent low, and climbed the last ten yards or so toward the light, finally emerging into the dove-gray morning.

The sun had been up for approximately fifteen minutes, and his day was already ruined, thanks to the woman who climbed out behind him, brushing dust from her skinny jeans and her bright yellow oversized top, which had big, white flowers on it. The woman dressed like summertime. She took special care brushing sand from the bag she'd gripped throughout her attempted escape as if it held the royal jewels. She turned back to study the cave's entrance, a nearly hidden crack between boulders that nobody would ever suspect hid just one of many secrets on this property.

It'd still been dark when he'd watched her running for her life, no more than a silhouette against the rising sun.

When she turned back toward him now, her image far outshone the one he'd conjured in his head to match the tall, shapely body. He'd noticed her cheerful top—it was impossible to miss. He studied her dark brown hair, which hung from a braid draped over one shoulder. Escaped tendrils curled around high cheekbones and eyes the color of the morning sky.

The morning sky?

He was channeling his prep school British Lit professor, who could wax philosophical about cafeteria lunches.

"You good?" he asked.

She was staring through the trees at the house.

When he was a kid, the old three-story Victorian hadn't been special. It'd simply been home.

After so many years away, he saw it with fresh eyes. Light-colored brick, steep roof with rounded shingles and gingerbread trim. Hexagonal turrets, eleven chimneys—fireplaces in every room, though most not functional now—and more gables than he'd ever bothered to count.

It was beautiful—if one could look past the peeling paint and sagging porches.

"It's like we're in another world." The woman's words were breathy with awe.

"A world five hundred feet from the one we just left. Come on."

He wouldn't hate it if she didn't follow. The last thing he needed was to get distracted.

But he was afraid those men were still looking for her.

The gravity of the situation was dawning on him, and the truth was much darker than the sun brightening the summer day.

"Stay low and move fast." He stepped out from between the trees, ducked to ensure he wouldn't be spotted from the shore below, and bolted to the nearest side of the house. He tapped the code to unlock the door, pulled it open, then stood aside to let her enter first.

She looked at Forbes, then at the steep staircase leading down into darkness almost as thick as the cave's. Licked her lips, which brought a reaction he was trying very hard to ignore. "Maybe I'll just...uh..." She backed away as if he might be a threat.

He could let her fend for herself.

But now she knew about the cave. She knew Forbes was here.

He needed to figure out how to get her not to tell the whole town what she knew.

"Look, I'm not going to hurt you," he said. "If I wanted to hurt you, I'd have done it already."

She blinked big, terrified eyes, taking another step back.

"You can trust me." He stuck out his hand. "I'm Ford. Ford Baker." Ironic, asking for her trust as he gave her his alias. But he'd used it most of his life, even if he'd never forgotten who he really was. "What's your name?"

"Brooklynn Wright." Reluctantly, she shook his hand.

"What were you doing out there?" He jutted his chin toward the ocean.

She hugged her backpack to her chest. "I'm a photographer."

As if that answered the question.

"I bet those guys are still looking for you."

She darted a glance toward the woods, then in the direction of the driveway before meeting his eyes. "What were you doing there?"

"Taking a walk."

She squinted. "I'd have seen you. You were in the cave. How did you know I was there? How did you know about the cave? Why would you—?"

"Are you coming or not?" He didn't owe her explanations, and he wasn't going to force her into his house. But he had a job to do, and she could ruin everything. "If you want to risk those guys catching you, go ahead, but I'd rather keep my presence here secret. So if you decide to leave and somehow manage to survive, keep the cave—and my presence—to yourself."

"Why?"

He blew out a long breath and crossed his arms, giving the door a pointed look.

He didn't miss the fear in her expression.

"I use this door because it's close." And hidden from the driveway and from the shore, but he didn't say that. No need to arouse more suspicion.

Forget that he'd just saved her life. Forget that she'd likely be dead if not for him. Apparently, that wasn't enough to garner her trust.

"If you'd rather"—he kept his tone even despite his annoyance—"I can go in and open the front door for you. But then you'd be out here alone, and if anybody happened by..." He shrugged, letting the implication hang between them. "You decide."

CHAPTER THREE

Brooklynn had never understood the expression about people's hearts being in their throats, until now.

Hers was trying to thump right out of her body.

The comfort she'd felt in this man's arms was long gone, chased away by the cold reality of a pitch-black cave.

And a man who looked like he was sorry he'd wasted his time on her.

If this guy was a madman who'd lured her here to chain her up in his basement, then refusing to climb down those scary steps would only turn his suggestion into a demand.

But really, what were the chances?

Nobody had known she'd be in the cove on this property at dawn. She'd only just had the idea the evening before.

She'd witnessed something she still didn't understand—a bunch of smugglers, she assumed, who also happened to be there at the same time as her.

A strange coincidence.

Being rescued by a lock-women-in-the-basement killer, who happened to be right where she needed him and knew about a secret cave?

That felt like one coincidence too many.

He probably wasn't a murderer.

And the people who'd chased her were still out there.

It wasn't as if she had a whole bunch of choices.

Sometimes, she wished she had Alyssa's analytical mind. Brooklynn's thoughts were taking her in circles.

Ford—were madmen ever named *Ford?*—raised his eyebrows.

"It's fine." Her voice was high and squeaky. She swallowed and tried again. "Lead the way."

He stepped through the door and pulled a string that hung from an overhead light fixture.

The bare bulb was blinding, and she paused until her eyes adjusted, then followed him down six steps into a basement.

Concrete floors and walls, bare rafters overhead with ducts and pipes snaking through them. A washer and dryer against one wall beneath a rough shelf that held detergent and fabric softener. That explained the scent of laundry.

Old furniture and stacks of boxes. Tools and discarded household items, including an old Westinghouse roaster that looked like it dated back to the fifties.

A wicker couch and love seat with floral cushions that belonged in the sunshine—in 1987.

A slightly newer-looking wrought iron café table and chairs.

No chains bolted to the walls. No handcuffs lying about. Even so, she trembled with terror.

The man crossed to the base of a wooden staircase with a rusty metal railing. "Go on up. The door at the top is unlocked."

She tried to move slowly, but fear fed fresh adrenaline into her veins, and she ran, practically hurtling to the top.

She burst through the door.

She was in a dark hallway with doors on either end. One was closed, the other open halfway, letting in enough light to give her hope. She hurried that way, pushed open the surprisingly heavy door, and stepped into a living area.

Straight ahead, windows showcased a view that had her halting. "Oh."

The sun glimmered on the Atlantic far below, which reflected a powder-blue sky. The cove that could've been her grave was bathed in golden light. The trees on the headland that jutted between here and town waved in the sea breeze, the pines on it nearly as high as the house where she stood.

In the cave, she'd known they were moving upward, and of course she'd seen this Victorian on the cliff, but it seemed higher from above.

"Coffee?"

She startled and spun, taking in the man who'd stopped behind her.

One corner of his mouth quirked as if it wanted to smile, but his eyes weren't on board. "Not sure how you forgot I was here in the one-point-six seconds it took you to bolt up the stairs."

Outside, he'd seemed like some combination of superhero and supervillain. In here, he looked like a nice, normal man. Well, a very handsome man.

And calling him *nice* was giving him too much credit.

He was over six feet. Broad shoulders, muscular arms that filled out his T-shirt perfectly. Strong jaw on a square face softened by a trimmed red beard that matched his short hair.

Her best friend in elementary school had been a little boy with red hair. Unlike Ford, her old friend hadn't even been cute by seven-year-old standards, but she'd always had a soft spot for redheads.

She'd never met one who looked like this.

Never mind the smirk he didn't bother to hide.

Now that she was inside, now that she was pretty sure Ford

wasn't a killer, she relaxed, inhaling a deep coffee-scented breath. "Do you have tea?"

After a curt nod, he closed the door they'd come through, and it disappeared into a dark paneled wall. If she hadn't known it was there, she'd have never found it.

Ford walked past her, going through an opening on the left, while she shifted to take in the interior of the house she'd always thought was the most beautiful structure in Shadow Cove.

If memory served, the mansion had been built in the 1870s. It still looked stately from afar, but from Dad's boat she'd taken photos with her zoom lens and seen the signs of wear and neglect.

Those signs were less obvious inside, at least in this room.

Tall windows framed with thick, ornate trim made up the ocean-facing wall. The other walls were wood-paneled. Not cheap laminate paneling, but rich dark wood, polished to a golden shine. The ceiling was crisscrossed by matching beams.

Pastel floral fabric covered the sofa, and a nearby chair-and-a-half and ottoman had a checkered pattern in coordinating mauves and greens. There were ornate tables with carved legs, lamps with lacy fringe, and a giant area rug over hardwood floors. Brooklynn guessed the wardrobe-style cabinet beside the oversized fireplace held one of those old, fat TV sets.

The room was clean and slightly feminine, and Brooklynn had the sense that time had stopped in the late eighties, maybe early nineties, and just restarted when she'd walked in.

"When you're finished gawking, your tea is ready."

She swiveled to find Ford leaning against the doorjamb between this room and the next, watching her, that enigmatic smirk on his face.

"Sorry. I was just..."

His eyebrows hiked.

She gestured to the room. "It's amazing."

Those brows lowered, though he seemed unsure how to respond.

"Lead the way." She followed him through an eating area tucked into one of the hexagonal turrets. It held a round glass table surrounded by six upholstered chairs. Windows boasted views of both the sea and the yard they'd run across from the cave.

It was gorgeous.

Ford had continued through another door, so she followed, entering a kitchen just as updated as the living room had been. The appliances were beige and predated her birth. The dark cabinetry had obviously been installed before the light-and-airy decor of the current decade.

Ford stood on the opposite side of an island she guessed had been added long after the house was built.

"Milk and sugar, I assume."

"No, thanks." She dropped her backpack on the counter and sipped from the mug. Earl Gray, one of her favorites. "This is perfect."

Maybe because she felt safe, everything that'd happened, and all that could have happened, suddenly turned her legs to jelly. "Mind if I...?" She didn't finish the sentence, just made her way back into the eating area and practically fell into a chair.

Two sips of the tea made her stomach churn.

Ford settled across from her, his narrowed eyes expressing what she hoped was worry or concern, though it looked a lot like irritation.

"I think it's all catching up to me."

His only acknowledgment was a low grunt.

"Do you have a cracker or something?"

He went to the kitchen and returned a moment later with a loaf of wheat bread, which he plopped on the table.

Some people possessed the gift of hospitality. Ford was *not* one of those people.

She helped herself to a slice of bread and tore off a bite. When she'd swallowed it, she asked, "Who were those guys?"

He shrugged.

She'd known her rescuer for about twenty minutes. But something in his countenance gave her the impression he wasn't being honest. "What were you doing out there?"

"What were *you* doing out there?"

"I was trying to get a shot."

"Of the people in the boat?"

"What? No. Of the sunrise."

"Thirty-five hundred miles of coastline in Maine, and you just happened to be on *this* property?"

"So did you."

"I'm supposed to be here. I wasn't the one trespassing."

"This house has been abandoned for as long as I can remember. How was I supposed to know somebody was here?"

"So it's okay to trespass as long as you don't get caught?"

This conversation was so bizarre, her body so drained from the adrenaline, the chase, the escape, the whole...everything. She couldn't help it.

She laughed.

He scowled. "You find this *funny?*"

"It's just... All of it." She gestured at the house, the windows, the ocean. "I should be home right now getting ready for work, and instead..." She giggled, sounding like a fool and not even caring. She often laughed when she was nervous or uncomfortable, and she was both right now—to the extreme. "I mean, you have to admit it's a little funny."

He didn't even crack a smile. "Taking pictures. Then what?"

"I heard a noise." Her amusement faded as she recounted

the events. Crossing the narrow headland, seeing those men on the dock. Them seeing her. "They were chasing me, and I was sure they'd catch me. And then you saved me." She held his eye contact. "Thank you."

He nodded, lips pressed closed.

A real conversationalist, this one.

The tea warmed her. She hadn't realized how cold she was until her fear and shock faded.

After another sip, she set the mug on the table, the sound too loud in the silence. "I guess I should call the police."

If anything, his scowl grew even scowlier. "No."

"What do you mean, no? Who knows what those men would've done if you hadn't rescued me?"

"I don't want anyone to know about the cave. I don't want anyone to know I'm here."

Brooklynn had heard rumors in town about someone at this property. "People have seen your truck. There's been speculation."

"So you *did* know someone was here."

"Contractors, maybe." At least that was the theory among townspeople. She hadn't paid that much attention. "I didn't know anyone was staying here."

"I want to keep it that way."

"But the police—"

"Won't do anything."

"You don't know that." She couldn't help the indignation in her tone. This outsider knew nothing about her hometown or their local police force.

A muscle in his cheek tightened. "Call them if you must, but leave me out of it."

"Why?"

"I rescued you."

"Meaning?" But she knew exactly what he meant.

She owed him.

She pushed back from the table and got to her feet. "Not that this hasn't been fun, but..."

He stood so fast that his heavy chair tipped back. He caught it before it fell. "You can't leave."

Fear spiked in her chest. "You plan to stop me?"

"No, not..." He ran a hand over his head, then gripped the back of his neck and held on. "Those guys are still out there."

She doubted they were. When they realized she'd escaped, they'd probably run. "The sooner I call the police, the better."

He opened his mouth, snapped it shut. "I'd rather you didn't tell them where you are."

"Are you a squatter or something? Do the owners know you're here?"

The smirk shifted, and for the tiniest microsecond, she thought he might smile. Wishful thinking.

"Yes. They know."

Again, she felt he wasn't telling her everything, but perhaps she didn't have the right to dig into his life.

"I'm sure they're long gone."

The man didn't talk much, but his face was a good clue as to what he was thinking. Right now, it told her he thought she was an idiot. "Based on what?"

"Based on..."

Well, based on...the fact that she wanted them to be gone. She'd escaped, so of course they would run. Wouldn't they? "I can't stay here."

He settled in his chair again, gesturing to hers. "It's safe here."

"How do you know? They'll look for me."

"If they come, I'll send them away. Worst-case scenario, they force their way inside. This house has lots of hiding places."

Fine. She was safe from her pursuers for now, but what about Ford? With that threatening scowl on his face, he looked anything but safe.

"Are you a local?" he asked.

"Are you?" she shot back.

He took a breath, blew it out. "No."

"Why are you here then? Are you a contractor?"

"I'm..." He seemed to wrestle with his answer. Or maybe he was fabricating a story. "This is between you and me." At her nod, he said, "I'm writing a book about unsolved mysteries in small towns."

She hadn't expected that.

Everyone in Shadow Cove knew the story. The family who'd lived here had been murdered. She'd heard a hundred variations of the facts and even more theories about who'd done it, but the killer had never been caught.

"You're trying to solve the mystery?"

"Just gathering facts about it and the family," he said. "But if I solve it"—he shrugged—"that would be good publicity for the book. You're obviously a local."

"Why is that obvious?"

"You didn't ask what mystery I was here to solve."

Good point.

"Have you been here long?"

"All my life."

That muscle in Ford's cheek ticked again. "I assume you know everybody in town?"

"Not everybody, but—"

"And they all know you."

"What are you getting at?"

Rather than answer, he asked, "How did you get here this morning?"

"I parked at the trailhead and took the path down to the cove."

He glanced toward the front of the house as if he could see through walls and doors and forest. The two-lane road diverged from the highway south of here, hugged the coast past this house and others, then met back up with the highway a couple of miles north. Farther south, a few other properties had been built on the seaside edge of the road, though this property had to sit on a couple of acres, putting the neighbors a good distance away.

A path led from the road between the Victorian and a neighboring property. It trailed down the rocky hill to the cove. It wasn't an easy hike, but it offered a fabulous vista. Of course, all of it was private property, but that didn't keep visitors away.

"You parked on the road?"

"In that sandy area by the trailhead."

"Tell me you drive a nice, nondescript Honda, preferably with dirt-covered plates."

"Not...exactly."

His brows lowered over angry eyes.

She might as well fess up—as if she'd done something wrong. Which she hadn't, even if the truth was inconvenient.

"I drive a Bronco."

"Of course you do. Any chance it's black?" Before she could answer, he straightened and glared at her. "It's orange, isn't it? That bright orange—"

"What's wrong with orange?"

"Aside from it being the most obvious vehicle in Shadow Cove? I mean, even *I've* noticed it."

"It's not like I've been trying to hide."

"The point is, you're not safe. If those guys were locals—"

"They aren't locals."

That smirk—Ford's resting-irritated-face—showed displeasure with a hint of condescension. It broadcast the question he didn't bother to ask.

"None of the men chasing me this morning were locals."

"You saw their faces?"

"Well, no. But the people of Shadow Cove are good, law-abiding citizens. They're not smugglers."

"You don't think bad guys can live in nice towns?"

"I'm not saying—"

"Right. Bad guys all live in bad-guy towns with names like Tombstone, or, I know. Gunpoint. Gunpoint, Wyoming. They scheme their evil schemes and then invade the sweet little Shadow Coves of the world to wreak havoc."

Those were the most words Ford had put together at one time since she'd met him. Funny that he'd managed a whole paragraph in order to make her look and feel stupid.

"Okay, then." She pushed back from the table. "That's my cue."

"Wait." He stood as well. "Sorry. I didn't mean—"

"Yes, you did." She snatched her backpack and moved toward the opening on the far side of the kitchen, which she hoped led to the front door.

"You can't just leave." Ford followed. "Where are you going?"

"To my bright orange SUV."

"They could be watching it. They probably are."

She didn't slow, not wanting his words to register. Or to be true.

"Please, stop."

She was halfway through a formal dining room—long French provincial table surrounded by ten matching chairs. The heavy drapes were pulled closed, blocking the natural light.

She turned to face him. "What?"

"You need to think this through."

"I own a business. The gallery isn't going to run itself." Of course, Jewel would be there this morning and could open it, but it was Brooklynn's responsibility.

And she was no more than a nuisance to Ford. She wasn't about to stay where she wasn't welcome.

"What gallery?"

She sighed. "A photography studio downtown."

Eyes closed, he nodded slowly. "Light and Shadows."

It shouldn't surprise her he'd name it, considering there was only one in town these days.

"I have things to do. I can't just hide here for the rest of my life."

His eyes opened. "You think well of the people who live in your town, and that's...fine. Great. I'm just saying, bad guys don't all wear black and carry sidearms."

Despite her frustration and fear, she couldn't help but smile at the image. "I don't know." She gave her words a lighthearted tone. "I thought they all had handlebar mustaches they twirled when they plotted evil."

Ford didn't smile back. She doubted he knew how.

"You need to think about your next move."

"I'll wing it." But she didn't walk away. She didn't want to admit that Ford might be right.

"Sticking your head in the sand *isn't* a plan."

Neither was staying here. Neither was doing nothing, not even calling the police, which seemed to be *his* plan.

"Your family is local?" he asked.

"Yeah." Close enough, anyway. But Dad was back in DC. For all his talk of retirement, he traveled as much as ever. Mom was in Paris overseeing the remodeling of their apartment there, and Cici and Delaney had gone with her. Alyssa had moved to Augusta a month before to be near her new boyfriend. Kenzie was in South Carolina, where she'd lived for years.

"You need to go somewhere they can't find you," Ford said. "And if everyone in town knows who owns that orange Bronco, then the people following you today could put it together, so that means—"

"I get it."

Even if her parents and sisters weren't out of town, she couldn't go to them without putting them in danger too.

But the business. The contest. Not to mention all the planning she'd poured into the Old Home Days celebration that would take place in a couple of weeks.

Brooklynn couldn't leave Shadow Cove at the height of tourism season. It was too important a time. She needed to be close.

She needed to go home.

But if she did, would the men who'd followed her this morning find her?

Ford was watching, studying her face. When she offered no solution, he said, "Make some calls, make a plan. Nobody knows this house is occupied. There're cameras set up all around the property, obvious enough that anyone can see them. If they're not afraid to risk getting caught on camera and show up at my door, I'll deal with them."

"I don't want to be a bother."

His smirk—he seemed to have a whole arsenal of them—told her it was too late for that.

She sighed. "Fine. I'll make some calls and...see what I can do."

Not that she had a clue what that would be.

BROOKLYNN FINGER-COMBED HER HAIR, which fell

in waves around her face. Rather than braid it again, she pulled it into a low ponytail.

After she'd agreed to stay until she had somewhere to go, Ford had directed her to a powder room—though he certainly hadn't called it that—tucked into a hallway off the foyer. Just large enough for a toilet and a pedestal sink, the bathroom walls were papered in a burgundy floral. The fixtures were shiny gold.

She stared at her reflection in the gilded mirror. Nobody would know by looking at her that she'd run for her life that morning. Her fear hadn't left any visible scars.

But at the memory of what'd happened at the cove, terror still thumped inside. She didn't want to think about what would've happened if not for the grumpy stranger who'd rescued her.

She had to find a place to go that wasn't too far from Shadow Cove in case she was needed at the gallery.

Nobody in her immediate family was in a position to help, but she had lots of cousins nearby. And while she wouldn't consider staying with her sisters, maybe one of the Wright brothers could give her shelter.

She started with the oldest. Daniel and his wife were moving to Shadow Cove. She wasn't sure of their timeline, though. She dialed his number and explained that she needed a place to stay—without giving him the whole story.

"We're on the road," Daniel said, "but we should be in Maine in a couple of days. We're staying at Mom and Dad's until our house is ready. They're up at camp, so there's plenty of room for all of us. Call Mom. I'm sure there's a key hidden somewhere."

Aunt Peggy and Uncle Roger would welcome her to stay with them, but the camp Daniel mentioned was actually a house on an island a couple of hours north, meaning they wouldn't be able to pick her up.

Daniel would, if she explained the situation, but that wouldn't be for days.

Assuming she could get to her aunt and uncle's house, it would probably be safe. But she'd need to get to her Bronco, which was probably being watched.

For now, that was a dead end.

She thanked Daniel and dialed Michael.

"We're in DC." His voice was deep, his words brusque, as usual. "We'll be back in Shadow Cove this weekend. You could stay at our place, but we've got someone house sitting while we're gone. It's a refugee family Leila met at the shelter. I don't know them well enough that I'd feel comfortable with you staying with them. Let me see if they can find somewhere else—"

"No. Don't do that." The last thing she wanted was to displace homeless people. "Thanks anyway."

"Why don't you stay with your parents?" he asked. "Everything okay?"

"Oh, yeah. Uh...it's just... It's a long story."

"Huh. Why do I get the feeling it's a story you need to tell someone?"

"It's fine. I'll let you know if I can't find a place." She ended that call quickly. Michael was a CIA agent, an expert at uncovering secrets. The last thing she needed was for the whole family to freak out, and Michael would definitely sound the alarm.

She started to dial Sam. The third Wright brother lived in Shadow Cove. He and Eliza would take her in, but with a five-year-old and a new baby, they had enough on their plates. And she wasn't about to put children in danger to protect herself.

Bryan and Sophie had left for Europe a week earlier, where they planned to work as missionaries to refugees.

Derrick, Jasmine, and the baby were out jet-setting somewhere. Well, flying the jet-setters around.

How did a woman with two parents, four sisters, an aunt and uncle, and six cousins not have anywhere to go?

She could call Grant. The fourth Wright brother and his wife used to be bodyguards, but Brooklynn already knew what he'd say, the same thing Ford had told her—get out of town and stay hidden. He'd demand she come to Coventry, which was farther away than Roger and Peggy's house.

Grant would pick her up himself or have one of his buddies —this particular cousin knew people everywhere—do it. They'd probably put her in protective custody. She'd be all but handcuffed for her own protection.

She loved Grant and Summer, she did. But his overprotectiveness would drive her batty.

For now, she wasn't ready to do anything quite so drastic.

What she needed was for those guys, whoever they were, to leave Shadow Cove and stay gone—or, even better, to be caught.

Which left her one option.

The only thing that raised Brooklynn's anxiety higher than being chased by smugglers was the thought of having to deal with Lenny.

If she reported what happened, her ex-boyfriend, a cop, would find out about it and make sure he was assigned to the case. And then she'd have to rid herself of him all over again.

She met her eyes in the mirror. "You can do this. Just set boundaries and don't let him push them."

Except Lenny wasn't exactly a stay-on-your-side-of-the-line kind of guy.

Seeing only one solution, she pulled out her cell phone, found the number, and dialed.

"Shadow Cove PD." The man's voice wasn't familiar, thank heavens.

"Right. Hi. I was taking a walk at sunrise in the cove in front of the Ballentine Mansion this morning, and I saw something suspicious at that old dock in the inlet there."

"Name?"

"You know the one. They call it the Haunted Inlet."

The moniker had always seemed absurd to her, but after this morning's events, she felt it wasn't creepy enough.

"*Your* name." The man's tone was less than patient.

"Oh. I don't want anyone to know who I am."

"Ma'am, I need it so I can file a report."

"They were moving boxes from a fishing boat to the dock."

He exhaled a frustrated breath. "Can you tell me what the fishing boat looked like?"

"Yeah. Hold on a sec." Thankful she'd brought her backpack to the bathroom with her, she found her camera and flipped through the photos. "It was white—well, more gray, but I think it was originally painted white. It had a long deck and a tall...cabin thing." Her sister would be embarrassed by her ignorance, but Brooklynn had never been as enthralled with boats as Kenzie.

"Go on."

"The tower thing was tall but only took up about a quarter, maybe a third of the top of the boat."

"The deck." His tone was droll. "So an old white fishing boat."

"I didn't get a look at the name, and I didn't see any markings on the side. But I did take a photo, so—"

"You might'a started there, lady. Send it to us."

She'd have to figure a way to do that without giving away who she was.

She copied an email address he rattled off into her notes

app. "They saw me and chased me," she said. "I managed to get away, but—"

"They chased you? You're saying you think you're in danger? Are you in a safe place?"

"Yes." For now, though she didn't add that.

"Where are you?"

"The point is, there's something going on at that dock. You need to...stake it out or whatever. You need to catch those guys so I can get back to my life."

"Ma'am, you need to file an official report, and I need that photo. This number works to call you back?"

Oh. Oh, no.

How had she not realized...? Of course they'd have a record of her phone number.

If Lenny saw it, he'd know Brooklynn had been the caller.

Fear crept up her spine. "I-I have to go. I'll see what I can do."

She ended the call. Fumbled her cell, which bounced off the sink and hit the tile floor. She sat heavily on the toilet seat and grabbed it. Not broken, thank heavens.

Lenny couldn't get involved. *Please, God, don't let Lenny get involved.*

Would he be able to track the phone? To find her?

She powered it off. But would that do it?

She needed to get out of there. If Lenny came...

Not that he'd hurt her, but he was the last person she wanted to deal with right now. Well, the last person, after the smugglers.

It said a lot about the man she'd thought she loved that she was nearly as afraid of him as she was of those men who'd sent her on the run.

She'd told Ford she wouldn't tell anybody he was here. But if Lenny traced her phone—which might not be legal, but he'd find a way—then he'd come. He'd see Ford, and he'd be enraged to find her with him. No matter what she told him, he wouldn't believe she and Ford had just met.

He'd make trouble, not only for her but for the man who'd risked his life to protect her.

She had to leave. If she could get to her car, she could go… somewhere.

She'd figure it out.

She stepped into a wide hallway lined with landscape photographs, which showed the area around this house.

Who had taken these? They looked professional, though the quality—or lack thereof—told her they'd been taken decades before.

Her panic faded as she moved deeper into the house, studying each image.

She turned at a corner, and light shone from a room at the end of the hall.

Ford had explicitly told her to return to the living room when she was finished, but curiosity pulled her toward that light. She needed to talk to him, and there was no time to wait.

Lenny could be on his way even now. He'd see her Bronco, and he wouldn't stop looking for her until he found her.

She peeked into a room lit by lamps and natural light coming through the east-facing windows. It was an office with the same dark woodwork as the rest of the house, but the chairs were leather, old and worn and inviting. A wall of bookshelves was built-in, filled with books.

A faded red-and-tan Persian rug stretched over the hardwood.

Ford was bent over papers strewn across a deep partner's desk that had to be antique. Plates were stacked on one side, the top one holding the remains of a sandwich.

She cleared her throat. "Sorry to interrupt—"

He spun so fast that her words stuck in her throat. "What are you doing here?"

"I was looking—"

"I told you to wait for me in the living room." He stalked toward her, and she shrank back.

Then stopped herself, standing her ground.

If Lenny hadn't taught her anything else, he'd taught her never to cower.

"I'm leaving. Thanks for your help." She spun and headed for the door, ignoring the heavy footsteps that thumped behind her.

"Someone's picking you up?"

"Nope. I'm just gonna run to my car, and—"

"Too dangerous."

"I'll risk it."

She marched past another hallway, around a corner.

It dead-ended.

She spun to find Ford standing a few feet back, arms crossed, smirk in place.

"Just show me, would you? I'm... I don't think straight when I'm angry."

"*I'm* making *you* angry?"

"You're not exactly dragging a Welcome Wagon."

He made a sound low in his throat that wouldn't have sounded more threatening if it'd come from a grizzly.

"Either move or get out of my way."

"Where are you going?"

"I'm not sure yet. Maybe my aunt and uncle's house."

"So you're just going to walk to your bright orange truck and hope nobody sees you?"

"You have a better idea?"

His lips pressed closed, and she had the strongest feeling he was trying very hard to keep words from coming out.

"I can't find anyone to pick me up, and I can't stay here."

"You *can* stay here."

"I can't... I'm not..." All thoughts dissolved as she processed that.

She couldn't stay here, but the fact that he'd offered when he so obviously wanted her gone...

She didn't know what to think about that.

"I have to leave." She sighed and looked at the beige walls. No artwork here, just brass sconces placed intermittently near the ceiling. They had lightbulbs in them now, but they must've once held candles.

Everything about this house made her want to stay and delve into its secrets.

"I know you said not to, but I called the police." She didn't glance at his face, not needing to confirm the scowl. "I made an anonymous report, but I didn't think about the fact that they'd see my phone number. They'll figure out it was me."

"From your number?"

His tone held curiosity, which surprised her. She'd only ever heard irritation and frustration from him.

"I had a relationship with one of the cops. If he sees it, he'll know. And he'll look."

Ford nodded, eyes narrowing.

"So I have to go."

She waited for Ford to say she couldn't leave. To say he didn't mind if she stayed, that she wasn't in his way.

To his credit, he didn't lie.

Because obviously he did mind her staying. She was in his way.

Technically, at the moment, *he* was in *her* way.

"Thank you for your help." She hefted her bag over her shoulder, a signal that she was ready.

He spun and led her to the front door—and then past it.

Down a hallway, around a corner, until they were back in the living room.

He opened the hidden basement door and descended the stairs into darkness.

Not total darkness, she realized as she followed. The bulb he'd lit earlier was still on.

He stopped beside the wooden staircase that led to the exterior door. "Cross the lawn to the front corner. You should be able to get through the hedge there. Stay in the woods until you reach where you parked."

"Okay. Thanks." She started to pass, but he stepped into her path.

Unlike when they'd first been in this scary, dank place, she wasn't afraid of him.

"You don't have to leave. I'd rather... I don't want you to get hurt."

"I'll be fine."

A moment passed.

And then he shifted, and she marched up the stairs and outside, where the morning sun hit her face.

She turned to him. "Thank you for everything."

He opened his mouth, then snapped it shut.

She had no idea what he'd planned to say, but it didn't matter.

Lenny was coming. She needed to leave.

She stepped outside into a yard she assumed used to be beautiful, though it was nothing but weeds and dandelions, their cheerful yellow flowers waving in the breeze coming off the Atlantic.

Brooklynn avoided the driveway flanked near the road by two stone pillars, jogging toward the tall hedge that separated the property from the road and the neighbors.

She couldn't be more than two hundred feet from her Bronco. She just had to get there without being seen.

Easy peasy.

She pushed through the thick bushes, moving slowly, thanks to the prickly branches that grabbed her clothes and her backpack.

Before stepping out, she peered along the road, then into the woods. Fear had her wanting to bolt to her car, but caution dictated she be sure nobody was out there.

She didn't move, just watched for movement, for anything.

But all was quiet.

She was just about to step out when she heard a car. Maybe it'd be safer to go when a car was driving by. Witnesses would keep her safe.

Unless that was the smugglers.

She backed into the prickly hedge.

A black car drove past, going more slowly than the thirty-five mile-per-hour speed limit.

The car had no plates.

Acid pooled in her stomach.

It pulled over on the side of the road between the hedge and her Bronco.

A man stepped out, then bent to talk to the driver. He was too far away for her to see his face.

If she weren't hemmed in by the hedge, she'd take a photo.

"I got it," the man barked, clearly responding to something the driver had said. "I'll find her."

Her breath caught in her throat.

It was them. They were still looking for her.

She'd nearly walked right into them.

She moved backward slowly, doing her best not to jostle the bushes and draw their attention.

And bumped into a solid chest.

CHAPTER FOUR

Forbes should've stopped Brooklynn from leaving. Not that he wanted her to stay.

He also didn't want her to tell anyone about him, the house, the cave...

He had a job to do, and Brooklynn Wright was a nuisance he didn't need.

But he didn't want her to die.

Which was why, when she was halfway across the yard, he'd jogged behind her. Just to make sure she made it to her Bronco all right. Once she drove away, hopefully to somewhere safe, he could quit worrying about her. She'd no longer be his problem.

Until then, he felt responsible for her. He felt a whole lot of things regarding the brunette, things he had no business feeling. Like wonder at the way she said what she was thinking without editing the words at all. And the way her every emotion showed across her face.

He had no idea how to deal with that.

He'd grown up steeped in secrets. Whereas Brooklynn Wright seemed completely open, completely guileless.

It was beautiful. It was...frightening in a way he couldn't explain.

He followed her to the edge of the hedge, watching her through the thick, glossy green leaves. Her bright yellow top wasn't exactly a stealthy outfit. At least she stayed hidden before exposing herself.

He was still there when she backed into him, creeping slowly enough that he hadn't realized she was moving until she was right there.

Which was how he ended up, for the second time in his life—and in the last hour—covering a woman's mouth to keep her quiet.

"Shh. It's me. It's me." His heart pounded, knowing she'd seen something scary enough to change her mind about leaving.

He kept his voice low, pulling her back against his chest. "Brooklynn, it's Ford."

She was stiff with terror.

"You're safe. Nod if you understand."

She did, and he removed his palm from her mouth and gripped her hand. Not for any reason except he needed to keep the connection, confirm she stayed with him.

With his other hand, he pushed branches out of the way until she'd disengaged from the hedge.

Her face was pale and...green. She seemed unsteady, whether from fear or something else.

A car crept past on the other side of the hedge.

Whoever she'd seen was about to drive right down his driveway.

He scooped her into his arms, earning a gasp of surprise.

Ignoring her reaction to him—and his to her—he ran. He reached the basement door and carried her to the bottom of the steps before he set her on her feet.

Then he crossed to the worst hiding place in the house. But there was no time to get her to a better one.

He opened the short metal door tucked into the concrete. "In here."

She looked at the space, which was as tall as his hip and half as deep. Concrete on three sides. Cold metal on the fourth. It latched from the outside, making it a tiny little prison.

Banging coming from the front door upstairs had her eyes popping wide.

"Get in."

"But—"

"I'll be back."

He didn't touch her, despite his eagerness for her to hide.

"You promise?"

"I promise." He made his tone as serious as he could. "I just need to get rid of them. You have your phone, right?"

She nodded, and he waited.

Until, at more pounding, she crouched and crawled into the tiny hiding spot.

He closed the door and latched it. Then pushed a couple boxes in front of it, just in case.

He hurried to the opposite side of the basement, where Dad had stored household tools on shelves over a wide wooden workspace. Forbes grabbed the tool belt he'd used a couple of times for small projects, fastened it to his waist, and stepped out the basement door.

He rounded to the front.

One man stood on the wide patio near the door. Another was standing on his tiptoes, peeking in the parlor window. A black Chevy was parked in the circle drive.

"Can I help you?"

Both men turned toward him.

The one on the patio jogged down the steps. He was

medium height and build with drab brown hair and nondescript brown eyes. Clean-shaven, he looked about as threatening as a ladybug. He marched toward Forbes, hand outstretched. "I'm Niles." He gestured toward the other man, who was coming up behind him. "That's Bernie."

Unlike Niles, Bernie was thick. Thick neck, thick shoulders, thick chest, thick thighs. Thick head? That remained to be seen.

"Ford Baker."

"We're looking for a woman," Niles said.

"Aren't we all?"

"Ha. Right. In this case, a particular woman."

Forbes made a show of looking around. "You think she's here somewhere?"

"You seen her?"

"Haven't seen anyone."

"You own this place?"

"Doing some work on it."

The man took him in, head to toe. "What time'd you get here today?"

"Kinda early."

Niles's eyebrows rose.

Bernie's mean smile revealed crooked teeth.

"We've been looking for her for a while," Niles said. "Didn't see you drive in."

"Yeah, well..." He shuffled from foot to foot, going for nervous. "I...uh... I've been staying here, but I don't want the owners to know. It's a long drive back to my place down near Lewiston." Though he'd learned to hide his Maine accent years before, he laid it on thick now. "The owners aren't here, so I figured..." He shrugged. "I really need this job, though, so..." He let the request hang.

Niles grinned. "I can keep your secret, but we need to take a look around, if you don't mind."

"I'm not supposed to let anybody in."

"You're also not supposed to be staying here."

"Yeah. But there's no woman here. I'd have seen her."

"Then you won't mind if we confirm that."

He did mind, very much. But he figured they would search, one way or another. This way, they'd think they had something on him and dispel any suspicion that he knew who they were or what they were up to.

"Why you looking for her?"

"She took something without our permission."

"She stole from you?"

Bernie's chuckle was dark.

Niles said, "Something like that."

As far as Forbes knew, Brooklynn hadn't taken anything from the smugglers. It was just an excuse.

"All right. Make it quick, and don't hurt anything."

Niles peered behind him. "Where'd you come from?"

"Basement."

Moving past him, Niles walked to the basement door.

Forbes should have thought this through better. There was nothing for it now.

"There's nobody there."

"Then it'll only take a few minutes."

Niles and Bernie climbed down the basement stairs while Forbes prayed Brooklynn had stayed put.

CHAPTER FIVE

Brooklynn held her own hand over her mouth, terrified she'd squeal and give away her hiding place.

Voices carried through the metal door that locked her in. With them, sounds of scraping and sliding boxes.

The men out there were almost as terrifying as the pitch-black darkness.

Something tickled the back of her hand, and she wiped it over her jeans.

Ants? Spiders? Cockroaches?

Get me out of here. Lord, get me out of here!

Every cell in her body screamed for her to escape. To pound on the door. To risk whatever was out there in order to get away from the invisible threats in here.

But she held very, very still. Not thinking about the bugs crawling in her hair. Beneath her shirt. Up her leg.

Please, please...

"I'm telling you, there's nobody here." That was Ford.

"Then you've got nothing to hide."

Footsteps on wood—they were going upstairs.

A door closed. Something moved on the ceiling over her head. Then nothing.

Silence.

For a long time. Too long.

What if something had happened to Ford? What if they hurt him, or killed him?

She needed to get out of there. Now. She needed to check on him and escape this tiny hole.

In the darkness, she opened her backpack and found her phone. Powered it on.

Tried to dial 911. Better to have to fend off Lenny than to suffocate. She'd deal with him. She'd deal with the smugglers. Anything to get out of this box.

She stared at her phone screen, at the zero bars that showed she had no service.

Time ticked by, second by second. Minute by minute. It felt like hours passed before she heard footsteps again.

Ford?

Was he dead? Were the bad guys still looking for her?

A scraping sound, and then the metal door swung open.

She crawled out, lurched to her feet, and crashed into Ford. "Thank you. Thank God. Thank you."

"Whoa." He held her at arms' length. "What's wrong?"

She backed up to brush away the bugs she hoped she'd only imagined.

But there was a spider crawling up her jeans.

Squeaking, she smacked it, then smacked at more.

"It's okay. It's okay. Just..." Ford looked around, then crossed the room. He returned carrying a man's button-down and a pair of shorts. "Take those clothes off and throw them in the wash. Put these on."

"What? I can't—"

He grabbed something in her hair, then brushed at her shoulders.

Spiders. Everywhere.

"Change. I'll wait upstairs. I'll...I'll have a plan." He thumped up the steps, leaving her some privacy.

She stripped out of her jeans and top and put the shirt he'd given her over her panties and bra, then added the too-big gym shorts, the waistband of which she rolled over three times so they wouldn't slide down.

On bare feet, she climbed the stairs to the living room.

Ford met her there. "Follow me." He barely looked at her, just spun and headed for the foyer and the sweeping staircase.

On the second floor, they hurried down a hallway like the one below, turned at a corner, and continued along a narrower hall. He pushed open a door. "There's a bathroom in here. Everything you might need." He seemed to be very careful not to look lower than her face. "I'll leave some clean clothes on the bed for you."

In case more spiders were crawling on what she wore, which seemed likely.

She shuddered. "Thanks."

She wasted no time, and though she longed to soak in the claw-foot tub, she went straight for the shower.

Only after she'd washed her hair—twice—did she allow herself to relax.

She was clean. She was safe from her enemies, two-legged and eight-legged and everything in between. For now, anyway.

She had no doubt those monsters would visit her in her dreams. Life had supplied her nightmares with a lot of fodder today.

The towel rack held two towels, one folded neatly, the other not so much. She touched it and found it damp. This was Ford's shower? Ford's room?

She used the dry one, then wrapped it around herself and peeked into the bedroom.

Empty, though Ford had left a pair of gray joggers and a blue New England Patriots T-shirt on the bed. The joggers had a drawstring, which she cinched tight around her waist. The T-shirt was way too big. She tied a knot at the waist to keep it from hanging below the sagging butt of the pants, then towel-dried her hair.

She was digging through her backpack, looking for a comb, when she remembered the phone.

She'd powered it on in the creepy hiding place in the basement. But she'd never powered it off.

She found it in the outside pocket and checked the screen.

Seven calls.

All from Lenny.

Dang it.

Stupid, stupid.

She turned it off again, but it was too late. He'd come looking.

Ford would probably hand her right over to him. She'd been nothing but trouble for the man who'd decided to step in and be her protector. No doubt he regretted that decision now.

If Lenny came, then…then she'd have to get out of town. Not just away from the smugglers, but away from him.

CHAPTER SIX

Forbes had been at his childhood home for three weeks.
Three weeks with zero visitors.
Zero interruptions.
Zero beautiful brunettes who made his heart race and his palms go sweaty like he was still the new kid at school.

The doorbell rang a second time in fifteen seconds, then his impatient visitor knocked.

Forbes was nearly to the front door when he heard a man's voice through the thick wood. "Open up. Police!"

He scowled, cursing said brunette even as he ran up the stairs to the second floor.

He reached his room and rapped his knuckles on the wood. "Brooklynn?"

When she opened the door, her wet hair hung well below her collarbones, dampening his favorite T-shirt, which she'd knotted at the waist over his joggers.

He'd thought the clothes he'd chosen for her would be baggy and shapeless.

Wrong again, Ballentine.

She was…anything but shapeless. And wearing his clothes, in his bedroom, next to his bed…

He swallowed, suddenly feeling parched and…and other things that had him wanting to move into the room and slam the door with his foot and take this total stranger into his arms.

Holy cow, he was in trouble.

He planted his feet firmly outside the door. "The police are here."

Her eyes widened, and she stepped back.

And fury rose inside, a fire even hotter than the one that'd already sparked.

"You're the one who called them. Why are you afraid?" The words came out harsh and angry. That anybody would frighten or harm this woman…

"I'm not scared, I just would prefer not to deal with him."

Him. Not *them*.

"The ex-boyfriend?"

Lips pressed together, she nodded.

"Is he dangerous?"

"No. I mean…" She blinked a couple of times. "No. Just…"

So yes. Yes, he was dangerous.

He worked to keep his temper under control. "What am I walking into?"

"He's not… He's a cop. He's not going to hurt anyone. He's just a little…stalkerish."

Stalker. Ish.

At that, Forbes squashed the last of his inappropriate feelings and moved past her to the wardrobe opposite his bed. He pushed his clothes out of the way and unlatched the compartment behind. "Get in here." When he turned, she was watching him with rounded eyes. "I'll try to get rid of him, but if he forces his way in or has a warrant…"

Downstairs, what had been faint knocking turned to pounding. "Open up!"

Brooklynn's eyes were saucers of fear.

"It's okay." He attempted to soften his tone. "This one opens from the inside. And there're no spiders, I promise." That didn't seem to lessen her worry. "I'll get rid of him."

When the pounding intensified, he decided to leave her to decide.

The cop was still banging when Forbes reached the foyer.

He yanked open the door. None of the words on his tongue would diffuse this, so he kept his mouth shut.

The uniformed cop on the other side looked furious. Behind him, a dark blue police car idled in the circle drive. "What took you so long?"

"I didn't hear you. You should knock louder next time."

The man's bushy eyebrows lowered. "Where is she?"

Forbes crossed his arms. "You're looking for a woman? You should try Webb's Harborside. I hear it's hopping at happy hour."

"I know she's here." The cop was a couple inches shorter than Forbes with tanned skin and dark hair. He straightened as if trying to make himself taller, bigger. "Her truck's parked"—he tipped his head to the road—"right over there. So I know she's here. If you don't cooperate, I'll have to take you in."

Forbes made a show of looking around. What he wanted to say—*you and what army?*—wouldn't go over well. "On what charges? Minding my own business?"

"Refusing to obey a police officer."

"Obey what order?"

"Tell me where she is."

"I can't conjure answers at your command."

The guy's skin reddened. He looked about one degree south of rage.

Forbes needed to dial it back. He could hear his grandmother's voice. *Use that big brain of yours for something besides filler for your skull.* "I'll tell you the same thing I told the other guys, I haven't—"

"What other guys?" The cop's unibrow lowered. "Someone else was here?"

Quick thinker, this one.

Forbes needed the police to be searching for the guys who were searching for Brooklynn. But he didn't need them thinking she was here. A fine line.

"Two guys came by earlier, said they were looking for a brunette. Said she'd taken something of theirs." He shrugged, leaning against the door jamb. "I told them I hadn't seen her."

If Forbes wasn't mistaken, genuine concern filled the cop's eyes as he glanced behind him toward the road.

The sun was high in the sky, a few puffy clouds overhead. The property, surrounded by forest and hedge, looked ill-treated. He'd hate to think what Mom would say if she saw her lawn like this. Grass replaced with weeds. Flowers dead. Bushes overgrown.

Of course, if Mom were still alive...

"Tell me about the men," the cop said.

Forbes did, sharing their descriptions and the names they'd given him—though he doubted very much they were really called Niles and Bernie.

The cop took down the information in a small notebook he'd pulled from his breast pocket. Old-school for someone who didn't look any older than Forbes's thirty.

"And they were looking for Brookie?"

"Brookie?" He repeated the name. "What kind of name is—?"

"What's your name?"

"Ford Baker. What's yours?"

"What are you doing here?"

"Repairs."

"What kind?"

"The house hasn't been lived in for decades. What do you think?"

"You see anything unusual this morning?"

"Aside from too many visitors?"

"Any boats?"

"Nope."

"Hear anything?"

"Nope."

The cop pursed his lips. "She's gotta be here, somewhere." He shifted, trying to spy beyond Forbes into the house.

Forbes centered himself in the doorway. "There's nobody here but me."

"I tracked her phone. It's on this property."

"Why don't you call her, then? If she's sharing her location with you, she can tell you where she is."

The cop's eye contact slipped.

"I see. She *isn't* sharing her location with you, Officer"—he checked the name printed on a gold tag—"L. Taggart. In which case, how did you track it?"

"I'm a cop."

Not an answer. Some cops might have access to that information, but surely it wasn't legal for them to access it without cause.

"I need to search the premises," Taggart said.

"Search the grounds all you want. If she's out there, I'm sure you'll find her. You wanna come in? Get a warrant."

"I'm trying to protect her."

"I'm trying to keep my job. I was told not to let anybody into the house. You'll have to take it up with the owners."

Taggart narrowed his eyes, seemed to be scheming. For a second, Forbes feared the guy was going to force his way in.

Forbes would be able to stop him, assuming Taggart didn't pull that gun holstered to his hip, but doing so would invite too much attention. Too many questions.

Forbes could just let him in, but Brooklynn's assessment was spot-on. This guy was stalker-ish.

Only without the *ish*.

He could practically see Taggart's gears moving, considering the ramifications of barging in. After a long, tense moment, he took a step back. "I'll need your boss's number to confirm your story."

"Wait here." Forbes slammed the door, found his wallet where he'd left it in the kitchen, and pulled a business card out. He opened the door again and handed it over.

The cop read it. "Ballentine Enterprises?" He looked up. "They still own it after all these years?"

Forbes shrugged. "I don't know anything about it. I just talked to the fellow who hired me."

Of course, *the fellow* was Tim, Forbes's assistant, and he wouldn't give anyone access to the house without Forbes's permission.

Officer Taggart would need a warrant, which no judge should issue based on an illegal phone trace and the proximity of her vehicle.

Though anything was possible, especially in a small town where everyone knew everyone.

"I'll call him. And search the property." The cop swiveled and marched down the steps and around the corner of the house.

After locking the door and then closing the blinds in the first-floor common rooms, Forbes took the stairs two at a time to give Brooklynn an update.

When he reached the top, he found her standing just out of sight.

"I told you to hide."

"I needed to hear. You had it under control."

"I did. But he could've..." Forbes didn't bother to explain all that could've gone wrong. "That was your ex?"

She nodded. Her face paled as she slid to the floor right there in the hallway.

Because things weren't complex enough, this woman needed to get the...the vapors or whatever.

She'd barged onto his property and into his life against his will. He'd now protected her three times. All he should want was for her to leave and never come back.

That was all he *should* want.

But he found himself sitting on the floor beside her. "You okay, Brookie?"

Her lips twitched. "I hate that nickname. And he knows it."

"Seems like a real catch. What's the L stand for?"

"Leonard. He goes by Lenny."

"He looks like a Lenny."

She nodded, then shook her head.

Tears dripped down her freshly scrubbed cheeks.

He had no idea why she was crying. Or what to say. Or what to do.

So he did what he'd have done if this were Rosie. He slid his arm around her shoulders and pulled her close.

Except Rosie had been a decade older than Forbes, his little boy arms not big enough to calm his big sister's heartbreaks.

Whereas Brooklynn curled against his chest. Despite her height and curves, at the moment she seemed small and vulnerable and oh, so soft. The logical, analytical side of his brain told him to push her away. To protect himself. To protect his mission.

But the rest of him told that killjoy to shut up as he tucked her head against his neck, reveling in her warmth. She smelled like his soap, a scent he'd never found the slightest bit attractive. But on her...

Dang.

He had no idea what he was supposed to do with this woman. One thing he knew: Having her here wasn't safe for Forbes.

But sending her away wouldn't be safe for her. And suddenly, he wanted more than anything to make sure she was safe.

CHAPTER SEVEN

Brooklynn needed to move. She told herself to sit up, to push away from Ford. To take care of herself.

To quit being such a nuisance.

But his chest was so broad and strong, the skin of his neck so warm against her cheek. Here, she found safety.

Which made no sense at all, considering that when he wasn't smirking at her he was scowling. He obviously didn't want her there. He certainly didn't want her in his arms. He was kind, and he'd seen her distress. This was nothing more than that.

She pushed away, swiping at her leaky eyes. "Sorry. I'm okay."

He stood and held his hand out for her.

She took it, allowing him to pull her up, enjoying the warmth of his touch.

Before releasing her, he gave her a narrowed-eye once-over, maybe trying to decide if she was going to collapse again.

She straightened and smiled. "I'm fine. Really. It was just... too much."

"Lenny."

"And...everything."

"He's still here, searching the property. I closed the curtains downstairs, but there're a lot of windows in this house."

"I'll be careful. Do you think he'll leave after he searches?"

Ford's only response was a shrug.

"I can't leave until he does."

"You're not going to try to get to your truck again. Can someone pick you up?" Even as he posed the question, his eyes narrowed. "No. That won't work. They could be watching the house."

They. Meaning...the smugglers, or Lenny.

An impossible situation.

He waited a few beats, then issued a short nod as if he'd just made a decision. He swiveled and headed down the hall toward his room. He passed that door and stopped at the next one, which he opened.

"You can stay in here."

"What? No, I can't—"

"Where are you going to go?"

"I just... I think..."

His eyebrows lifted, accompanied by that almost constant smirk.

"My aunt and uncle's."

"They going to pick you up? They can keep you safe?"

"No, they can't pick me up, but if I can get to their vacation house, I'll be safe there." Except it was too far, and she didn't want to ask them to drive back downstate to get her. "I just need to figure it out. I just need a little more time."

"Will they be able to protect you from the people chasing you?" Far from gentle, his tone was frustrated. "What if the smugglers are watching the house? What if they follow you? What about the stalker."

"He's not a..." Her voice faded.

"Does Lenny know about this aunt and uncle?"

Unfortunately, Lenny knew too much about her. Back when they were together, before she understood what kind of person he was, she'd shared everything about her family.

No place in Shadow Cove would be safe. Peggy and Roger's house wouldn't be safe. Even their island-camp wouldn't be safe, not from Lenny.

She'd need to find a hotel somewhere, and not close by, either. As a cop, Lenny could get far more information than most, especially in the town where he lived and worked. He was well-respected and well-loved by the locals. Brooklynn hadn't even shared the details about their relationship with her family, much less friends. Only Lois knew the truth.

So. A hotel far away, too far to be able to manage the gallery...

The gallery!

"Oh, no."

"What?"

"I forgot..." She pulled her phone from her pocket but hesitated. If she powered it up, and if Lenny was still tracking it, then he'd know she was here. He'd find her.

Ford's hand slipped over hers. "Don't. You can use mine. It's in my office."

She looked up at him, and he let her go, stepping back. He seemed as surprised by his sudden touch as she was.

He continued down the hall, deeper into the house. "Don't just stand there. Come on." He didn't even look over his shoulder when he issued the command.

Wasn't like she had that many choices. She hurried to catch up with him. At the end of the hall, he pulled a tall cabinet door she would have assumed opened to a linen closet.

But he flicked a switch, lighting a narrow spiral staircase.

A secret passageway.

Add that to the house's mysteries, of which there were clearly many.

Ford started down, so she followed.

"How long have you been here?" She aimed the words at his back.

"Few weeks."

"How did you find all the hiding places?"

He reached the bottom and opened a door.

She followed, stepping into a cedar-lined closet facing a row of hanging coats. She closed the door behind her, and it disappeared into the wall, hidden from sight.

She stepped past the coats and into a bedroom she hadn't seen before. The bed and bureau were covered with sheets

Ford hadn't answered her question.

She followed him into a hallway. "Did you just poke around? How did you know that was there?"

"The owner told me."

"Who was that? Like, a distant relative of the Ballentines?"

He didn't answer.

She tried a different question. "Are there more secret passageways?"

Not only did he not respond, he picked up speed.

She was practically running to keep up, a puppy eagerly chasing its owner.

The thought gave her pause, and she slowed. So what if she lost him? She'd find him again.

He disappeared into a room. It was the office where he'd been working before. They'd come from the opposite direction.

She stopped in the entry as he retrieved his cell phone from the desk.

"I just need to call the gallery to make sure it's open and they don't need me."

He walked toward her, cell phone in his outstretched hand.

She reached for it. "And then I'll figure out a ride."

He closed his fingers around the phone and drew it back. "You're staying here."

"No. I'm...I'm going to go..."

He didn't open his hand, just waited.

"Every problem has a solution. I'll figure out the solution to this one." Just saying the words brightened her spirits. God always made a way. All her life, He'd guided her. And He wouldn't stop today. He was her protector, after all. Her strong tower. Her fortress.

She needn't worry. She only needed to ask Him to open the doors she was meant to walk through. To pray that His will would be done.

It was a prayer He loved to answer.

As hope filled her heart, Ford's frown turned to a grimace. "I told you the solution. Stay."

"You don't really want me here."

"I'm not going to send you into danger."

It said something about his character that he didn't lie by protesting.

"If my safety were assured—"

"Until then, you're staying."

"I have no choice in the matter?"

He muttered something under his breath. She picked up the words *time* and *woman*. She was pretty sure she heard *irritating* as well.

"I didn't catch that."

"You're not a captive." He opened his palm. "Take it. Call whoever you want. Do...whatever. You wanna get yourself killed or...stalked or whatever, be my guest. Or...*don't* be my guest, if that's what you want." He jiggled the phone in his palm. "I'm just trying to help."

Once again, irritation enabled him to string together

multiple sentences. Apparently, if she wanted to get him to open up, all she needed to do was annoy the tar out of him.

Good to have a plan.

She took his cell, tried and failed to unlock it, then held it back out.

He snatched it, put in the code, making no effort to hide it. It was the digits in the corners of the keypad, beginning with three.

Easy enough to remember.

He handed it back. "Get that?"

"Thank you."

He turned back into the office, paused with his hand on the door for two seconds, then continued—without shutting her out.

Monumental progress, that.

After unbuckling a tool belt from his waist that she hadn't noticed before, he dropped it on a side table and settled behind the desk. He'd told Lenny he was there to make repairs. Apparently, the tool belt was part of his...costume, for lack of a better word.

She dialed the gallery.

"Light and Shadows. This is Jewel."

"I'm so glad you're there."

"Omigosh, Brooklynn?"

"I'm sorry I wasn't—"

"I've been so worried about you! You wouldn't believe the rumors. They said you witnessed a crime or something? And now you're on the run?"

So much for her anonymous tip. News traveled too fast in small towns.

Brooklynn stepped into the office and settled on a leather chair, putting the phone on speaker so Ford could hear.

His gaze flicked up, and he gave her the teensiest nod, almost as if he approved.

"Say that again, Jewel?"

"A cop came in demanding to know where you were, said he thought you were in danger. He practically accused me of hiding you, like you're some kind of criminal. He wanted me to unlock your apartment for him, but I refused."

"Let me guess. Officer Taggart?"

"How'd you know?"

She'd hired Jewel a few months before, which was after Lenny had given up on her—or was convinced she really would seek a restraining order if he didn't leave her alone. She'd never needed to fill her employee in on the ugly details of her previous relationship.

"What'd you tell him?"

"That I didn't know where you were." She sounded defensive. "Which I didn't. And still don't."

"That was perfect. Even if you did, though, do me a favor. Never tell him anything about me, okay? Even if he claims it's police business. If he says that, tell him you'll talk to someone else, but not him."

"Is that...? Did he do something?"

"No, no. I did witness something unusual, though I didn't see any faces, and I have no idea what they were up to." As Brooklynn said the words, she thought of her camera. Had those men seen it?

Could the photos help figure out what was going on?

She needed a way to study them—and her camera's small screen wouldn't do it—and then to send them along to the police.

"I hope you don't mind," Jewel said, "but after he left, I checked your apartment, just to make sure you weren't there and hurt or something."

Ford looked up, curious, she supposed, as to why her

employee would do that. She hadn't told him that her apartment was on the second floor above the gallery.

"That's why I gave you the key," Brooklynn said, "in case of emergency. I assume you didn't see anything that worried you?"

"No. It looked like it always does."

Nobody had broken in. Yet. But if that was the plan, they'd probably wait until after dark. She hated the thought of those men pawing through her things.

"I'm going to have to lie low for a little while. Can you handle the gallery?"

"Sure thing. Where are you?"

Across the room, Ford shook his head.

"You'll be better off if you don't know," Brooklynn said. "Suffice it to say, I'm safe."

"Whose phone are you on?"

"I borrowed it from a stranger."

Nodding, Ford turned his attention to the papers on the desk.

"All right, well... Of course the whole town needs you today of all days."

"What do you mean?"

"Besides that cop, Ms. Whitmore called."

Lois was the widow of Arthur Whitmore, the photographer and namesake of the award Brooklynn hoped to win.

"She wanted to know how your shoot went this morning."

Brooklynn had forgotten she'd texted her mentor the night before, asking her to pray for favor. "Okay, I'll call her."

"And Graham Porter came in wanting to talk to you about the Old Home Days booths. The self-important windbag talked for twenty solid minutes, as if I have nothing else to do."

"Sorry about that."

"Oh, it's fine. He did what he always does, pretending to be interested in your photos for his hotel. But we both know he's too cheap to pay for anything valuable."

Brooklynn was grateful that her only employee saw value in her work. She wished more people did.

"And Elvis stopped by."

Ford looked Brooklynn's way again, eyes narrowed.

Brooklynn imagined his reaction if she told him this particular Elvis was a woman, a sixty-something former flower child who ran a souvenir shop that sold handmade jewelry and seashell art.

"And don't forget you got a call from the mayor last night. He wanted an update on—"

"Yeah, I know." Ian Prescott had roped her into chairing the Old Home Days planning committee. She worked with him and other local business leaders to put together the annual gathering.

Never mind that she'd barely survived the day. Life went on. Somehow, she'd have to figure out how to manage everything from where she was.

"And Owen came in, said he heard a rumor that you were in trouble."

"Did he say where he heard that? I'm trying to figure out who started the rumors."

"He didn't, just asked me to tell you he's available if you need help."

"That was nice of him. If he comes back, let him know I'm fine—and that he doesn't need to worry Delaney with any of this." Owen and Brooklynn's younger sister had been dating for a few months. He seemed like a nice guy, though Brooklynn didn't know him that well.

"Will do. Is there anything else I can do for you?"

"Actually, yeah. Could you call Frizzel Automotive and have them tow my Bronco to their shop? Ask them to leave it around the back of their building. It's parked at the top of the trailhead just north of the Ballentine mansion."

"Sure. I'll take care of it." Jewel gave Brooklynn a rundown on the day's sales—which were zero, so that didn't take long. "But one couple seemed really interested in the seagull picture. They said they were going to think about it."

In other words, *Thanks, but no thanks.*

"That's it for now," Jewel said. "You take care of...whatever it is you need to do. Stay safe."

"Thanks." Brooklynn ended the call.

"She seems competent," Ford said.

"She is, very. Her family owns Webb's Harborside, but she got tired of working for her brother." Brooklynn was beyond grateful that she'd finally hired someone to help her with the gallery.

Still, she didn't feel comfortable going very far away, even if someone could take her in. "I could go to a hotel."

Ford's lips pressed together. He wasn't scowling or smirking. He wasn't smiling, either. After a minute, he shook his head. "They'll see you leave. Those smugglers searched the house and the property and didn't find you. As far as I can tell, they've moved on. Lenny gave up the search, but he could be staking out the driveway. You're safe here. If you leave, you'll put yourself in danger. I see no reason for you to do that. This house is big enough for both of us."

She was almost ready to agree, then remembered the conversation she'd overheard earlier. "You told Lenny that you're not allowed to let anyone inside."

Ah, there was that smirk. "Who's going to tell on me?"

"I don't want to get you into trouble."

"It's not...Nobody's trying to kill *me*."

Kill?

Did he really think those people had wanted to kill her?

Her reaction must've been displayed on her face because his eyes flashed, more frustration than sympathy. "Whatever. I'm just saying, you're safe here. Stay or don't stay. I don't care." He focused on the paperwork on the desk.

Leaving her to sit there, stymied.

If she stayed, it might get him in trouble, and it was obvious that she was the last thing he wanted to deal with. Even so, he was sacrificing his own preferences to keep her safe.

"That's so sweet of you."

He didn't even bother to shoot her a glare.

"You're really quite wonderful, aren't you, under all that anger."

"Do you mind? I'm trying to work." But she was pretty sure she caught the tiniest smile fighting to break through his facade.

It seemed her grouchy friend was a lot like this old mansion. A little rough on the outside, but filled with beauty. And secrets.

The thought of staying, of ferreting out some of the house's mysteries—and the man's—had her fingers tingling with anticipation.

Not that she had time for that.

She needed to get back to work. Between the gallery, the contest, and the Shadow Cove Old Home Days festival, she had a million things to do.

But as long as she was stuck in the Ballentine Mansion, she might as well enjoy herself.

She swiveled and left the office, taking his phone with her. She just needed to make arrangements, and then this could work.

As long as nobody figured out where she was staying—not those scary smugglers and not Lenny—then she'd be safe.

CHAPTER EIGHT

Forbes didn't protest when Brooklynn left him alone in the office, even after he realized she'd taken his phone.

He didn't need it. He was elbow-deep in his father's old files, desperately looking for some clue as to what Dad had been up to before that terrible night.

It was evening by the time he heard a soft knock. His stomach was growling, his eyes crossing, thanks to all the dull real estate information he'd been perusing.

He looked up to see his unwanted guest standing in the doorway. She still wore his joggers and Patriots T-shirt, looking very comfortable—and far too attractive—in the oversized clothes. She'd braided her hair, which hung over one shoulder. And she was smiling as though all were right with the world.

Maybe she was, as Grandmother would say, *touched*.

Crazy. Nuttier than a Payday.

Though he guessed she was in her mid-twenties, she looked about seventeen at the moment, exactly the kind of girl who wouldn't have given him a second glance back in high school.

Not that he cared. Not that he was looking for a girlfriend.

Girlfriend?

For crying out loud, what was it about this woman that gave him these wild thoughts?

Her head tilted to one side. "What?"

He shook himself. "What *what*?"

"What what *what*?" Her grin widened. "I feel like we could do this all day."

"Maybe you could. I'm busy."

That smile wavered but didn't fade. "Thought you might be hungry."

He was, very. He bookmarked the paper he'd been reading and closed the file—a contract from a few months before the murders. Probably had nothing to do with anything. "I'll fix us something."

"I already did. I hope you don't mind."

Did he mind that she'd helped herself to his kitchen, cooked a meal without his permission?

Nope. Not one bit.

"I made *croque monsieur* sandwiches. I used all your Gruyère. Hope that was okay."

Forbes's assistant had ordered the fancy cheese, but he hadn't touched it.

"Would you bring me a plate?" He'd meant for that to sound like a request, but it came out more like a demand. "I usually work while I eat."

"If you're hungry, you can join me at the table, where we'll eat like civilized humans." She nodded to the pile of dirty dishes he'd been meaning to return to the kitchen. "Grab those when you come." She swiveled and marched out.

She had a lot of nerve ordering him around.

On the other hand, the prospect of a hot meal certainly wasn't objectionable.

He found Brooklynn in the kitchen, cutting two sandwiches in half.

She shot him a grin over her shoulder, apparently already over their tiff, then went back to plating their dinners and adding a handful of potato chips to each serving. "I looked for ingredients to make a pasta salad or a green salad, but the only lettuce you had was wilted. I tossed it. Grab the drinks, would you?"

Two glasses had already been filled with water.

"I was going to make iced tea." She carried the plates into the breakfast room.

The curtains were pulled closed—had been since Taggart's visit—but the chandelier and the lamp on the china cabinet cast yellow light, making the room look cheerful despite the lack of evening sun.

"I couldn't find any that wasn't Earl Gray." She was still talking about tea. "Not that that wouldn't make good iced tea, but I wanted to save it for mornings." She set the plates on the table, sliding into one of the chairs. "You don't have any lemonade or soda."

"Water's fine." He settled across from her and lifted one of the sandwiches. It was ham and cheese but with some kind of sauce on top.

She cleared her throat, and he looked up.

"I usually pray before I eat."

"Oh. Sure. Go ahead."

"Unless you want to. Do you pray?"

"No. I mean, yes, I pray." Sometimes. Though he doubted anyone listened. "But no, I don't want to. I mean, out loud." He clamped his lips shut.

Her smile didn't dim. She hadn't stopped smiling since she'd announced the meal. Did she have a secret? Had she discovered some mystery?

Surely she wasn't that happy. Nobody was *that* happy.

"I'll do it then." She bowed her head and offered a simple

blessing, then asked God to protect them and the property. "And help Ford find what he's looking for. In Jesus's name, amen."

Hearing her speak his alias in prayer, guilt pricked his conscience. He'd gone by the moniker since he was a child, but Ford Baker wasn't who he really was.

Did he owe Brooklynn the truth?

No. If anyone owed anyone, she owed him, not vice versa.

Even so, the guilt didn't fade.

"Well, dig in," she said.

He bit the sandwich, enjoying the salty ham and cheese paired with the creamy sauce and the crusty bread. It was nothing more than a fancy grilled cheese. But also, one of the tastiest sandwiches he'd ever eaten.

He might be ruined for normal grilled cheeses for the rest of his life.

After wolfing down one half and most of the chips, he sipped his water, catching her watching him from the opposite side of the glass table.

"What?"

"I take it you like it?"

"It's fine." He set the glass down, adding, "Thank you."

"You're welcome."

Niceties managed, he resumed eating.

"Why do you tell people you're a handyman?" She'd barely made a dent in her sandwich and didn't seem at all hurried. "I'm sure the town would roll out the Welcome Wagon if they knew why you were here."

"That's the last thing I want."

"Because?"

"When people find out I'm investigating an unsolved mystery, they get curious. They start coming around."

"I guess you have some experience."

He shrugged, not wanting to lie again. He didn't have experience with it, but he guessed how people would react.

"Either they'll want to know what I've learned or they'll want to share their theories—or both."

"You're not interested in their theories? Or you just don't like people that much."

"I'm interested, but I want to formulate my own ideas before I hear from others."

"So you will eventually ask the locals what they remember?"

"Depends on what I learn."

"But if you do, then you'll have to admit you were lying. Do you really think that's going to generate a lot of goodwill?"

"I've met four people." All that very day, and two of whom were smugglers. He decided not to point that out. "I don't care about goodwill."

"Right." She laughed, the sound lighthearted and free, completely incongruous with the conversation. "I probably could've guessed that. But you know the old saying about catching more flies with honey." As the words came out, her nose wrinkled. He assumed she was thinking of the spider incident.

Which brought the memory of Brooklynn after she'd taken off the insect-infested clothes. He'd known, intellectually, that she wore shorts beneath his button-down, but the shorts hadn't shown. What *had* shown were long, shapely legs.

Everything about this woman was a distraction.

"Speaking of insects, I put my clothes and the ones you let me borrow—the other ones, obviously—into the wash. They're taking forever to dry."

"It's an old dryer." He lifted the second half of his sandwich.

"I bet you'd learn more in an hour at The Salty Frog than you'll learn all day long holed up in that office."

He set his food down. "The what?"

"It's a restaurant, coffee shop, bar, depending on what time of day you get there. Been there since before I was born. It's where a lot of locals hang out."

"I'll try it, if it comes to that." He lifted the sandwich again.

"But not yet."

He didn't stifle his sigh. "Not yet."

"Because you want to formulate your own opinions, which I get. But the people who were around at the time can probably tell you more than those papers in the office."

He lowered his meal once more. "I know you think all the people of Shadow Cove are above reproach, that not a single one of them could be involved in...whatever you saw this morning. And I'm sure it's never crossed your mind that one of them could've had anything to do with the murders that happened in this house twenty-five years ago. But somebody knows something. I'd rather not paint a big target on my back just yet."

If anything, her smile only broadened.

"What?" She was the most annoying person he'd ever met.

"I have a theory about you."

He inhaled, counted to three, then exhaled slowly.

He was supposed to ask her theory—that was what she expected. But he didn't feel like playing games.

He lifted his sandwich and took a huge bite. Waiting for her to share her stupid theory and telling himself he wasn't curious.

"If somebody was involved in the murders back then," she asked, "what makes you think they still live here? Wouldn't they leave town?"

He swallowed and wiped his mouth with a napkin. "Why would they? They got what they wanted and never got caught."

"Well, because...because don't guilty people run?"

"Running makes you look guilty."

"But also keeps you out of prison."

Except nobody had gone to prison. Nobody had ever paid for his family's murders.

"You don't think the murderer is still here?" Brooklynn's cheerful demeanor faded. "After all these years."

"Maybe. They might still live right where they did before. These particular guilty people—"

"You think there're more than one?"

"I don't know."

He did know. But he couldn't say so. And why was he having this conversation?

He ate the rest of the sandwich, lifted the plate, and headed for the door. "Thanks for dinner," he called over his shoulder.

"You're welcome. I was wondering if I could ask a favor?"

He slid his plate into the dishwasher, knowing he could either hear the favor here or back in the office. Since he wanted her to leave him alone, he opted to hear it now.

She moved into the opening between the breakfast room and the kitchen. "Could I borrow your computer?"

"No."

"No? Just...no?"

Since his answer had been clear, he saw no reason to expand on it. He closed the dishwasher and started to leave.

"Wait." Of course she followed. "I need to send the photos I took this morning to the police."

He spun around so fast that Brooklynn nearly crashed into him. Her eyes were wide.

"You got pictures?" he asked. "Of the people who followed you?"

"I don't think they're very clear, but it's hard to tell on my camera's tiny screen. I thought—"

"Come on." He marched away, his heart thumping.

Maybe Brooklynn had caught the faces that had eluded Forbes for months. He'd had cameras installed to surveil the dock, hidden high in the trees. Unfortunately, the angle made it impossible to make out faces. He'd considered lowering the cameras, but he'd worried doing so would be noticed, or that the cameras themselves would be seen.

Brooklynn had surely had a better angle.

In the office, he moved the files he'd been reading to one side of the desk, then opened his MacBook and powered it up. "How do you transfer the pictures? I don't have an SD slot."

"My camera connects to Wi-Fi."

He gave her the network name and password, and she got it hooked up.

"Do you mind if I sit?"

He did mind a little, but moved out of the way. They were her photos, after all.

She settled in the chair, and he stood behind her and watched the screen over her shoulder. He should've brought one of his larger displays from his home office back in Boston. He was cursing the small laptop screen now.

The first images were of the Atlantic just as the sun peeked over the horizon. She was scrolling through them quickly.

"Those are...wow."

He guessed she was smiling at the compliment and angled forward to see her face, picking up her distinctive scent.

Her expression was as serious as he'd ever seen it. Lips pressed closed, eyes laser-focused on the images. Nose scrunched.

He studied the photographs again.

They looked great to him. "Are you not happy?"

"Huh?" Her eyes flicked to him. "Sorry. I was just..." She seemed barely aware that he was there as she advanced the photos.

And then stopped. Her breath caught.

She'd captured the sun shining through a cresting wave.

The deep teal color contrasted beautifully with the gunmetal-gray water surrounding it. There was a cliff in the background, a seagull diving on one side.

The other photos had been good. This was spectacular.

And was that...? He leaned forward to get a better look.

"You caught a fish." He heard the words he'd said and shook his head. But she had, in the image. There was the unmistakable shape of a fish, a silhouette in the wave. "Did you do that on purpose?"

"Are you kidding?" She laughed, though the sound wasn't lighthearted. More...awed. "I could take a million shots and never do that on purpose. That's...that's—"

"Amazing."

"The power of prayer." She looked up at him and seemed to realize what he'd said. "You think so?"

"Not that I know anything about photography, but I'd buy that."

She turned to the screen again. "Maybe. Maybe it'll work."

"For?"

"Oh." She shook her head. "Nothing. It's not important."

He got the feeling that it was, indeed, important. But perhaps not so much as catching the men who'd chased her.

She continued scrolling until she reached the end of the sunrise shots.

The next photograph showed boxes, or maybe they were crates, being unloaded from a white fishing boat.

He counted five men. Four hauling boxes, the fifth standing near a Polaris, angled away from the camera.

"The guy who saw me isn't in the shot. He was below me on the cliff."

But she'd gotten the other men. "Can you zoom in on their faces?"

She did, starting with a heavy man holding one side of a

crate that, based on its size compared to the man, was probably about three feet tall. Forbes thought it was the thick-headed guy who'd been on his porch that morning. Bernie, he'd said his name was.

The guy holding the other side of the crate wasn't familiar. His features were hard to make out in the shadows. It was impossible to tell hair color or eye color. He was taller than Bernie—six feet or more—but thinner.

Brooklynn scrolled to zoom in on the man pushing the dolly away, but he was facing the forest.

The other dolly-pusher's face wasn't clear. He was looking at the man at the edge of the forest, near the vehicle. He acted like an overseer.

Oh. That was Niles. His face was the easiest to make out.

No more information than Forbes had already had, but now there were pictures. Proof of what he'd suspected—that someone was using his family's private dock for nefarious purposes.

Just like all those years ago.

Bernie and Niles couldn't have been more than children back then, but who were they working for? Or was it possible these were different smugglers, unrelated to those who'd killed his parents and sister?

"I told the police officer I talked to this morning that I'd forward these." Brooklynn's voice pulled him back from his speculations. "I'm going to have to get them onto my phone, and then—"

"You can't use your phone."

"I used yours to call my sister. She accessed mine remotely and installed a VPN. She promises it's safe."

"How does your sister know how to do that?" That was some pretty high-tech stuff. What if she got it wrong?

"Alyssa's a cyber-investigator." Brooklynn looked over her shoulder at him. "Before that, she worked for the NSA."

"Oh." He hoped he schooled his features at the news, but if Brooklynn's sister decided to cyber-investigate him, would she discover his real identity?

He hoped Brooklynn hadn't asked her to do that. And he also hoped that a woman who used to work for the government's most intrusive agency wouldn't decide to look into her sister's rescuer herself.

Brooklynn's smile was back, but she didn't say anything, just turned her focus back to the computer and sent the photos to her phone. "Alyssa told me not to send the photos directly, just in case. Apparently, everything leaves a footprint."

"So...?"

"I'll send them to her, and she'll forward them for me."

"Would you send them to me too?"

Her eyebrows lifted. "Why?"

"Technically, that dock is on this property. Maybe what's going on there is related."

"To murders that happened decades ago?"

He shrugged, going for casual. "You never know."

She sent the images, then stood and handed him his phone back. "Thank you for letting me use it. And the laptop, and for everything."

They were standing too close, but there wasn't a whole lot of room behind the desk. Her nearness messed with his head. If she was going to be staying in his house, then he'd need to get accustomed to her.

Hadn't happened yet.

"Sure." He cleared his throat. "Anytime."

The words brightened her smile, and he realized he'd literally refused to let her use the laptop about ten minutes before.

Since he couldn't think of anything to say, he said nothing.

"I was poking around in the room you told me I could stay in, and there are some clothes I think might fit me."

Rosie's clothes.

He absorbed the emotional throat-punch.

He must've schooled his features well because Brooklynn continued.

"They're small. I think the room must've belonged to a teenager, which..." She shuddered, and her smile dimmed considerably. "I guess it's pretty distressing to think of what happened to her. But at the time, I was just happy to find something to wear. I took the liberty of throwing some of them in the wash, so I can return your clothes to you tomorrow."

There was no way to explain the rage that bubbled inside at the *liberty* she'd taken.

How could she know what those clothes meant to him? It was his own fault for lying to her about who he was. And for putting her in Rosie's old room. This house had twenty bedrooms. He could've put her anywhere. He'd chosen that one because it and the master bedroom at the end of the hallway, unlike the rest of them, had been cleaned and dusted. He'd washed all the linens to remove the musty scent, wanting to feel some sense of normalcy. Some sense that he hadn't actually lost everything that mattered that terrible night.

He planned to search those rooms thoroughly, soon. When he thought he could do so without getting maudlin and melancholy. His parents' bedroom might produce something helpful. He doubted there was anything useful in Rosie's room.

"I can tell that you mind."

"It's fine. Do you have everything you need?"

"I'll make it work, unless you don't want me wearing her things."

There was no reason for her not to, though Brooklynn was

inches taller than Rosie and had the curves of a grown woman. He couldn't imagine anything of Rosie's would be comfortable.

"I will need soap and shampoo in the shower in there. And some kind of moisturizer."

"Write down what brands you like, and I'll take care of it. Let me know if you think of anything else."

"Okay."

"FYI, the house has a burglar alarm which I set before bed and anytime I leave. The sirens blare—you won't miss it. If you hear it, hide. There's a compartment behind the wardrobe, like in my room."

"Okay."

"Or you can go into the spiral staircase, or, in a pinch, the basement."

She shuddered, and he fought a smile. Spiders.

"I mean the stairs going to the basement, or even just the hallway. The doors on both ends are hidden."

"Lots of options."

There were more, but he wasn't in the mood to show her all the house's secrets. "Do not leave without telling me. You could set off the alarm."

"I won't."

"You have my cell phone number now. If you can't find me, text." Not that he planned on doing much outside the house, but if he got wind of someone at the dock or elsewhere on the property, he'd investigate.

Though it felt like the conversation was over, she didn't move, letting her gaze roam the office. "I'd love to help you with—"

"I'm good. Thanks. There's an upstairs living area. Just go past your bedroom to the end of the hall, where the spiral staircase is. You remember?"

"I remember."

"There's a TV in the room on the left, and lots of books." Forbes's mother had loved to read. She never met a book she didn't like—and didn't need to own, usually in hardback. "Help yourself."

Brooklynn seemed like she wanted to say something, but after a minute, she backed up.

Halfway to the door, she turned. "I really would like to help."

"I'll let you know if I think of anything you can do." Which he wouldn't. The only way she could help him was to keep her distance so he could focus.

Maybe she read that in his expression, because hers dimmed, and she walked out.

~

THE NEXT MORNING, Forbes grabbed his keys and headed down the long hallway that led to the attached garage.

Attached now, but what held cars had first been a barn, then a carriage house off to the side of the main building. His parents had built a wing connecting the original house to the garage, which added another few thousand square feet to the mansion.

In retrospect, it seemed an unnecessary expense, but Dad had wanted Grandmother to have her own suite of rooms. Mom had talked about turning the place into a bed-and-breakfast someday, though Grandmother had suggested that would have to wait. Forbes smiled as he remembered his grandmother's words. "Over my dead body."

Ironic that Grandmother was still alive, while the family home had stood empty and decaying for decades.

Burglar alarm set, Forbes climbed into his truck and maneuvered his phone into its holder, ensuring the proper angle before he exited the garage.

Was it smart to leave Brooklynn here alone?

Maybe not, but there'd been no attacks overnight, no intruders anywhere on his property, and no more unwelcome boats at his dock. He'd checked the multiple video feeds that linked to his phone, just to be on the safe side. If anyone broke in, Brooklynn should have plenty of time to hide before they found her.

Niles and Bernie had searched and turned up no evidence that the brunette they were looking for was at his house. As far as Forbes could tell, they'd moved on.

Even so, as he drove down the long driveway, he prayed for her safety.

As if God might be listening.

The sun was low on the horizon, turning the sky various shades of pink and coral, as pretty a sunrise as Brooklynn had captured the previous morning. But clouds were rolling in from the west, and the forecast called for a stormy evening with the temperature dipping into the fifties.

It would take Forbes a half hour to make the trek through Portland. He should get to the superstore at seven, right when it opened.

He turned onto the two-lane road, not at all surprised to see a police car parked off the edge of the opposite side.

The driver followed him.

Though Brooklynn needed some supplies, that wasn't the only reason Forbes was making this trek into town. Usually, he had everything he needed delivered.

The cameras covered every inch of his property, but that view didn't extend to the road—an oversight he would fix, if he could figure out a way to do so without alerting the very people he needed to watch. He wanted to know if the house was being surveilled, and if so, by whom.

The police car told him the house was definitely being

watched, and thanks to the sun beaming through the windows of the car behind him, he had no trouble seeing the driver.

It was Lenny, Brooklynn's stalker.

Because they didn't have enough to manage with the smugglers and murderers.

Not that Forbes was one for speeding, but he was very careful to keep his speed below the limit.

He wasn't surprised when, as he was slowing to stop at the intersection to the state highway, the lights flashed behind him.

Here we go.

Rolling down the window, he pulled over onto the strip of dirt beside the narrow country road. He tapped his phone where he'd set it up earlier, then located his driver's license and papers.

By the time Lenny the Stalker approached, Forbes had both his hands on the steering wheel. No need to give this guy any excuse to claim he feared a threat.

He watched in the rearview as Lenny peered into the bed, then the backseat of his pickup before he stopped outside Forbes's window.

"Morning, Officer Taggart."

"Where you headed?"

"Portland."

"For?"

Since it was none of Taggart's business, he didn't bother answering.

"License, registration, and proof of insurance."

Forbes handed them over. He'd had his name legally changed years before so nobody could connect him to the mansion or Shadow Cove. "Was I doing something wrong?"

Studying the paperwork, Lenny said, "You crossed the yellow line."

This country road didn't have a yellow line.

Forbes didn't bother to point that out.

They both knew what this was.

"I guess you didn't find your friend on my property yesterday."

The cop's eyes narrowed. "Mind if I have a look in your truck bed?"

"I'll ask the same question as the one I asked yesterday when you demanded to search the Ballentine Mansion. You have a warrant?"

"Don't need a warrant if I have probable cause."

"Which is?"

"I saw movement when I walked up. Seems like maybe someone's under there."

Forbes was thankful he hadn't unloaded the truck after he'd picked up the supplies to replace some second-story flooring, ruined after a roof leak. Not that he'd be installing it—he'd leave that task to a professional.

"Unless boxes suddenly grew arms," he said, "that seems highly unlikely."

"Maybe there's a fugitive taking refuge without your permission. Seems you'd want to know."

"Has there been a prison break? I hadn't heard."

Taggart smiled, though the expression held no amusement. "Stay put for your own safety, sir. I'll have a look."

"So there's no misunderstanding, I am *not* giving you permission to search my vehicle."

His smile was smug. "I'll take that as permission." Pocketing Forbes's license and paperwork, Taggart moved to the bed of the pickup. He didn't say anything, just reached over and yanked the blue tarp.

It was held down by a few heavy stacks of hardwood, though, so the action didn't have nearly the flourish the cop was going for.

He scowled, and Forbes managed to contain a snicker.

Taggart climbed over the tailgate, jostling the whole truck, to check under the tarp.

Forbes lifted his phone from its holder to make sure the video caught the cop's actions through the rear window.

Obviously, Taggart found no lurkers, brunette or otherwise.

He hopped off the back and returned to Forbes's window, frowning at the phone Forbes now angled toward him. "Put that down."

"I have the right to take video in my own vehicle, officer L. Taggart of the Shadow Cove PD. In case you're wondering, it's been running this whole time."

Taggart's stare flicked from the phone to Forbes's face, and Forbes guessed he was trying to decide if he should smash the thing under his foot.

Tightening his grip, Forbes added, "It's saving to the cloud."

The man's scowl turned murderous.

"I'll take my license and paperwork."

Forbes could feel the man's rage as he handed the items back.

"I assume you tucked the tarp back around the boxes?"

"You assume too much." He swiveled and started back to his car.

"Officer Taggart?" Forbes made his voice just loud enough.

The man didn't turn around, but he looked over his shoulder. "What?"

"I don't know where your friend is. I'm sorry she's missing, but if you're worried about her, you're wasting your time with me."

"We'll see about that."

"You're getting a pass this time. If it happens again, I'll have no choice but to report you to your superiors." He let that simmer, then added, "I won't be bullied."

The man stalked back to his police car and drove away.

Forbes ended the video, ensured it had indeed uploaded, and then sent a link to his assistant with a brief note. Too brief, and no doubt Tim would want more details, but he didn't have time for that now.

He shoved the edges of the plastic sheet beneath the heavy boxes, then resumed his trip to town.

The cop wouldn't be so bold again. Forbes couldn't have asked for a better outcome.

As he headed toward Portland, he left the brief victory over Taggart behind. The cop might be put off, but those men who'd chased Brooklynn obviously wouldn't worry about Forbes's cell phone camera.

At least Brooklynn was safe at his house, for now.

CHAPTER NINE

As predicted, Brooklynn's nightmares had been populated with shadowy killers, giant Lord-of-the-Rings-sized spiders, and a creepy Hogwarts-style castle, complete with moving staircases and talking portraits.

She'd finally slept a few unbroken hours, then woke when the sun was well over the horizon. After her shower, she dressed in the now clean outfit she'd worn the day before. Though she'd washed a few of the things she'd found in the room, she wasn't quite ready to wear the garments of a murdered teenager.

The house was quiet as she made her way down the main staircase and into the kitchen. A note on the counter told her Ford had gone shopping.

For some reason, the image of the enigmatic man wandering around the grocery store struck her as amusing. He seemed somehow above all that normal human stuff.

He'd made a pot of coffee and drunk a cup, based on the dirty mug in the sink. He'd left a clean mug and a couple of tea bags on the counter beside the teapot.

She filled it with water and put it on the stovetop to boil, then emptied the dishwasher she'd run the night before. The lack of plates and bowls in the sink told her Ford hadn't eaten before he'd left.

If she had any idea what time he'd be home, she'd fix breakfast for them both. She'd wait a little while before fixing herself something, just in case he was hungry when he returned. Maybe he'd sit and eat with her like he had the night before.

The man was mysterious and secretive. She supposed she should be grateful he'd offered her shelter for the time being, but she wanted more than just shelter. She couldn't help but be curious.

She could imagine her little sister Cici's reaction to Brooklynn's thought.

Curious? The word you're looking for is nosy.

Cici called it like she saw it.

Brooklynn was scanning the contents of the fridge and pantry when the sound of footsteps reached her.

Fear sent her heart racing. She grabbed a knife from a block on the counter and spun to face her intruder.

Ford stepped in from the dining room, multiple sacks hanging from his hands. When he saw the knife, his eyebrows hiked. One corner of his lips quirked as if he might, eventually, with a little provocation, crack a smile.

"You scared me."

"Evidently."

She slid the knife back into its slot as he settled the bags on the counter.

"You've been busy." She peeked at the contents. "Is this everything?"

"One more load. I'll get it."

She put the groceries away. Lots of produce, a few boxes of pasta, jars of both marinara and Alfredo sauce. Condiments she'd searched for the day before but hadn't found. Oatmeal. Eggs, bacon, sausage. Steak, chicken. A roast.

Lemonade, large tea bags for iced tea, and more Earl Gray. Oh, he'd even bought a different black tea. Salted caramel? Sounded yummy.

She smiled at the packages of sliced ham and Gruyère. Apparently, he'd liked the sandwiches she'd made for dinner.

He returned with two twelve-packs of drinks—one cola, one sparkling water—and more sacks hanging from his wrist.

He stowed the cases in the pantry, then handed her the sacks. "I thought you might... I just guessed." His face turned an amusing shade of pink.

She peeked inside and understood why. He'd bought her a couple of sports bras and underwear.

She couldn't help imagining him wandering around in the lingerie section.

He must've guessed the direction of her thoughts because he grunted. "You said the teen's clothes were small."

"This was very thoughtful of you. Thank you."

Another grunt as he filled his mug with coffee.

"Hungry?"

He turned, nodded.

"Eggs and bacon?"

"I can cook."

"But unlike you, I have nothing better to do." Which wasn't strictly true, but there wasn't a whole lot she could accomplish without her computer. That was a problem that needed to be solved.

She'd made some calls the evening before, reaching out to the people who'd left messages with Jewel. All of them had heard that Brooklynn was in trouble and asked what happened and where she'd been.

Graham, who owned the biggest hotel in Shadow Cove, practically grilled her for details about what she'd seen.

Elvis, owner of the shop next door to the gallery, had

worried drugs would flood into the community. "Back in my day, we experimented, dabbled here and there."

Brooklynn pictured the sixty-something woman as a hippie, her long, straight hair parted down the middle, bellbottom jeans, and a multicolored polyester shirt.

"Not that they were good for us, mind you," Elvis was quick to say. "But they weren't laced with poison like the drugs nowadays. I know you're holed up somewhere... nearby?"

Brooklynn, of course, hadn't told her where she was.

The mayor had assured her that he'd directed the police chief to put his best men on the case. "We'll get you back soon," Ian had said. "Not sure we can pull off Old Home Days without you."

Good to know where his priorities lay.

Only Lois Whitmore seemed truly concerned. "Call Leo. He'll figure out the best way forward."

Leo was the chief of police—and Lenny's father. He was also an old friend of Lois's.

"I might do that."

"Do you have his direct number?" When Brooklynn said she didn't, Lois rattled it off. "Did you get that?"

"It's in my phone."

"Call him, dear. He'll help you. And if there's anything I can do for you, just ask."

"I'm safe for now. There is one thing, though. I'm worried my mother's going to find out what happened." Lois and Mom had been friends as long as Brooklynn could remember.

"You know she'll want to know."

"Yeah, but I'm afraid she'll rush back home, which could put her in danger. And if she does, Cici and Delaney will come too. They need to stay in Paris for the time being."

"I hate to break this to you, dear, but they're going to find out. I won't talk to them without your permission, but you'd be wise to get ahead of it."

"I will, but when she freaks out and calls you, talk her off the ledge, will you? I'll do my best to assure her that I'm safe, but I'd appreciate your backup on that."

"I'll do what I can. So... Did you get it? The picture?"

Excitement bubbled inside. "I did. It's perfect, exactly what we planned."

"Wonderful! I can't wait to see it."

The contest was the least of her worries at the moment, but if she won the prize money, she could keep the gallery door open. And the prestige of winning the contest wouldn't hurt business.

She was considering how to break the news to her parents when Ford interrupted her thoughts. "If you don't mind cooking, I'd eat."

"Great. Maybe you'll let me use your computer again later?"

"More pictures to look at?"

"To work. I need—"

"No. I'm sorry, but I can't do that."

Of course not. He probably had something super-secret on his laptop he was afraid she'd discover.

Right. Because historians were just *that* interesting.

He sipped his coffee, then set it on the countertop. "I'll get you a laptop."

"I can't afford—"

"I have an extra one. I'll have it delivered."

"From your house? Where is that?"

As if he hadn't heard the question, he started for the door, saying over his shoulder, "Let me know when breakfast is ready."

The more he tried to hide, the more she wanted to uncover his secrets.

BROOKLYNN'S COMPANION was as forthright at breakfast as he'd been during their other conversations, which was to say, not at all.

Ford was a puzzle Brooklynn worried she'd never solve. Rather than let that frustrate her, she gave up asking him questions. After their meal, she washed the dishes, then cooked some rotini and set it in the refrigerator to cool. She'd fix a pasta salad for lunch.

With no more excuses to put off the inevitable, Brooklynn called her family. The conversation went exactly as she'd expected—with Mom worrying, Cici demanding answers Brooklynn didn't have, and Delaney diffusing the tension.

Fortunately, she managed to convince all three of them that she was safe—without telling them where she was—and that she would be safer if they stayed in Europe.

That task finished, she had nothing to do.

She wandered around the first floor, opening closed doors and peeking into closets. This place made the seven-bedroom house where she'd grown up seem quaint. She found no more hidden passageways.

With that thought, she went around pushing on wooden paneling and shifting books on bookshelves in hopes she'd find magic levers and moving walls.

No deal.

This sleuthing thing was harder than it looked, especially when she wasn't looking for anything in particular. Just...secrets.

At the end of a long corridor in the opposite direction from the office where Ford worked, she came to a door with a keypad beside it.

It was the alarm, and the little *disengaged* light was lit. So...it should be fine.

She opened the door and discovered a gigantic garage.

Considering the high ceilings and overhead loft, this must have once been a barn.

Fascinating.

She stepped inside, and her gaze snagged on a steep wooden staircase that led to the loft that had probably once held hay. She climbed and found a beat-up cradle with some broken spindles, a chest of drawers, and an area rug wrapped in plastic. There were boxes of toys and games that looked like they had come straight out of the fifties. She found balls and bats and gloves. A badminton set, a croquet set.

Remnants of generations of happy families.

The thought made her eyes sting with tears. Years of Ballentines had lived here. Fathers and mothers and sons and daughters. And then a horrific crime, and the place had been empty since.

Was it really so easy to wipe away a family like chess pieces swiped from a board?

As if they'd never mattered at all.

Except they had mattered to someone. Suddenly, she had a better understanding of Ford and what made him tick. Even the locals rarely talked about what'd happened at the Ballentine Mansion twenty-five years before. But Ford hadn't forgotten. The secretive, curious man was determined to uncover the truth.

If only he'd let her help.

From the loft, she got a sense of the size of this garage—large enough to hold far more than the two cars below.

Two cars... How odd when only one person was here.

A beat-up blue pickup truck sat beside a red Cadillac sedan. The two vehicles were worlds different from one another. Did they both belong to Ford? If so, why had he brought both of them? And, logically thinking, how?

She climbed down the stairs, thinking that Ford didn't seem like the pickup-type. Maybe the truck went with the tool belt—a prop to back up his claim as a handyman.

But the man inside the house didn't seem the red-Cadillac type, either.

Weird.

She reached to peek beneath a tarp in the truck bed and found boxes of flooring. Why would he have that, if he wasn't really a handyman? Was that part of his prop?

The truck's cab was clean, though it showed the vehicle's age. In the glove box, she found the registration and proof of insurance, both in Ford's name.

The Cadillac was just as tidy but much newer. She found the proof of insurance in the glove box. This car was registered in Massachusetts to...

She stared, blinking. Confused.

Marie R. Ballentine.

Ballentine?

As in, the Ballentine Mansion? As in, the family that used to own the property?

She'd assumed they'd sold it. Apparently not. Even so, why was the car here?

The Cadillac might not be brand new, but it hadn't been here since the murders. That much was obvious, considering the fancy screen on the dashboard. It was clean and shiny and smelled fresh, meaning it hadn't been parked very long at all.

It didn't make sense.

Brooklynn climbed out and closed the door, suddenly certain that if Ford found her, he'd be furious. She hurried back inside, down the long hallway, and to the main staircase. She climbed to the second floor, her heart pounding all the way.

She'd discovered something Ford didn't want her to know.

Not that she was afraid he might hurt her. He'd proved that

much, anyway. But she needed Ford, she needed this sanctuary. She'd gotten comfortable here. She wanted to stay until this whole crazy thing blew over.

If Ford discovered her nosing into things, he might just order her off the property. But the more she knew about this place—and the man who lived here—the less she wanted to leave.

CHAPTER TEN

Forbes leaned back in the creaky leather chair and squeezed the bridge of his nose.

His father's old files had revealed nothing. He'd left a lot of handwritten notes, but Forbes couldn't make heads or tails of them.

Three weeks of reading until his eyes crossed had garnered exactly zero helpful information.

The police had perused all of Dad's paperwork after the murders, then shoved the files back into the cabinet haphazardly. Forbes had spent his first hours in this office putting them in chronological order.

Not that he hadn't reveled in reading his father's notes, seeing the real estate empire through Dad's eyes. After he'd finished college, Dad had had nothing but a lot of education and a huge dream.

Grandmother had told Forbes that his grandfather didn't believe in passing on wealth to the next generation or even giving them a hand up until they proved themselves. So when Charles went to his dad and asked for a loan to use as a down payment on his first property, Grandfather had refused.

"'If you want it badly enough, you'll find a way.'" Grandmother had affected a man's voice, repeating her husband's words from a generation before. "I never told your father, but Henry and I did not agree on this. We had the money. What would it hurt to give some to our only child?" Then Grandmother had smiled.

Forbes remembered it so clearly because she was a woman who'd rarely smiled in those days.

"Henry was probably right, though. That place he wanted to buy was a rundown, rat-infested converted brownstone in a lousy area of Roxbury. By the time Charles raised the down payment, it was, mercifully, off the market. Condemned, I think." Her lip had curled, though a hint of that rare smile remained.

Dad had found a way. His first property was an apartment building in Watertown, just outside Boston. He'd bought it, fixed it up, then converted it to condos and sold each separately. According to the file Forbes had studied, he'd made six figures on the deal, though he'd made pages of notes about what he would do differently next time.

Dad had invested his profit in two apartment buildings. Some he turned to condos. Others he kept as rentals, which gave him needed cash flow.

By the time Mom and Dad married, he was a millionaire. Within a few years, he'd turned the first million into twenty-five.

When Grandfather died a few years later, Dad had made more money than his dad had ever dreamed. He moved his family back to this property. Rosie was three at the time. Forbes came along a few years later.

This was the only home Forbes had ever known.

He glared at the stack of folders. Details about every deal Dad had ever made, but nothing that pointed to what had happened that terrible day. Nothing obvious, anyway. There were a bunch of scribbles that required a key to figure out, but there was no key. No way to decipher what Dad had meant by them.

There had to be something, somewhere. Because Forbes's family's murders hadn't been random.

His father had been involved in...in whatever the killers were doing. It had been a smuggling operation. At least, that was Forbes's theory. The smugglers had used the dock in the inlet, just like the smugglers had the day before.

Though Forbes hadn't understood everything he'd overheard that day, he'd known that Dad had not only been acquainted with the people who'd barged into their house, but he'd known why they were there.

Forbes tried not to think about that part, but every once in a while, when he let his guard down, the memories intruded, and he'd be faced again with the knowledge that, in some way, Dad had been responsible for their deaths.

But how? And how had a man who took such meticulous notes about every deal he'd ever made not left anything about what those killers had been doing?

Forbes hoisted the files and carried them to the two-drawer file cabinet that held the old, useless fax machine and a printer they'd stopped producing ink for early in this century.

He should toss the things out with the trash. He would, too, along with all of these old files. Eventually.

Forbes struggled to part with any of his family's things. This house and the memories it contained—even the useless and outdated ones—were all he had left of them.

Before returning the files to the cabinet, he felt around the bottom of the drawer to make sure he hadn't missed anything.

As he was slotting the files into the organizers, the question Brooklynn had asked the previous day came back to him.

How did you find all the hiding places?

He'd said the former owners had told him, which was true. His family had shown them to him.

That was just the kind of slip-up Forbes couldn't make around Brooklynn or anyone else. Which was why that moment on the spiral staircase kept coming back to him.

But now, when he heard the question in his memory again, he realized what his brain had been trying to tell him.

Yes, Forbes knew about the hiding places because he'd lived in the house. His parents had shown him and Rosie some. He and his sister had found a few on their own.

But were there more?

One of his ancestors had built this mansion—and all its secrets—so many generations before that nobody knew what, if anything, he'd been trying to hide. Family lore had it that the original American Ballentine had designed a castle in Europe in the mid-eighteen hundreds and filled it with hidden nooks and secret passageways to protect the royal family from their enemies.

Nobody knew which country the builder had been from, nor which royal family he'd been trying to protect. Nor did anybody know why, years later, he'd included all the secrets in his own home on the peaceful shores of Maine.

Forbes wondered if maybe his great-great-plus-grandfather had just been eccentric, perhaps even a bit playful. Sort of like Forbes's own father.

Or maybe, like Dad, his ancestor had had something to hide.

Were there hidden nooks he and Rosie had never found in places they'd never thought to look?

Forbes stood in the center of Dad's office and turned in a slow circle.

When he was a kid, unless Dad was behind his big desk, this room had been locked.

It wasn't until Forbes was an adult that he realized how strange that was. What was Dad trying to keep from them?

Or perhaps, shield them from?

Maybe this office hadn't given up all its secrets. Little though Forbes wanted to prove his suspicions about Dad correct, he needed to know what happened that night.

Even if the truth hurt—and Forbes had no doubt it would crush him—he needed to know. He needed to bring their murderers to justice.

If this room contained a secret, Forbes needed to find it.

~

FORBES SPENT an hour searching the walls, then the desk, for secret compartments. He found nothing.

When his phone dinged with a text, he was glad for the reprieve and snatched his phone off the desk.

It was from Tim.

> The delivery driver is there.

Giving the text a thumbs-up, Forbes headed for the foyer, where he accepted the box his assistant had sent and then climbed the central staircase. He hadn't seen Brooklynn since lunch and assumed she was watching television or reading.

The sound of music increased as he approached the family room. He stopped in the doorway to assess the situation.

Brooklynn wasn't watching TV. The music came from a record turning on Mom's old player, a big band tune that stirred a vivid memory.

Mom and Dad had been taking ballroom dancing lessons, and they'd put on the music to practice. What started as a stilted waltz ended in a cheek-to-cheek slow turn. Dad's expression had been filled with love.

Mom's reflected pure joy.

Forbes had stood in the entry, watching, unwilling to interrupt the moment. Even as a little boy, he'd understood the beauty of it.

The image was so fresh and unexpected that it took his breath away.

He forced his eyes open, worried Brooklynn had seen.

But the space was empty. A light shone through the door of the connected office, a room he hadn't set foot in since he'd returned to the house.

He crossed to the open doorway, taking in each memory like a jab to his flesh.

Mom's narrow antique writing desk. A wall of white bookshelves that held not the most beautiful books or the most expensive, but the ones she liked the best.

In front of the windows, there were two armchairs Mom had recovered in white fabric with black...drawings of some kind. She'd told him once the pattern had some fancy French name, but he couldn't remember. A footstool—recovered in black-and-white check—was in front of the chairs.

The desk held nothing but a can of Pledge and a rag.

He inhaled, but his mother's scent was gone. All he smelled was lemon and...Brooklynn.

She was seated on one of the chairs poring over an oversized book in her lap.

"What are you doing?" His voice was loud and echoed off the walls.

She startled, eyes wide when she looked up. "You scared me."

"What're you doing poking around where you don't belong?"

"Cleaning." She nodded to the things she'd left on the desk. "But I noticed the pictures and—"

"What pictures?" He moved forward and realized the thing in her lap wasn't a book at all, it was a photo album. He spied a pile of others on a side table.

He breathed through his rising anger.

Her ever-present smile faded. "I saw that"—she nodded to a photograph on the bookshelf—"and it made me curious. When I found these—"

"Those are private family property." He barely glanced at the photo she'd mentioned. "What are you even doing in here?"

"I was bored, and I thought—"

"The TV, the five thousand books in this house weren't enough of a distraction for you?"

"I've never been yelled at for cleaning."

"This is not your house."

"You said I should stay in the family room, so—"

"I said you could use that room." He pointed toward the door. "I did not say you could come into this office. I did not say you could go through the family's things. Their photos are personal. They're none of your business."

He expected her to blanch, or blush, or apologize profusely.

Instead, she sat back and squared her shoulders. "Said the guy going through *all* their personal things."

"That's different."

"Why?"

He didn't answer the question. It was none of her business.

"If you want to find their killer, I'd think you'd welcome help."

"I don't need your help." He set the box he'd carried upstairs on the desk and held out his hand. "Give it to me."

"Or is the real reason you're upset because you're one of them?"

He froze. "What are you talking about?"

"I saw your photograph."

"Mine?" Pulse racing, he prayed she didn't hear the worry in his tone.

This was not okay. This interloper could not know who he really was. Nobody could. That would ruin everything.

It would put Forbes in danger.

Worse, it would put *Brooklynn* in danger.

"Are you going to deny it?"

Think, Ballentine.

The most recent of those photos would be nearly twenty-five years old. He'd only been eight when his family was murdered.

He could fix this.

"Show me."

She eyed the books on the floor but didn't move to pick them up until he settled on the chair beside her.

She grabbed the album on top of the pile.

They were scrapbooks, the photos glued into place, many with captions.

Handwritten by his mother.

Another gut punch.

Brooklynn turned the pages quickly, and he tried not to see the images of his parents and Rosie as she passed them as if they didn't matter.

Finally, she stopped. "There." Her tone was gentle as she pointed to a photograph. "Tell me that isn't you."

He braced himself.

And looked at the photograph.

It'd been taken in the adjoining room on Christmas morning. Their decorated tree stood in the background, and though most of it was out of the picture, he could practically smell the spruce.

Tasha, Rosie's calico kitten, was in the foreground playing with discarded wrapping paper.

Dad was seated in his recliner.

Rosie was behind the chair, bending low enough to fit in the frame.

Eight-year-old Forbes stood beside his dad, whose arm was wrapped around his waist.

They were all three smiling at the camera, at Mom.

He let the image settle, breathed through the pain that felt as acute as a physical blow, and considered his answer carefully.

When he was sure the truth wouldn't show on his face, he looked up. "It's not me."

Her mouth opened, then snapped shut. She licked her lips, seemed to be trying to figure out how to get him to come clean. "I didn't realize there was a second child."

"His name was Forbes. He wasn't home at the time of the murders." Another lie, one that'd been repeated a thousand times. Only a single cop had known what really happened. "He'd gone to his grandmother's."

"Just tell me the truth."

"I'm telling you everything." Everything it was safe for her to know, anyway.

This was a secret he'd kept for nearly twenty-five years. He'd promised he'd never tell.

He wasn't about to betray Grandmother because of a too-attractive brunette who couldn't mind her own business.

"I'm related to the Ballentines."

There.

That was true without being the whole truth. "Which is why I'm determined to figure out who killed them."

Her eyebrows rose in perfect mirrored question marks. "You're *related*?"

He tapped the photograph. "There's a resemblance, but it's

not that strong. I mean, I know what I looked like as a child, and that isn't it."

The lies were stacking up like bricks, hopefully creating an impenetrable wall.

"Have you met him?" Brooklynn asked. "He is your relative, after all."

"After the murders, he disappeared. Our grandmother sent him away. She changed his name. She won't tell anyone where he is, not even me."

Brooklynn started to say something, then must've thought better of it.

She didn't believe him, that was clear. But he wasn't going to confirm her suspicions.

"I've been given permission to go through the family's things," he said. "You haven't. If I can't trust you—"

"I found something you might want to see."

"I doubt there are any clues in the family photo albums."

She set the top one aside and picked up the one she'd been perusing when he walked in.

These weren't family photos, he realized. In fact, he'd never seen this album before.

"The picture on the bookshelf made me curious," she said, turning page after page.

As she flipped through the pages, he saw mostly adults, some posed, some caught mid-conversation. They were at events—dinners, meetings. Some showed outdoor gatherings downtown or at the small town common.

Her remark registered, and he looked at the photo on the bookshelf that she'd indicated earlier. It was a posed shot of his parents, probably taken a few years before their deaths. It had a brownish background, the kind one would find in a studio. "What's special about that picture?"

"The photographer. Arthur Whitmore."

Forbes lifted the frame and peered at the tiny gold logo in the bottom corner. *AW Photography*.

"He was my mentor." Brooklynn pointed to a photograph in the album of a bunch of men and women posed shoulder to shoulder in two rows. There was a line of windows on one side of the room. Ornate crown moldings told him this wasn't some bland meeting room.

"A lot of the people in these pictures are locals who've been in Shadow Cove as long as I can remember. This"—she tapped one of the faces—"is your...is Charles. Your uncle, I guess." She flicked her gaze to Forbes, but he didn't reply. "I recognize him from the other album. Thought you might want to know some of his acquaintances."

Forbes had already spotted his father. He leaned closer to the book. "Who are they?"

Had Brooklynn come across a real lead?

Had one of the people in that photo been involved in the smuggling scheme? Had one of them been behind his family's murders?

Brooklynn tapped a face in the back row, a tall middle-aged man with a square chin and a receding hairline. "That's Graham Porter. He owns the Wadsworth Inn, that big beachside hotel south of downtown."

Forbes remembered seeing the place. Henry Wadsworth Longfellow was born in Portland, which explained the name.

"How long has he owned it?"

"As long as I can remember."

The name was familiar. "Didn't he need you for something yesterday?"

"I called him back this morning. We're on the Old Home Days committee together."

"Did he ask where you were? Was he overly curious?"

She considered the question, then shrugged. "He did ask

where I was, but I don't think he really cared about the answer. His booth will sell lobster rolls, and so will Logan's—he owns Webb's Harborside. Graham wanted me to tell Logan he'd have to offer something else." She shook her head. "As if everyone should bend to Graham's will."

"Was he surprised that you refused?"

"Maybe? I can't believe he even asked. Since Logan signed up before he did, I suggested the Wadsworth could sell something else."

Maybe Graham was more interested in Brooklynn's location than he'd let on. Maybe the lobster roll situation was an excuse to try to figure out where she was. "Go on."

The man beside Graham was a few inches shorter and considerably older. "His name was...Johnson or Jackson. Something like that. He passed away a few years ago."

"What did he do for work?"

"No idea. All I ever saw him do was drink coffee and yell at the TV over the bar at the Salty Dog, but I guess he probably owned a business at one point."

"Why do you say that?"

"I guess because most of these people do, or did, if my memory serves."

The next person looked even older, and Brooklynn didn't know his name or his profession. Then came Forbes's father.

"Did he own a business?" she asked. "Charles Ballentine?"

"Yup."

Forbes didn't offer more, though it surprised him that Brooklynn didn't realize Forbes's father was the founder of Ballentine Enterprises, which built industrial properties all over New England.

Forbes remained the largest single shareholder and held a seat on the board, even though he only attended meetings as a voice on the phone. Nobody knew Forbes Ballentine was the same person as the historian called Ford Baker.

Maybe the caution was no longer necessary, but the people who killed his family had done it for a reason. Grandmother feared Forbes could be their next victim.

Dad stood beside a tall, elegant woman.

"That's my mother, Evelyn Wright."

"Oh." Forbes studied the blonde, who was probably around the same age as Brooklynn was now. She was tall, like her daughter, but very slender where Brooklynn had curves Forbes should try harder not to notice. "You have her eyes."

"So they say."

Whereas Evelyn had a sort of elegant, regal beauty, Brooklynn's beauty seemed more natural, as if it emanated from her very being.

And there was a thought he'd keep to himself. "Did your mother own a business?"

"She was an interior designer, though I think she mostly did it for fun. She was involved in a lot of clubs and events in town, though, back then."

He tapped the man beside Evelyn. "Your father?"

"No. Dad's not in the picture."

"Did he own a business?"

"Not back then. He worked for the government."

That information pricked a memory.

We know you're working with the government. We need a name.

That was it.

Just one line, uttered by one of the murderers just moments before Dad was shot.

What had Dad said?

Forbes couldn't remember. But his heart thumped as if he'd hit on something important.

Was it possible Brooklynn's father had been involved? "What did he do?"

She sat back, her head tilting to one side. She studied Forbes as if she couldn't figure him out.

"What?" he demanded.

She smiled. "It's just rare I run across a local who doesn't know who my father is."

"I'm not a local."

"Point taken. My father is Gavin Wright. He was tapped to head the CIA back"—her gaze flicked to the album—"probably about a decade after that was taken. He turned it down, though, and started—"

"He's a defense contractor."

"You do know him."

"Of him." Forbes hadn't associated the gorgeous—if nosy— brunette with the talking head he'd seen on the news more than once. "I wonder if he knew Charles. He must've, if your mother did."

"Maybe." Brooklynn lowered her focus to the album again. "Dad was gone a lot. I'm sure my mother would remember your parents more than he would."

"Not *my parents*." The denial rolled from his tongue off-handedly.

Maybe the Wrights had been a part of...of whatever Dad had been into.

For all Forbes knew, Evelyn or Gavin Wright had killed his parents. Just because their daughter was beautiful and guileless didn't mean her parents were. Especially if one had been a spy.

Brooklynn tapped the last person in the back row. Unlike the rest, all of whom were clean-cut and wore business attire, this guy had a thick, scruffy beard and wore a faded plaid shirt. He looked like a brute of a man with wide shoulders and a thick neck. The rest were looking at the camera, but this one's gaze had flicked to Evelyn, and his expression was far from innocent.

"That's Shane Dawson," Brooklynn said. "He's a fisherman. Or…maybe a lobsterman. Something like that."

"He seems…taken with your mother."

"Hmm. Yeah. He's a little creepy." She leaned in. "Huh."

"What?"

"He kind of looks like one of the guys from the photo yesterday." She pulled her cell phone from her pocket and zoomed in.

Forbes's gaze flicked from the sixty-something guy in the photo to the younger man hauling the crate. "You think?"

"Same square jaw," she said. "Same squinty eyes. I mean, obviously, it's not the same person, but it could be a relative."

Forbes's heart thumped. "Does Dawson have a son?"

"I hardly know him, but I can find out."

"I'll do it. I don't want anyone thinking you're involved."

She looked up, a tiny smile on her face. "I am involved. I took those photographs. Anyway, I'll ask my sister. Alyssa will find out everything we need to know."

Forbes didn't want either one of these Wright women involved, but Alyssa's skills could be very helpful. "All right. If she doesn't mind."

That settled, Brooklynn looked at the photo again. "Shane and Graham are friends, or at least business associates. I've seen them together a lot."

Forbes scanned back to Graham, an elegant, almost fussy-looking man. What could he possibly have in common with the rough-looking fisherman? And what kind of business could they have?

Perhaps Dawson supplied lobster for the hotel's restaurant. Was that all it was?

"How do you know all these people?"

"Chamber of Commerce." Her tone definitely didn't convey

enthusiasm. "I joined after I opened Light and Shadows. If I had to guess, I'd say this photo was taken at a Chamber meeting."

"Based on?"

She shrugged. "They're business owners, and they're in a meeting room at the Wadsworth. That's where the Chamber meets today, and this isn't a group that likes change."

Turned out, his houseguest was a fountain of information. He should have taken notes.

She moved her finger to the front row and indicated a woman. "I don't know her, though she looks familiar. This one though." She tapped the next person. "This is Elvis Harper."

"Elvis?" He'd heard Brooklynn say that name the day before and had imagined a man with dark hair wearing a pale-blue leisure suit. Not a fifty-something woman in an outfit that would've looked right at home in the sixties on the corner of Haight and Ashbury. Was her jewelry made of... He leaned closer.

Seashells?

"Elvis owns the shop next door to mine," Brooklynn said. "She's sort of an odd duck."

"Sort of?"

Brooklynn smiled. "Nice lady, though. Wouldn't hurt a fly."

Maybe. "Didn't your assistant say she was looking for you yesterday?"

"I called her this morning. She'd just wanted to visit, I guess."

"Did she ask where you were?"

"I gave her the same story I gave everyone else, that I'm staying with a friend. She told me she'd 'send peaceful thoughts.' So if you're feeling extra peaceful, you have Elvis to thank."

This was getting weirder all the time. Obviously, Brooklynn

didn't suspect her business neighbor, but Forbes wouldn't discount Elvis based on her hippie persona.

Brooklynn pointed to the next person, the first of the three men in the front row. "That's Mr. Webb." He was a tall man with blond hair and a wide smile. "He owned Webb's Harborside."

Forbes noted the past tense. "Did he sell it?"

"He died a few years ago. His family still owns it."

Brooklynn pointed to the next person, who had a ring of gray hair around his bald head, sharp blue eyes, and a friendly smile. "That's Arthur Whitmore."

"The photographer." Forbes's gaze flicked to the photo he'd returned to the bookshelf.

"He was one of the kindest men I've ever known." She leaned back. "I got a camera for my ninth birthday. I loved it. Went around taking pictures of everything—people, landmarks, flowers, birds... If I could frame it, I'd snap it.

"I got stacks of pictures back from the lab—you remember when you had to actually develop them?" At his nod, she continued. "I thought they were amazing. They weren't, of course." Her grin was self-effacing. "But I think, looking back, that they were good for a child's first attempt. I was so proud of those pictures. I showed them to my parents and declared that I was going to be a photographer when I grew up. Mom took me seriously and introduced me to Mr. Whitmore. Over the course of the next few years, he taught me everything he knew about photography. He even taught me to develop my own photos and gave me access to the darkroom in his studio.

"Sophomore year of high school," Brooklynn continued, "I had to do a project for art class. I decided to study the history of Shadow Cove, and with the paper, I added photographs of our local landmarks. Arthur was so impressed that he turned the paper and photos into a full-color book, which he sold at his booth during Old Home Days." Her smile was shy. "I was so proud of that, even if only a few copies sold." She tapped his face on the photo. "I owe so much to him."

"I assume he's no longer with us?"

"He passed away a few years ago. He left me all his equipment. It's out of date now, but I keep it anyway."

"You said your mom took you seriously. What about your dad?" Not that it was his business.

Brooklynn's smile faded. "Suffice it to say, Dad wasn't impressed."

Forbes didn't ask, just waited for her to continue.

"He wasn't mean or anything," she said after a long pause. "But you know... Mom oohed and ahhed over my photos. Dad said they were fine but that photography was a hobby, not a real job. That I'd better figure out how I was going to make money so I wouldn't be a 'nuisance to society.'"

"Nice."

She shrugged as if it didn't matter. "He wasn't great about the dad things. He wasn't around as much as Mom, and he didn't really know how to deal with five daughters."

"Five?"

"I'm the second. Alyssa—she's the oldest—is the one who used to work for the NSA. Cici and Delaney are with Mom in Europe, and Kenzie lives in South Carolina when she's not off sailing the world."

Five daughters who needed their father. Five daughters Gavin Wright had neglected.

Forbes's father had owned a multimillion-dollar corporation, and he'd traveled a lot. But when he'd been home, he'd been a great dad. Good and kind and gentle and generous.

Of course, Dad had gotten his whole family killed.

If Forbes was ever blessed with a family of his own, he would be involved with his children, even more than his own father had been. And unlike Dad, he would protect his family above everything.

Which was why Forbes couldn't think about romance. Because he'd been in danger since the day he'd witnessed those murders. He wouldn't drag any woman into the nightmare that was his life, no matter how beautiful she might be.

No matter the way Brooklynn's grace and generosity showed in her eyes.

Or the way this nosy, beautiful, kindhearted trespasser made him yearn for things he couldn't have.

CHAPTER ELEVEN

"Anyway." Brooklynn cringed at her too-perky tone, trying to brush off her father's words as if they were irrelevant. As if the hurt they'd caused were a thing of the past.

Which wasn't even close to the truth. Twenty years later, she was still trying to prove she was more than just a nuisance to society.

She tapped the next person in the photo. "This is Arthur's wife, Lois. She's a good friend of Mom's, and after Arthur died, she took over as my mentor. She's not a photographer herself, but she used to run Arthur's gallery, and she's given me a lot of business advice."

Ford leaned in. "She was younger."

"Almost twenty years. Lois was his second wife." Brooklynn pointed to the chubby, curly-haired man beside Lois. "That's Hollister Briggs. He's an accountant." Even though she and Hollister had been in the Chamber together for more than a year, he'd hardly said more than hello to her. She got the sense he wasn't quiet so much as just...listening. Watching everything.

"And this"—she moved on to the next person—"is Maury

Stratton. She's a Realtor." Brooklynn looked up at Ford and rolled her eyes. "Not just a real estate agent, but a *Realtor*. Apparently, there's a difference. One piece of advice—don't ask her the difference because she will explain in excruciating detail."

Though he didn't smile, there was a tiny quirk at the corner of his lips. "I'll keep that in mind."

"Maury used to be married to Lois's brother. He moved away years ago, but those two are close. She runs the Shadow Cove Historical Society. She'd be a good resource for you. She has her hands in everything." Brooklynn pointed to the next person, a stocky man in his thirties at the time the photo was taken. "That's Leo Taggart. He's the police chief now."

"Taggart? As in your stalker?"

"Lenny's not a stalker, just...persistent."

"Brooklynn." The way Ford said her name had her looking up. His brows were lowered, his lips pursed. "Someone who's so persistent they follow you even after you tell them to go away? We call that person a stalker."

Right. Well...

She knew that. She knew Lenny had pushed it too far. She wasn't sure why she still balked at the term.

"Speaking of," Ford said, "your friendly neighborhood cop was staking out the house when I left this morning." He explained how Lenny had pulled him over and illegally searched under the tarp on the bed of Ford's truck. "I got a video of the whole thing."

Despite the guilt his words brought, Brooklynn didn't share that she'd also searched his truck—and the garage, and the Cadillac.

"He was looking for you, obviously," Ford said.

Her guilt dissipated, and fear crept in. She shouldn't be afraid of Lenny. He'd never hurt her, but he'd been so hard to get rid of the first time. The thought that she might have to go through it again...

"He knew you might be hiding *from him*," Ford said, "which tells me everything I need to know about this guy. You need to stop making excuses for him and come to terms with the kind of person you're dealing with."

Obviously, Ford felt passionately about this. And very irritated, considering all the sentences he'd strung together.

"You're right. I used to have feelings for him, so it's hard."

"I threatened to report him to the police and send the video, but if the chief is his dad—"

"Leo would take it seriously," she said. "I think, anyway. Lenny left me alone when I threatened to report him. He respects his father."

"Maybe. But that didn't keep him from sitting outside my house or pulling me over."

"He's worried about me, that's all. He says he still cares about me." She was embarrassed to say what Lenny claimed.

That he loved her. That they were meant to be together. That they were soulmates.

It was laughable, considering how he'd manipulated and belittled her when she dated him. She'd had to threaten to get a court order to get rid of him. And now that she was in danger, he could claim he had no choice but to hunt her down.

To protect her.

To *possess* her, more like.

"I'm sorry he gave you a hard time." Brooklynn worked to keep fear out of her voice.

If Ford's skeptical expression could be believed, he didn't buy the way she played down the problem. "That's why I went out this morning, to see if he'd stop me, and to warn him off if he did. If you want to go somewhere, as long as you stay hidden in my truck so he doesn't see you—assuming he's still staking out the driveway—he won't dare pull me over again. You should be safe."

A wave of affection for her grouchy host rolled over her. And then she realized what it really meant. That he wanted her to leave. That she was too much of a nuisance. "I can find a place to go. Alyssa said—"

"I don't want you to leave." He sounded annoyed. "I mean, I don't care if you stay. I just want you to have the choice."

"Oh. Okay. That was really clever, and thoughtful of—"

"But no more snooping." He looked around the office, then shook his head. "That's the deal."

Brooklynn could've denied she'd been snooping, but it would be a lie. And she could've assured him she wouldn't do it again.

But that would probably also be a lie. She was too intrigued by the mysterious mansion.

"Tell me about Lenny's father," Ford said, as if the matter were closed.

"He seemed nice enough when Lenny and I dated. I think he's a decent guy. And he's a good cop."

"Did his father own a business?"

She looked at the photo again. "If he does now, I'm not aware of it, but maybe he did back then. Or maybe he was invited to speak to the group on behalf of the police department. We have speakers sometimes."

She continued to the rest of the people in the picture, but she either didn't know them or they'd moved or passed away. When she finished, she sat back. "I can go through the rest of the album and see if there's anyone else I recognize. I mean, it's not like I have anything else to do."

"Actually, you do." Ford stood and lifted the box he'd carried into the office with him. "I got a computer for you."

"Are you serious?"

Her disbelief had his smirk turning to a frown. "I told you I would."

He'd said that, but she hadn't expected him to do it, certainly not within a couple of hours.

She opened the box and spied an Apple laptop. "This is perfect. It's okay if I get online?"

"Just be careful that you can't be tracked here."

"Of course. I'll call Alyssa and get it connected to a VPN. This will be so helpful. Thank you."

The tiniest hint of a smile crossed Ford's face, and he quickly turned away. He was working very hard to hide his real self behind that grumpy demeanor.

He might not be Forbes Ballentine—though he looked an awful lot like the little boy in the photos she'd seen—but he was keeping secret his connection to this family, a connection she'd already guessed from the fact that Marie Ballentine's car was in the garage.

The question was, why?

And if he learned she'd discovered his lies, would he boot her from his property?

Or worse?

~

A FEW MINUTES LATER, Brooklynn was setting up the laptop at a small writing desk in the family room when Ford stepped into the doorway.

"I wanted to ask who the other people were who looked for you or called you at your shop yesterday morning."

"Let's see." Brooklynn thought back to her conversation with Jewel. "Ian Prescott. He's the mayor."

"Tell me about him."

She wasn't sure what Ford wanted to know. "He's about my height and always wears a suit, even in the summer."

By the way Ford crossed his arms, that wasn't the sort of information he wanted.

Not that she could offer much more. "He's an attorney. His parents were solidly middle-class, but he's got a lot of money."

"From where?"

"His work, I assume. Maury—historian, Realtor—told me he paid full price for a house on the hill."

"Which hill?"

"You know, that hill overlooking town. I always call it Sam's hill because my cousin Sam lives up there. The houses up there have great views, and Maury said Ian bought one of those. I get the feeling he has higher political aspirations than to be the mayor of a small town."

"Why?"

"I guess because he's already the mayor, but he still acts like he's campaigning. Lots of handshaking and baby-kissing, you know?"

"What did he want?"

"To ask me about Old Home Days."

"That project's keeping you busy."

"You have no idea." It was killing her. The committee had nominated her to organize the booths, and she'd been foolishly pleased, as if it meant they trusted her. Now, she understood it wasn't that at all. Nobody wanted to deal with the booths because it meant dealing with every single business owner in town.

"What did he want to know?" Ford asked.

"No idea. I called him back this morning, but he hasn't returned my call."

"Is he always so involved?"

She couldn't figure out where this conversation was going. "This is the first time I've ever worked on the event, so—"

"I'm asking if he's called you a lot this year?"

"This was the first time."

Ford nodded. Maybe his frown deepened a little, but it was hard to tell, seeing as how he was always frowning.

He was a handsome man. How much more handsome would he be if he'd ever learn to smile?

"Anyone else?"

"Owen Stratton."

"Stratton? Isn't that the real estate agent's last name?"

"Maury. Yeah." Ford had a good memory. "Owen's her grandson. He's dating my sister, Delaney, and I guess he heard I was in trouble."

"How did he hear? Your call to the police was anonymous."

"He's a volunteer EMT and has friends in the police department, so maybe he heard from one of them. Besides, it's all over town."

"Is Owen friends with Lenny?"

Why did Ford keep coming back to Lenny? "They know each other, but if they're friends, I'm not aware of it."

"What's Owen do for work? Aside from the volunteer thing?"

"I think he works on the docks? I've seen him down there a few times with Shane."

"The fisherman or lobsterman." At her nod, Ford said, "Does everyone know everyone?"

"It's a small town."

He acknowledged that with a grunt. "I can make dinner."

"I plan to, unless you want to cook."

"I don't. Help yourself." He tossed out a "thanks" and then walked away.

He was back in seconds. "No snooping."

"How about cleaning?"

Lips pressed closed, he glanced down the hallway. "The other wing. Not the family's rooms."

"Fair enough." He started to walk away, but she called him back. "Ford?" When he filled the doorway again, she asked, "Can we turn on the heat? It's getting chilly." Clouds had moved in, and though she hadn't stepped outside all day, it was obvious by the cool air seeping through the old windows that the temperature had dropped.

"This house still has electric heaters." Ford adjusted a thermostat near the door. "Feel free to turn it up in your bedroom too."

"Thanks."

He walked away, and this time, he didn't come back.

The room filled with the scent of dust from the heater but warmed up pretty quickly. She checked her weather app. Rain was coming, and the temperature was supposed to dip even more, down into the fifties.

Thank goodness for heat.

Brooklynn got caught up on paperwork for the gallery, spent an hour trying to organize the booths for Old Home Days, which was much more complex than it sounded. She should've listened to Lois and refused the job. She hadn't because she'd thought, seriously? How hard could it be to manage fewer than a hundred vendors?

In retrospect, the answer was—*incredibly* hard.

She wanted to get it done so she could focus on more important things like the Arthur Whitmore contest. Arthur had been a top New England photographer, his photographs featured in newspapers and on national magazine covers. Because he'd been a Shadow Cove local, the contest would take place the weekend of Old Home Days. All the entries would be displayed in the Whitmore Gallery booth.

Lois oversaw the contest but had professional photographers judging all the categories. Brooklynn wanted to win the landscape category, and one entry would win the grand prize.

That was the prize that came with money—five thousand dollars. It wasn't a huge amount, but it would make a world of difference to her business.

The winning photograph would be announced at the Whitmore booth at the small-town festival, of course. But because of how well-known the Whitmore prize had become, the winning photographer would be written up in newspapers all over New England—and in photography journals all over the country. If Brooklynn won, it wouldn't just be a boon to her name and her work. It would mean free publicity for the Light and Shadows website.

As much as she loved the walk-in business that came with seasonal tourists, she needed more sales if she was going to keep the lights on twelve months a year. And she wanted to prove to her father she could support herself with her work. To prove she wouldn't be a drain on her family's finances for the rest of her life.

She checked the entry requirements carefully, then ordered the photograph to be printed in various sizes at her favorite lab.

It was done. She'd either win or not win, but she was out of time.

If Arthur were still alive, he'd ask if she'd done everything she could. Knowing she had, she could practically hear her old mentor telling her to trust God with the outcome.

Capturing His beautiful world is reward enough. If people want to buy your photos, that's just icing on the cake.

Translation: Don't worry. Much easier said than done when you had a mortgage to pay.

If she shared her fears with Lois, she would remind Brooklynn of how talented she was.

If the judges don't see that, then they're fools.

Maybe not fools, though. Beauty was subjective. She might get the best shot of her life, but that didn't guarantee the judges would even like it.

Lord, You know how much it means to me. Please, let my photograph win. Save my business, my dream.

Either He would or He wouldn't. Now that the prints had been ordered, it was out of Brooklynn's hands. She needed to quit fretting about it.

She closed her laptop, grabbed the Pledge and the rag she'd found earlier, and headed down the hall. She had time to get some cleaning done before she needed to start dinner.

And if she happened to find something interesting along the way, who could blame her for doing a *little* snooping?

CHAPTER TWELVE

Forbes had scoured every inch of his father's office and found exactly...nothing.

It was maddening.

Dad had to have left something about the smugglers he'd done business with. He'd kept meticulous records regarding every other aspect of his real estate enterprise. Surely, surely he'd recorded information about the people who ran a smuggling operation through his property.

The Network.

That was all Forbes knew. He had a fleeting memory of one of the murderers—the woman—using those words.

"The Network trusted you. You betrayed us."

But who was The Network? What had they trusted Dad to do? Had Dad really betrayed them? He'd vehemently denied it. He'd begged them to believe him. He'd assured them that nobody in his family knew anything about it.

But they'd shot him. And Mom. And Rosie.

And Forbes had done nothing to protect them. He'd hidden like a coward.

He knew what his therapist would say. *You were eight years old, Forbes. What could you have done?*

Something. He could've done *something*.

He could have tried to get to a phone. He could have tried to protect his mom and his sister. If he had, maybe he'd have died with them. Probably. But he wouldn't have had to live with this guilt and regret.

But Rosie had shoved him into the hiding place, and there he'd stayed.

Even now, so many years later, he could see his father's body fall. See his lifeless eyes.

Forbes hadn't seen his mother's murder or his sister's, but he had never forgotten the sound of the gunshots.

He'd stayed in his hiding spot, listening to shouts. He didn't remember most of it, but one phrase had lingered.

Find it. We have to find it.

They hadn't found it, whatever *it* was. Sirens had cut their search short. They'd escaped moments before the police swarmed the house.

Forbes stayed hidden, even then. Too terrorized to emerge from his hiding place.

It wasn't until Grandmother came to the house the following day that he dared leave the little cubby hole in the family room. She'd coaxed him out, and then she'd taken him away.

Grandmother had protected him. The old woman was far braver than Forbes had ever been.

What had the killers been searching for? And where had Dad hidden it?

A flash of light had him turning toward the window.

Thunder cracked.

Though it was only eight o'clock, it looked dark enough to be midnight.

Another crack of lightning, and the power went out.

What in the world?

He stood in the center of the office and waited, sure it would come right back on. But it didn't, and thanks to the thick cloud cover, it was even darker inside than out.

Had everyone in town lost power, or just him?

Had someone cut his electrical line?

He didn't move. Just listened to the wind howl, the thunder rumble. No sounds of breaking glass or doors opening. No voices. No intruders.

His state-of-the-art alarm system was engaged. If anyone tried to get in, thanks to a backup battery, it would sound despite the lack of power. They should be safe.

Where was Brooklynn?

They'd eaten dinner—she'd broiled steaks, which had been delicious. He thought she'd gone back upstairs to resume cleaning.

Forbes pulled his handgun from a drawer in Dad's desk, ensured the safety was engaged, and shoved it into his waistband, just in case. He owned a holster for it, but he didn't think he was actually walking into a gunfight. Besides, the holster made him feel like some Old West train robber.

He moved into the long hallway, using his phone's flashlight to keep from crashing into walls, and went up the hidden spiral staircase to the second floor.

He peeked into the family room. "Brooklynn?"

No answer. It was warmer in there, but that wouldn't last without electricity. He closed the door to keep the heat in.

He headed away from his family's bedrooms toward the north wing, where he'd told her she could clean. Nobody in his family had used those rooms. He raised his voice. "Brooklynn?"

"In here!" Her voice was faint over the storm.

He moved faster, but there were a dozen rooms on this end of the hall. "Where exactly?"

"Polo!" she called.

Like they were playing a game.

Silly woman.

He was thankful she couldn't see the smile creeping across his face. He schooled it, just in case, but decided to play along. "Marco!"

"Polo." She sounded closer.

He continued more slowly. "Marco?"

"Polo?" She replied with the same questioning tone, the sound coming from an unused sitting room. He pushed the door open and stepped inside, scanning with his phone's flashlight. She'd turned on the heat, making it warmer than the chilly hallway.

She'd plopped down in the middle of the floor. This room had no windows, no natural light at all.

"Comfortable?"

"Oh, yeah." She pushed to her feet. "Best seat in the house." Was her voice shaky? Surely she wasn't afraid of the dark.

"Does your phone not have a flashlight?"

"The battery died." She brushed off her pants. "I've been meaning to ask you to borrow a charger, but..." Her voice trailed.

He guessed she was the kind of person who let her phone die regularly.

"Thanks for coming for me. Another rescue mission! You're like one of those lifeguards on *Baywatch*."

Like it was 1995.

She added, "Sans the Speedo, of course."

What was he supposed to say to that? He came up with zero responses. "What were you doing in here?"

"Cleaning."

He scanned the room again. His flashlight skimmed the bottle of Pledge and the rag but landed on a spiral notebook in the middle of the desk. "What's that?"

"I found it. I thought you might want to see it."

He crossed to the desk and flipped the top open. It was a ledger of some kind, filled with Father's handwriting. Beside it were a couple of cassette tapes.

His heart thumped. How had she come across this? He'd searched this room already, and law enforcement had searched the entire house.

Which meant...

"Where?" He spun to face Brooklynn, accidentally flashing the light in her face.

She squinted and took a step back.

He lowered the beam. "Where did you find it?"

"Um..." Based on the wavering single word, she was nervous to tell him. "The desk drawer had a false bottom. Once I figured that out, it was just a matter of finding the way in."

"How did you know?" He was tempted to flash the light in her face again, to judge her expression as she answered the question.

No need for her to feel like she was being interrogated, even if she was.

"It's just that the house has some secrets, so I thought maybe there were more." When he didn't let her off the hook, she added, "I didn't mean to pry. I just... I was curious."

"I specifically told you not to snoop."

"I wasn't snooping. I was—"

"Cleaning? You were worried the secret compartment might be dusty?"

She shifted her feet but said nothing.

"Come on." After grabbing the ledger and tapes, he marched to the door and down the hall to the family room, the whisper of her footsteps following. He pushed the door open and stepped aside so she could precede him.

When she passed, she didn't look up. Was she embarrassed or frightened? Maybe a little of both?

He didn't want to frighten her, but she needed to quit nosing around in his business.

Even if she had found something he'd missed.

Though this room had a wall of windows, they didn't let in much light. The sun had set, and the moon was hidden behind clouds. Nothing but an occasional flash of lightning brightened the space.

"Sit."

She froze. "I think you've mistaken me for the family dog."

Nothing about Brooklynn said *dog*.

And anyway, dogs were obedient.

He blew out an audible sigh. "Would you please sit down so you don't crash into something and break a bone or an antique lamp?"

"Why, thank you, kind rescuer." He heard a smile in her voice as she settled on the sofa near the fireplace.

The woman was cheerful to a fault.

He checked his phone and confirmed that the power was off in most of Shadow Cove. Then, he scrolled the video feeds. His security system was working and all seemed...

Wait.

Was that...? It looked like someone was lurking outside the garage. Or maybe a fallen branch had blown in the heavy wind.

He didn't want to worry Brooklynn, and if someone was out there, if they breached the building, the alarm would sound.

"Don't move," he told her. "Just...just stay there until I get back. If you hear anything unusual..." He crossed to the hiding space he hadn't peeked into since that terrible night so many years ago. He swung the grate open.

He didn't look inside. Never wanted to see in there again. "You can hide in here."

"Ooh, another secret."

"Just stay put." His words were too gruff. When she said nothing, he added, "Please?"

"With no flashlight, where am I going to go?"

There was no telling with this woman. "I'll close the door to keep the heat in. I'll be right back."

"Okay, but Ford? Don't be long."

She sounded as nervous for him to leave her alone as he was. Sure, the alarm system would alert him if anyone came. But could he get back to her in time?

∼

FORBES MADE his way down the steps to the basement and to the door that let out into the side yard, opposite the garage. Silently, he paused the alarm long enough to step outside, knowing it would re-engage in seconds.

He killed his flashlight and stowed his phone. The wind whipped, and rain stung his face.

Heart thumping, he pulled out his handgun.

That shadow on the video feed had probably been nothing. Even so, he proceeded cautiously.

He crept toward the back of the house. He couldn't differentiate the sound of the surf from the heavy wind whipping through the trees.

On the far end of the house, he rounded the garage.

The side door was open just a crack.

Thanks to the storm, Forbes couldn't hear anything coming from inside. He glanced through the window in the door.

Two flashlights were moving around near the vehicles.

He backed away and pressed against the wall. What should

he do? He could try to trap them in there, but the last thing he wanted was to get into a shootout. He had to assume they were armed, and there were two of them and one of him. They were inside and he was out. If they killed him, nothing would stop them from breaking into the house.

They could find Brooklynn.

Thick, wild bushes poured out of what used to be a pretty flower bed. They'd be easy enough to hide in. When Forbes heard the voices moving toward him, he ducked behind the bushes and watched.

Two figures stepped outside. It was too dark to make out faces, but Niles's voice carried on the wind. His words were impossible to make out.

The taller man had to be Bernie.

Tweedle-Dee and Tweedle-Dum.

They bent low and jogged past Forbes toward the driveway and the road. When they were a good twenty feet past, he cocked his weapon and shouted, "Hey!"

"Run!" one shouted.

They both broke into a sprint.

Forbes aimed high and just to the left of the shorter one. He fired.

Niles hit the ground. The bullet hadn't come within ten feet of him, but he was smart enough to know one could.

Bernie, the moron, kept running.

Forbes aimed for just north of his ear and fired again.

The big man dove.

"Stay off this property!" Forbes yelled to be heard over the wind, never revealing his position. "Next time, you'll leave in a body bag."

He counted to ten, dripping in rainwater. They might as well get as wet as he was. Finally, he shouted, "Go. Don't come back!"

They both hopped to their feet and bolted toward the road.

Forbes hoped he'd made an impression.

When they were out of sight, he let himself in the garage. Everything looked fine.

He checked his pickup truck's engine, then that of Grandmother's Cadillac. He checked the brake lines. Both undisturbed. No ticking bombs. No booby traps.

He saw nothing worrisome at all, which was...worrisome.

What had they done?

He had no idea, and the not knowing bothered him almost as much as the intruders themselves.

~

AFTER FORBES CHANGED into dry clothes, he made a quick stop in the kitchen, then grabbed an armful of wood from the stack in the garage. He wasn't worried about kindling. This wood had been dead for twenty-plus years. It would burn way too fast.

He was practically jogging, Brooklynn's fearful tone when she'd asked him to hurry playing on a loop in his mind. Nothing would happen to her as long as she stayed put.

But this was Brooklynn.

Making the odds she'd start snooping fifty-fifty. Maybe seventy-thirty.

At the family room and carrying an armful of logs, he kicked the closed door.

"Ford?"

"It's the boogeyman. Open up."

The door swung open. Thanks to the darkness, he couldn't see her face, but he didn't need to. He conjured her smile in his mind's eye.

"I always pictured you bigger, with claws." She took the

phone from his hand—her fingers were colder than his—and lit the way to the fireplace with his flashlight.

"Common misconception. We boogeymen get a bad rap."

"Did you just make a joke? Are you bantering with me?"

"No."

"I love to banter. Bantering is my favorite."

He dropped the firewood, thankful she couldn't see his smile.

This woman.

She was incredibly irritating. And funny and sweet and happy.

Stop that.

Nosy. That was what she was, and he couldn't have it.

He put the sack that'd been hanging from his wrist on the coffee table, then found the box of matches Dad had always kept on the mantel and set them down as well. "Light the candles, please."

"On it."

While she rustled in the plastic, he took the weapon from where he'd tucked it at the small of his back and set it on a side table near the windows.

"Is that a gun?"

"Yeah." He took a breath and blew it out. "Your friends Niles and Bernie decided to take advantage of the power outage. I saw them on one of my video feeds."

She gasped. "What happened? I thought I heard...I thought it was thunder. Did you—?"

"I scared them off. Don't worry." He'd do enough worrying for both of them. "If they come back and try to get in the house, the alarm will sound. We're safe."

He turned the knob to open the flue, realizing too late that he hadn't grabbed anything to warm the chimney or light the flame.

He must've grunted because she asked, "Something wrong?" She sparked a match and lit a candle, but the light barely penetrated the darkness.

"I forgot newspaper." He pushed to his feet, suppressing a sigh. "I think there's some in the garage."

"There's a ream of paper in Grace's office." She nodded to the closed door. "It's useless, old and yellowing. I'm sure it would work." She stood. "I'll grab it."

"Stay here. Where is it?"

"Bottom desk drawer, right side."

"The drawers were dusty inside?"

"Terribly."

"Hmm." He should call her on her snooping again, but at the moment, he was just glad he didn't have to return to the garage. The walls were too thin, and it was already getting cold out there. Summers in Maine could be colder than winters in many parts of the country, especially when the wind whipped like it did tonight. The new wing of the house was better insulated, but there were no working fireplaces. He'd had this one inspected before he'd moved back. It was the only one in the house he dared to light.

He found the paper right where Brooklynn had said and set to work building the fire.

Brooklynn was busy doing something behind him, but he didn't look to see what.

As predicted, the old wood lit right up. It was throwing heat into the room within a couple of minutes—and enough light to show him what she'd been up to.

She'd moved the coffee table and sofa so they faced the hearth, blocking the rest of the room's furniture.

Okay, then. Apparently, she was chilly.

He made his way to a club chair in the corner and dropped into it.

"What are you doing? Come sit with me." She patted the space beside her. "It's warmer over here, and I opened the snacks. Good thinking, by the way."

She'd torn a box of crackers at the corners so that the cardboard was flat and laid out the things he'd brought up in a spread like they were at a cocktail party. Two of the bottles of water he'd brought were open.

"What is it about sitting in front of a fire that makes me want to eat?" She chose a cracker and added a slice of cheese. "I wasn't even hungry until I saw the fire. Now, I'm looking for marshmallows and graham crackers."

He leaned toward the food but was too far away to reach it.

"Sheesh, Ford." She tapped the cushion again. "I'm not going to bite you, not while I'm eating, anyway." She punctuated the statement with a bite of her snack.

It did seem silly to sit so far from the heat.

"Don't be a scaredy-cat."

He couldn't help himself.

He chuckled.

She gasped again. "Oh, my gosh. Did I make you laugh? Where's a video camera when you need it?"

"Shut up." He stood and settled beside her so he could reach the food and feel the heat. Not because he wanted to be closer to her.

"You're safe there until we run out of food," she said. "Then, all bets are off."

"I'll take my chances." He grabbed a handful of crackers and cheese slices and sat back to enjoy them.

"For me," Brooklynn said, "it's the history, I think. When I was a kid, if we had a fire, it was for a reason. Christmas morning or a game night. And of course when we lost power, we had to light the fire to stay warm. If we lit a fire, it was an event, even if the event was a storm. Mom always had the stuff for s'mores. We'd have hot chocolate and popcorn—if the electricity was working. If not, then crackers or...whatever she could find. If we lost power in the summer, Mom claimed we *had* to eat all the ice cream or it would go bad." Brooklynn smiled, shaking her head at the memory. "Only as an adult did I realize ice cream would last in a freezer for hours."

In the fire's glow, her face was golden, her hair radiant.

Couldn't she just be normal for two seconds? Did she have to give off that...that annoying, tempting glow?

Everything about her drew him. Her sweet voice. Her kind demeanor. Even her cheerfulness wasn't as irritating as it should have been.

She was his opposite in every way. Where he was closed off, she was an open book. Where he was quiet, she was chatty. Where he was serious, she was lighthearted.

They couldn't be more different. They would never work.

He focused on the flames, which were much less dangerous than the woman at his side.

"Did you grow up around here?" she asked.

"No."

"Ooh, tell me more."

He shook his head and ate another cracker.

"Where did you grow up?"

He took his time swallowing, hoping she'd give up waiting for a response. When she didn't, he said, "Massachusetts."

"So specific. Wow. Do you have siblings?"

"No." Another lie, but Ford Baker had no siblings. He figured the only way to get Brooklynn to stop asking questions was to ask his own. "Tell me about your sisters."

"Well, there's Alyssa. You know about her. She's a year older than I am." While Brooklynn described her four sisters in detail, Forbes listened, really listened. He had nothing else to do, after all, and Brooklynn's voice just made him...happy.

Which was stupid, and which he wouldn't admit to under threat of death.

She spoke about each sister with great affection, then went on to describe her mother. "I always wanted to be just like her. She's so elegant, my mom. And she makes everybody feel right at home."

"You do that."

"You think so?" Hope filled her voice, as if he were right on the verge of making her year.

"Sure. You're nice."

Nice?

That single word didn't begin to describe Brooklynn.

"I do try to be nice. I like people to like me."

Yeah. That fit.

"But I'm not elegant. Mom's just got this way about her that makes everyone take notice when she walks into a room. I swear, in a past life she was a queen."

A past life? "Are you a Hindu or something? Into some New Age—"

"I'm kidding." Her laugh was lighthearted. "I'm a Christian. I'm just saying, she was born to be royalty, you know what I mean? Alyssa's like her, with that long pretty blond hair. I'm nothing like that. I've always been... I don't know. Just ordinary. And also... Too much."

"Too much of what?"

"I don't know."

At the shift in her tone, Forbes looked at her. "What's wrong?"

"Nothing."

"Obviously something. You're not smiling."

"I don't *always* smile."

"You do unless something's wrong."

She licked her lips, and the sudden rush of warmth Forbes felt had nothing to do with the burning logs a few feet away.

"I don't know what makes me too much, but I've always had the sense that people think I am. Just...too much. Too much to deal with. Too much trouble. Even you think that."

"I never said that."

"I snoop."

"That *is* annoying."

"See? Too much."

"That doesn't make you 'too much.' It makes you nosy."

"Too nosy. Too much. It's fine." This time, her laugh was forced. "I am who I am. I can't help myself."

"You could try *not* snooping."

"Hmm." She made the sound as if she were considering the option. "I *could,* theoretically. But in practice... I'm not sure."

At least she was honest.

Far more honest than he'd been.

"How did you find the hidden compartment in that desk?"

"Oh. If I didn't know the house had secrets, I probably wouldn't have. But the dimensions inside the drawer didn't match the depth."

"How did you see that?"

"I don't know." She shrugged. "It was obvious."

It hadn't been to him. She'd also noticed the resemblance between Bernie and Shane Dawson, which he hadn't picked up on at all. And he'd seen Bernie face-to-face, not just in a grainy photograph.

"You see what others don't see," Forbes said. "Which makes sense."

"How so?"

"You know, because you're an artist."

She sat back and scoffed.

"What?"

"I'm not an artist," she said. "I just take pictures. The art, the beauty, is already there."

"You see what others don't see and capture it. You evoke emotions with your work. A painter does that with paints. A poet does it with words. You do it with a camera."

"It's not the same. A painter has skill. A poet... I mean, I can barely *read* poetry, much less write it. That's crazy skill. I just point and shoot."

"You're being ridiculous. You don't really believe that." He hadn't meant the words to come out angry.

To be fair, he hadn't meant the words to come out at all.

She crossed her arms and stared into the flames.

"What?" he demanded. "What are you thinking?"

"Nothing. It's nothing."

"Just tell me."

She looked his way, head tilting to the side. "Do you find that annoying? When you ask a question and get no response, or just a one-word answer that doesn't actually explain anything?"

"Whatever."

"Because I imagine that might be a little frustrating."

"I was just making conversation."

"No, you were expecting *me* to make the conversation so you could sit there silently. Maybe it's my turn to be the mysterious one, mmm? Ever thought of that?"

"Nobody forced you to talk."

She pressed her lips together.

Not sure if the darkness hid the way his cheeks burned, he stood and added another log to the fire. Sparks crackled and rose. He used the poker to position the log, keeping his face averted so she couldn't guess what he was thinking. Telling himself not to ask again. That he didn't care.

There was a story. There had to be a reason a woman who

owned a gallery and filled it with her own art didn't consider herself an artist.

He shouldn't care.

The problem was, he did care, and it did matter how this amazing woman saw herself. She thought she was too much.

From what Forbes could tell, everything about her was just right.

CHAPTER THIRTEEN

Ridiculous.

Ford had called Brooklynn ridiculous, then expected her to explain herself. As if she owed him an explanation. If she told him what she was thinking, she'd only prove what he already thought about her.

Ridiculous.

That pretty much summed it up, didn't it?

Ford had scarfed almost all the crackers she'd set out, along with most of the cheese, so she replenished the makeshift charcuterie board, wishing she had some grapes, maybe a bowl of olives to make it look pretty.

Ford would probably suggest that made her an artist, as if everyone in the world couldn't present food on a tray.

Okay. Maybe she was the one everybody in the family insisted put together the charcuteries and set the table for a fancy meal, but only because she liked doing it, and she had experience. And maybe she understood scale and color. She liked making things look pretty. That didn't make her an artist.

She was smarter than to use that word to describe herself. She knew who she was, what she was, and what she wasn't.

Ford settled beside her and reached for the crackers. But he didn't take any, just sat back again. "I went to boarding school."

The words were out of left field, apropos to nothing, but she quenched her surprise, afraid she'd scare him back into silence.

"That's different."

"My great-aunt raised me. She came from money, and in her day, all wealthy young men went to boarding school, so..."

"Where were your parents?"

His lip quirked. "They were...busy."

"Was this an aunt on the Ballentine side of your family?"

"No. Other side." He grabbed a cracker and the last slice of cheese and ate them, taking his time chewing.

She'd pushed too hard. She sipped her water to keep from pressing him for more information.

"I didn't like it very much," he finally said. "Boarding school. It was cold. The buildings were drafty, but it was more than that. It seemed like the kids all knew each other and didn't need another friend. I wasn't good at fitting in. Too quiet."

"Really? I'm shocked."

He ignored her. "The teachers were strict. The classes were challenging. My aunt expected top grades, and I had to work hard to achieve them. This was a sort of...cream-of-the-crop type of place. Only the smartest were allowed entry, so even though I'm...you know."

"Super smart?"

He shrugged. "I was born with a good intellect. Like some people are born with artistic ability." He looked at her, eyebrows hiked. "There's no shame in knowing who you are, who God created you to be."

He seemed to wait for her to say something, to admit she was talented or artistic or whatever, but she snagged on something else. "You're a Christian?"

He studied the fire. "I believe in a Creator. When I was a kid, I put my faith in Jesus."

"But?"

He shrugged. "Life happens, and God doesn't show up."

"God doesn't have to 'show up.' He's always with us."

His smirk told her what he thought of that. "If He does nothing, then He's about as helpful as a gun with no bullets." Ford nodded to the weapon he'd left on a side table. "At least that thing's loaded. It can *do* something. It's more effective than a God who watches impassively. I believe He exists. I just don't think He cares a whole lot."

Ford had spoken more words in a row to her in the last ten minutes than he had since she'd met him. The last thing she wanted was to shut him down. Challenging his beliefs might do just that, but maybe it was worth the risk.

"Yesterday," she said, "when I was being chased by those men, and you were there? That was God showing up."

"For you."

"Well, yeah. But the point is, He is involved. He cares. I was praying for help, and He brought you. Scared the stuffing out of me, but you... God used you to save my life."

His only response was a slight shrug.

She wanted to question him more about his faith, about why he'd lost it, about what had happened to him that had hurt him so. But she sensed he wasn't ready to go that deep with her.

"Were you in boarding school until you graduated?"

"Yup."

"Did you make some friends? Did you eventually feel like you fit in?"

"I got involved in sports and clubs. I knew people. They knew me."

"That's not exactly friendship, though."

He rubbed his lips together, seemed to be contemplating what to say. Maybe how much to share.

After a minute, he exhaled. "I had a friend for a couple of years. Kid named Matty. I used to go home with him for weekends sometimes. When my aunt traveled, his family would let me stay with them. They lived on a huge piece of property out in the Berkshires. He had a bunch of sisters, and we'd play games and..." Ford's voice trailed.

"Sounds like fun."

"One year at school, some older kids targeted him. I don't know why. My friend was tall but skinny, not at all athletic. A few older kids started picking on him. I tried to stick up for him, but it was my friend and me against five older, bigger boys. There wasn't much either one of us could do. I thought... I was young and stupid, and I still believed adults could fix problems. I told Matty to tell a teacher. He didn't want to, thought it would make things worse. But things were pretty bad. They'd knocked him around, bruised him. And I just..." Ford shook his head, his lips pressing together.

"You were smaller and outnumbered." Brooklynn kept her voice low, barely wanting to interrupt the flow of his thoughts. "What could you have done?"

"When one of them pushed Matty hard enough that he fell and fractured his wrist, I decided to tell the headmaster myself. I was trying to help. The problem was, the ringleader of that little gang of bullies was the son of the school's biggest donor."

"So what? Surely the parents would have wanted him to be reprimanded."

"Bullying was grounds for expulsion. Those were the rules the school itself had set. So they couldn't exactly call him on it without following through on the prescribed punishment. They had a stern talk with the kid and his little thug followers. The next night, thinking he was the one who'd reported them, they beat Matty so badly that he ended up in the hospital. He never came back."

"Aw, Ford." She leaned toward him and rested her palm on his arm. It was warm and muscular, and she dropped her hand immediately. "I'm sorry. That's awful."

He shifted out of her reach. "It's fine."

"It's not fine. It's terrible, and I'm sorry you had to deal with it. What happened to Matty after that?"

"His parents enrolled him in a private school near where they lived. As far as I know, he was happy there."

"Did you two lose touch?"

"I didn't. He did. He never got past it." Ford stood and poked at the burning logs, then added another, though the room was plenty warm.

"Didn't he understand you were trying to help?"

"He landed in the hospital."

"Yeah, but—"

"Wanting to help, trying to help... The point is, I *didn't* help." He stood with his back to her, head lowered as if in shame.

Because of the actions of one kid trying to help another.

She studied his beautiful silhouette. He had straight, broad shoulders, but they weren't broad enough to carry all the burdens piled up there. He needed to know how to let them go. To release them to the Lord.

Of course, he didn't trust the Lord. How did people without faith survive the trials of life—even a normal life? And it sounded like Ford's hadn't been normal at all. Parents too busy to care for him. Raised by an aunt who'd sent him off to school to deal with pressures no child should face.

"If you had it to do over again," Brooklynn asked, "what would you do differently?"

He faced her. "I don't..." His voice trailed, and he looked

over her head as if a good answer hovered in the darkness behind her. "I don't know."

"If you'd done nothing, the bullying wouldn't have stopped."

"Maybe it would have, eventually."

"Did those boys suddenly become kind, upstanding citizens of your boarding school?"

His lips quirked. "After he left, they moved on to another kid, but the teachers watched more closely. They weren't as bad."

"So telling the headmaster actually did help."

"Didn't help Matty. For him, I made things worse." He returned the poker to its stand. "I prayed about that decision. I thought God would help, and He didn't."

"He isn't a genie, you know. You don't just automatically get what you pray for. Maybe it was better for Matty to go home."

"Yeah, it was. Which proves my point. God worked that out for Matty because God was on his side. Just like he used me to save you yesterday because He's on your side. He's never been on mine."

"That's quite a lesson to take from one bad experience."

"One?" His voice was too loud. He faced the fire again. "You have no idea."

Those last words were uttered so low she barely heard them.

"I'd love to know, though, if you want to talk about—"

"I don't."

"Okay." She'd pushed too hard, and he'd retreated into his shell. The thought that he might never open up to her hurt, physically hurt. She wanted to know more about this man who carried the world on his broad shoulders. She wanted to know everything about him.

He was secretive and mysterious and short-tempered and broody. But beneath that, he was a boy who'd only wanted to help his friend. A man who'd risked his life to save hers. Who'd stood up to criminals—and a cop—to protect her.

He was so many things she admired. She wanted to know him better.

And she wanted him to know her.

CHAPTER FOURTEEN

What was wrong with him?

Forbes never told anybody that story. In the years since Matty had left school, Forbes had never told a soul. Not even Grandmother.

He loved his grandmother, but she wasn't exactly maternal. She'd have told him to buck up and get over it. Since bucking up and keeping quiet about things was his way, he'd seen no need for the pep talk.

And yet, here he'd gone and spilled the second-worst most shameful secret of his life. Somehow, between the darkness and the fire and Brooklynn's beautiful, mesmerizing eyes, he'd lost his ever-loving mind.

He was going to have to face her eventually. He needed to change the subject. Was there a natural segue from *I got my best friend beat up?*

Not surprisingly, nothing came to mind.

"I once referred to my photos as art."

At Brooklynn's softly spoken words, Forbes turned to face her, waiting for her to continue.

"Lenny laughed at me."

Anger, hot and sharp, filled his mouth. He clamped his lips closed to keep from spilling it onto the amazing woman who didn't deserve it.

"He told me any idiot could take a picture. 'Including my four-year-old nephew.'" She'd affected a male voice, then smiled like it was all some big joke.

"It's not funny. Any idiot can carry a gun, too, but it takes skill to know how to use one."

Her smile faded. "That's true. I wish I'd thought to say it."

"You shouldn't have *had* to say it. You shouldn't have been with a man who put you in the position to have to defend yourself."

She looked down. "You're right. It was stupid."

"Don't do that." Forbes settled beside her again. "Don't make his insecurities about you."

She lifted her gaze and nodded. "You're right."

"You're too agreeable. Maybe I'm not right. If I'm not, you should tell me. Don't just agree with everything."

"Okay." She cleared her throat. "But you *are* right, in this case. I shouldn't have let him treat me that way."

"What else did he say?"

"You don't want to talk about him."

"I'm not a guy who makes conversation for no reason. I asked because I want to know."

She bit her lip and looked at the fire. "It's been years since we dated. I shouldn't still let his words affect me. I don't know why I can't let it go."

Forbes knew why. "Wounds leave scars, and deep scars never fully fade. You trusted him. You loved him, I guess." He paused, hoping she'd deny it, but she just shrugged.

It did something to Forbes to know this woman had loved that pile of excrement—a man who'd trampled on her love.

What was the penalty for punching a cop? Would it matter if the guy was off-duty?

Forbes might just risk prison for the satisfaction.

"What else did he say?" He tried to make his voice gentle, though *gentle* wasn't exactly his modus operandi.

"He said I should get into portrait photography. Not that there's anything wrong with that, but it's not..."

"Art?" he supplied.

"It's not what I love," she said. "He implied that only very talented photographers could make a living at landscapes."

"The guy's a moron."

"You know what? You're right." She smiled, getting into it now. "You know what else he said? He said, 'Who do you think you are, Ansel Adams?' Which...whatever. I mean, I'm not Ansel Adams, but the way he laughed as if he'd made a very clever joke, when he knew, he *knew*, how much I admired Adams's work. I told him how I wanted to do with digital photography what Ansel Adams did with film. He knew that. He said that just to hurt me."

"More than to hurt you, Brooklynn."

She narrowed those clear blue eyes, tipping her head to the side as if she wasn't sure what he meant.

"Taggart knew exactly what he was doing," Forbes said. "I have a vague idea of who Ansel Adams is, but not knowing everything about him doesn't make me feel small or stupid. It just makes me acknowledge that I don't know everything. A guy like Taggart? He probably needed to pretend, to fake it. You knowing something he didn't know and doing something he couldn't do? I bet that killed him. I've known my share of Lennys. Insecure little boys who can't stand being outshined by anyone, especially a woman. He had to cut you down to feel good about himself. He had to cut you down because he didn't want you to realize you were too good for him. Guys like that aren't worth your time."

He wasn't sure what reaction he expected. Maybe defensiveness. Maybe an exuberant nod at his brilliance.

He wouldn't have hated that.

But she smiled her joyful smile, her wide eyes reflecting the firelight, gleaming as if she had a secret.

"What?"

"You keep proving my theory true."

He growled, sounding like the boogeyman she'd accused him of being.

Her smile just widened.

Okay, fine. "What theory?"

"When you get angry or feel passionately about something, you talk in full sentences, even paragraphs."

He clamped his lips shut and faced the fire.

She was right.

This woman could read him like a trifold brochure.

He was waiting for her laugh, but her hand slid around his forearm. "Hey, Ford?"

"Hmm?"

"I like that about you. You're like an iceberg. There's so much beneath the surface, and every time I get a peek of it, I see how beautiful it is."

Beautiful?

There was an adjective he'd never aspired to.

He must've made a face because she gave him a little squeeze. "Maybe that's not the right word, but...actually, it is. Because when you get angry and passionate, it's usually not because someone's hurt you. It's because someone's hurt someone else. Me, in this case. That's righteous indignation, and it's beautiful."

He grunted, which was just one step above the growl. He needed to work on his communication skills. "If you say so."

"I do. Trust me. I know beauty. I am an...artist, you know."

Her eyes twinkled as if the admission filled her with joy. Her hair fell in waves all around her face, shining in the light of the fire. She was, quite simply, the most gorgeous creature he'd ever seen.

He didn't stop to think, didn't *want* to think. Just slid closer and brushed a tendril behind her ear.

She shivered, though the room was plenty warm.

Her reaction lit a fire inside him to rival the one in the hearth just a few feet away. He slid his fingers into her silky hair, loving the way her curls wrapped around his hand.

Loving the way she leaned into his touch.

Loving...all of it.

He held her eye contact, waiting for her to push him away. But she didn't.

She held very, very still.

He leaned forward, feeling her breath on his face, needing to feel her lips against his.

The lights flashed on.

The sudden brightness shocked him out of the crazy trance.

He jerked back.

Brooklynn's eyes widened in surprise. Or...hurt?

What was he thinking, almost kissing her? Had he lost his mind?

Apparently, because he wanted to curse the stupid electricity that'd ruined the moment.

He expected her to be angry, to lash out at him for taking advantage. But her expression softened. She squeezed his forearm again. "It's okay."

What was okay?

Was it okay?

He didn't know, but he needed out of that room, away from this woman, before he did something he couldn't take back.

CHAPTER FIFTEEN

Brooklynn replayed that moment a hundred times.

It wouldn't have been wise to let Ford kiss her. She knew that. She was attracted to the man—who wouldn't be?—but *feeling* a physical attraction and *acting on* one were two very different things. Being holed up in this house with him and depending on him for her physical safety were not good precursors to a healthy relationship.

And anyway, who was talking about a relationship? It would've been a kiss. A good kiss, she was certain, but a very bad-idea kiss.

Probably.

Though she would have enjoyed it.

She ran a brand-new cordless vacuum she'd found in the closet with the cleaning supplies over the old hardwood floor of a guest room on the second floor, across from the office where she'd found the notebook the night before. It was mindless work, which was not the distraction she needed from the almost-kiss.

She'd slept fitfully, giving up right after dawn. Rather than wait on Ford for breakfast, she'd prepared boxed blueberry muffins and added a crumble topping. For someone who was only here temporarily, Ford had a well-stocked pantry. She'd scarfed one muffin while it was still warm and left the rest in a bowl on the counter before retreating to the second floor.

Not that she was trying to avoid him.

She just needed to get her head on straight.

For all the awkwardness after the power came on the night before, Ford had remembered her need for a phone charger and brought her one before fleeing, tossing a quick "G'night" over his shoulder as he headed for the stairs.

This morning, she'd checked her messages, responded when she needed to, before she resumed her cleaning. She'd scoured four rooms in this wing already and was on the fifth when her phone rang.

She checked the caller ID and then swiped to answer. "Hello?"

"Brooklynn? Are you all right?"

It was Lois, though she didn't sound like herself. "I'm fine. What's wrong?"

"You're safe?"

"What happened?"

"We had a power outage last night. Bad thunderstorms."

Brooklynn didn't share that the power had gone out where she was, not wanting Lois or anyone to know she was so close.

"Is it still out?" Maybe they hadn't restored the whole town's power yet.

"No, but while it was out, some men broke into my house." The older woman's voice shook. "They demanded to know where you were."

Brooklynn gasped. "Oh no. I never thought... I'm so sorry. I would never put you in danger."

"I know, dear, and I'm fine." Her voice was stronger now. "It was three men, and they wore masks. They didn't hurt me, just scared me. When the power came back on, they took off."

Brooklynn's heart thumped with fear, imagining what her poor friend had gone through.

And fear that those men were as determined as ever to find her. "Did you call the police?"

"Lenny and his partner came, and I gave them a statement. Lenny insisted I tell you to call him for an update. He seems to believe for some unknown reason that you won't answer his calls." The last was deadpanned. Besides Ford, Lois was the only person Brooklynn had confided in about her trouble with Lenny. She'd been the one to suggest Brooklynn file a report against him.

"Leo wouldn't put up with that from any of his officers," she'd said, *"and believe you me, he definitely won't put up with it from his son."*

Considering that Lois had known the police chief all her life, Brooklynn had trusted her instincts, and she'd been right. Just the threat of reporting Lenny to the police had gotten him to back off.

"Who's Lenny's partner now, do you know?" Brooklynn asked.

"It's that younger one, the new guy? Charter or Chambers?"

"Church. Nathan Church."

"That sounds right. You ought to call *him*."

She needed to check with the police, anyway, to find out what they'd learned since she'd sent the photos. "I will. I'm so sorry it happened. I can't imagine—"

"Don't you worry about me. I'm going to stay with my niece and nephew until this blows over."

Would it blow over, though? Lois couldn't stay hidden forever.

For that matter, neither could Brooklynn.

"Don't they just live in Portland?" Brooklynn asked. "Maybe you should go farther."

"I have a business to run. And I refuse to live in fear. I'm more worried about you. Let me know if there's anything I can do to help you."

She wouldn't get her friend more involved than she already was, but she saw no need to say so. "Sure thing."

"By the way, we got your photograph for the contest." Lois's voice brightened considerably. "What an amazing shot. If you don't win, those judges are blind and dumb."

"I'm sure there are a lot of great entries."

"None as perfect as yours."

"And you're not at all biased."

"Well..." She drew the word out, humor in her tone. "I suppose it is a good thing I'm not one of the judges."

Brooklynn ended the call, checked in with her mom and sisters to let them know she was safe, and sent a text to Owen, Delaney's boyfriend, who'd called and texted her a few times to check on her. She assured him she was all right.

And then she dialed the police department. She gave her name and asked for Officer Church.

"One moment."

Less than a minute later, a man came on the line. "Brooklynn? Are you all right?"

At the sound of Lenny's voice, she was tempted to hang up. "I asked for Nathan."

"He stepped away."

Sure he did.

"Are you safe?"

"I'm fine." She wanted to call him on stalking her the previous day, but if she did that, he'd know exactly where she was. "What happened to Lois last night?"

He related the events from his perspective, and Brooklynn

couldn't help picturing the whole thing. Lois lived in a two-story garrison-style house a mile or so from town on a little country road. It sat on two acres, far enough from the neighbors on either side that, this time of year, their houses weren't visible through the trees.

Lenny told her that, about an hour after the power went out, three men had burst through the door leading to the garage.

"Lois admitted she never locks the garage door that opens outside," Lenny said. "Looks like they picked the lock that leads to her kitchen. She'd gone to bed. They dragged her out and made her sit in the living room and demanded to know where you were."

Brooklynn squeezed her eyes closed, trying to block the image of her sixty-five-year-old mentor surrounded by masked men.

"Did they hurt her? She said they didn't, but..." But would Lois have told her?

"Fortunately, no. They threatened to, though. Where are you?"

"I'm safe."

"Brookie, just tell me—"

"Don't call me that. I hated it before, and I hate it now."

His sigh was long-suffering, as if she were being unreasonable. "You need to tell me where you are."

"What have you uncovered? Any idea who they were? Or what's going on at the inlet?"

"Until you file an official report, I'm not authorized to share information with you."

"Can I file a report over the phone?"

"You need to file in person."

She didn't know if that was true or not. "I'm not coming in. Those people are still looking for me."

"Just give me the address where you are." His tone was so reasonable, as if it were the perfect solution. "I'll come to you."

Was he keeping her in the dark as some sort of power trip? As a way to find her?

Brooklynn didn't know, and it didn't matter. She wasn't telling him or anyone where she was. "Did you get any information from the pictures? Were you able to identify—?"

"I'm not authorized to share—"

"Sure you're not." Typical. When they'd been dating, he'd given her all sorts of information—not because he wanted her help. He'd liked sharing his cases, liked giving her an idea how good he was at his job. How competent and talented. Never once had he suggested he wasn't *authorized* to tell her.

"Why do you have to make everything so difficult?" His words came out too loud. He lowered his volume before adding, "How can I take care of you if—?"

"I don't need you to take care of me, Officer Taggart. I need you to tell me what's going on."

She was sick of his *trust me, I know what's best for you* attitude. As if she couldn't be trusted to make her own decisions. As if she had nothing to offer or add to a conversation. As if she were irrelevant, and too much trouble.

She wasn't going to let him get away with it anymore.

"I can't do that."

"Then I guess there's no point in us talking at all. Bye, Lenny." She swiped to end the call before he could say another word, then ignored the phone when it rang seconds later.

Her hands were shaking, and not because of Lois's late-night invaders. She prayed she'd never have to talk to Lenny again.

She looked around the now-sparkling guest room. She'd stripped the bed and sprayed fabric freshener on the mattress to eliminate a musty scent. She'd wiped down all the furniture and vacuumed the floor. And of course, she'd snooped, but she'd found no hidden compartments or secret passages.

After gathering the linens, she swung the door open to find a man on the other side.

Gasping, she dropped the blankets and stepped back, pressing a hand to her chest.

Ford stood in the hall, fist up like she'd caught him one second before he knocked. He lowered his arm. "I didn't mean to scare you."

"It's fine." Though her heart was pounding. "You didn't... I'm fine."

"Okay. Good. And, uh, good morning." He gathered the sheets and blankets from the floor. "Thank you for breakfast. The muffins were...good."

"Good." Apparently, everything was *good* today. "I'm glad you liked them." Was this awkward enough?

"I haven't had a chance to wash these." He jiggled the linens in his arms.

She'd guessed that already, based on the musty odor she'd found in much of this wing of the house. It was as if someone had just walked out and never come back. They hadn't covered furniture or made any effort to protect the valuables. They'd abandoned clothes and household goods and antiques and a thousand leftovers from a thriving family.

She understood, of course, how that could've happened. What she didn't understand was why nobody, in all the years since the murders, had come back to deal with it.

Not that it was her business.

"Find any more secrets?" His lips twitched in what she'd decided was the closest thing she'd ever get to a smile.

"Not today. How about you?"

"I'm making progress."

"Yeah? What did you find out? Anything new, or are you putting pieces together of stuff you already knew?"

"Sorry. It's my business."

Of course it was. Heaven forbid anybody should tell her anything. Never mind that masked men were threatening people she loved. Never mind that somebody was trying very hard to find her.

Ford said nothing else.

"Did you need something?" she snapped.

He blinked. "I made lunch."

"Oh." She felt like a jerk for being rude. "Sorry. Is it lunchtime?"

He lifted one shoulder and let it drop. "I'm hungry."

"I guess the muffins weren't enough."

"They were fine. I can cook, you know." He started down the hallway, pausing to gather the rest of the linens she'd tossed into a pile to take downstairs. Then, he opened a closet door and dropped the blankets and sheets inside.

"Is there a washer and dryer in there?"

"Laundry chute. You coming?"

She closed the guest room door. "I was coming to find you."

He slowed a little so she could catch up.

"Remember I told you about my friend Lois?"

"Whitmore, widow of Arthur? She's your mentor and used to manage Arthur's gallery."

"Good memory." She didn't hate that he'd listened so closely.

In that respect, he was much better than Lenny. Not that she should be comparing Ford to her ex-boyfriend. "She was the victim of a home invasion last night."

He looked in Brooklynn's direction, brows lowered. "She all right?"

"Yeah. The intruders demanded to know where I was."

That brought a scowl.

"When the power came back on, they took off."

He started walking again, more slowly. "Why would they leave because of the power? Did she recognize them?" He paused to let Brooklynn precede him down the center staircase. "Or did she have some way to contact the police once the lights were on?"

"I assumed they were afraid she'd recognize them, but she said they wore masks."

"Then how could she? Did she recognize voices?"

"I think she was pretty traumatized. Maybe she'll remember something today she didn't think of last night."

"Does she know a lot of people in town?"

"Mostly older people. Now that she's retired, she doesn't interact with the public much. She doesn't have kids of her own, and Arthur's don't live nearby. She's in her sixties, so I'd say she knows people she grew up with, but aside from me and my sisters, I doubt she knows a lot of younger people."

"Why do you assume the people who terrorized her were young?"

"Oh." Brooklynn considered the question, then shrugged. "I guess I just don't see any sixty-something men invading a home. Even if one were behind it, wouldn't they hire someone? The people who followed me sounded younger."

"But they were here," he said. "What time was it?"

"I don't know exactly."

"Whoever it was, they were aware of her connection to you."

That had Brooklynn stopping in place.

She hadn't thought of that. Not that it was a secret that she and Lois were friends, but it wasn't public information. Meaning, whoever had broken into her house knew enough about Lois—or Brooklynn—to understand their relationship.

Which meant the intruders, and the people who'd followed her, weren't strangers or outsiders. They were locals. Or at least someone they worked with was.

Ford watched her processing but didn't say anything.

Brooklynn swallowed a fresh wave of fear—along with a healthy dose of sadness that someone she knew was behind this.

But who?

She continued toward the kitchen, picking up a scent she couldn't place that, under normal circumstances, would have had her mouth watering. As it was, she felt a little sick.

And claustrophobic.

She needed out of this house. Out of this situation.

"Your friend called the police?" Ford asked.

"Yeah." She cleared her throat, trying to make her voice sound normal. "I tried to reach Lenny's partner, but Lenny took the call. He wouldn't tell me anything. In that respect, you and he could be twins separated at birth."

"I'm nothing like your stalker."

Stalker.

She didn't argue this time. She needed to keep in mind who Lenny really was. And no, Ford didn't seem to have stalker tendencies, but in other ways? "Right. Because where he keeps things from me, you're an open book."

"I have a... I'm trying to..." He clamped his lips closed and continued to the kitchen. "Come."

She froze.

He disappeared through the door, sighed loudly enough that she could hear it, and then poked his head into the doorway. "Will you please help me?"

"Happy to."

Ford went straight to the stovetop and scooped a big spoonful of noodles onto a plate. "Could you get us drinks? Please?"

She joined him in the kitchen. By the looks of things, he was a messy cook. An empty noodle box, spice containers, and a half-full jar of something—the label was turned away—were surrounded by dirty pots, dishes, and silverware.

"Lemme guess. You're expecting the servants to clean?"

"Something like that."

Chuckling, she filled two glasses with ice and water, then carried them toward the breakfast nook.

"We're not eating there."

She paused and watched as he put the two plates onto a large tray and added silverware and napkins.

"What am I missing?" He seemed to be talking to himself.

She was the one missing something.

"Salt and pepper." He answered his own question, snatching the shakers, then grabbed a bottle of soy sauce from the counter. He opened the pantry and shoved something into his pocket. "I think this is it. Come on." Halfway to the far door, he turned and again said, "Please?"

He was trying to be polite. That was something.

"Where are we going?"

"I'll show you. Trust me."

He led the way back up the stairs, down the hallway toward the family bedrooms, and through a narrow door she'd assumed opened to a closet.

She shouldn't assume anything in this house.

They climbed a staircase that rose two flights. At the top of the second, Ford turned back to her. "Stay close to the wall, and you should be fine."

"Why? What's happening?"

With all the craziness of the last few days and the news she'd received in the last half hour, a wave of fear rolled over Brooklynn as Ford reached for the knob on yet another door.

Leading to...she had no idea what. Did she trust this man?

If not, she was in too deep to save herself now. She'd go where he led and pray he didn't lead her into trouble. Or to the men who'd terrorized her friend.

∼

BROOKLYNN FOLLOWED Ford onto a small rooftop patio that had her pulling in a lungful of clean, fresh air, inhaling the scents of summer and sea.

She hadn't realized how stuffy the house was until she stepped into the sunshine.

The patio floor sloped downward toward a waist-high wrought iron railing, but the angle was nothing like the pitched roofs surrounding it on three sides.

Beyond the rail, she spied the cove where she'd taken photos two days before, the headlands on either side jutting into the Atlantic. She stepped in that direction, but Ford grabbed her arm. "You don't want to be seen."

"Oh, right. Thanks." Once again, the man had protected her, this time from her own awe.

How did she keep doubting him when he kept proving himself to her over and over? He wasn't only protective, though. This...this was one more piece of evidence proving his thoughtful, generous nature.

"I figured you were getting cabin fever." He set the tray on a small café table between two chairs right beside the door.

Were they the same table and chairs she'd seen in the basement when he'd rescued her? She thought so, meaning he'd found them and carried them up three...no, four flights. They were clean, so he'd wiped them down. And swept the rooftop.

She dropped her head back, closed her eyes, and lifted her face to the sunshine. "This is glorious."

"It's kind of messy."

She heard the closing of the door, and then the glasses were lifted from her hands. After another full breath, she opened her eyes and looked at him. "Another wondrous secret."

He set the glasses on the table, then removed the plates and silverware from the tray. "You don't get out much, do you?"

She laughed. Had she been annoyed with him before? Whatever irritation remained flew away on the breeze, along with her fears and worries.

"It's a widow's walk," Ford said. "Not exactly a secret, considering you can see it from the beach. Have a seat." He waited until she did before settling across from her.

"Was the original owner of this house a sailor?" Widow's walks were designed for people to watch for their loved ones' return from long voyages, thus named because so many never made it home.

"No idea. My research doesn't go back that far. He was obviously eccentric. Maybe he just wanted the rooftop view."

"It is lovely." She regarded the Asian dish that smelled so good. "What is this?"

"Pad Thai."

"I'm impressed."

"Don't be. The sauce came out of a jar. All I did was cook the noodles."

"And slice and sauté the vegetables." She used her fork to unearth a bite of pork. "And cook the meat."

He shrugged. "I needed a break. Seemed only fair, since you've done so much cooking."

She swirled her fork in the rice noodles but paused when he cleared his throat.

"Should we ask a blessing?"

"Oh, right." She smiled, nodding toward him. "Go ahead."

His flash of surprise had her hiding a grin. He bowed his head. "Lord, thank You for the food and the sunshine. Help us figure out what's going on, and the people behind it. Keep Brooklynn safe. In Jesus's name, amen."

"Amen." She smiled at him. "Thank you. I'd sort of like you to stay safe too."

"I'm fine. Eat."

"Loquacious, as always."

Taking her first bite, she closed her eyes to savor the flavors. Salty and spicy and sweet. She swallowed and wiped her mouth. "Delicious."

Another shrug.

He ate a couple of bites, then set his fork down. "I wanted to apologize for last night. I got a little…carried away."

"No need to apologize. You carried me right along with you."

She'd said the words to lighten the moment, but his ever-present scowl deepened.

"It's not that I don't… I mean, you're obviously very attractive."

When he said it, it sounded like an accusation. "Thank you. So are you."

He huffed. "The point is, I'm just not…" He seemed to struggle to finish the sentence.

"Interested in women?" She added humor to her voice.

"What? No. I like women. I didn't mean…" He mashed his lips closed.

"So I'm attractive, but not for you." She smiled to show she was teasing.

"Stop putting words in my mouth."

But it was so much fun.

He tried again. "I'm saying I'm not in a place where I can get involved."

"Right. You don't live here. Where do you live?"

"Boston."

"Practically the other side of the planet."

He took a giant bite of his noodles.

She took a smaller one, then sipped her water. "You have a girlfriend?"

"No."

"Wife?"

That earned a glare.

"Yeah, you don't seem like the type to cheat. Or almost cheat, in this case."

Now he ignored her, not even looking up.

Frustrated or rattled? Maybe a little of both.

"Don't worry, you haven't broken my heart."

"Just trying to apologize. You don't have to make it so hard."

Exactly what Lenny had said, but coming from Ford, she found it amusing. "That wasn't hard for me at all. It was the most fun I've had all day."

"You don't like to clean?"

"Nobody in their right mind likes to clean. But I have to do something. I've done everything I can for the gallery and Old Home Days from here. Fortunately, Jewel is managing the day-to-day, but I can't stay gone much longer. I have work to do. And I need to take photos." She'd restrained herself from taking pictures inside the house, though she'd considered it many times. Not that she'd sell them, but if she could... She could envision a whole series on this house, secret hiding places and passageways and all.

He lifted his gaze to hers, eyes narrowed. "You can't go back to work until this is over."

"I'm tired of people telling me what I can and can't do." Her irritation was back. "Especially when they don't trust me to tell me anything else. *Just keep Brooklynn in the dark. She doesn't need to know anything. She can't possibly help.*"

His eyes narrowed, and he returned to eating.

Fine.

She did the same.

It was hard to stay annoyed with someone who'd made such a delicious meal. She added a little soy sauce and stirred it into the noodles.

"I'm investigating Charles Ballentine."

Her gaze lifted and met Ford's. She didn't ask, just hoped he'd keep talking.

"It's not that I don't trust you, it's just that I don't usually talk about what I'm doing. I tend to work alone."

"Really? Because you seem like such a people-person."

He swallowed another bite, then set down his fork. "I believe he knew his killers, so I thought if I could figure out who he was doing business with, maybe I'd be able to follow the clues to what he was into that got him killed."

"You don't think it was random?"

"Why him? Why this house, this family? There was a reason for it."

"But the police—"

"Didn't care that much."

That had her back straightening. "You think a triple murder wasn't enough to get their attention?"

"I think…I think maybe one of them was involved."

"In murder?" The second word came out too loud and too high-pitched.

If he noticed, he didn't remark on it. "It's just a theory. The cops searched the place, but they found nothing."

"How do you know what they found?"

"I have a copy of the police report. It's very thin."

"Okay, but if clues were hidden in hiding places, then they were, you know, hidden."

"You found one yesterday."

"I knew they existed. If the cops didn't, then they wouldn't have known to look."

"But Charles's mother knew about them. She'd lived in the house for years. She told the police, but still they didn't find anything. They should've worked harder to unearth them. Instead, they decided early on that it was about the robbery."

"I didn't realize anything was taken."

"Grace's jewelry. Most of it was pretty commonplace—valuable, but not worth killing over. But she had an antique ruby necklace worth a couple hundred grand."

"That could motivate some people to kill."

"I don't think it was about the necklace. The house was filled with valuables that weren't touched. I think one of the killers grabbed her jewelry box because...why not? Why not take that after they'd taken lives?"

"Was anything else stolen?"

He shrugged. "There was nobody left to say."

"The little boy—"

"He was eight. Would he have known about hidden stashes of cash?"

"Okay. But your theory that a cop was involved... That's quite a stretch. Maybe the police looked but failed to find anything useful."

"If they were serious about their investigation, they would have found something. You're not a cop, and you found a ledger I've spent weeks searching for."

"I'm special."

That brought the telltale twitch that told her she'd amused him. "True. I hadn't found it. But they were professionals. So they were either incompetent or covering up the truth."

"You're a professional, aren't you? I mean, not a cop but someone who digs up secrets? Is this your first unsolved-mystery book?"

He swallowed. "Yeah."

"And you didn't find the ledger."

He returned to his lunch.

Was Brooklynn making a mistake in trusting the police? Even Lenny the Stalker, for all her issues with the man, took his job seriously.

Or was she wrong about him—again?

Were the local cops incompetent? Or worse, corrupt?

CHAPTER SIXTEEN

Forbes worked to keep his gaze on his plate. Watching Brooklynn savor the meal he'd prepared for her brought far too much enjoyment.

He'd bought her a handful of T-shirts to go with the yoga pants, and today she'd chosen a bright pink one. He'd vacillated about the color, but remembering the yellow top she'd worn when they met, he'd guessed she preferred bright colors. He didn't hate that he'd guessed right. Her hair was braided, a few strands framing her face. She wore no makeup, not that she needed any.

She looked gorgeous.

He'd cleaned up the widow's walk and hauled the furniture upstairs because he'd needed a distraction. He'd needed to think, and sometimes that was best accomplished when he did something with his hands.

And maybe he'd gone to the trouble because he'd known she would like it. Another thing he'd guessed right about, considering her appreciative gazes at the view and the little mews of pleasure as she ate.

If he were a different man with a different past and a future filled with hope instead of the murky darkness he'd never been able to see past... If there were any way at all to make it work, he might consider trying to keep Brooklynn around. Not that the effervescent woman would want to be with a miserable jerk like him.

Even so, he wanted to make her happy, or at least a little less *un*happy, while she was trapped in his house.

"Tell me about him." She sipped her water, then added, "Your uncle."

Forbes set his fork down. "Charles grew up here. A Ballentine ancestor built it, and it's been in the family ever since. The family's got some money."

"Strangely enough, I figured that out myself."

"You'd be surprised how many families own expensive properties who are barely scraping by financially. The upkeep on a house like this is pricey. Just the taxes force some families to sell."

"But not the Ballentines. They've held onto it, even though nobody's lived here for years."

His ever-practical grandmother claimed she'd held onto it for him—his legacy—but he suspected it was more than that. Though this house was the setting of great tragedy, before that it had been a home filled with love.

Forbes couldn't share any of that.

"Charles's grandfather owned a shipping company, which his dad, Broderick, inherited. He added logging to the enterprise. Charles wasn't interested in either business."

"Did his father mind?"

"Not that I know of." Forbes was careful to talk about this like an outsider, though it felt strange. He never talked to anybody about his family. He'd spent his entire life hiding his past and his true identity. But Brooklynn was involved now, and she needed more of an understanding about what was going on.

Plus, he wanted her to know him better, even if she didn't realize how much of himself he was revealing.

"Aside from paying for college," Forbes said, "Broderick gave Charles no money but plenty of encouragement. Charles started buying real estate, sometimes to flip, sometimes to rent out. By the time he moved back here with his wife and three-year-old daughter, Rosie, he was a multimillionaire."

"I bet his father was impressed."

"He died before they returned to Maine, but he lived long enough to see his son succeed." Forbes wished he'd met his grandfather. If Grandmother's opinion hadn't been too jaded with time, the man had been kind and generous. Even when he'd refused to help Charles start his business, he'd done it not to hurt him but to help him learn that he didn't need anyone's help to succeed.

"What about your cousin?" Brooklynn asked.

Forbes took a sip of water, reminding himself to stay in character. Never in his life had he felt guilty for not being honest about who he really was. It was for his safety, after all. And, as Grandmother said, he didn't owe anybody the truth about his past.

He'd never doubted her, but now, with Brooklynn across the table, with her open, expectant expression, guilt niggled his conscience.

"Forbes was ten years younger than his sister," he explained. "I understand Grace had a couple of miscarriages between them."

"Aw, I bet that was hard."

Forbes assumed so, though his parents hadn't talked about it in front of him. Grandmother had told him about the miscarriages, how his mother had called Forbes her miracle baby.

"Charles owned real estate, but you said they moved back to Maine. Where did they live before?"

"Boston area."

"Was that where most of his real estate was?"

"Started there, but he expanded all over eastern Mass, then into New Hampshire and southern Maine. He had an office in Boston where his employees worked. He'd moved on to industrial properties by then, which required more day-to-day involvement than the residential properties. Charles moved into contracting. At the time of the murders, he had three huge construction projects underway."

"Do you think the murders were related to one of those?"

"I've gone over all the books and talked to his former employees, and by all accounts, everything was aboveboard. There'd been no threats against him or his company, no lawsuits except the typical run-of-the-mill stuff, all of which were settled out of court. None of which was contentious. His manager at the time told me that Charles was well-respected among New England developers, that his employees and peers were shocked and devastated when they heard the news."

"What about Grace?" Brooklynn asked. "Could the murders have been related to something she was doing?"

"I can't imagine how. Grace didn't work outside the home. She raised her kids and took care of this place. She was involved in local charities, the women's club, that sort of thing."

"She sounds a lot like my mother. I bet Mom would remember her. I could ask."

The last thing Forbes wanted was for anyone to know he was looking into his family's history. "Not without giving away where you are."

"Oh. Right." Brooklynn's head tilted to the side. "Did you learn anything new today? Did the notebook I found help at all?"

He swallowed a bite of pasta. "Yes and no."

The slight lift of her eyebrows told him he hadn't satisfied her curiosity.

"It's a ledger written in Charles's handwriting, but it wasn't in his office. He went to a lot of trouble to hide it, which tells me he was doing something illegal or at the very least, immoral. But I haven't figured out what."

"It didn't offer a lot of details, did it? Just dates and dollar amounts and other numbers with no explanation."

A flash of frustration had his hands balling into fists.

"I know, I know." She lifted her palms defensively. "I shouldn't have looked at it. It's not my business. Blah, blah, blah. I was just curious."

"The word is *nosy*."

"If not for my nosiness, you wouldn't have the ledger." She winked and added, "You're welcome."

"I wasn't thanking you."

"I'm assuming a level of politeness you've yet to exhibit." She gazed around the space. "Except you've more than made up for your rudeness with this lunch. Underneath all the grumpy bluster, you're really very kind, aren't you?"

"Just wanted to get outside, that's all."

Her smile was brighter than the sunshine. "Your secret's safe with me."

"Right. From the woman addicted to snooping."

"It's not like I'm telling anybody what I learn."

"Are you going to stop?"

"What do you think?"

He sighed, and she laughed her lighthearted, all-is-right-with-the-world laugh. Frustrating woman.

Frustrating, and way too enticing.

∞

FORBES NEEDED TO PROTECT BROOKLYNN, not develop feelings for her.

He'd worked with his share of beautiful women, but none of them had elicited these feelings in him. He needed her to stop digging into his family's life, into his business.

On the other hand, she had been helpful. She'd shared the photos she'd taken of the men at the old dock. She'd seen a resemblance between Bernie and Shane Dawson he'd never have noticed, giving him a new lead to investigate. And she'd found the ledger.

She could be a good resource, someone to bounce his ideas off of.

Forbes wasn't accustomed to having anyone on his side. He was used to going it alone. He didn't even tell Grandmother much. She'd lost her only son that terrible day, not to mention a daughter-in-law she'd loved and her granddaughter. Grandmother wasn't fragile or delicate, but she was desperate to know who murdered them and why. He didn't want to get her hopes up.

Brooklynn had no skin in the game. He could tell her what he knew with little risk. She'd already done so much for him. Between cooking and cleaning and finding the ledger...

He owed her more than a thank-you. He owed her information about what he was up to.

He owed her the truth.

The only person alive aside from his grandmother who knew his real identity was his therapist, and she'd known who he really was since he was eight years old.

The headmaster from his boarding school had known, but he'd died a few years past.

Forbes had never confided in anyone else.

It wasn't such an easy thing to trust someone with the truth about who he was, knowing he would open himself up to questions he wasn't prepared to answer. But Brooklynn wasn't pushy. Nosy, but not pushy.

He could trust her.

"I need to tell you..." He lost his nerve and changed tack. "I don't mind. The snooping, I mean."

Her eyebrows rose, brightening her already-joyful expression. "It's nice to have permission."

"All I ask is that you show me anything you find."

"Deal." She pushed her plate away. "That was delicious."

He dug in his jacket pocket and held out a foil-wrapped truffle.

"My hero!" She snatched it and unwrapped it. "This is exactly what I was craving."

He'd noticed that she liked dessert after every meal. One cookie, one piece of chocolate. Never a lot, just a bite of something sweet. He'd had a fresh load of groceries delivered that morning, including a bag of chocolates and a package of cookies.

Just for her. Because...because he liked her.

"If you think the murders were related to something Charles was doing, do you have a theory about what that was?"

"At this point, all I have are guesses." He finished his last bite of noodles, then unwrapped his own chocolate and popped the whole thing into his mouth.

How much should he tell her? How could he share what he knew without telling her where the information came from?

"There were rumors at the time of their murders about a smuggling ring here in Shadow Cove."

"I never heard that."

"You were a child, and it was a long time ago. I've heard people refer to the group as "The Network."

"Who? What people?"

"Just...people."

"You can't tell me?"

"No."

She squinted, studying him closely. "So you have talked to people in town."

He considered the question and answered carefully. "I've heard from a few, yes." That was honest enough. He'd heard the term from the murderers themselves. "I believe that the smugglers used the dock on the property, the place where the men were unloading the other day."

"The Haunted Inlet."

"The...what?"

"That's what locals call it. And this is Mystery Mansion."

"I didn't know that." How...disconcerting. The home that was the site of all his greatest memories, along with the most horrifying event of his life, had been reduced to a couple of creepy nicknames.

Brooklynn's head tilted to the side. "I'm surprised that the people who told you about The Network didn't mention the town's monikers for this property."

"The point is that what you witnessed confirms the information I received. The Network is back and operating again."

"Who told you that?"

He considered various answers and decided to stick with the truth. "I received an anonymous note."

"That's weird. Why would they send it to you? Because you're related? But wouldn't they send it to Marie? The grandmother?"

"Whoever sent it must've heard I was researching what happened here."

Another lie.

The sender had addressed the note to Forbes at the Ballentine Enterprises office.

But who'd sent it? And why?

Brooklynn sucked in a breath, her eyes widening. "Oh,

wow. The person you talked to must've told someone you were investigating. Or maybe that person sent the note? That means...that means they're involved somehow."

"If so, then why would they tell me?"

"But if they aren't involved, how do they know?"

"No idea." His tone was short because she was asking all the questions he'd yet to answer.

Why would someone involved alert him? But if they weren't involved, then how did they know? And why him? Why not tell the police?

Brooklynn stood and stretched, gazing out at the ocean. "It feels so good to be outside."

Standing quickly, he touched her arm. "Don't go to the railing."

"I know." She glanced up at him, her voice gentle. "Thank you for this. I didn't realize how much I needed it."

"No problem."

Her smile was shy. "You went to a lot of trouble for my sake, and it means a lot."

He wasn't sure what to say to that.

"Did you request old police files?" she asked. At his nod, she turned back toward the view. "Maybe someone in the records office told someone." She tilted her head to the side. "Ian Prescott would have known, or his secretary, but she's in her seventies and a strong believer. She's been teaching Bible study at my church as long as I can remember. I can't imagine her being involved in anything nefarious."

"What about the mayor?"

"He seems like a good guy, but he's a politician, so..." Brooklynn shrugged. "How would I know?"

"More likely it was someone at the police department. That's where I made the records request."

"Is that why you don't trust them?"

"It's one reason." The bigger reason was that none of them had found out who'd killed his family. And...he'd always had the sense that one of them had worked with The Network, though he couldn't explain why he believed that.

So many of his memories surrounding the murders were murky, so he had to trust his instincts.

"Truth is," he said, "I have very few definitive answers at this point."

"But you must have theories."

"Nothing that's panned out."

Brooklynn wandered to the wall and leaned against it, her gaze on the horizon. He stayed beside her, just in case she forgot and stepped forward. They couldn't see the shore from where they stood, just the dark water and the blue sky.

He needed to tell her the truth. Not that the truth would offer much more information. He didn't know who'd tipped him off about The Network. He didn't know who'd been involved back then, nor who was involved now. Though he'd been looking for answers for weeks, he knew little more than he'd known when he arrived here.

It was frustrating beyond belief. It was even more frustrating to not know who'd tipped him off. Was it someone who wanted to help?

Or someone who wanted to expose him?

He'd worried that was the case, but after staying in the house for weeks, he no longer thought that. If he'd been lured here by murderers, they'd have killed him by now. He'd come face-to-face with Network members, and he was still alive, so he doubted the note had been sent by enemies.

Besides, if enemies knew who he was, then they could've taken him out from his Boston home.

Grandmother had been careful to leave no trail after she'd legally changed Forbes's name.

But somebody knew who he was.

Grandmother was still sharp, but a nurse at her retirement home had told him she'd had a few memory lapses. Had she told someone?

He couldn't imagine her sharing a secret she'd kept for so long. And even if she had, how would the information have gotten to the person who sent him the anonymous tip?

The package he'd received had included photos of the house and the inlet, along with a typed note that read simply, *They're back. Don't miss your chance for justice.*

Forbes had craved answers since he was eight years old, but he hadn't even known where to start.

Finally, he had an opportunity to bring his family's murderers to justice—and the strength to come back to this house and face all its ghosts.

Brooklynn had gone quiet, but now she looked up at him. "If the men I photographed the other day work for this network, then...then that means they could be the same people who killed the Ballentine family."

"That's my assumption."

"Wow." She sounded shocked by her theory. "I mean, I knew they were dangerous, but..." She blinked a couple of times, then gazed at the beauty surrounding them. She licked her lips, swallowed. "You're saying the people who followed me *murdered* three people? Including a child?"

Rosie had been eighteen, so not technically a child, but close enough. "Not the same people," he said. "Remember, the murders happened almost twenty-five years ago. The people you photographed were too young."

"You think they work for the same people?"

He was convinced of it. Brooklynn looked frightened, but she needed to understand the peril she was in. "Even if they're not the same people, they're dangerous, considering how they searched for you. And what they did last night."

"Lois is lucky to be alive."

Brooklynn wasn't wrong. The thing was, Forbes didn't understand why Lois was still alive. These weren't exactly merciful people. But maybe this new...generation, so to speak, was less vicious than the last. Or... "Maybe they thought she'd be more useful alive than dead."

"Which means she's still in danger. This is all so convoluted. I thought it would all just...just blow over. But it's not going to, is it?"

He shook his head, unsure what to say. It seemed Brooklynn was just now coming to terms with the seriousness of the situation. Her optimistic disposition had tricked her into believing all would work out, all would be well.

In Forbes's experience, nothing worked out for the best. Nothing went well.

She covered her mouth as if the horror had just occurred to her. "Lois could've...she could've *died*, and she's still in danger." Brooklynn's eyes filled with tears. "I feel terrible. I shouldn't have allowed my curiosity to get the best of me when I heard those voices. But"—she waved toward him, her pitch rising to a squeak—"you're right. I'm nosy. I should've just minded my own business. And now Lois is in danger. My sisters, my parents. Thank God they weren't in town. Everything's all messed up."

Her eyes reddened, and tears dripped down her cheeks.

He didn't think, didn't consider the ramifications, just wrapped his arms around her and pulled her close.

She came willingly, burying her cheek against his chest. As if his hug opened a crack inside her, the tears turned to weeping. She circled her arms around his waist and held on.

"None of this is your fault, Brooklynn."

"Lois is in danger because of me." Her volume was low, her pitch high. "They're all in danger because of me."

She wasn't concerned about her own safety, just that of her loved ones.

"There's nothing wrong with being curious." Unlike hers, his voice was husky. She was feeling overwhelmed with guilt. He was feeling overwhelmed with a thousand other emotions, many of which were inappropriate, considering the situation.

She could worry about others all she wanted.

He worried about her.

It felt right to have her in his arms, as if she belonged there. As if she'd stepped into a void he hadn't even known existed. Kind and cheerful. Even when her life was at risk, she thought of others first.

She made him want to be a better man. She made him want to be worthy of her.

He inhaled her scent, floral and distinctly *Brooklynn*. A subtle scent that overpowered his senses. "You couldn't have known. You're the one who's in danger. You're the one those killers are after."

The words didn't help. Her tears turned to sobs that wracked her body.

He was terrible at this comforting thing. "I'm just saying, you have to keep yourself safe. Worry about yourself."

That was how the world worked. Take care of yourself. Let others take care of themselves. Because when you tried to help others, you just screwed it up.

Life had taught him that. He couldn't solve anyone else's problems, and when he tried, he only made it worse.

It couldn't happen with Brooklynn. He had to figure out how to keep her safe.

He was going to take care of her whether she liked it or not.

CHAPTER SEVENTEEN

Brooklynn never wanted to leave Ford's arms.

Her world was falling to pieces, but in his arms she felt safe. In this house, on this property, she felt protected from all the scary things in the world.

The killers who'd chased her.

Even Lenny couldn't find her here.

The safety made her feel terrible, knowing that she'd put Lois in danger. *Thank You, Father, that she's still alive. Thank you for sparing her life.*

But what if someone else got hurt because of her? What if Lois had been killed? What if the killers tracked Alyssa down, or Mom and Cici and Delaney came back to town? What if Kenzie showed up?

Dad could be in danger, though he traveled with security, as did Mom.

Brooklynn and her sisters had all refused to be guarded twenty-four seven. Maybe she should call Dad and ask for a security guard. If she left this safe haven, she'd do that. But she didn't want to leave. She didn't want to move out of Ford's protection.

Or his arms.

The thought brought her up short. What was she doing, letting him hold her like this?

She leaned away, and he stepped back.

"You okay?"

"Yup." She swiped her fingers under her eyes, though there was little moisture there. Ford's T-shirt was damp with her tears. "Sorry. I'm okay. Really." She cleared her throat.

He watched her as if terrified she'd fall apart again.

She attempted a smile, though fear and worry still hummed in her blood. "So, what did this network smuggle?"

"I don't know. I'm hoping the ledger offers some clues, but I haven't figured it out yet."

"Let's look at it together. Maybe I'll see something you didn't."

His lips pressed into a thin line, and she braced for the coming rejection. He didn't want her help. He wanted her out of his business.

"It can't hurt," he finally said. "I can use all the help I can get."

Wow. He could be taught. She tamped down the triumphant feelings, not wanting him to see.

Carrying their empty glasses, she followed Ford back down the staircases to the kitchen, where they rinsed the dishes and tidied up. Though Ford was his usual, quiet self, he seemed... Peaceful wasn't the right word, but maybe a little less grouchy. Almost as if sharing his struggles and comforting her had lifted some of his burden.

Yeah, right.

More likely, she was seeing what she wanted to see.

She wanted Ford to like her. Silly as it was, she wanted him to be thankful she was there, not lamenting his unwanted, too nosy houseguest.

They were headed to Charles's office when her phone dinged with a text.

> It's Nathan Church. Call when you have a minute.

"Someone important?" Ford asked.

"It's Lenny's partner. Maybe he has information for me." She called the unfamiliar number. When he answered, she said, "It's Brooklynn."

"Thanks for calling me back so quickly."

She recognized Nathan's voice, though she'd only spoken to him a handful of times. He was about two years her junior, in his mid-twenties. Brooklynn remembered him as a shy, chubby kid, but the last time she'd seen him, he'd turned the extra weight into muscle.

"Do you have some news for me?" she asked

"I got a message that you called. Are you safe?"

"Yeah." They reached the office, and Ford stepped aside so she could enter first. She nodded her thanks, then said to Nathan, "I'm safe." She didn't mention that she'd spoken to Lenny and he'd refused to tell her anything.

Ford touched her arm to get her attention.

She looked at him, ignoring the zing of energy that tried to distract her.

"Can you put it on speaker?" Ford kept his voice low.

She did, keeping her gaze on the phone so she could concentrate. "Can you give me an update?"

"We're looking for the boat," Nathan said, "using your photograph to ask around. As far as we can tell, it doesn't belong to any of the local fishermen, but we're hoping one of them will remember it. The images of the people were too grainy for us to get anything helpful, but we sent them to the state police lab.

Unfortunately, they're pretty backed up, so we won't hear anything back for weeks."

Ford's eyebrows lowered. He didn't like that.

"We've also been keeping our eye on the Haunted Inlet. There's been no activity there since you reported the incident a few days ago."

"Do you think they just...moved on?" She couldn't help a little spark of hope.

Shaking his head, Ford settled in the leather chair on the opposite side of the desk.

"Unfortunately," the cop said, "what happened to Mrs. Whitmore last night tells us they haven't."

"Oh, right. Of course."

"The guys who broke into her house demanded to know where you are. You were wise not to tell anybody, and I don't mind that you haven't told us. However, I would like to know if you're alone or with someone."

"I'm with someone. I'm not alone."

"Good, good. Name?"

That had Ford's head shaking hard enough she feared he'd give himself a headache. In case she didn't get the message, he mouthed, *No*.

"Sorry," Brooklynn said. "The person who's helping me doesn't want anyone to know...they're involved. They're worried they'll get pulled into this."

"Multiple people, then?"

"No. I'm just trying to honor his or her privacy."

"I see." His tone told her he didn't see at all. "The problem is, if I can't get in touch with you, I won't know where to start looking."

"Someone knows where I am. Someone not in my family, and not the person I'm with." Brooklynn wasn't about to put her sister in anyone's crosshairs. Not that she didn't trust

Nathan, but police reports could be hacked or stolen or leaked.

And maybe she was paranoid, but as the daughter of a CIA agent and a sister of a former computer hacker, she knew nothing was truly private.

Nathan said, "If I don't know who—"

"If something happens to me, this person will know where I've been, and he or she will contact you."

"Could you give me your friend's contact information?"

She didn't have to look at Ford to know what he thought about that. "Sorry. I'm trying to honor everyone's wishes."

Nathan blew out a frustration-filled breath. "No problem. I understand. Is this person you're with someone you know well? Someone you know you can trust? Because whatever happened at the inlet obviously wasn't a one-time thing, and if that's the case, then... I have a gut feeling that people in Shadow Cove are involved. I mean, if not, then why here? There are a thousand inlets on the coast of Maine. Why that one?"

"Well, I mean... it's hidden and unused."

"So well hidden that hardly anybody knows it exists. Locals know, though. You need to be careful about who you trust."

She lifted her gaze to Ford, who held it. He didn't smirk, there was no lip-twitch-smile. Just a serious expression that communicated...what?

That he understood why she'd wonder about him, and that he wasn't afraid of her questions.

Ford could be trusted. There was no fear in his expression. There was no malice. No duplicity.

He'd saved her life. He could've killed her that first day, and nobody would be the wiser. And that comforting embrace on the roof...

No, she wouldn't distrust Ford Baker. He was exactly who he claimed to be.

"I trust the person who took me in," Brooklynn said. "I'm safe here."

"If you say so. There's one more thing." Nathan paused to inhale, then blew out the breath. "I'm saying this unofficially, okay?"

She looked at Ford, who shrugged.

"What?"

"I get the sense that Lenny has not gotten over you."

She wasn't sure how to respond to that, so she said nothing as she settled onto one of the chairs on the visitor's side of the desk. The files Ford had been going through the day before were stacked neatly in one corner. In the center was the ledger she'd found. On the side opposite the files was the photo album that held the photos of the people in town.

"He's my partner," Nathan said, "and I really like the guy, but where you're concerned, he's a little...irrational."

Ford's lips pressed closed as if he were fighting not to add his own opinion of Brooklynn's ex-boyfriend.

"I've noticed," she said.

"I'm just saying, I understand if you feel...hesitant to call the police if you believe he might respond. This is my personal cell phone number, so if anything happens, or if you remember something, call me directly. You don't have to work with him."

"Okay, but... How do you know that about Lenny?"

"I wasn't sure, but he told me he was staking out that old, abandoned mansion, thinking you'd taken refuge there. He searched the property and gave the contractor there a hard time."

Ford wrote something down and turned the note so she could see.

"Someone's staying there?" she asked. Because, as Ford reminded her, she shouldn't know that. "I had no idea."

"How'd you get away from the people who followed you?"

"I hid. There's an outcropping of rocks, and I managed to wedge myself in tight. It was sunrise, and I was in the shadow. They ran right by me. I stayed there for hours until I knew they were gone."

"You're lucky they didn't find you."

Ford pulled the notebook back to himself and wrote something down. He slid it back to her.

Be careful. He's fishing.

She felt that too. "It wasn't luck. God protected me."

"Okay." Nathan said the word like he wasn't convinced but couldn't be bothered to argue the point. "Anyway, there was something almost...desperate about Lenny's need to find you. He's told me a few times that he believes you two are going to get back together. My gut tells me he's...uh...a little too invested, let's say."

"Not sure what that has to do with anything," she said.

"I'd like to know." Nathan's words took on a *you can trust me* tone. Lenny used to do that. Was it a skill they taught at the police academy?

"If he's been stalking you," Nathan said, "then I need to know so I can keep an eye on him. I'd rather get him to stop on his own than see him reprimanded. Or fired."

"So this is unofficial," she said. "Right?"

"For the moment, if you want it to be."

Ford gave her a go-ahead nod.

"Okay. He was sort of...stalking me."

Ford's eyebrows lifted, and she sighed

"I guess not 'sort of.' It wasn't until I threatened to report him and get a restraining order that he left me alone. Though, to be honest, I've had the feeling for a while that he was watching me. Like, I'd look out my apartment window and see him across the street. But that coffee shop is there, so..." She shrugged, not that Nathan could see her. "The point is, he'd left me alone. I tried to report the crime anonymously, but I guess your system made note of my phone number. I don't want to have to turn him in, but I'm not going to put up with it again."

"I'm sorry about...all of that," Nathan said. "Lenny said he likes to sit there to watch the town walk by, but now that I think about it...he was mostly watching the gallery."

Just as she'd suspected, but how was she supposed to call him on that? He was a cop in Shadow Cove. It was his job to be there, looking out for the locals.

"Thanks for telling me," Nathan said. "I'll back you up if you ever decide to file a report against him. The chief's reasonable. You can trust him to do the right thing, if it comes to that."

She hated to think how Lenny would react if she turned him in.

The fear of that reaction had kept her silent for too long. If Lenny tried to force himself into her life again, she'd report him to the police.

And suffer the consequences.

"Back to business," Nathan said. "We've got patrol cars driving by your building at night. We've informed local business owners and people who live downtown of the fact that there was some trouble at the inlet and to keep their eyes out for strangers. There've been no credible reports at this point, and no trouble at your apartment."

"That's a relief."

Ford shook his head. He didn't have to say anything for her to guess what he was thinking. Some variation of *a lot of good that'll do*.

She didn't disagree.

"I've been doing a little research," she said. "Did you know there were rumors about a smuggling ring at the Haunted Inlet back at the time of the Ballentine murders?"

Ford tapped the desk to get her attention, then swiped his finger across his neck, telling her to stop talking.

"Uh...no," Nathan said. "I think that was before I was born."

She wanted to mention The Network, but Ford had trusted her with the information, and she didn't want to abuse that trust. "It's probably nothing, just an old rumor."

"I'll look into it. I'll call if I learn anything. If you need me, call me at this number, anytime. Stay safe, Brooklynn."

She thanked him and ended the call.

"You shouldn't have told him about the smugglers," Ford said.

"Why? He's a cop, and he wants to help."

"Or to get information out of you. Now, he knows you're doing some armchair investigating."

"You think Nathan is involved?" Her tone was a little mocking, but she couldn't help it. "Obviously, you've never met him. He's the twenty-first-century version of Timmy Martin."

"Who?"

"Timmy Martin." She waited for the recognition to dawn on Ford's face. "You know, 'What is it, boy? Is Timmy stuck in the well?'"

"I have no idea what you're talking about."

"The TV show. Everybody knows *Lassie*."

"Wasn't Lassie some kind of famous dog?"

"Wow." She shook her head in mock horror. "Not a fan of reruns, I guess."

"I wasn't allowed to watch TV. The point is, you don't know if your Timmy guy is trustworthy."

"His name is Nathan, and I went to school with him. He's a nice kid."

"He's a grown man, and for all you know, Lenny was listening in on that conversation. For all you know, Nathan is trying to figure out where you are so he can tell the smugglers."

"You're—"

"What do you think, Brooklynn?" Ford demanded. "That if you've met somebody, they must be good? Ted Bundy had a girlfriend. Jeffrey Dahmer worked in a chocolate factory. Just because *you're* nice doesn't mean everyone is."

"Obviously." She stood abruptly. "There's nothing wrong with seeing the best in people."

He stood, too, and came around the desk. "There is if those people are criminals and murderers."

"They're not."

"Because you're such a great judge of character." His sarcasm was thick. "Said the one who fell in love with a stalker."

His words were a blow.

She stepped back, not even sure how to respond.

His eyes widened. "I'm sorry. I didn't mean—"

"Yes, you did."

His mouth opened, snapped shut. He seemed at a loss for words. Too bad he hadn't felt that way thirty seconds before.

The problem was, he was right.

She was a terrible judge of character. She liked people. She trusted people, and when they disappointed her, she forgave easily.

She hated conflict, and she wanted everyone to like her.

Which made her...a fool.

She'd been a fool to forgive Lenny so many times, to think he would ever treat her with respect.

She'd been a fool to believe Ford would see her as a help, not a nuisance.

She'd been a fool to believe she could be more than the burden to society her father believed her to be.

She was just...a fool.

Tears burned. She swiveled and headed toward the door. Not wanting him to see how much he'd hurt her. Not wanting to be a burden or a nuisance or any of the things she knew she was, and couldn't help but be, no matter how hard she tried.

"Brooklynn."

"It's fine."

He took her hand, his touch gentle. "It's not fine. I'm sorry."

She could've yanked away. He held her hand loosely, giving her the option.

"Please, don't go."

At the kindness in his tone, so contrary to his harshness a moment before, tears spilled over and down her cheeks.

Crying twice in the same day. In the same *hour*. In front of this man who already saw her as weak.

She didn't want him to see her tears.

And she didn't want to leave.

He shifted to stand in front of her. "Please." He swallowed again. "I'm sorry. I'm just worried about you. I don't want you to trust the wrong people."

"Maybe I already am." She swiped tears from her face, then looked up at him. "Nathan seems to think so. You want me to distrust him. He wants me to distrust you. Seems I shouldn't trust anyone."

His gaze roamed her face, probably seeing the remnants of tears. He blinked and stepped back, dropping his hand from her arm.

"You're right. I'd prefer you distrust everyone than trust anyone. The cop's not wrong. Only a local would know about your relationship with Lois Whitmore. Whoever sent those thugs to her house last night knew about your friendship with her. You can't trust anyone."

"'Anyone' includes you, you know."

"That's fair. If you want to leave, I get it. My offer stands. I can take you anywhere you want. You just can't go home. Not until it's safe." He backed up and leaned on the desk. "I'm really sorry about"—he waved toward her chair as if their conversation hovered there—"my stupid remark. I was just…"

"Being stupid?"

There was his lip-twitch. "What else is new?"

"You're not stupid. You need to work on your cultural references, but I can forgive that."

His expression sobered. "Can you? Forgive me? I was… I think I'm a little…" He shook his head, grunted. "It's nice you trust everyone. It's nice you're so…nice. Also, stop it."

"Stop trusting people. Got it. Can I write that down?"

He ignored her sarcasm. "Why are you smiling?"

She hadn't realized she was. But he'd apologized, something her ex-boyfriend would never have done in a million years.

Not that she was comparing them. Not that Ford would waste his time on someone like her. "I guess I'm just a happy person."

"You're in danger. You're trapped in this house with me. You're being stalked by a jerk. You're just…" He seemed to grope for a word, landing on, "…impossible."

"I'm happy."

"It's annoying."

"You love it."

He looked away, and she could swear he almost smiled.

CHAPTER EIGHTEEN

There'd been a moment, a brief moment, when Brooklynn had looked at Forbes like he might be an enemy.

It made sense, considering she'd only known him for three days, and all she knew about him came from what he'd told her.

Meaning most everything she believed about him was a lie. She seemed discerning enough to know something wasn't right, even if she didn't know exactly what.

Forbes. Ford. They were the same person. He was using his alias, sure, but his personality was the same.

Except Ford wasn't Forbes. Ford wasn't one of the five hundred richest men in America. Ford didn't own a majority stake in a Fortune 100 company. Ford was an illusion, a creation of his grandmother.

Ford Baker was a historian writing a book about unsolved mysteries who paid the bills working as a freelance handyman and dabbled in real estate.

He must've inherited his father's knack for investing because Ford had become a millionaire by the time he was thirty. Not that Ford...Forbes...needed the money. It was just a cover story. Real estate was the thing he did to kill time.

Forbes's whole life had felt like killing time, just waiting until he could find out who'd killed his family. Find closure and move on.

Ford wasn't writing anything to publish, of course, but he had been researching unsolved mysteries—one mystery in particular. To satisfy Ford's curiosity—and Forbes's obsession—Ford spent time with other historians, with college professors, and with private detectives, learning their methods, discovering how they uncovered secrets.

While keeping his own secrets hidden.

He'd played the role of Ford Baker, ordinary guy, for so long that he'd felt comfortable in it.

Being in this house, surrounded by memories, his false persona felt distant. Here, he was Forbes Ballentine.

That was why he desperately wanted to tell Brooklynn the truth. It was why his alias, which had rolled off his tongue since he was eight years old, now felt like sand in his mouth.

His whole life had been a cover story. Lie, pretend, hide. Nobody could know who he really was.

He couldn't get close to anyone. Ever. No serious relationships, no close friendships.

He'd never cared before. Sure, in college he'd met a woman he'd thought he could love. But even then, he hadn't felt compelled to tell her the truth.

It was Brooklynn and her cheery attitude and honest disposition and...

Everything. It was everything about her that made him want to be himself. Or a better version of the man he'd become.

Her footsteps sounded in the hallway—she'd gone to the restroom—and he turned as she stepped into the office.

"I'm so proud of myself." Her voice was, as always, filled with joy. "I didn't get lost once!"

"Congratulations."

"I know, right. This place is amazing. I just want to explore and find out all its secrets." She slid into a chair across the desk. "Did you figure out the mystery while I was gone?"

"Uh, no." He'd barely looked at the ledger, just stared out the window and wished everything were different.

"Let's see it, then." She pulled it close and studied it.

He wasn't a pro at upside-down reading, and the desk was wide. So he stared at her, at the way her braid draped over her shoulder, the way curls framed her face. At the tiny wrinkles on her forehead that appeared when she was trying to figure something out.

He needed to stop.

He had two choices. Sit across from her and try to resist her beauty, or sit beside her and try to resist her enticing scent.

Neither option was ideal, but beside her, at least he could look at the ledger.

He rounded the desk and settled in the second guest chair. "Can you share?"

"I had four sisters. Sharing was never my strong suit." She slid the ledger closer to him. "But I can try."

"Don't strain yourself."

She chuckled, shaking her head.

He shouldn't banter with her. Shouldn't joke or laugh or let his guard down in any way. If he did, she'd slither through whatever crack he allowed, and then he'd be a goner.

Focus, Ballentine.

He tried. Really, he did.

But he'd stared at the first page of the stupid ledger for hours the night before. All he saw were dates, dollar amounts—

assuming those squiggles were supposed to be dollar signs—and other numbers that made no sense. The first line read:

3/4/99 650 × 4 $10.5M

Not exactly a paltry sum.

The other lines were similar. The numbers were slightly different, but all had the same pattern. A date, three digits multiplied by single digits, and then a dollar sign and high number.

There were only four lines, one a month for four months. His family had been murdered on June twentieth, seventeen days after the last date.

"Let's assume," Brooklynn said, "that Ballentine was smuggling drugs."

Drugs.

This was why Forbes couldn't make heads or tails of the journal.

Because of course his father wouldn't be involved in drug smuggling. Antiquities, tobacco, or liquor, to avoid the taxes, maybe.

But not drugs.

And yes, he saw the irony of counseling Brooklynn not to trust her friends while he refused to believe the worst about his father.

Brooklynn didn't look up, didn't see his reaction.

"And let's assume they were using the same size crates to smuggle back then as they used the other day. They looked like three-foot cubes, each carried by two men off the boat, then moved with a dolly."

"Big men," Forbes said, thinking of the so-called Bernie. He closed his eyes and remembered the photograph he'd been shown. His guess was, those crates had been heavy.

"Strong men," she added. "So, what would fill three-foot cubes and be heavy enough that two strong men would struggle to haul it?"

He had no idea. "Let me do some research." He nodded at the four lines. "See if you notice any patterns."

Not that there was much data to draw from.

She reached for his notebook, moving into his personal space for a pen.

Her hair tickled his arm, causing a reaction that tingled to his toes.

He snatched the pen and plopped it on top of the ledger, probably too hard.

"Sorry," she said.

"It's fine." He pulled his laptop close, opened an AI browser, and typed in the question, *How much would a 3x3 crate of drugs weigh?*

AI gave him a list of multiple drugs and their weights.

Heroin weighed thirty to forty pounds per cubic foot. Meth, forty-two to fifty-five pounds. Fentanyl, fifty to sixty.

A three-foot cube had twenty-seven cubic feet, meaning each of those numbers would have to be multiplied by twenty-seven.

Forbes did the math.

Calculating for each of the drugs, he doubted any of them fit the bill. Few men could lift eight hundred pounds and carry it as the men in the photos had, much less the sixteen hundred pounds fentanyl would weigh. Assuming the boxes were filled to the brim. Assuming there wasn't filler or something on top to hide the drugs.

Marijuana was much lighter. But would that much marijuana have a value in the tens of millions?

A quick internet search proved his guess was right. It couldn't be marijuana.

It could be heroin. Or cocaine. Or...or any number of things.

If Brooklynn's theory was correct, then the smugglers had been moving serious drugs.

How, how could his father have been involved in something like that?

Maybe Brooklynn's theory was wrong. But what else could it be?

"Are you okay?" Brooklynn asked. "You're pale as flour."

"I'm fine."

"Are you sure? You look...I don't know."

"I said I'm fine. What did you learn?"

She blinked at his harsh tone. "Nothing on the first page, nothing that you wouldn't have seen. The shipments came once a month. They got gradually larger, then abruptly stopped a few weeks before the murders. But I did see something else."

She tapped the ledger sheet, not the list, but a tiny doodle in the corner. "Have you ever seen that before?"

He'd seen it, sure. He'd paid no attention. He studied it now and realized it was a tiny sketch of a bird in flight. "It's just a doodle."

"Was Charles an artist?"

"You call that art?"

"It's detailed, a seagull. The tiny feathers along the back of the wings, longer at the tips. See how the wings are bent like that? It's diving."

He'd seen a squiggle. She'd seen a bird in flight.

She flipped to the next page and tapped another doodle he'd ignored. It was the same thing, a tiny bird, but this one was inside a circle, the beak poking out on the bottom right side.

There were similar doodles on the next few pages of the journal.

"Weird that they're all the same," he said.

"You're sure he wasn't an artist?"

"Maybe he wanted to be." Forbes had no memory of his father ever drawing anything, though, so that didn't feel right.

"Maybe." Brooklynn nodded to the stack of files Forbes had yet to put away. "Did he doodle a lot on those?"

Forbes thought back. "I didn't pay attention. I think there were some doodles, yeah."

"Do you mind if I look?"

"What difference does it make?"

She took out her phone, took a photo of one of the tiny drawings, and then enlarged it on her screen. "This isn't random. This is a specific image, drawn multiple times. You say he's not an artist. Was he on the spectrum, do you think?"

"Are you asking if he had autism or Asperger's?" Forbes needed to hide his irritation, considering that Ford would find the question fascinating.

Since nothing ever got by Brooklynn, she winced at his tone.

He tempered it. "I've seen no evidence of that. Why?"

"Maybe OCD? It's just odd that he'd always draw the same thing. Six times in one journal, which was written over the course of months."

He saw her point.

"It must mean something." She nodded to the pile of manila folders Forbes had yet to put away. "Did you see similar doodles in any of his other papers?"

He thought back to the reading he'd done for days on end. He'd been focused on the words, not the scribbles. But there had been some. And if Brooklynn was right, then they might mean something. "I wasn't paying attention. We can look for them after we go through the ledger."

She turned the page. "This is a list of letter pairings."

"Yeah, I saw." Similar to the notations on the previous page, these had not all been written at once. They were in different ink colors and thicknesses, some more legible than others, as if his father had jotted them down over time. "They're not abbreviations for any weights or measures, as far as I can tell. I doubt they're federal agencies, since most of those have three or more letters. Maybe they're state agencies?"

She tapped one of the pairings. "No states begin with B."

"Are you sure?" He reached for his laptop to ask AI.

Brooklynn said, "Alabama, Alaska, Arizona, Arkansas, California..."

She knew the states. In alphabetical order.

"Are *you* on the spectrum?"

She laughed. "We had to memorize them in grade school, and once I commit something to memory, it's there forever."

He'd memorized his share of useless stuff, but he'd let most of it go years ago. "Let's say they're people's initials," he said. "That eliminates hundreds of millions of people. In a world of eight billion, that's not exactly helpful."

"Right." She bit her bottom lip. "If some are locals, then G.P. could be Graham Porter."

The hotel owner. "Or George Parker. Or Gigi Perkins."

Brooklynn ignored him. "Is that an E?"

"Looks like E.H. Could be your friend Elvis, the flower child."

"She wouldn't be involved in drug trafficking."

"Not all bad guys wear black hats, Brooklynn. And not all bad guys are *guys*."

She flashed a glare. "I know that. I also know Elvis. She wouldn't hurt a fly."

"Maybe, but she could've been involved, not knowing the danger she was putting people in. We don't even know what this list is about. Maybe it's victims. Or customers."

"So Elvis was a...a pusher?"

"It's possible." Forbes jotted both Graham's and Elvis's

names in his notebook, then pointed at the next letter pairings. She couldn't identify an N.P, an L.S., or a B.D.

The next pairing caught his eye. "O.T. Didn't you say something about an Owen?"

"Owen Stratton, Delaney's boyfriend. He would've been about five at the time."

"Probably not our killer, then. What about...Taggart? His father's name is...?"

"Leonard—Leo. Lenny is named after him."

"No names starting with O? Lenny's mom, maybe?"

"His mother left when he was little. Lenny respects his dad, but he told me once that he blames him for the divorce. Apparently, Leo was unfaithful, which doesn't surprise me."

"Why do you say that?"

"He's kind of a player, Leo Taggart. His last girlfriend was younger than Lenny."

"Nice." He'd never understood men who chased younger women. He craved a partner who was his intellectual equal. Someone smart and beautiful and...

"Lenny's no prince," Brooklynn said, "but he's nothing like his father in that respect. Anyway, last I heard, his mother lives out west somewhere. Lenny doesn't have much of a relationship with her."

"You don't know her name?"

"No idea."

"How about F.W.?"

"F.W." Brooklynn tilted her head to the side. "If I remember correctly, Jewel's father was named Frank."

"Is that the one who owned Webb's Harborside?"

"Good memory. His wife is Fiona. She and the kids own the restaurant now."

Fiona was still alive, then. Forbes wrote the names in his notebook. Then realized... "Jewel's your assistant."

"She manages the gallery."

"Her father could've been involved." His heart thumped. "Her mother could be now. You've been communicating with her."

"I trust Jewel."

"Maybe you shouldn't."

"I have to trust somebody, Ford."

He winced at the name, at the irony. "But you haven't told her where you are or who you're with, right?"

"And *you* have to trust *me*. I said I wouldn't."

"Just making sure."

Brooklynn had no names to go with the rest of the initials. Maybe none of the people she'd mentioned were involved. Maybe they all were.

He'd look into every one, just to be sure.

The next page had notations, some referring to the initials on the previous page.

> L.S. CRYPTIC COMMENT AT CC MTG
> O.T. COERCED?
> STEER CLEAR OF F.W. DANGEROUS.
> G.P.? GREEDY BUT INVOLVED?

They went on like that, notes about most of the initials, confirming Forbes's guess that they referred to people.

So many people.

Had Dad been trying to figure out who all was involved in The Network? If so, why? To have something to use against them? Blackmail material?

Or maybe he was afraid he'd get caught and wanted to have information to turn over to the police to get himself out of trouble.

If so, then Dad was a drug smuggler *and* a back-stabber.

The thought was so distasteful that Forbes sipped his water, wishing he could wash away the flavor.

The next page of cryptic notes made no sense.

What were you up to, Dad?

More importantly, why?

Between what he'd earned and what he'd inherited, Dad had been worth hundreds of millions of dollars. Had it really not been enough?

Was the money more important than his family?

Beside him, Brooklynn made a low *hmm*. "I wonder if he was trying to extricate himself."

He snapped his gaze to her. "What do you mean?"

"Maybe he wanted out. Maybe he was threatening to turn over everything he knew if The Network didn't let him go. And maybe...maybe that's why they killed him. Maybe they killed Grace and Rosie to make examples of them so nobody else would try to get out."

Forbes thought back to that terrible day, to the moment before Dad was shot. *"The Network trusted you. You betrayed us."*

"That's a good theory." His heart was thumping. For the first time in the weeks since he'd arrived, he had real leads. And a possible explanation for what'd happened that day. Maybe the initials and the names they'd put with them would lead to something.

There was only one thing Forbes wanted, one thing he'd lived for since he was eight years old.

Justice.

~

FORBES WAS BACK on his father's side of the desk, researching the names he and Brooklynn had come up with.

He'd been at it for forty-five minutes but hadn't found anything illuminating when her cell phone rang.

She looked at the screen, said, "It's Alyssa," then answered. "Hey, sis." After listening for a minute or so, she reached for Forbes's notebook, glancing at him for permission.

He slid it toward her, and she jotted something down.

"Perfect." She listened for another few seconds. "You're the best. Seriously. I'll get back to you."

She ended the call and looked at him, her expression bright. "Shane Dawson has a nephew named Bryce."

"How do you know that?" He had a good idea what her answer would be, and frustration vibrated in his chest.

"Alyssa. I told you, she's brilliant. She can find anything on—"

"You had no right to ask her."

Brooklynn's lips twisted into a smirk. "Did you find that information on your own?"

"No, but—"

"It took her about ten minutes. Even the Lone Ranger had Tonto."

He'd heard of the Lone Ranger, but who was Tonto?

She must've read his confusion. "His sidekick. Like Robin to Batman."

"Your sister is not my sidekick."

"You're right. And neither am I. We're both capable of things you obviously aren't, so stop being so stubborn about it and accept help." Her phone dinged with an incoming text, and she glanced at it. "Unless you don't want to see this."

"What is it?"

Her eyebrows lifted. "Are you admitting you need help?"

"Whatever." He shouldn't sound so surly, considering Brooklynn and her sister had learned more in three days than he'd learned in three weeks.

That was exaggerating it a bit. He'd learned an awful lot, but he'd hit a wall, a wall that the Wright sisters had barreled right through.

He held out his hand for the phone and read the texts.

There was a photograph with a note.

> Is this your guy?

He tapped to enlarge the picture. It was a mugshot of the so-called Bernie.

Another text came in.

> Bryce Dawson. 27. Arrested in 2022 for possession and assault. Took a plea deal—probation and 90 days in rehab. Nephew of Shane Dawson.

The next text included Bryce's address in Portland.

> Shane has no arrests. His brother, Michael, Bryce's father, arrested 2x for OUI, 1995 and 2002.

OUI... Operating under the influence of either alcohol or drugs.

> Mother Laurie Renee Smith. Record clean. Bryce's parents never married.

The next text included a document.

He flashed the screen to Brooklynn to let her read what her sister had said. "Mind if I open the attachment?"

"Go ahead."

He scanned it, seeing a full report on everything Alyssa had learned about Bryce Dawson. Education, work history...

He forwarded the photograph and the document to his own

phone, then handed Brooklynn's cell back to her. "I could never have gotten that information on my own."

"You admit it!" She flashed her million-dollar smile. "See? I'm more than just a nosy houseguest."

She was so much more than that. Fun and happy and cheerful and helpful and...

And he couldn't remember why he'd ever resented her presence.

He should say that, tell her how grateful he was that she was there, how much he enjoyed having her around. But he didn't know how to do that without sounding...hokey or like a flatterer.

All he managed was, "Thanks."

Her smile brightened even more, as if he'd made her whole day. "You're very welcome. Alyssa asked me if there was anything else she could help with, so I thought I'd pass along the rest of these names." She flipped back through the notebook to the list he'd made from the initials. "She can check if any of them have a record."

"How does she have time for this? Doesn't she have a job?"

"This is her job."

"Right. Find out what her rate is, and—"

"She's not going to charge us."

"I am going to pay her. That's nonnegotiable. And I expect confidentiality."

Brooklynn looked like she wanted to argue, then shrugged. "If you prefer to pay for something you could get for free, who am I to argue? Alyssa can use the business."

That settled, Brooklynn took a picture of the notebook page Forbes had filled with names and sent it to her sister, then tapped a text faster than he could type on his laptop.

They had a solid lead, an actual name to go with an actual photo of a person he knew was involved.

Bryce Dawson was too young to have been involved in

Forbes's family's murders, but if Forbes's theory was correct, then he worked for The Network.

That reminded him...

"Brooklynn?"

She looked up from her phone.

"Tell your sister we're looking for a man named Niles, or maybe someone with a name that starts with N. In your photos, he was the one on the beach, looking like a manager." Forbes described what he remembered about the man who'd searched the house with Bernie/Bryce a few days before. "It's not a lot to go on, but maybe he's a son or family member of one of the people the journal referred to."

"Gotcha. I'll send his picture. And text Bryce's name to Nathan."

He pulled the pile of files closer and started flipping through them, looking for doodles and feeling like an idiot. Who cared if his father liked to draw birds?

When Brooklynn set her phone down, he slid half the pile to her. They worked in silence. Whenever he found the doodle, he turned the page horizontal and set the file aside.

He was surprised at how often he found them.

After half an hour, he started to believe that this wasn't as futile an exercise as he'd first thought.

When he finished the last file, he looked up to find Brooklynn watching him.

When he caught her eye, she looked away. Did her cheeks pink?

"You got through the stack?"

"Yup." She eyed his files with papers sticking out sideways. "Mind if I—?"

"Go ahead."

She slid them closer and studied the doodles. "All seagulls."

"I noticed."

"See any patterns?"

"All the doodles are on the back sides of printed reports. The front sides are typewritten, of course, but the doodles are with handwritten notes, unlike the other content."

"Same with my pile."

"And the content doesn't match." He skimmed through the files and pulled one sheet out. "For instance, this file is related to a construction project in Reading, Mass. An office building built back in the mid-eighties. But the dates on the...doodle-note are in the late nineties."

"I'm seeing the same thing. The dates don't match, and there are initials, like we saw in the ledger." She opened one of the files she'd looked at. "Like this one."

He held his hand out, and she gave it to him.

The first line read,

MM (G-BAZZ) CAHAL—XSC

This was why he hadn't focused on the notes when he'd gone through the files. Because they made no sense.

"MM Bazz?" He looked at Brooklynn. "That mean anything to you?"

"Nope."

He googled it and got nothing helpful. Then he googled the second part. "CAHAL could be a name. It's a character in some show." He blew out a breath and added *boat* to the search, which sent him to boat sales websites.

Brooklynn was looking over his shoulder. "Maybe shipping or maritime?"

He typed CAHAL SHIPPING.

"Bingo. CAHAL is the maritime code for the port in Halifax, Nova Scotia."

"That's gotta be it. And SC is Shadow Cove. So whatever... this referred to was smuggled from Halifax to here."

Didn't exactly narrow it down, but it was more than he had known ten minutes before.

He studied the next line. Similar gobbledygook, though it seemed all of the shipments came from Halifax. Maybe G Bazz was the sender? But what kind of name was Bazz?

Frustrated, he pushed the papers away. "Obviously, this made sense to Charles."

"Maybe..." Brooklynn yawned. "Sorry. Maybe if we put everything together, a pattern will emerge."

Forbes checked his watch. It was past dinnertime. They'd been holed up in here for hours. "We need to rest."

She nodded, but the smile he'd expected didn't come. "There is one more thing." She tapped one of the doodled seagulls. "I think I recognize it."

His fatigue vanished as adrenaline flooded his veins. "What do you mean? What are you saying? From where?"

"I don't know. But I'm sure I've seen it before. It's a logo for something. I just... I've been racking my brain, and I can't remember."

He typed *What company uses a seagull logo* into his search engine and was rewarded with a clothing company.

He studied the logo. It was a seagull, but it was completely different from the one Dad had doodled.

Could they be smuggling clothes? From Google, he learned that people had been caught smuggling fake designer-brand clothes and purses.

He'd much prefer to think of his father smuggling clothes than drugs, but how could a three-foot cube of dresses and leather goods weigh hundreds of pounds?

Or be worth tens of millions?

Much as he'd like to believe it, he seriously doubted that

theory. Besides, the clothing company with the seagull logo didn't sell designer products.

This was so frustrating.

Couldn't Dad have just written a note? *If I turn up dead, I was killed by these people, and this is why.*

Would that have been so hard?

Brooklynn covered a yawn. "I'll figure it out. I just need to rest and think."

Answers rarely came during the information-gathering process. Usually, they came later, when he focused elsewhere and let his brain work things out in the background.

"The information needs to simmer," he said.

"To slow roast, so to speak. Also, I'm hungry." She grinned and pushed to her feet. "I'll go start dinner."

She'd already done so much for him, he wasn't about to let her cook. He didn't know how to thank her. He didn't know how to express his gratitude. All those words seemed to cling to his tongue, unwilling to be released.

All he managed was, "You like pizza?"

CHAPTER NINETEEN

Brooklynn carried plates, silverware, and napkins to the family room, where Ford was crouched in front of the fireplace, lighting a flame.

Despite the day's sunshine, the house was chilly. Worried someone would peek inside and see her, Ford had kept all the blinds and curtains closed. Nice for safety, but he'd never turned on the heat. By the time the sun went down, it was downright cold.

She set the things on the coffee table. "Another fire?"

"Just thought we should burn the wood I hauled up last night so I don't have to take it back down."

He settled where he'd sat the night before, opened the pizza box on the coffee table, and shifted a piece onto a plate, which he handed to her.

"Thanks." She nibbled a bite, savoring the salty meats, crisp veggies, and spicy sauce. Her stomach had been growling for hours. She hadn't realized how much energy it took to solve a mystery.

Ford finished his first bite. "Good pizza."

"The best in town." She sipped her water to wash down the

bite. "You must have some great stories. Tell me about other mysteries you've investigated. Have you solved any?"

He took his time swallowing and wiping his mouth. "Nope."

She waited for more, but apparently, he had nothing to add. "Whoa. Don't overwhelm me with information."

His lips did that twitching thing. "This is the most interesting mystery I've studied so far."

"How do you decide which mysteries to write about?"

"I focus on mysteries that occurred in old houses. And I look for mysteries that happened in the late twentieth century or the early twenty-first."

"Always murders?"

"Not...officially."

"Meaning?" When he said nothing, she asked, "Can you give me an example?" Sometimes, making conversation with Ford was akin to getting the perfect shot. It took patience and determination and a whole lot of luck.

She could give up, but like the perfect shot, when she managed to get him to talk, it was incredibly satisfying.

He set one ankle over his opposite knee. "Back in the late eighties, a two-year-old girl was snatched out of her second-story bedroom from an old plantation house in Georgia."

"That's awful." She couldn't imagine the pain of losing a child that way. "Do you know who did it?"

He rubbed his lips together. "Nothing definitive, but the girl's mother was an alcoholic, and neighbors reported their suspicions that she was abusive. They heard her screaming sometimes. There were even a few police reports, though nothing ever came of them.

"My theory—and that of others looking at the mystery—is that the mother killed the child, possibly by accident."

That was even more distasteful than the idea that somebody had snatched her.

"Rather than confess," Ford said, "she hid her daughter's body and claimed she'd been kidnapped. The mom's brother was the sheriff. Maybe he knew she did it and wanted to protect her. Maybe he couldn't imagine his baby sister doing something so terrible. Either way, he investigated her claim of kidnapping and never entertained any other theories."

"So she got away with it?"

"If she was guilty, then yes. Even though she wasn't arrested or convicted, can you imagine trying to live with that?"

Brooklynn couldn't, but there were people who would kill a child without blinking an eye. Alyssa and Callan—and his daughter, Peri—had come against just that kind of person.

"The woman and her brother inherited the house from her grandparents. It was empty for years while she was in college. She got pregnant and came home with a baby. She never told anyone who the father was.

"When she reported the little girl missing, she named the baby's father, claiming he must've taken her. But she only had a nickname, didn't know how old the man was, and didn't know where he lived. Also, she'd always claimed she never told the father she carried his child. Even if he'd found out somehow, why kidnap her? Why not try to get custody legally? That theory had more holes than a sieve, in my opinion. Especially when the father was never located."

"More reason to believe she did it. She still claims innocence?"

He looked toward the windows, though the twilight evening was hidden behind curtains. "She committed suicide a couple years after the girl's supposed kidnapping. Her suicide note read, *I can't live with it anymore. I'm sorry.*"

"Oh, a confession?"

He shrugged. "Maybe she couldn't live with not knowing

where her daughter was, but that seems wrong. Wouldn't a mother always hope she'd find her baby?"

"Maybe she wasn't emotionally capable of handling it."

"I think she did it, but there's no way to know. The girl's body was never found. She could still be out there."

"How awful for the family to never get that closure. Did you meet the brother? What does he think?"

Another shrug. "He's hard to get a read on." His answer showed no enthusiasm or curiosity.

For someone who investigated unsolved mysteries, he didn't seem to care that much.

Except she knew he cared about this house's secrets.

"Tell me about another one."

"I'm tired of thinking about mysteries tonight."

Obviously, Ford wasn't in the mood to talk. "You want to watch TV?"

He'd finished his fourth slice of pizza and wiped his hands. "You're a big fan."

"When I was a kid, we weren't allowed to watch much, and when we did, Mom monitored the programs carefully. We watched a lot of reruns because she said most of the current programs were filthy." Brooklynn felt a smile at the memory. "Of course, we thought that was ridiculous, but looking back, she had a point."

"Once I grew up," she said, "I cared less about TV. Who had time for it? But I live alone now, and the evenings can be long." She shrugged like it didn't matter. "You probably spend your evenings reading Shakespeare and...biographies of dead people."

His lips tipped up and...

Oh, my. Was that a real smile? His very handsome face transformed, making him absolutely gorgeous.

If she could, she'd spend the rest of her life trying to coax that smile out of him.

Okay, maybe not *the rest of her life*. Talk about hyperbole.

"Not Shakespeare," he said. "All that poetry and thees and thous. But biographies are fascinating."

"Aha! I knew it."

He looked away, still smiling. Maybe a little embarrassed, which made him even more attractive. How was that even possible?

"Okay," she said, "favorite biography of all time."

"Impossible. There are too many to choose from." He named a few people she'd never heard of. He must've noticed her confusion because he sighed. "Ever heard of John Adams?"

"He makes beer, right? No, wait. That's Sam."

Ford's jaw dropped.

"I'm kidding." She laughed, waving off his shock. "Of course I know who he is. Founding Father, second president of the United States."

"There's a great biography of him. Sort of long, but—"

"Oh, I know which one you mean. There was a miniseries about him based on a book."

Forbes chuckled, an actual genuine chuckle—with a grin and sound and everything.

She did her very best not to react.

"I'm guessing the book is better than the movie," he said.

"We can watch it, and you can tell me. Though it's probably five or six hours long."

His eyes widened as if the thought of watching that much television was abhorrent. "Let's pick something...uh..."

"Shorter?"

"Whatever you want."

She found the remote and turned on the TV—a modern

flatscreen that had to have been recently purchased. "If you don't watch TV, why do you have this? Or was it already here?"

"The owner provided it. I watch the news sometimes, mostly to keep me company in the evenings." His head dipped side to side. "It does get quiet being alone all the time."

They were similar in that, anyway.

She turned the TV on, and a twenty-four-hour news channel was showing video of some tragedy. Car accident, plane crash, forest fire? She didn't watch long enough to find out, scrolling the guide until she paused on an old Cary Grant movie that was just starting, one of her favorites.

"Ever seen it?"

He read the title and perked up. "It's about a builder?"

"Not exactly, but it's funny." She started the movie—*Mr. Blandings Builds his Dream House*—and hoped Ford would enjoy it.

They both settled back, and somehow as the movie progressed, they inched closer to one another until their shoulders were touching.

Ford's attention never strayed from the screen. Everything he did, he did completely, even this.

Where she could be flighty and spontaneous, he was organized and intense.

She'd seen the black-and-white movie more times than she could count, which explained why she spent more time observing the man beside her than the comedy.

In all the time she'd spent with Ford, he'd never let his guard down. There was something about the movie, the fireplace, the whole...situation, that seemed to encourage him to relax. He wasn't scowling or even frowning. The worry lines etched in his forehead smoothed out.

She'd already been attracted to him. Now she felt drawn to him in a way she'd never felt toward another man. He was mysterious and closed off, just like this house. And like the house, stately and dignified, but beneath that veneer, the man had secrets she was compelled to uncover. If only he wouldn't work so hard to hide them.

They were nearly finished with the movie when his phone rang. He checked the caller ID, then shifted away from her as if surprised to realize she was there. He stood abruptly. "I need to take this."

And apparently, he needed privacy, because he stepped into the hall and closed the door.

She paused the movie, stood and stretched, then added another log to the fire. Not that she was cold, but the flames were so friendly.

He returned a few minutes later, and his walls were back up. If anything, his worry lines were etched deeper.

"Everything okay?" she asked.

"That was the manager at Marie Ballentine's retirement community. I'm her closest family, so I'm her emergency contact. She was taken to the emergency room yesterday after a fall. She's home now. They wanted to make sure I'd been notified."

"Is she all right?"

"She was released a couple of hours ago and took a taxi back to her place. That's why they reached out to me. They figured I'd have been there if I'd known. Which I would have." His lips pressed tightly closed, frustration wafting off him. He swallowed, looking beyond Brooklynn. "I need to go see her tomorrow, but I can't leave you here on your own."

"I'm sure it would be fine."

"Are you? Because maybe those guys who chased you are just waiting for me to leave so they can search the place again."

They hadn't given up on finding her here. And she didn't

relish having to hide in some spider-infested hole until Ford came back.

Or calling the police and dealing with Lenny.

"You'll have to come with me," he said.

"Out there is more dangerous than in here."

"Out there, I can protect you. If I leave you here, anything could happen." By the way his expression darkened, she guessed he was not happy with the arrangement. "You'll have to come with me. There's no other way."

CHAPTER TWENTY

After Tuesday's storm and Wednesday's cool, crisp air, Thursday morning brought summer temperatures. It was already in the seventies—both the temperature and the humidity—when Forbes and Brooklynn left the estate.

Not long after they hit the state highway, Forbes noticed the tail.

Ten minutes later, the black Chevy sedan was still there.

It stayed a few cars back, and under any other circumstances, he'd think nothing about it. But he'd seen that car before, parked in his driveway when Bryce Dawson and the so-called Niles had demanded to search his house.

How long had they been staking out his property? Or had they attached some sort of tracker to his truck? Was that what they'd been doing in the garage the other night, not trying to get into the house but finding a way to track him?

Were their cohorts sneaking onto his property right now?

His cell phone hadn't pinged an alarm.

"Can I come out now?" Brooklynn was tucked in the narrow space between the passenger seat and the backseat bench.

A glance behind told him she was sitting up and watching him over the console.

"Stay low. We're being followed."

He couldn't see her reaction and managed to stifle the urge to look.

"Are you gonna try to...lose them?"

Lose them. Like he was about to start a high-speed chase.

He checked the speedometer—five miles over the speed limit. He didn't want the thugs to know he'd spotted them. "Don't worry. If they follow me all the way to Marie's, I'll take care of it. You'll be safe."

"Okay."

No hesitation in her voice, no worry. No questions. Just *okay.*

She trusted him.

Her confidence in his ability to protect her felt better than it should. And worried him.

What if he failed?

All he'd wanted for years, decades, was to find the people who'd murdered his family. Until now, he'd have sacrificed almost anything to get justice for his parents and sister.

But he wouldn't sacrifice Brooklynn. He hated that she was in danger. If it came down to choosing between justice for the dead or protection for the living, he'd choose Brooklynn.

It would be excruciating to give up on justice, but losing her would kill him.

Simple as that.

The night before, he'd managed to get absorbed in the comedy, enjoying the laughter, the silly jokes, the escape from his worries.

Until he'd realized Brooklynn had somehow ended up close enough that their arms touched. He'd blame her for scooting closer, but he'd somehow drifted her direction. Once he noticed the warmth of her, the feeling of her tucked against his side, it'd taken every ounce of self-control not to wrap her in his arms and kiss her.

Until this was over, he couldn't allow any distractions.

He probably could've safely left her at the house, but he wanted Grandmother to meet her so she'd understand Forbes's desire to tell her the truth.

He couldn't share who he really was without getting Grandmother's okay, not after the promises he'd made. Not after the sacrifices Gran had made for him.

But he couldn't lie to Brooklynn anymore.

Maybe she'd hate him when she learned the truth, but if he fessed up, if he explained, then...maybe not. They could still be friends. Someday, if he ever found the murderers, they could be more than friends.

Forbes could have a real family, a real life, out of hiding.

It felt...impossible. The person he was now, his talents and faults. His personality. His fears and dreams. They'd all been shaped by that one terrible night.

Who would he be when he finally exposed the murderers and their crimes?

He wanted to know. He desperately wanted to move past the murders.

Brooklynn had barged into his life and his house and his thoughts.

Considering he could count the number of hours he'd known her, his feelings for her should scare him. But something about this whole thing seemed almost God-ordained.

Not that he believed God cared about him. But if He did, if Forbes could redeem himself in his own eyes and in God's...

Maybe there was hope.

He exited the highway, and the Chevy followed.

Forbes snaked along the streets of Portland, hoping to lose them.

"Are they still back there?" she asked.

"Don't worry." He turned into the driveway that led to the retirement home and stopped at a guard gate, rolling down his window. In front of him, the spike strip was up.

They took security seriously at this retirement community, which was why Grandmother had chosen it.

The guard recognized him. "Morning, Mr. Baker."

"Hey, Russ." Forbes handed over his ID. "Listen, someone's been following me. They're in a black Chevy sedan."

The man's gray eyebrows lowered.

"You know how important Mrs. Ballentine's security is," Forbes added.

"Gotcha." He peered behind Forbes, likely seeing Brooklynn, but he didn't say anything as he spoke into a walkie-talkie. Then he opened the gate. "Thanks for the heads-up. We'll take care of it."

Forbes waited for the spike strip to lower before continuing past the guard and onto the manicured grounds. The road wound between tall trees, past flowerbeds and walking trails to the main entrance.

After parking, he opened the back door for Brooklynn. She'd dressed in navy yoga pants and a gray T-shirt two sizes too large, which she'd knotted at her trim waist. Her hair was tucked up into a baseball cap he'd found in Dad's closet.

The drab clothes and old hat did nothing to hide her beauty.

She reached back for her backpack and hiked it over her shoulder. She hadn't wanted to leave her camera at the house, just in case the thugs broke in.

"Keep your head down." He guided her toward the front doors. "I don't want your face on the cameras."

"I remember." She glanced around, and he followed her gaze. This place dripped wealth and beauty like rainwater. It was a perfect summer day—and only the second time Brooklynn had been outside since she'd been chased by smugglers, yet there was no joy in her voice when she added, "Are you sure it's safe?"

"The guard will stop them from coming in. They're very good at what they do."

She rubbed her lips together. The fear didn't leave her eyes.

Not that he wanted her to be nervous, but it was good that she was. She needed to keep her guard up.

In the foyer, he greeted Cheri, the receptionist, pulling out his ID.

She swiped it in the scanner, giving Brooklynn a quick once-over. Cheri was usually cheerful, but her expression dimmed.

"This is Betty." Forbes indicated Brooklynn. "She doesn't have her license on her."

Brooklynn smiled her million-dollar smile. "I lost my wallet." She rolled her eyes. "I need to get one of those wallet-cases for my phone."

Cheri's lips pursed. She glanced at Forbes. "You know the procedures."

"I do. She's my sister, and Mrs. Ballentine is looking forward to seeing her. I was hoping you could make an exception."

Just like that, Cheri's smile was back. "I understand." To Brooklynn, she said, "Just stay with your brother."

"Will do."

"Please send Dr. Shelley to Mrs. Ballentine's room," he said. "I'd like to speak with her."

"I'll let her know."

The electronic lock clicked, and Forbes opened the door.

Brooklynn stepped through, pausing to look around. Her

gaze landed on a group of women gathered in one of the side rooms.

"What's going on in there?" she asked.

As if he'd know.

She headed that direction, and a woman waved her in.

"Are you in the market for a wig, dear?"

"Oh, no." Brooklynn laughed. "Just curious."

"The word is nosy," Forbes muttered.

Somehow, the woman heard him and laughed. "Oh, darling," she said, "Let a woman shop."

He saw no point in responding to that.

Brooklynn called, "Have fun" and ducked out.

He led her down the hallway toward Grandmother's room. "You remind me of a kitten that used to hang around my boarding school."

"I love kittens! I always wanted one."

"Ever heard that old expression about curiosity and cats?"

"A bunch of old ladies shopping for wigs aren't going to hurt me. Not like your admirer."

"What are you talking about?"

"Cheri, the receptionist. If looks could kill, I'd be bleeding out."

"She was just doing her job."

Brooklynn laughed. "Are you really so clueless? No wonder you're not married. Cheri was practically drooling."

"You're crazy." Wasn't she? He'd never been good at reading people, and not being good at things irritated him. "You're doing a lousy job keeping your head down."

She looked up at him and smiled. "Now that we're inside, I feel safe again."

"But you're not. There are cameras everywhere." He'd told her that, but a reminder seemed in order. This place had great security, but anyone could hack a system, and he didn't want her enemies confirming that she was here with him.

"You're right." She ducked her head as if she were in trouble.

They passed doorways decorated with wreaths and welcome signs, skirting strategically placed sitting areas where he'd never seen anyone sitting. They turned at a corner and walked a long corridor, finally reaching Grandmother's room at the end.

He knocked, then checked the door. It was locked, as it should be.

A moment later, it opened, and Grandmother stood on the opposite side. She was dressed in one of her comfortable velour outfits. She wore her typical jewelry—diamond earrings, diamond necklace, and the wedding ring he'd never seen her without, despite the fact that his grandfather had died before Forbes was born. Grandmother's hair was perfectly styled, as usual.

But a bruise blackened her eye and marred her cheek, and she wore a brace on her hand.

She plastered on a smile, though it was hesitant. Her gaze flicked from him to Brooklynn and back. "I didn't know you were coming."

"I tried to call." He bent to give her a hug and held her a second longer than usual. "You didn't answer your phone."

"They told me to rest, so I turned it off." She patted his arm and stepped back. "I was following the doctor's orders." She rested a cool hand on his cheek. "I asked them not to call you."

"Why? *You* should have called me."

"I'm fine." She turned her attention to Brooklynn.

"Aunt Marie," he said, giving her a pointed look, "this is a friend of mine, Brooklynn Wright."

Brooklynn held out her hand to shake. "It's nice to meet you, Mrs. Ballentine."

Grandmother took her hand in both of hers. "You too, dear. I'm sorry he dragged you along to check on me. One little fall isn't going to kill me." She stepped out of the way. "Come on in."

Forbes followed Brooklynn inside, leading her through the smallish kitchen to the living room. It was just large enough for a sofa and a chair.

Grandmother remained in the kitchen. "Shall I put on some tea?"

He said, "No thanks—"

"—That would be lovely," Brooklynn said.

Grandmother started the electric kettle.

"Go sit down." He urged her toward the sofa. "I'll take care of it."

"I can make tea."

"I know you can. You can also sit with our guest—and let me serve you."

She tapped his forearm, giving him a little smile before she returned to the living room.

While she questioned Brooklynn about everything from her career to her family—she apparently knew the Wrights and even remembered Brooklynn's parents—Forbes prepared the tea. He'd been a little worried that Grandmother might reveal who he really was, but she seemed as sharp as ever. She'd kept up the ruse for decades. Lying was old hat to both of them.

He set two cups of tea, the matching cream and sugar dishes, teaspoons, a glass of ice water, and a plate of shortbread cookies onto her favorite tray and carried it to the living room.

"Here we go," he said.

They helped themselves, continuing their chat.

He gave them a few minutes, then cleared his throat. "Enough stalling. Tell me what happened."

She laughed. "You act like I've committed a felony. I lost my balance and fell."

"Where?"

"In the lunchroom. My legs were a little shaky. I reached for a chair to steady myself, but I missed. It was nothing serious."

"If it wasn't serious, then why did they take you to the emergency room?"

"Oh, you know this place." She waved off his words with a flick of her hand. "Always worried about getting sued."

"Or," he said, "they were worried you'd seriously hurt yourself. Obviously, you hit your head."

She touched her cheek gently, then dropped her hand as if she could hide the brace. "It's nothing. A little bruise, a little sprain." Her gaze flicked to Brooklynn, telling him silently that she wouldn't discuss it further in front of a stranger.

"Brooklynn, would you mind—?"

A knock cut him off, followed by a call through the door. "It's Eileen." She was one of the nurses.

Grandmother started to stand, but he got to his feet first. "I'll get it."

She sighed. "Go ahead and ask all your questions, even though I told you I'm fine." He heard the slight reprimand in her voice, along with a hint of affection.

She hated growing old, but she loved him, and she loved that he cared.

After he found out how Grandmother really was, he'd ask Brooklynn to give them some privacy, then talk to Grandmother about telling Brooklynn his true identity, a request he'd never made before.

He opened the door to Eileen. "Where's Dr. Shelley?"

"In her office. She asked me to send you in."

"Can she not come here?"

The young nurse shrugged. "She just said—"

"Fine."

He didn't like leaving Grandmother and Brooklynn alone, but it seemed the doctor was giving him little choice.

After telling the women where he was going, he headed back down the long hallway, praying Grandmother really was all right. And that she'd agree he could tell Brooklynn the truth.

Today.

CHAPTER TWENTY-ONE

Marie Ballentine had impeccable manners. Unlike her great-nephew, she chatted easily and put Brooklynn at ease, or tried to, anyway.

She was an elderly woman who'd been released from the hospital less than twenty-four hours before. Even so, she'd gotten up this morning, done her hair, put on her jewelry, and even added a dab of makeup. The woman was dressed in a cute leisure outfit Brooklynn guessed had come from Chico's or Neiman-Marcus.

Meanwhile, Brooklynn felt like a slug in her ugly, baggy clothes and the hat that hid her hair. She hadn't cared before, but now, meeting this woman who meant so much to Ford, she wished for one of her dresses, or even a pair of slacks and a silky blouse. She wished her hair were down. She wished she wore makeup.

She wished she looked like herself. "How long have you lived here, Mrs. Ballentine?"

The woman set down her teacup with a shaky hand. "Not long. When Ford came to Maine, he wanted me to come too. Not that I have to do what he says, mind you." She gave her a pointed look, as if to say, *I have a mind of my own.* "But he's the only family I have left, and I didn't want to be too far from him. Of course, he asked me to move into that house with him, but...." She looked at a photograph on an end table, and Brooklynn followed her gaze.

It depicted a tall man in his sixties beside a regal-looking woman—Marie in her younger days—along with Charles, Grace, and baby Rosalie.

Brooklynn brushed the woman's arm. "I'm sorry about your family. I imagine the grief never goes away."

She turned back to Brooklynn, her head tilting to the side. "He told you about that?"

"A little."

"You two are an item, then?"

"No, no." She didn't know how much she should say about how she'd met Ford, if anything. "We're just friends."

"I see." Though the woman seemed skeptical.

While they talked, Brooklynn took in the apartment. Like the retirement home's common spaces, this room dripped with luxury. There were photographs and books and lots of personal touches.

She loved the fact that Ford's aunt wore diamonds with her casual outfit. She loved that, despite this tiny space, she behaved like the queen of her own castle.

She was telling a story about her late husband when her words trailed off. She seemed to slump in her seat.

"Are you all right?" Brooklynn leaned closer. "Mrs. Ballentine?"

The elderly woman looked at her, and her eyes popped wide. "Who are you?"

"Uh...I'm Brooklynn. I came with Ford. Your nephew?"

"I don't know you." Her volume rose, and she looked terrified. "Where's Forbes?" She looked around. "Where is he? He was just here."

"It's okay. I'm a friend of his." Brooklynn's great aunt used to have similar episodes, after she was diagnosed with dementia. Brooklynn had taken care of her from time to time. Now, she brushed her hand across Mrs. Ballentine's forehead. It didn't feel hot. She gripped her wrist to check her pulse. It was neither racing nor sluggish. There didn't seem to be any immediate danger, thank God.

"I need Forbes." Mrs. Ballentine looked around as if the man might materialize in the room. "Where did he go?"

Brooklynn didn't know if Forbes ever visited his grandmother, so she assumed Mrs. Ballentine was looking for Ford. "He'll be right back. Why don't we get you into bed? Would you like that?"

"Well, yes. I suppose." She tried to stand but wobbled.

Brooklynn wrapped her arm around her waist and supported her as they walked through an opening into the bedroom. The bed was neatly made, so Brooklynn had her sit on a small chair while she pulled the covers back.

She didn't protest as Brooklynn moved her to the bed, slipped off her shoes, and pulled the covers over her.

"Find Forbes," she said weakly. "I need to talk to him about...something."

"I will. I promise." She'd find Ford, anyway. Right away. Obviously, the concussion had affected Mrs. Ballentine more than anyone realized.

Her eyes closed. Had she fallen asleep already? Her breathing was steady. She looked older than she had twenty minutes before, but otherwise, the same. No drooping, nothing that indicated a stroke.

She turned toward the living room, but her gaze caught on an array of framed pictures on the bureau.

She recognized Forbes, the little boy from the photos she'd seen at the house.

His age progressed in the rest of the photos. From eight to ten to a teenager to a college graduate to...

To Ford.

She blinked, trying to work out what she was seeing.

Ford *was* Forbes. Just as she'd suspected. And just as he'd denied. She'd believed his denial.

He'd lied to her. She'd asked him if he was Forbes Ballentine, and he'd looked her square in the face...

And lied to her.

The truth rang in her head, a buzz she couldn't shake off.

He'd lied to her about who he was. About everything.

She didn't understand. All she knew was that the man she'd trusted to protect her couldn't be trusted at all.

She stepped out of the bedroom and grabbed her backpack, but she couldn't leave without notifying someone that Mrs. Ballentine needed help.

What should she do?

After considering the question and all the possible answers, she made a decision.

She tapped a text to Alyssa, then opened her ride-sharing app and ordered a car.

When it was on the way, she searched for a notebook and pen, finding both in a kitchen drawer. She left a note on the counter.

Finding one of the bright red *pull in case of emergency* cords she'd seen earlier, she pulled it, then slipped into the hallway to wait.

CHAPTER TWENTY-TWO

Forbes had waited outside the doctor's office for ten minutes before he'd been allowed to enter. The woman had apologized for making him wait—a call she had to take, apparently—then gave him more details about Grandmother's fall and diagnosis.

"She did have a bout of memory loss last night," Dr. Shelley said. "She forgot who I was and where she was. She was demanding to see Forbes. That's her grandson, right?"

Her words had worry churning in his middle. "Weird she'd ask for him. He's not around."

"We assumed, since we've never met him."

"Why isn't she in the hospital? She should be—"

"She's all right. This happens when people get older. We're optimistic that, with enough rest, she'll be back to normal soon."

"Meanwhile, you're just leaving her by herself? What happens if she forgets where she is when she's alone? What happens if she panics and gets hurt again?"

"We're keeping an eye on her. We don't have enough staff to—"

"Take care of the people you're paid to take care of?"

"Mr. Baker, we do what we can."

He didn't like that answer and wasn't going to pretend he did. He stood. "Is there anything else I need to know?"

"We're taking good care of your aunt."

He didn't dignify that ridiculous comment with a response. If they were taking good care of her, she wouldn't have fallen.

"Next time something happens, I expect you to notify me immediately, not the next day. Immediately."

The doctor nodded once. "I'm sorry they didn't get in touch with you sooner. I'll make sure the staff knows you're to be informed."

He ground out, "Thank you," and left the office.

He was making his way down the long hallway when Dr. Shelley called out to him from behind. She was rushing toward him.

"Your aunt pulled the emergency cord."

"What happened?"

"I don't know." She reached him, and he hurried alongside her.

Grandmother's door was open when they arrived.

Please, let her be okay.

Brooklynn was with her. She'd take care of her.

A nurse and two staff members were in the living room.

Dr. Shelley moved into the bedroom, and he followed. Grandmother was tucked into bed. There was no sign of Brooklynn.

He shook off worry about Brooklynn to focus on Grandmother.

She was sound asleep.

A nurse followed them in, scooted past Forbes, and held something out to the doctor. "She was disoriented and weak."

The doctor took the piece of paper and read it, then handed it to him. "I think this is for you."

Forbes read the handwritten note. Read it again. On the top, Brooklynn had written exactly what the nurse had said, that Grandmother had been disoriented and weak. Brooklynn had helped her into bed, and she'd fallen asleep immediately.

Below that, she wrote,

> SHE FORGOT TO LIE.
> —B

Forbes's heart dropped to his knees.

Brooklynn knew. Grandmother had told her. And Brooklynn...

He looked around, already knowing what he refused to believe.

She was gone.

CHAPTER TWENTY-THREE

As soon as Ford...no, *Forbes* ran past the alcove where Brooklynn had hidden, she'd returned to the entry foyer, where the women were still shopping for wigs, laughing like children as they tried them on and examined themselves in handheld mirrors.

When Brooklynn stepped in, the one who'd welcomed her earlier brightened. "You change your mind?"

"I think so."

The selection was more suited to old ladies. Short hair, most curly, in all different colors. She found a silvery-gray one in a straight shoulder-length bob. "I'll take it."

"Don't you want to try it on?"

She laughed. "It's for my mother. She'll love it. You don't have any wig caps, do you?"

The woman did, and Brooklynn bought both, paying way more than she could afford to spend. But if it kept her alive, it'd be worth it.

She thanked the vendor, then turned for the door, where walkers and canes had been left. An idea solidified in her mind. She knew what she had to do.

After shoving the wig and cap into her backpack, she hurried to the double doors and looked for her Uber.

Wasn't there.

The receptionist asked, "Did you call for a ride?"

"I did."

"I'll tell the guards."

A minute later, a small SUV pulled around the circle drive. A woman stepped out. "Brooklynn Wright?"

"That's me."

She settled in the back, allowing herself to relax for the first time since her terrible discovery.

Hot tears pricked her eyes.

He'd lied to her. Ford...Forbes...had lied, over and over.

For all she knew, everything he'd told her had been a lie.

Why, though? Why not tell her the truth? She was the innocent one in all of this. She had done nothing to betray him. She hadn't told anyone about the cave. She'd kept her whereabouts a secret.

Was that it? Did he not want her to leave because he didn't trust her not to blab about him and the house? Or was it worse?

The smuggling operation. Was he in on it?

She couldn't imagine, but an hour before, she wouldn't have guessed what a skilled liar he was.

Ford Baker, historian and handyman, she'd come to know and trust.

She knew nothing about Forbes Ballentine except that she couldn't believe a word that came out of his mouth.

She was a fool. A stupid, stupid fool.

CHAPTER TWENTY-FOUR

Forbes paced at the end of Grandmother's bed, watching as the doctor examined her. Grandmother hadn't stirred, despite the crowd in her bedroom. Her steady breathing told Forbes she was resting. He'd rarely seen her asleep. All her worry lines were smoothed out, the tension in her jaw relaxed.

He hated for her to wake up, but at the same time, he needed to ask what had happened that sent Brooklynn running. Assuming Gran would even remember.

Probably not.

Forbes needed to find Brooklynn.

But he also needed to stay.

He needed...he needed help.

Lord, heal Grandmother. Protect Brooklynn. For her sake, help me find her.

Because God wouldn't do it for Forbes's sake. He'd proved that over and over.

Today was further proof. Forbes had needed Grandmother to hold it together for twenty minutes, but God hadn't given him that. It was like the Almighty held a grudge against him. Not that he didn't deserve it.

"Forbes?"

Grandmother's voice was weak and wobbly, nothing like the strong woman who'd raised him.

"He's right here." Dr. Shelley moved away, indicating for him to take her place. As he scooted past her, she gripped his arm and whispered, "Play along. Don't upset her."

Right. Play along that he was Forbes, not Ford, when he actually *was* Forbes, and Ford didn't exist.

His whole life was one big, convoluted story. No wonder he was alone.

He sat on the edge of the bed. "I'm here."

She looked weak and vulnerable, but the strength in her grip when she took his hand encouraged him. She was still in there. "I think I said something—"

"It's all right." The last thing he needed was for her to alert the hovering healthcare workers as to his real identity. He turned to the doctor. "Would you mind stepping out, please?"

She left, ushering her nurse along with her. There was no door between this room and the next, so Forbes kept his voice low. "What happened?"

"I don't know. I just have a feeling…" Her words trailed.

"It's all right, Gran."

She wasn't a trailing-words kind of woman. She always said what she meant and meant what she said. Her confusion broke his heart.

"I can't remember her name."

"Brooklynn."

Her lips relaxed. "Yes. I was afraid I'd conjured her. She's lovely, though I'm not a fan of her wardrobe."

Only Grandmother, after a medical emergency, would comment on a woman's clothing.

"She claimed you two are only friends. Are you? Or...or did I mess that up?"

"Don't worry about Brooklynn, or me." He kissed her forehead, something he'd never done with his staunch, always-in-control guardian. "You take care of yourself, and I'll handle Brooklynn."

"Can she be trusted?"

If she'd asked him a half hour before, he'd have told her that Brooklynn was completely trustworthy. But now that she'd learned the truth—and not from him—he had no idea. "What matters is that you're taken care of."

Grandmother's eyelids drooped, and she blinked. "I'm so tired."

"Of course you are. Go to sleep. Call me when you wake up, okay?"

Nodding, she closed her eyes. Within seconds, her breathing evened out once more.

He watched her sleep, praying God would protect her and heal her. Then he returned to the living room.

Dr. Shelley said, "She's having—"

"Not here." The last thing he needed was for Grandmother to wake up and hear them talking about her. He marched to the door and held it open until the doctor preceded him into the hall. He unlocked the door, then closed it. "For what we're paying for this place, I expect better care."

The doctor straightened, squaring her shoulders. "This is not a nursing home, Mr. Baker. It's assisted living."

"Not that 'assisted,' apparently. I want a nurse with her one hundred percent of the time until she's completely recovered."

"That's not a service we offer. If you want her moved to the nursing home—"

"No." Grandmother would kill him. "I'll pay for it. Hire someone. Someone trustworthy."

She seemed to consider the command, her gaze jumping from him to the closed door. "That's not something we normally do, but in this case…"

This case—because Grandmother was a Ballentine, and her fortune was widely known.

"I'll find someone," the doctor said.

"Until you do, have a nurse stay with her." Before she could tell him how short-staffed they were, he said, "I'm willing to pay whatever it costs."

"I'll see what I can do. Bouts of memory loss aren't uncommon with concussion victims, especially elderly ones. I expect her memory to return, but of course we'll monitor her. If anything changes, we'll take her back to the hospital."

"See that you do. And inform me immediately. Immediately, no matter what she says."

"Of course."

He needed to go.

He needed to stay.

He'd purposefully lived his life without anyone depending on him, and now he was responsible for the care of two women. One was dealing with dementia.

The other one was missing.

"I'll check in with you this afternoon."

At the doctor's nod, he swiveled and marched back to the lobby, praying Brooklynn was still in the building. But she wasn't in any of the sitting areas.

When he stepped into the foyer, the wig saleswoman was dragging a plastic case toward the door. He hurried forward and pulled it open for her.

"Thank you."

"Did you see my friend? About my age wearing yoga pants and—"

"Oh, yes. Darling girl. She bought the prettiest silver wig.

Straight hair cut into a bob"—she brushed a hand just above her shoulder—"with a full crown." Now, the woman gestured over the top of her head, maybe in case he didn't know where a wig was worn. "She said it was for her mother."

They both moved into the reception area. He let the door close and crossed the space to open the exterior door. "Did you see where she went?"

Before the saleslady could answer, the receptionist said, "She left in an Uber."

"Did she say where she was going?"

"Sorry." Cheri looked genuinely distressed that she couldn't help. "She didn't say."

Of course not.

"Thanks." He followed the saleslady out and jogged to his pickup.

But he had no idea where to go. Where to look.

He closed his eyes and prayed for direction. Maybe this time, God would answer.

When he opened his eyes, he had one idea, and it wouldn't work. But what did he have to lose?

He dialed Brooklynn's number, thankful he'd taken it down days before.

She rejected the call.

He dialed again.

Rejected.

Anger and frustration had him balling his hands. Rather than calling again, he tapped a text.

> I was going to tell you today.

He stared at his screen. The message went from *Delivered* to *Read*.

And then the dots flashed, telling him she was responding.

> How is she?

>> Tired. They said episodes like that aren't unheard of with concussion victims, especially at her age.

Brooklynn's only reaction was a thumbs-up. No other response came through.

>> I needed to talk to her about you. I made her promises.

This time, his text wasn't even marked as read. He added one more line.

>> You can trust me, Brooklynn.

That text got an immediate response. A little *Haha*. As if anything about this was funny.

>> Please, be careful. Don't let your anger at me deceive you.

He waited for something. A thumbs-up, a thumbs-down. A string of expletives.

After a moment, he decided he'd get nothing at all.

And then, a text came through.

> Don't worry, FORBES. I'm not going to tell anybody who you are or what you're doing. I'll keep your secrets. You don't have to hold me captive anymore.

Captive. Was she insane?

>> I was protecting you

> You were protecting YOU.

Stubborn, hard-headed woman.

Fine. She didn't trust him. She didn't want his protection. Problem was, he'd vowed to protect her, and he wasn't going to break that vow just because she didn't want him around anymore.

He shifted into drive and headed toward Shadow Cove.

CHAPTER TWENTY-FIVE

Brooklynn stared at her reflection in the department store restroom mirror. She'd changed into a cheap pale-blue jogging suit—nothing like the fancy clothes Mrs. Ballentine had worn—and bright-colored slip-on sneakers. After shoving her hair into the tight wig cap, she'd added the wig, then followed the steps on a YouTube video to apply makeup to make herself look old. Now her skin was paler and grayer. She'd rubbed in fine pencil lines to give herself wrinkles and even added some to her neck.

Her eyes were already red-rimmed from crying, which enhanced the effect.

She looked like...herself with bad makeup and a wig.

But to a stranger, to someone who didn't look closely, and from afar, it would do.

She shoved a pebble she'd picked up into her shoe to give herself a limp.

There were perks to having CIA agents in the family.

She'd purchased a giant bright yellow faux-leather purse and put her things inside, backpack and camera and everything else.

She made a note to thank her mother for the credit card number she was letting her use. She doubted anybody was tracking her purchases, but just in case, it seemed wise not to use anything authorities—or bad guys—could employ to find her.

After ordering a car to meet her at a different door from where she'd entered the Maine Mall, she hobbled out of the bathroom, leaning on her new cane. The pebble in her shoe did its painful job, keeping her limping.

She met the driver, and forty minutes later, reached her gallery in downtown Shadow Cove.

Fear bubbled inside of her. What was she doing? Was she crazy?

No. She wasn't going to lose her nerve. It would be fine. She was in her hometown, surrounded by friends. Nobody would hurt her here.

And anyway, it had to work.

Simple as that.

Her other option was to return to Forbes's house, and she couldn't do that, no matter how many times he called and texted.

Claiming he'd planned to tell her the truth. Right. As if he hadn't had enough time to do that in the hours and days she'd spent with him.

His excuse—that he'd wanted to tell his grandmother first—rang true, but how could she forgive his lies?

She thanked the driver, using an older-person voice. It didn't sound authentic at all. She prayed nobody would ask her any questions.

The bells over the gallery door jingled as she let herself in, inhaling the familiar scents of vanilla and history.

Here, surrounded by her photographs, she felt at home. And safe, even if it was an illusion.

Jewel was talking to customers but called over her shoulder, "Be right with you."

Brooklynn waved to indicate she'd heard, moving along the walls and gazing at the artwork as if she'd never seen it before.

Normally, she loved having customers, but today she wanted the couple to leave. It was the height of tourism season in Shadow Cove, though. If she managed to survive the mess she'd gotten herself into, she'd need all the customers she could get.

Jewel rang up a sale, promising to have their selection delivered within two weeks. When the couple walked out, Jewel called to her. "Can I help you?" She showed no sign of recognition.

"Just browsing," Brooklynn said.

"Let me know if I can answer any questions for you."

What she needed was for Jewel to get distracted so she could slip up the stairs. Not that she suspected her assistant of anything, but better to keep her presence here a secret from everyone.

A few minutes later, the phone rang, and Jewel stepped into the office to answer it.

Brooklynn used her key to open the door in the back corner. She'd painted it the same color as the walls and, with a few art pieces on it, most people didn't even realize it was there.

After closing and locking it again, she flicked on the light switch and climbed the staircase, careful of the creaky ones, to the second floor, where she let herself into her apartment.

She'd done it. She'd come home.

Her apartment was just as she'd left it. Tidy, open and airy, comfortable. Some of her favorite photographs graced the walls, adding color and interest. She'd spent too much money to remodel and decorate this space. It'd been mostly Mom and Dad's money, but she was paying them back.

No matter how much she wanted to crawl into bed and cry herself to sleep, she had to do what she'd come to do and get out. There was no time for the heartache that battered her emotions.

Walking lightly so Jewel wouldn't hear her footsteps, Brooklynn hurried to her bathroom, where she removed the itchy wig and cap and braided her hair to keep it out of her face. Then she perused the text Alyssa had sent.

She hadn't found any more information on Bryce Dawson or his friend, the so-called Niles. But she'd sent a boatload of information about the man who'd pretended to be Ford Baker after Brooklynn had texted.

Forbes Ballentine was the chairman of the board of Ballentine Enterprises, but he'd never attended a meeting in person. Instead, his representative—a man named Tim Lakewood—took notes for Forbes, who ran his company over the phone.

Nobody had seen Forbes Ballentine since he was a child. Nobody knew what he looked like. Even the assistant, Tim, claimed to have never met him in person.

According to a magazine article about him, Forbes Ballentine was a recluse who avoided all interactions with people. Some said he was an agoraphobic living in the Ballentine house in Boston, having food and necessities delivered. Others said he'd never left the Shadow Cove mansion, rambling around in the old place all by himself for decades, living with the ghosts of his family.

Ridiculous, of course, but in the absence of information, foolishness prevailed.

The man Brooklynn had met was quiet and grumpy, but he was no agoraphobic. He'd faced cops and killers without fear.

She skimmed an extensive list of businesses owned by the Ballentines. Import companies, logging enterprises, real estate.

The Ballentine fortune was worth over a billion dollars.

The man who claimed to be a historian who dabbled in real

estate and worked as a handyman to pay the bills was, in fact, a billionaire.

She could hardly wrap her head around it.

Not that it mattered. Billionaire or not, he was a liar.

Even as the harsh word crossed her mind, she winced at it.

Not a liar. A man who'd lived his entire life in hiding. Maybe she could give him a little leeway because of that.

After a quick snack, Brooklynn shoved her phone into her pocket, grabbed her backpack, and headed for the stairs that led to the attic.

Ford Baker might've been a lie, but the smugglers who'd chased her had been very real. If she wanted her life back, she had to figure out who they were.

∼

BROOKLYNN HAD PURCHASED the building that housed her gallery a couple of years before. On one side, an alley led to a narrow road parallel to Center Street. On the other side, her gallery and second-story apartment shared a wall with Elvis's souvenir shop. Beyond that, multiple businesses were housed in this single building, one of which was Maury Stratton's real estate office.

It wasn't the real estate office that mattered to Brooklynn today, but the Shadow Cove Historical Society, which was located on Maury's second floor.

When Brooklynn had first seen this attic, she'd been amazed. Not that it was unusual, with its exposed rafters and plywood floors. What captivated her was the sheer expanse of it. No walls separated the different spaces, so she could see all the way to the far side of the building at the end of the block—a good hundred yards away.

It was hot and stuffy, as she'd expected it to be. She crept softly, not wanting to give her presence away. Unless someone heard her, she shouldn't see anybody in this barely used space.

She hadn't walked to the far end since she'd moved into the space. It was filled with boxes and crates and old furniture, most of which were so dusty she wondered if the owners even remembered the things were up here.

Signs on doors leading to staircases indicated the businesses below. At the far end, she found the one with a handwritten note that read *Stratton Realty*.

This was it. She turned the knob, not surprised to find it unlocked. She and her neighbors locked their exterior doors, of course, but they trusted each other. Nobody would take advantage of this shared attic space.

A twinge of guilt had her hesitating, but only for a moment. She needed to do this, and she needed to do it secretly. She'd apologize to Maury later.

Brooklynn let herself in and tiptoed down the stairs, then paused outside the door to the small room that housed the historical society.

Guests used a staircase that rose from the foyer, right outside Maury's office. Nobody would use this one. These hidden staircases were dark and dingy, unsuitable for tourists and customers.

Brooklynn listened for a few moments, then opened the door.

A creak had her pausing, but nobody reacted.

She let herself in, closing the door behind her.

It'd been a while since she'd been to the town's historical society, a couple of years at least. But the dusty bookshelves were exactly the same as they'd always been. An antique desk sat in the middle of the room with a couple of chairs pushed beneath it. Other chairs were stacked in a corner.

Silently, she put her backpack on the floor beside the table and crossed to the bookshelves to search.

She needed to find the book Arthur had produced from Brooklynn's high school art project. She had a copy of it somewhere, but not in her apartment. It was probably at her parents' house, but she couldn't figure a way to go there without being discovered. The house was surely being watched, and the only way to get through the gate was to tap in the code. While doing that, she'd be seen for sure.

No. This was the better choice, even if it involved breaking and entering, or...well, just entering. Probably a misdemeanor at worst, not that Maury would press charges.

The woman was a friend to her family, and the last thing Brooklynn wanted was to put a target on anyone else's back.

A few minutes later, she slid the book out of the stacks and carried it to the table in the center of the room, bending over it because she didn't want to risk the noise of a chair scraping across the floor.

She flipped from page to page, certain the distinctive seagull logo was in here, somewhere. She remembered seeing the outline of it floating in the pungent developing chemicals at Arthur's lab. She could visualize it hanging from clothespins in his old darkroom.

She skimmed past the town's first church, complete with a bell tower and steeple, and the forties-era World War II monument in the town common. Photos of old buildings had captions explaining when they were built and who'd first owned them. There was an animal pen made of stacked rocks, where early settlers would put sheep and cows at night to protect them from predators.

She turned to photos of the harbor and the text explaining the fishing enterprises that had built the town. She studied the boats, thinking maybe the logo was painted on a side or decorated a sail.

But no.

The next page's picture displayed downtown from the grassy area that ran along the middle of Center Street. The next photo had been taken from the sidewalk. In the foreground was the hanging sign advertising Arthur's gallery. The camera was aimed down the hill toward the cove, so that the other shops' signs looked layered like bricks. The picture had been taken in springtime, and flowers overflowed from pots and window boxes.

At the time, she'd been so proud of the photo. She'd needed to borrow a ladder to get it just right. Now, she saw all the things she'd done wrong. Even so, it was visually impressive.

Wait.

She leaned closer and peered at the top sign.

Arthur Whitmore Photography.

To the left of the words was a seagull logo.

No. It couldn't be.

She pulled out her phone and checked the picture she'd snapped of the doodles in Charles Ballentine's ledger and files.

They were the same, right down to the seagull's beak and the way it interrupted the circle surrounding the bird.

It couldn't mean anything. Of course it couldn't. Arthur couldn't have had anything to do with the murders at the Ballentine Mansion.

He'd been a sweet, tender man, a Christian who'd go out of his way to help.

He wasn't a smuggler or a killer. No way.

But...but why else would Charles have drawn the exact same logo, over and over?

A logo that had been changed so long ago that Brooklynn had forgotten all about it.

What could it mean?

Rather than worry over it here, she returned to the stacks. Back when she'd worked on her art project, she'd researched the history of Shadow Cove. There was a book somewhere about the Ballentine Mansion.

She skimmed the titles, hoping to find it. Hoping maybe there'd be information in it that could help Forbes.

His name still felt foreign.

She was so focused that she didn't hear the footsteps until it was too late.

She stepped away from the bookshelves an instant before the door opened.

"...lucky that you were there. Just help me get set up, and you can..." When Maury saw Brooklynn, she gasped and froze.

"What's wrong, Grandma?"

Though Brooklynn couldn't see Owen, she heard the alarm in his voice.

Maury's eyes were wide. She covered her chest with one hand and exhaled. "Good heavens, dear. You scared me to death." Her surprise shifted to worry. "I didn't hear you... How did you get in?"

"Grandma, this stuff is heavy."

"Oh." She stepped out of the way, and Owen hauled two cardboard boxes into the room.

He stopped when he saw her. "Brooklynn? What are you doing here?"

She picked up the book she'd left lying on the table and held it against her chest like a shield. "Can I help?"

He dropped the boxes on the table. "What's going on?"

She considered making up a story, but what would explain her breaking in? She had to tell them the truth.

"You didn't see me," she said.

Maury's eyebrows lifted.

Her grandson's lowered.

"I mean, obviously you did."

"You look terrible, dear." Maury moved closer. "Are you ill?"

Brooklynn still wore the old-lady makeup. She laughed, the sound forced. "It's fine. I'm fine. It's just... I needed to get into my apartment, but I didn't want to be seen."

Owen said, "You think makeup will keep anyone from recognizing you?"

"With a wig and cane..." She shrugged. "I didn't have a lot of choices."

"Okay." Maury's word was drawn long. "Why are you here?"

"For this." She wiggled the book in her arms. "I don't know where my copy is. I'm sorry I scared you. I came in through the attic. I didn't think you'd mind."

"I'd have preferred to give you permission than have *you* give *me* a heart attack."

"I didn't think anybody would be here."

"We have a meeting. If you're that interested, you really should join—"

"What's the holdup?"

The words came from the stairwell, quickly followed by Graham Porter, whose shiny bald head reflected the overhead lights. "You said you'd be gone two..." His words trailed as he caught sight of Brooklynn. "Hey, you're back. I didn't realize. Have you had a chance to move my booth at Old Home Days? I refuse to share space with—"

"I can't talk about that right now." She needed to get out of there before the rest of Shadow Cove traipsed through. To Maury, she said, "Can I borrow this book? I promise I'll return it."

"Of course, dear. Is there anything else I can help you with?"

"Nope. Just this." She backed toward the interior staircase, then had a thought. "Do you remember a logo in town? A seagull surrounded by a circle?"

Graham's chest puffed out. "At the Wadsworth, we've never strayed from our original logo." It was a silhouette of Henry Wadsworth Longfellow, which they probably ought to stray from, but she didn't say so. "It's about tradition," Graham continued, "and honoring those who've—"

"Right." Brooklynn cut him off before he started one of his legendary lectures. She shifted the book under her arm, pulled out her phone, and showed Maury the photo she'd taken of Charles's drawing. "Is that familiar at all?"

"Sure, sure. Arthur used that logo until he changed it to that stylized A. If you ask me, the seagull was better, but it was similar to another one in town. I don't know if he was asked to change it, or—"

"Whose logo?" Brooklynn usually wasn't rude, but getting into a conversation about history with the president of the historical society wasn't likely to be brief.

Maury tapped her upper lip. "Hmm. It was a boat, wasn't it?" She directed the question at Graham. "I remember seeing it by the docks."

He stepped forward and peered at Brooklynn's screen. "The charter company," he said. "We at the Wadsworth used to recommend them to our wealthier patrons from time to time."

Brooklynn's heart thumped. A charter company would own plenty of boats that could smuggle goods.

To Brooklynn, Graham said, "You should talk to Taggart or Prescott. They owned it."

By Taggart, he couldn't have meant Lenny. To clarify, she asked, "Leo?"

"Ayuh," Graham said, "I think Ian owned a share. They

closed up shop in the early two-thousands. Their families go back."

Didn't all families around here? She used to think of her town as one big family.

Now it felt more like a spiderweb, everyone connected to everyone else, the silky fibers hidden until they trapped the innocent.

She shook off the creepy notion.

At least she had a lead, one that didn't point to her old mentor. "Thanks, you guys. I'll let you have your meeting." To Maury, she said, "I apologize again. I'll explain everything when I can."

Carrying the book, Brooklynn turned and reached for the knob, but a voice stopped her.

"Don't forget your backpack." Owen held it out to her. "Where are you going?"

He'd been observing so quietly that she'd forgotten he was there. She took her bag. "Thank you."

"Delaney's worried about you," Owen said. "Is there anything I can do to help? Can I take you somewhere or—"

"Thanks for asking. I'm fine, really."

"You have a safe place to stay? It's not safe there." He nodded in the general direction of her apartment.

"Yup." Or she would, as soon as she figured out where it should be. Alyssa's, maybe. She could hole up there.

"You let me know if you need a ride." He stepped forward and wrapped her in a hug, whispering, "Let me know if there's anything I can do."

"I will." Her eyes burned with tears. She hardly knew Delaney's boyfriend, but that didn't stop him from offering her comfort.

Brooklynn stepped back and ducked into the stairwell and scooted up the stairs.

All she'd wanted was to get in and out without being seen, and instead, she'd bumped into three townspeople. As kind as all of them had been—especially Owen—she couldn't shake the thought that Ford—Forbes—believed Shadow Cove residents might be involved with The Network.

Their information about the seagull logo lent credence to his theory.

Were her friends and neighbors...criminals? Maybe killers?

As Brooklynn made her way back to her apartment, she prayed. *Protect the innocent, Lord. Let Maury, Owen, and Graham not tell anybody they saw me. Keep them safe. Keep the whole town safe. And if any of them are involved in this terrible smuggling operation, expose them.*

Almost against her will, she added, *Keep Forbes safe and help him find what he's looking for.*

CHAPTER TWENTY-SIX

By the time Dr. Shelley called, Forbes had been cruising Center Street for hours as if Brooklynn might just appear in front of him.

He parked on a side street and answered.

"I hired two nurses on your behalf," the doctor said without preamble. "They'll each take twelve-hour shifts."

"When do they start?"

"One's already here." Dr. Shelley gave him the nurses' names and a rundown of their experience. "They come highly recommended from one of the visiting nurses organizations in Portland."

"Thanks for handling that."

"Mrs. Ballentine woke up from her nap to find one of them in her room, and she's not happy."

As if Grandmother had sensed him talking about her, his phone buzzed with an incoming call. "That's her. I'd better answer."

"Good luck." The doctor sounded amused as she ended the call.

He took a deep breath and pressed the accept button. "Good afternoon, Gran."

"Don't you *Gran* me. Why do I have a babysitter?"

"Not a babysitter, a nurse. And you know why."

"Because of a silly fall? Old ladies fall all the time, young man. I will not be treated like a child."

He absorbed that, inhaling a breath, exhaling it slowly. "Do you remember what happened this morning?"

"Of course I remember. You brought a guest to see me. Was she with...with these people?"

He pictured Grandmother waving toward the nurse. Hopefully, the woman wasn't easily offended.

He had no idea how much he'd be paying her nurses, but he figured they deserved every penny and more.

"No, ma'am. Brooklynn is a friend of mine, or was. Do you remember what you told her?"

That brought a long beat of silence. "I-I don't remember much." The belligerence was gone as she added, "The doctor told me I fell asleep?"

"You had a little memory loss. I think you referred to me as Forbes, maybe called me your grandson. She figured out who I really am and that I'd been lying to her."

"Oh. Oh, dear."

Like earlier, at the retirement home, his strong, regal grandmother sounded very much the opposite.

"It's okay." Though it wasn't yet, he spoke with a soothing tone. "I'm trying to find her now and make it right."

"We can't let anyone know the truth. Tell her how you look like your cousin and I confuse you two—"

"I'm not lying to Brooklynn again. She knows the truth, and I'm not going to—"

"Have you forgotten...?" He heard shuffling, then a door closing. "You could be in danger."

"Brooklynn Wright didn't kill our family, Gran. She's younger than I am."

"Her folks—"

"Even if her parents were involved—which I highly doubt—she didn't tell them where she was or anything about me. And she won't."

"You don't know that."

Brooklynn had texted him hours before, promising to keep his secrets. He believed her.

"What would you have me do, Grandmother? Assassinate her?"

"Don't be ridiculous."

He took a breath to temper his voice. "Brooklynn knows who I am, and I'm not sorry. I'm not going to lie to her. She's too smart to fall for more lies from me, even if I could find her. Which I can't, so this conversation is pointless."

Suddenly, Forbes remembered Brooklynn's theory about him, that he only spoke in paragraphs when he got angry or passionate.

He'd definitely given his grandmother a paragraph-full.

"Sorry, Gran. I didn't mean—"

"You have feelings for her."

Not a question, so he didn't feel compelled to answer.

After a moment, she said, "All right, then. If you trust her, I trust her. Find her and tell her how you feel."

Just like that?

"Really?"

"You were bound to meet somebody someday, and you're not the kind of man to keep secrets from those you love. If this woman means something to you, then tell her the truth."

Wow. He'd expected more pushback. He'd expected Grandmother to want to know everything about her. That she trusted Forbes's judgment that much both surprised and pleased him.

Unfortunately, it wasn't going to be that easy. He hadn't told Grandmother about the smugglers. About how Brooklynn had taken pictures of them. About how he'd protected her, or about how she'd been at the house for days.

He hadn't told Grandmother anything like that because none of it mattered.

Heaviness lifted from his shoulders as that thought registered. The smugglers, The Network...

If he never found his family's murderers, he could live with that.

If he could convince Brooklynn to give him another chance, maybe...maybe the two of them could try a relationship. Maybe there could be more than just attraction and friendship between them.

Maybe he could have the family he'd always craved.

He could never be Forbes Ballentine, not if Grandmother was right and he was still in danger.

There were so many unknowns, and he hated unknowns.

But he cared about Brooklynn. A lot. In fact, though it was crazy to say so, he thought he could love her, someday.

Could he forget the past and focus on the future?

Could he leave justice to God?

If he let go of his need to know who'd killed his family, could he hold onto the woman he was falling for?

Maybe.

But the better option was to find Brooklynn, get her somewhere safe, and then take down The Network for good.

God willing, he could have both Brooklynn and justice.

∼

FORBES SHOULD JUST DO what Brooklynn wanted and leave her alone.

He should certainly *not* still be lurking on Center Street, looking for a tall, older woman wearing a shoulder-length wig with a full crown.

He assumed it wasn't a real crown, with diamonds and such.

Of course, because he was looking, he'd swear he'd seen a hundred sixty-plus women in the hours he'd searched. None who looked anything like Brooklynn.

Where are you?

After grabbing a hot dog, chips, and a soda from a fifties-style diner, he parked on the opposite side of Center Street from her gallery. He ate and watched the people who went in and out.

Someone stepped in the way, and a knock sounded on his window. The man backed up enough to be seen.

Forbes stifled a curse word, then rolled the window down. "Taggart."

"It's Baker, right?"

He dipped his head. The cop wasn't wearing his uniform today, just jeans and a short-sleeved golf shirt. "Want to search my truck again?"

"What are you doing here?"

He lifted his cup. "Enjoying my dinner. How about you?"

"Seems to me, if you were here to take in the view, you'd be facing it." He gazed down the hill toward the Atlantic.

"Parking isn't a crime."

"But stalking is."

"You would know, I guess."

The man's eyebrows lowered in the center, creating a dark brown V, like an angry emoticon.

"Because you're a cop." Forbes forced a smile.

"Funny you're here."

"Why? Is this your spot?" He looked around. "I don't see a no-parking sign."

"You trying to be smart?"

"Some of us don't have to try. It just comes naturally."

He didn't react to that. "Parking's limited during the tourist season. Move along."

Forbes gave Taggart a long look. "Must be frustrating to still be on traffic duty at your age. Bet you thought you'd be a detective by now."

He acted as if he hadn't heard, but his face reddened. "I said, move along."

"I don't think I will." Forbes settled back and sipped his Coke. "Is there a law against sipping a soda?"

"Maybe that's really alcohol."

"Arrest me and find out. And then I'll sue you for harassment."

The cop's phone played a sound, and he glanced at it, then glared at Forbes. He leaned in and lowered his voice. "You know where she is, don't you?"

"Who?"

Lips pursed, he watched Forbes for so long that it started to feel awkward.

Forbes wouldn't blink first.

"Stay out of my way." Taggart stormed away.

Forbes scanned the area but didn't see his cruiser anywhere. The man crossed the street and slowed, meandering along the sidewalk.

Well, that was the most entertainment he'd had all afternoon.

Unfortunately, Forbes was losing hope of finding Brooklynn.

She must not have come home, or if she had, she wasn't leaving again.

He had no idea where else to look. Maybe she'd had one of her family members pick her up. He prayed she was safe and would stay that way.

He sent her a text.

> Let me know you're safe, and I'll leave you alone. If you need me, call or text anytime. I'm sorry.

He watched the screen but got no indication that she'd read the messages.

She would or she wouldn't. He had no control of that.

Let her forgive me, Lord.

Except that was a selfish prayer, and God never answered those, not for Forbes anyway.

He took his time finishing his dinner—mostly to irritate Lenny, assuming the man was still watching him—then shifted and pulled into traffic.

CHAPTER TWENTY-SEVEN

Brooklynn stepped back into her apartment and froze.

Something wasn't right.

She wasn't safe.

She didn't know how she knew and didn't pause to evaluate. Silently, she ducked back into the stairwell.

A voice stopped her.

"Come on in, Brookie. It's too late for that."

If she'd been worried before, Lenny's voice sent her anxiety spiking.

She considered continuing downstairs to the gallery, but she wasn't in costume, and as much as she loathed her ex-boyfriend, she couldn't let herself be seen by anyone else in town. If she climbed back to the attic, he'd just follow her. He'd probably been up there already. Back when they'd been dating, she'd shown him the space. How long had he been in her apartment, waiting like a spider for its lunch?

The thought brought a shudder, but it was Lenny. He was a jerk. He was possessive to the point of creepy. But he wasn't trying to kill her.

She stepped into the living room, where he was sitting on

her couch, arms stretched across the back, feet propped on her coffee table as if he belonged.

"What are you doing here?"

"I saw the light on." He dropped both feet to the floor. "Since I didn't think you were home, I figured I'd better check it out."

She'd left the light on?

No.

She hadn't touched the lamp, and it hadn't been on when she'd walked in earlier. It was now, though, which was what had alerted her that something wasn't right, though she hadn't registered it at the time.

"You're lying." She crossed her arms. "How did you know I was here?"

"Believe it or not, Brookie—"

"Don't call me that."

"—you make mistakes, just like the rest of us. You left the light on, and I saw it from outside."

By his attitude and his tone, he might as well have said, *stop being irrational and trust me. I've got it under control.*

All too familiar.

How many times had Lenny deceived her to her face and then pretended she was crazy when she called him on it.

She'd had it with being lied to and treated like a fool. She should've known better than to trust him. She should've known better than to trust Forbes.

Nobody could be trusted.

"I'm calling the police."

"I *am* the police."

"Not when you're committing a crime." She pulled her phone from her pocket.

He was off the couch before she got it unlocked. He grabbed her wrist and, with the other hand, snatched her cell, which he pocketed. "There's no need for that." When he settled his free hand on her shoulder, she shrank away.

A look of hurt crossed his features. He slid her backpack off her shoulder—including the book she had stored inside—and set it on a side chair.

"I want my phone back." She held her hand out. "Now. Or I'll scream. Jewel will hear me. She'll call the police and have half the town up here in a matter of seconds. And if you think for one hot minute that I won't press charges, you're even crazier than I thought."

He blinked. Lips pursed, he held her phone out to her, and she snatched it, gripping it tightly.

"I just wanted to make sure you're okay," he said. "That's all."

"I'm actually *not* okay when I come home to find a man in my apartment. Get out."

"Stop being ridiculous. It's just me."

Just him. As if that should make her feel better.

What should she do? Scream or dial 911 and alert everyone that she was here—potentially including the men who'd tried to kill her?

Or try to get Lenny to leave without making a scene?

She'd hear him out for now, but she wasn't ruling out calling the police or screaming. She'd do what she had to do.

"How did you know I was home?" she asked. "And don't tell me the light tipped you off. It's not even dark out yet." Her gaze flicked to the windows. The sun was already setting? She'd been gone longer than she'd realized. Even so, that dim living room light wouldn't show through the windows.

Lenny shifted from foot to foot, looking less like the tough cop he was and more like a little boy who'd been caught misbehaving. "I was worried about you, that's all. I want to protect you."

"How, Lenny? How did you know?"

He looked at her front door, which led to an outside staircase in the back of the building. "I uh..." He swallowed. "I installed a camera so I'd know when you got back."

"Where exactly?"

"There's one above that door, and one"—his gaze flicked to the interior staircase—"in the gallery facing the stairs."

Fury set her hands trembling. "Where in my gallery exactly?"

"It's a small camera. I installed it on the bottom of one of the frames on the door. When the door moved—"

"Let me get this straight. You were 'worried' about me"—she added air quotes to emphasize how ridiculous it sounded—"so you spied on me?"

"It's not spying. It's not like I installed them in here."

"But you *are* in here. So how do I know that? How do I know you haven't put them in my kitchen or my bedroom?"

"I would never!" His eyes popped wide, then narrowed. "You know me better than that."

"Do I? The man I thought I knew wouldn't break into my apartment or install cameras to watch me. How'd you get in?"

The little boy was back. "I...it's a little lock-picking kit. I just... What if you were in here and hurt, or worse? I needed to know."

"If you thought that, then why not enter legally? Tell Jewel your worries and ask her for the key?"

The answer was obvious. He wanted to see her. He wanted to wait for her and corner her. Again, the thought brought to mind a spider, sending shudders down her spine.

"Everyone else believed your story," he said, "that you had gone someplace safe. But I didn't buy it."

"Why?"

"Because...because you've got a life here. I didn't see you just taking off."

She hated that he knew her that well. She hated that she'd ever been honest with him, giving him ammunition to weaponize her vulnerability.

"Your optimism is amazing, but sometimes it gets you in trouble."

Like when she'd believed Lenny loved her. Like when she'd trusted Forbes to be honest with her.

Yes, her optimism was a problem.

"I was afraid," Lenny continued, "that you'd come home, hoping the men who'd chased you would leave you alone. And" —he gestured toward her as if she'd made his point for him— "here you are. So I was right. Where have you been, anyway?"

"Where I go is none of your business. What I do is none of your business. My safety is none of your business. My *life* is none of your business. Get out."

"Brookie—"

"Get. Out."

When he didn't move, she walked past him, her pulse thumping in her ears. She needed to get somewhere safe so she could call Nathan. His partner would talk him down and get him out of her apartment.

Lenny's footsteps followed. "Where are you going?"

"To the bathroom. That okay with you?"

He grabbed her hand, but she yanked out of his grasp and bolted.

She made it to the bathroom and locked the door behind her. Had she outrun him? Or had he let her go? She didn't know.

"I'm calling the police."

"No need." His voice sounded from right on the other side of the door. "I'll leave. I didn't mean... I'm sorry I scared you."

"Next time you want to *not* scare a woman, maybe don't break into her apartment."

His sigh was heavy. "I was worried, that's all. I would never hurt you. I love you."

"I won't put up with your brand of love." She softened her tone. "It's over, Lenny. It's been over for a long time." She needed to be honest, and forceful. She needed him to understand that she meant what she said. So even though she didn't want to hurt him, she added, "You need to leave, now. And don't come back."

She clasped her hands together to minimize their trembling and prayed he'd do as she said.

For a long moment, there was nothing but silence. And then, his footsteps retreated. A door opened, and closed.

He was gone, for now.

But not forever. She sat on the edge of the tub and dialed Nathan. He'd offered to help her with Lenny. It was time to take him up on it.

∽

AFTER SHE EXPLAINED to Nathan exactly what had happened, he assured her he'd keep an eye on his partner. "Worst-case scenario, I'll talk to the chief."

"His father," she said.

"In the department, even to Lenny, Leo is the chief. He'll take care of it."

Assuming the man could be trusted, but he'd been an owner of the charter company with the seagull logo. Maybe he'd been involved with The Network.

Was he still? Was Leo Taggart the reason the operation had returned to Shadow Cove? Was he the reason that nobody had been arrested yet?

When she asked about Bryce Dawson, Nathan said, "We're looking for him, but he hasn't gone home or to work all week. Portland PD is on it. When Dawson pokes his head out of hiding, they'll catch him."

"What about the other men in the picture?"

"Still no word."

How could it take so long? Could someone working for the state police be in on it?

She was getting paranoid, but could anybody be trusted?

"How about his friend, the so-called Niles?"

"No leads there yet. When we find Bryce, we'll get his partner's name. Hang in there, Brooklynn. We'll figure this out."

They'd better because she needed to get back to work and on with her life. She needed this to be solved before her mother and sisters returned to Shadow Cove.

Maybe she should call Dad. He could apply pressure. He'd find Bryce and his cohorts. He'd keep her safe.

But he'd be furious that Brooklynn had gotten herself into this mess. He'd probably send her far away, and if she mentioned needing to manage her gallery, he'd scoff as if it didn't matter.

It mattered to her. She needed to do this without Dad's interference.

"You can't stay at your apartment." Nathan pulled her back to the conversation. "I can pick you up and take you anywhere you want to go."

But if the police were compromised, and if Nathan let slip what he was up to...

She hated distrusting people she'd known all her life, but too many people had proved untrustworthy.

"I'm all right. I have a plan." The seed of a plan, anyway.

"Let me just—"

"Get Lenny to leave me alone. For now, that's all I'm

asking." She ended the call, changed back into her old-lady costume, and with her bag and cane, climbed the stairs to the attic. She needed to get out of the building without anybody else spotting her—or trying to stop her.

She crossed to the door leading down to her neighbor's store and let herself in.

Shadow Cove was busy this time of year, and tourists who spent their days at the beach or on the water often came to town for dinner and shopping.

Elvis Harper's store should be busy enough for Brooklynn to blend in. The first floor was filled with kitschy souvenirs and more expensive goods, many made by locals.

The second floor housed toys and games, plus inflatables and boogie boards for playing in the surf.

At the door leading into the store's second floor, Brooklynn paused to listen.

Voices came from the other side. Children playing, some whining. One parent promised ice cream for good behavior.

Brooklynn eased the door open, catching sight of a little boy kneeling beside a small table, playing with a wooden train set. She hobbled down the staircase, hurried to the exit, and stepped into the warm, muggy evening.

Gazing at tourists and locals, she searched for threats, but nobody paid her any mind as she made her way up the street, away from the cove at the bottom of the hill.

The downtown buildings were painted in pastel colors that gleamed in the twilight. She passed the old library, now a bookstore owned by Darcy Webb, Jewel's sister-in-law. Wife to Logan, owner of Webb's Harborside.

More silky threads in the spiderweb that was Shadow Cove.

A few blocks up, she reached the major cross street that snaked to the highway. Here, the buildings were farther apart, separated by untamed forest. She walked a block to the north and reached the new library.

Though it was probably a decade old, when she stepped inside she inhaled the new-construction odor that lacked the familiar scent of old books. This was larger than the original town library, brightly lit and shiny.

The librarian didn't look up from her task, and Brooklynn didn't announce her presence, not wanting to be recognized. She headed for the section near the door that held books about Maine, the coastline, and Shadow Cove.

It took some digging, but she found the book she'd remembered from her high school project on her hometown, which referenced the Ballentine Mansion. She settled in a little reading nook in the back.

Had the mansion's eccentricities been mentioned? Could Forbes's enemies know about the secret hiding places if they did any research at all?

Maybe.

She'd barely had time to process what she'd learned that morning, that Ford was Forbes. That the man she knew had lost his parents and his sister to murder. That he was trying to solve their murders, not because he was writing a book but because the killers needed to be brought to justice.

She didn't want Forbes to get hurt. If somebody could learn about the house's secrets, then she needed to let him know.

And maybe there were more secrets he didn't know about.

After skimming the first few chapters and finding nothing helpful, she reached the center section of glossy photographs.

She stopped on one and stared. It wasn't people or old images of the mansion. It was a blueprint of the house's first floor.

Notations with arrows pointed out the secret staircase and

the hidden hallway that led to the basement door. Other arrows pointed to hiding places and hidden compartments.

All the secrets were right there for anybody to find. But a caption at the bottom of the page told her this was the only sheet of the blueprints uncovered, that the rest of them had gone missing.

She checked the book's copyright—mid-nineteen seventies, decades before The Network had started operating.

Even if they got ahold of this book, they wouldn't know anything about the hiding places on the second and third floors.

She snapped a photo of the page and texted it to Forbes.

> The first-floor hiding places aren't safe, but the blueprints of the other floors seem to have been lost.

He responded immediately.

> We need to talk.

> No. I just wanted you to see this.

She added the information she'd learned about the seagull logo.

> I haven't found the logo of the charter boat company, but it's a lead you could follow. Also, Nathan says Bryce is still missing. No info on Niles from him or Alyssa.

Her phone vibrated. It was Forbes.
She ignored it. But he called again. And then he texted.

> After we talk, I'll leave you alone. But considering everything, I deserve the opportunity to explain.

She squeezed her eyes closed. She didn't want to talk to him, but he'd saved her life, maybe more than once.

Perhaps he had earned the right to a conversation.

A moment later, he texted again.

> Please?

Fine.

Aside from the librarian, the library was empty. Leaning on her cane, the pebble in her shoe reminding her to move slowly, Brooklynn made her way to a small room off the back, closed the door softly, and dialed.

Forbes answered with, "Thank you for calling."

"You wanted to explain."

"Can we talk in person? Let me take you back to the house."

"Just say what you have to say."

She braced for an argument, but he didn't pressure her.

"I was going to tell you today, but Grandmother—"

"You're blaming your grandmother for lying? Very nice."

"I'm not blaming her." His tone was hard. "I'm just explaining. My legal name is Ford Baker, has been since I was eight years old. That wasn't a lie."

"Why?"

"Grandmother feared I was in danger, so she—"

"No. I mean, why were you going to tell me?"

"Oh. Because... You know why, Brooklynn." The words were softer now. "Because you mean something to me."

How could one sentence both warm her heart and send ice to her veins?

She didn't know how to respond. It was possible he was being honest with her.

It was just as likely he was lying, considering he barely knew her.

She didn't know him at all.

"Why does your grandmother think you're in danger?"

"I'll tell you that, but not over the phone."

And there it was. Dangle a carrot to get her to do what he wanted.

She'd been manipulated too many times to fall for it again.

"I'm not going to tell anybody who you are, Forbes. I'm not going to tell anybody anything, so you don't have to keep lying to me. You don't have to pretend this is something it's not."

"I'm not..." He blew out a breath. "I'm worried about you. I've spent the entire day searching for you."

Heat burned her eyes, and she squeezed them closed. "Sorry you wasted your time."

How she wished he really cared about her. How she wished she could trust him. But how could she trust a man who'd lied to her from their very first meeting?

He had an agenda, and he was worried that she'd mess it up. Simple as that.

"I promised to keep your secrets, *Forbes*, and I will. One of us can be trusted."

"I'm looking for you because you're in danger. I care about you."

"I can take care of myself. You can cross me off your list of things to do." She ended the call and slumped in a chair.

What was she doing here, trying to help him solve his mystery? She needed to trust the police to figure out what was going on.

She needed to get out of town until this was all over.

She would, as soon as her stupid tears stopped.

∽

IN THE LIBRARY BATHROOM, Brooklynn took the pebble out of her shoe, figuring she wouldn't see anybody else tonight, then checked her old-lady makeup. It was waterproof, so her tears hadn't washed it away.

She adjusted the itchy wig, reminding herself to play her part, though she probably wouldn't see anyone she knew between the library doors and the Uber she'd called to pick her up. It would deliver her to her Bronco parked at Frizzel Automotive a couple miles down the road. She'd grabbed her extra set of keys at her apartment.

She would just...drive away, which was what she should've done on Monday when this whole thing started. She should never have stayed at the mansion.

Studying her image in the mirror, she saw a sixty-something woman with Brooklynn's red-rimmed eyes looking back at her.

She shouldered the yellow purse, grabbed her cane, and pulled open the bathroom door.

The hallway was darker than it'd been before.

She reached the entrance to the large room with rows of bookshelves. The lights were out.

Was the library closed?

She glanced at her phone's clock. It was seven forty-five. Maybe the librarian had decided to close early? Odd that she hadn't done a sweep to make sure nobody was there.

Great. This was Brooklynn's reward for sneaking in. Hopefully, no alarm would sound when she snuck back out.

The front-facing windows let in a little light from the glow of the town and the fading sun. Cane swinging at her side, she headed that direction, aiming for the bright-red exit sign over the front door.

A noise stopped her.

"This way," a man whispered.

"I'll guard the door," another answered.

Brooklynn recognized those voices.

She'd heard them from the inside of a very dark cave. And then again from inside a spider-infested box.

Bryce and Niles had found her. But how?

She shifted to the end of a bookshelf just as, on the other end, a man shined his flashlight between the stacks. When he moved on to the next aisle, she dashed in the other direction.

Her heart was thumping so hard that she feared he'd hear it.

In a corner between a wall and a shelf, she watched the first man's flashlight beam toward the hallway where she'd just been.

There was probably an exit in that direction, which he'd find—and watch.

The other man said he'd guard the front door.

She was trapped.

Silently, she crept toward the librarian's station. If she could get there and out of this very open space, she could call 911.

Staying low, she reached the counter, rounded to the narrow opening, and slid behind it. It was darker back here with no windows to let in light. She moved slowly, careful not to bump herself, the cane, or the cumbersome old-lady purse into anything.

She prayed they'd give up and go away.

A door opened and closed.

"Don't just stand there. Search for her." This was a new voice. There were three of them. "She's gotta be here somewhere."

How did they know?

Someone must've seen her come in. But who? And how did they recognize her?

She crawled behind a rolling cart of books and opened her phone, aiming the screen away from the men. After checking twice to make sure it was silenced, she started to dial 911.

But stopped, fearing they'd hear the operator's voice on the line.

She texted Nathan instead.

> I'm trapped in the library. They're here. Help!

He responded with a thumbs-up that felt all wrong, considering the situation. But he was on it.

Shoving her phone into her pocket, she prayed the police would arrive before the men found her.

It was too dark back here to make out much, but red glowed from around a corner at the back of the room. An exit? The guard might be there.

But he might not.

A thump, followed by a low curse word, came from the direction of the librarian's desk.

Someone was closing in.

She couldn't wait. She had to try.

Slowly, slowly, she crept toward that red glow. Around carts and boxes and chairs and desks, careful not to bump anything.

Her foot caught something soft, and she looked down.

It was a leg. A leg connected to a body, lying on the floor.

No.

She crouched to confirm her suspicion.

It was the librarian. Brooklynn found her neck and felt for a pulse. It was there. Faint, but there.

She wasn't dead, thank heavens.

Creeping toward the door, she prayed the woman would stay unconscious until this was over.

She followed the back wall to an open doorway, then peeked into a hallway.

There was an exit just a few feet away.

On the other end...

"Got her!" A man bolted her direction.

She lifted the cane like a bat and swung at his head.

It connected. He paused, unsteady.

Glared at her, murder in his eyes.

She jabbed the cane again, this time hitting his forehead.

He fell back, and she lurched for the door.

He reached out, grabbed the cane. She let go of her only weapon, pushed through the exit, and bolted outside.

"Help!" She screamed, running toward the front of the building. If her Uber driver was there, she could escape.

But when she rounded the corner, a man spotted her and shouted, "Over here!" He sprinted toward her.

She shifted and pushed herself faster.

The structure next door was dark.

Beyond that were more empty office buildings. If she could make it to the B and B across the street...

But she wouldn't. No chance.

Somebody needed to drive by, to give her cover or stop and help. Where were the police? She needed a stranger, someone.

Footsteps closed in behind her.

Her foot landed partly in a hole, and she twisted her ankle, stumbling. Pain shot up her leg, but she pressed on.

A hand gripped her wig and yanked it off.

A scream crawled up her throat, but terror cut off her air.

An *oof* and a thud had her glancing back. Two men, on the ground.

Before she could register what was happening, one popped up, wrapped an arm around her waist, and propelled her forward. The man dragged her behind the building and toward the forest.

She fought, trying to get away.

"Stop. Brooklynn. It's me."

Forbes?

He was here? Saving her—again?

How? How had he found her?

They reached the edge of the sparse forest as shouts rang behind them.

"Down! On the ground!" Forbes urged her, and she went to her knees, then face down on the damp forest floor.

He lay on top of her, his body warm and sheltering. "Shh-shh." The sound was barely more than a breath in her ear. "Don't move."

She was sucking in air, trying to be quiet.

"I've got you." The words infused confidence, as if Forbes's presence was all she'd required.

But the men were closing in.

He shifted against her. She craned her neck and caught the glint of a handgun as he pulled it from beneath his jacket.

"Where'd she go?" A man's voice was too close.

"I don't know." This one sounded woozy. Forbes had obviously done more than just knock him over.

"How could you lose her?"

That voice was familiar, but the words were uttered so low that she couldn't place it.

But she had a bad, bad feeling about it.

"Find her," that same familiar voice said.

"I'm working on it."

They were coming. Everything inside her trembled with terror.

Forbes was poised and ready. If someone spotted them, Forbes would shoot. And then the men would know exactly where they were. Could Forbes fight them all off? Or would he be killed? Would she?

A man was coming, moving slowly, swinging his flashlight ahead of him, checking his phone screen every so often.

The light skimmed over Forbes's arm, but he wore a dark

jacket. Dark jeans. That must be why he was lying on top of her, not just to shield her, but to hide her outfit.

But it probably showed. And her sneakers, so bright. What a fool she'd been to think she could slip in and out of town without notice.

But the man didn't see them, just continued past, moving deeper into the woods.

He was slight with blond hair, and she recognized him from the photos she'd taken. Niles.

Nearer the road, other men were calling out to each other occasionally. Frustrated sounds of failure.

Forbes, handgun out, whispered, "Don't move."

Before she could respond, he was up and creeping silently. Following Niles.

He was a few feet behind him when Niles started to spin. "Hey—!"

Forbes lunged, and his handgun came down hard against the man's head, cutting off his shout.

Before Niles could regain his equilibrium, Forbes grabbed his weapon and tossed it, then slipped an arm around his neck and squeezed.

Horrified, Brooklynn covered her mouth with both hands, watching, as Forbes slowly lowered the blond man to the ground.

Seconds passed. Long, long seconds.

Was Forbes killing him? Would he do that?

To keep her safe, he would.

When Niles was lying flat on the damp bracken, Forbes returned to her. "Come on."

She was too scared to move, but she couldn't stay there, either.

He helped her up and urged her through the woods, going behind the library until they were a good hundred yards past it.

The voices behind her faded until she could no longer hear them.

Only then did she and Forbes return to the two-lane highway that extended the length of this section of coast. They crossed and slipped into the alley parallel to Center Street. Though she wanted to run, he kept a steady pace, holding her hand as if they were out for a stroll.

Her gallery and apartment were four blocks ahead. Was that their destination?

Surely not.

About a block down, Forbes let go of her hand and pulled keys from his pocket.

Ahead, a red sedan's lights blinked.

She reached the passenger side and settled inside.

He rounded the car, climbed in behind the wheel, and hit the gas.

CHAPTER TWENTY-EIGHT

A mile from downtown, Forbes could breathe again.
Thank You.
There was no way they would've gotten out of that without God's help. But they weren't safe yet.

He glanced at Brooklynn in the passenger seat. She was on the phone with the 911 operator, explaining what happened. "I texted Nathan Church, asking for help, but none ever came."

The 911 operator must've said something because Brooklynn snapped, "I was hiding. I had to be quiet." She glanced his way, then put the call on speaker.

"You're safe now?" the operator asked.

"No thanks to the police, yeah. A man must've heard my shouts. He fought a couple of the guys, giving me time to get away."

"Where are you now?"

"I'm safe, and I'm getting out of town."

When she ended the call, Forbes said, "Thank you for keeping me out of it."

Brooklynn's only response was a nod. She had one hand

curled around the edge of the console in a white-knuckled grip. The other was pressed against her stomach. Her eyes were wide, her gaze fixed on the side mirror, clearly afraid an enemy would find them here.

But nobody had followed.

"Are you hurt?" He'd seen her stumble, and she'd been limping.

She reached toward her foot but stopped before she touched it, turning to him. "How did you find me?"

"When you texted, I guessed you were at the library. The lights went out as I was walking up. I assumed it was closed—and you had left—until I saw men circling the building."

Again, he breathed a prayer of thanksgiving.

After his confrontation with Lenny in town, Forbes had headed back to the house.

By the time he'd gotten there, he'd decided he wasn't giving up on finding Brooklynn. Until she told him she'd left Shadow Cove, he was going to do everything in his power to keep her safe, even if it meant behaving as badly as—or worse than—her stalker.

Thanks to Lenny's spotting of the pickup, Forbes had switched to Grandmother's car.

This time, before he drove back to town, he remembered to search both cars for trackers, thinking perhaps that was why the men had broken in the night of the storm.

He'd almost given up when he finally found a small, black apparatus attached to the underside of his pickup. It took a flathead screwdriver to pry the magnet from the metal.

Once he knew where to look, it took much less time to find the tracking device on the Cadillac. He left that one on a workbench in the garage and pocketed the one from the pickup before climbing behind the wheel of the luxury car.

He turned north and stopped at a service station a few miles up the road, where he filled the tank and grabbed a cup of coffee.

A minivan drove up, headed away from Shadow Cove. It stopped at one of the pumps, and a woman and two little kids came in. She ushered them to the bathrooms in the back.

Outside, a man pumped gas into the minivan.

The stop at the bathroom told him they weren't close to home. Tourists, he hoped, headed farther up the coast.

Coffee in one hand, Forbes headed back to the Caddy, nodding a greeting to the driver of the van.

When he turned to hang up the nozzle, Forbes pressed the magnetic tracker to the inside of his wheel well.

Then, he tossed his coffee into a trash can, muttering, "I'd rather fall asleep driving than drink that."

The father chuckled, heading for the door.

Back in the Caddy, Forbes had turned toward town, where he'd parked in the alley so nobody would connect him with the car. Wearing a baseball cap and a black jacket, he'd kept his head down and found a bench across the street and a block down from Brooklynn's gallery.

He'd had no idea what else to do. When Brooklynn texted him the photo, he'd guessed she was at the library and walked in that direction.

It was sheer luck—or maybe all God—that he'd gotten there in time.

Beside him, Brooklynn's breathing had settled, but a glance told him she wasn't back to normal yet.

"You're safe now. It's okay."

"Did you... Did you kill that man?"

Was that what she was worried about? The man would certainly have killed her, if he'd had the chance. "I put him in a sleeper hold."

"Oh. Like...like Jack Bauer?"

"I have no idea who that is."

"From 24. The series?"

This woman and her television shows. "I put pressure on the veins in his neck until he passed out. I didn't cut off his air. He probably woke up a few seconds after we slipped into the woods."

"Oh. Good." That second word was tentative, as if a little part of her wished at least one enemy had been taken out. "How do you know how to do that?"

"Years of martial arts training."

He didn't tell her that he'd taken the lessons since he was a child so that he'd never again run and hide when others were in danger. He didn't tell her that the only thing that had made the nightmares stop was the belief that he could defend himself and his grandmother.

He didn't tell her about the arsenal he'd amassed over the years or the hours and hours he'd spent in target practice.

He didn't tell her that he'd dedicated his entire life to two things—discovering who killed his family and preparing for the moment he caught up with them.

"I'm glad you didn't kill him." Brooklynn's voice was weak.

In the days he'd known her, he'd never thought of her as weak. She'd been stronger than he'd ever have guessed by looking at the gorgeous, cheerful, curly-haired brunette. It was as if her optimism had been a shield protecting her from fear and worry.

And now, it seemed, her shield was falling away.

"I would've killed him if I'd had to." He angled around a wide corner, hugging the waterline, then met her eyes briefly. "To protect you, I would have killed him. Considering how hard they're trying to find you, they're not planning to leave you alive." Or at least not in a condition where she could tell. He didn't want to think about all the things smugglers could do with such an attractive woman.

"It's just... I don't understand." Her voice wavered. "I already sent the photos to the police. I hoped...I thought they would leave me alone."

"Maybe they don't know about the photos. Or maybe they think, photos or not, you can identify them."

"I can't, though! I hardly got a look at them."

He kept his response steady. "They don't know that."

"I know." The words were sharp and thin, like cracked laminate, no longer protecting what was beneath. "I just want it to be over." Her voice broke, tearing through his resolve.

He slid his hand over hers on the console. "I'm sorry." He didn't know what else to say. He'd give anything for it to be over. For Brooklynn to be out of danger and his family's murderers brought to justice.

He drove slowly past the mansion's driveway, peering between the hedges at the house.

No cars in the driveway. No strangers lurking about.

Maybe it was foolish to come back here, but he didn't know where else to go. Like Brooklynn, he wanted—he needed—for this to be over. And the answers were in his house. On his property.

Leaving would mean giving up. He could do that. He *would* do that, if he thought Brooklynn would be safe. But she wouldn't, not until everyone involved in The Network was brought to justice.

He pulled over onto the gravel shoulder two miles beyond the mansion. The moon was low in the sky, glimmering off the black Atlantic waters beyond the low stone wall separating the road from a rocky decline.

He checked his security system on his cell phone.

"What are we doing?" Brooklynn asked.

"Just making sure I've had no visitors."

"We're going back to your house?" Was that fear in her voice?

"Only if it's safe." He scrolled through camera views, seeing the familiar scenes—the front, garage, side, and back doors, the forest near the entrance to the cave, the dock, the beach.

There'd been no alerts, no activity all night.

"All is well."

"They'll look for us." She swiveled and peered through the rear glass as if bad guys might careen around the corner any second.

"I think they've convened in town." He kept his tone calm, which didn't reflect how he felt at all. "Also, they have no reason to believe you've been staying with me. Remember, nobody's been able to confirm that."

She pulled her knee up on the seat to face him. But she didn't let go of his hand. "They broke into the garage the other night. They must think—"

"They left a tracker on the truck and on this car."

She stiffened, her eyes wide.

She loosened her grip on his hand, but he held on.

"I found it. I took care of it." He explained how he'd attached the tracker to the vehicle at the gas station. "They'll believe I'm gone. And you were last seen in town. Nobody got a look at me at the library. I hit both guys from behind. They won't know it was me."

"But..." She closed her eyes. "Niles turned toward you."

"I hit him before he saw me."

"You think." Her eyes opened again. "But what if you're wrong?"

Forbes replayed the scene in his head. "He didn't see me. I made sure of it."

"But—"

"Only Lenny suspects you've been staying with me." Forbes told her about his run-in with her ex-boyfriend in town. "He's why I drove Grandmother's car. I didn't want him finding you through me. So unless he's involved, I think we're safe."

"Not Lenny, I don't think. But Nathan."

"I heard what you told the 911 operator. You reached out to him?"

"From the library. I was trying to call in the cavalry."

But there had been no police near the library. None had come even after they'd escaped. No sirens, no lights.

Forbes swallowed hard. He'd always believed that someone in the Shadow Cove PD was involved with The Network at the time of the murders. "How old is Nathan?"

"Younger than I am."

Then he'd been recruited by someone, and that someone was probably also a cop. Which meant...

"Who did you send the photos to?"

"Oh!" Her eyes widened. "I sent them to the police department email address, but Nathan was the one who told me they'd been forwarded."

Had they, though? Or had Nathan—or whoever else at the department was involved—kept them from sending? Or done something to make them unreadable?

That would explain why The Network was still after Brooklynn. If the photos were corrupted, then the information on her camera—and in her head—was the only evidence of the operation going on at the dock. And the only record of who was involved.

"We need to find out if the state police actually have the photos," Forbes said.

"Or just send them again."

"But if they're not logged correctly, will they be admissible in court?"

"Would they be if they'd been sent to an email address?" She sounded doubtful. "Let me..." Her voice trailed as she tapped a text message.

"Alyssa?" he guessed.

"My cousin Grant. He's a police detective in New Hampshire. He'll tell me what to do." She sent the text, then stared at the phone as if he'd respond in seconds. Giving up, she lowered the phone. "He'll get back to me as soon as he gets this."

"Good idea, asking him." Forbes had thought he was prepared to ferret out the mystery on his own, but he didn't have any of the contacts Brooklynn had.

She'd been a godsend.

Oh. Huh. He'd need to think about that—and rethink his theory about the God whose love Forbes had doubted for so long.

"Any idea how they found you?"

She uttered a short laugh. "I might as well have dropped breadcrumbs."

"Meaning?"

She sighed. "Going home was a bad idea. I thought, with the costume... I needed to see something at the historical society." She explained how she'd broken in through the attic—ingenious, and it should've worked. But she'd been seen by three people.

She didn't seem concerned about any of them, but hadn't she said Graham and the fisherman—Shane—were friends? And Shane was Bryce's uncle, so could that man be trusted? Was the hotel owner connected to The Network?

"And then I got back to my apartment," she said, "and Lenny was there."

Acid crawled up his throat. "At your door? You let him in?"

"No. Inside. He let himself in. He'd installed cameras so he'd know when I got back. And then used a lock-pick to get inside."

"Brooklynn, that's unacceptable. He needs to be—"

"I know, I know. I got him to leave, but then, to be on the 'safe side...'"

Her air quotes made him worry about what was coming.

"I texted Nathan and told him what happened. He'd offered to help with Lenny, and I thought..." She blew out a breath. "I'm so stupid."

"You're the farthest thing from stupid. You're supposed to trust the police. That you can't in this case is their problem, not yours."

"You're much nicer than you seem."

Surprise had a chuckle escaping. "Am not."

"Are too." The amusement leached from her voice. "I was careful, leaving through Elvis's shop. Nathan must've been watching. And recognized me despite the costume."

That made sense.

Brooklynn glanced at her phone again. "Maybe I should go to his house."

"Whose?" Not Nathan's obviously, so... "Lenny's?" He couldn't help the sharp tone. "Are you—?"

"No. Sorry. I was looking to see if Grant texted back. I mean him, my cousin."

"Oh. Right." Forbes hated that idea, but not because it was a bad one. He hated the thought of her leaving. "I can drive—"

"No."

"How else—?"

"No, I mean... I can't do that to Grant and Summer. They can protect me, but their baby's due any day. I can't just barge in on them."

"You think they'd mind?"

"I think they'd take me in and never tell me if they minded." She sighed. "I hate this. I hate being a burden, a nuisance."

"You're neither of those things. You're a...you're a blessing." Those were words he'd never said to another human in his life, but it was true, even if it felt weird on his tongue. "Just come back to the house with me."

"But those guys—"

"They might assume I was the one who helped you. If they come to look for you, you'll hide, and I'll take care of it." Which was easy for him to say. Easy for him to ask her to trust him. "I get it if you don't want to, but you need a real plan."

Maybe it was time to stop putting off the inevitable and let her go.

"If not your cousin's house," he asked, "then where? You must've had a plan before they followed you to the library."

"I was going to get my car and drive to Alyssa's in Augusta."

He opened his phone's map. "Address?"

"I-I don't want to go there."

Did that mean she wanted to stay with him? He couldn't help the flash of hope her words brought.

"I'm afraid I'll put her in danger, and she's been through enough lately."

"Then where?"

"I don't know. There's nowhere safe. There's nowhere I won't put someone I love in danger. I just... I can't think straight. I'm not used to being chased by men who want to kill me, and... This is all so..." Her voice shook again. "I guess a hotel? Or maybe just the bus station. I'll go to Boston."

On a bus?

To the city, by herself?

Forbes rubbed his lips together, hating that idea. "No."

"What do you mean—?"

"You'll come home with me. When you make a better plan, I'll help you follow through with it. But I'm not dropping you off at the bus station and sending you out on your own. I can drive you to Boston if that's what you want. Do you *want* to go to Boston?"

"Not really."

"Okay, then. Tomorrow, I'll take you anywhere. For now, you'll stay." He did a U-turn and returned to his driveway. As before, there was no sign of intruders.

They'd be safe here. And if they weren't...

Then she'd hide, and he'd take on the killers.

～

ALL THE BLINDS were closed in the kitchen, all the drapes pulled shut.

The house was just as Forbes had left it, no signs of intruders, inside or out.

He sliced cheese and apples, then grabbed grapes from the refrigerator. He put those on a tray, adding a sleeve of crackers and a couple bottles of water.

He carried the food upstairs to the family room, where he closed the blinds and curtains before jogging back down to check on Brooklynn.

He'd still been turning off the car and closing the garage when she hurried inside to the bathroom.

She was still in there when he returned from upstairs.

He didn't want to leave her alone, not with that limp. Should he linger out here, or wait, or...what?

After a few minutes, he knocked. "You all right?"

"Yeah."

Despite the wobbly answer, just hearing her voice calmed him. She was here. She was safe, and he'd keep her safe, no matter what.

The water ran, then shut off. Finally, she opened the door.

She'd taken off the wig cap and washed off the makeup that made her look old. Her skin was freshly scrubbed, though paler than usual. Her hair was a mass of frizz and curls. Messy and somehow...

Far too touchable.

He wished they could get back to where they'd been the night before, so close. Almost-kissing close.

He wanted to bury his face in those curls and get lost in them.

He took a step back. "You're..." Beautiful, but he shifted to, "Hungry?"

She shook her head. "Not even a little."

"Have you eaten?"

She shrugged.

"I got us a snack."

"I'm not... It's just that I might need..." She lifted her left leg, and he saw the issue.

Her ankle was swollen to twice its size.

"I think I sprained it."

"Hmm. Or worse."

"No, it's just... I can walk, if you'll help."

He offered his forearm. Leaning on it, she took a step forward, grimacing.

The pain on her face sent acid to his stomach.

He wrapped his arm around her waist, and she took another painful step.

He couldn't stand it.

He swept her into his arms.

She squealed, sounding somehow both frightened and whimsical, grabbing him around the neck as if she didn't trust him not to drop her. Her bright yellow bag dangled from her elbow. "I can walk."

"Mm-hmm." That was the best he could do, thanks to the

affection and attraction rolling over him. He headed toward the kitchen.

"Put me down."

"I will." When he was finished drinking her in. Inhaling her scent. Enjoying the warmth of her.

He reached the foyer and angled through the formal dining room and into the kitchen, where he set her gently on the counter.

"I could've made it," she said.

He stepped back and crossed his arms. "You're very stubborn."

But she was also wonderful. Amazing. Perfect.

"I'm sorry, Brooklynn."

Her eyebrows hiked.

"For lying to you. I know I said it. I've said it a few times, but I'm not sure you've accepted my apology. It didn't feel like lying at first. I've gone by Ford Baker and told the story about being a historian for so long it feels real to me sometimes. But there came a point with you when it wasn't okay anymore. I wanted to tell you. I almost did, on the roof, but I'd made Grandmother a promise. I needed to introduce you to her, get her...blessing, I guess."

"Did she give it?"

"She did. She likes you."

"I'm glad." But Brooklynn didn't smile. "I understand why you did it."

"But can you forgive me?"

"I can. I do. Just...no more lying, okay?"

He nodded, swallowing all the things he wanted to say, unsure how to say them, not knowing if he should, if he had any right to.

So he turned his attention to her injury, lifting her injured leg to the counter. "Nice shoes." They were multicolored slip-on sneakers.

"I thought they looked old-lady-ish."

He slipped off the one from her injured leg, feeling her calf tighten beneath his hand. He moved to take off her sock, needing to get a look at her injury and make sure nothing was obviously broken, but before he'd even touched it, she sucked a breath through her teeth.

"I can cut it off."

"No, no. It's fine." But her face was white as milk.

"It's not a problem. Just—"

"I said it's fine!" Her eyes popped wide. "Sorry. Sorry. You're trying to help, and I'm—"

"In pain. No need to apologize." He turned toward the wall behind him. Mostly cabinets, but... "You see that dent on the refrigerator?"

"Uh-huh."

"Focus on it. Don't take your eyes off it." He leaned over her knees so she couldn't watch what he was doing. "Can you still see it?"

"Yes."

He ran his hands gently down her calf. "I put that dent there when I was about six. Me and my thick skull."

"Ouch." But the way she said it, she didn't mean her ankle.

"It's okay. Unlike the fridge, I wasn't permanently damaged." His hands were at the top of her socks.

She flinched, but this couldn't hurt. "You strike me as the type to wear multicolored sneakers."

A beat passed. Then she said, "I like bright colors, but come on. Those are garish."

He managed to roll the top edge of her sock over. "When you get older, I see you in bright purple pants. Not jeans, but those polyester things with elastic waistbands."

"Not a chance."

He rolled the sock gently over the swollen skin, feeling heat coming from her wound, her muscles tensed as she worked to stay still. "And sparkly jackets," he added, "like with those little round...things."

"Sequins?" she squeaked. "You think I'll wear sequins?"

"And felt hats. You're definitely the felt-hat type. With feathers, just for the fun of it." He rolled the sock over her heel. "Or those weird topless visors."

Maybe her hair would still be long in thirty years, streaked with gray. She'd be gorgeous. Her smile lines would be permanent proof of a happy life.

Gently, gently, he rolled the sock to the end of her foot and pulled it off.

He turned to her, finding her much closer than he'd imagined. So close that, if he leaned forward, he could press a kiss to those perfect lips.

He swallowed and backed up, lifting her sock like a prize. Then, to make her smile, he swooned as if the scent were getting to him. "I think I might pass out."

"Shut up." But she laughed. Then, her head tilted to the side. "You're pretty good at the nursing thing."

"If you tell anyone, I'll deny it."

Her smile was tender. She studied him as if he were a puzzle she wanted to solve. "Thank you, Forbes."

He grunted, sounding like a Neanderthal.

He needed to do something besides stare at her.

He filled a zipper bag with ice, then put a bottle of ibuprofen in his front pocket. He shoved a kitchen towel in his back pocket. "We'll wrap it after you ice it for a while. Do you need anything else?"

"Crutches?"

A smile tugged his lips up.

This woman, in the middle of all the chaos and craziness, could still make him smile.

He loved that about her.

The thought sent the irrational joy invading his rational mind running for cover. He loved a lot of things about Brooklynn, but none of that mattered. He'd lied to her. She didn't trust him, and even if she managed to forgive him, both of their lives were in danger.

There was no room for the wild emotions that had his thoughts bopping around like they were trapped in a pinball machine.

He handed her the ice pack. "If you'll hold that... Is it okay if I carry you upstairs now?" He asked as if she had a choice, which she didn't.

"I'll allow it." Straightening, she nodded in a dignified manner, which was...very cute.

This time, she came willingly into his arms, and he enjoyed every moment of closeness as he carried her from the kitchen to the second-floor family room.

He settled her on the couch, then propped her ankle on pillows. "You comfortable?"

"Yes. Thanks."

He took the bag of ice, wrapped it in the towel, and laid it on her ankle.

At the moment of contact, she sucked air through her teeth.

He got it situated, then glanced at her face. "Pain or cold?"

"Yes?"

"Fair enough." He grabbed a throw blanket and laid it over her. "That'll help with the cold, anyway."

"The tablets you stuck in your pocket will help with the pain."

"But if you don't eat, they might make you sick." He filled a plate from the food he'd carried up earlier and handed it to her.

The corner of her mouth lifted in a smile. "You're very bossy."

"Stubborn patients make bossy nurses."

Her eyebrows hiked.

Memories of his own childhood injuries and illnesses overwhelmed him, and he focused on the room, the space, the here-and-now.

The furniture was still out of place after their evenings enjoying the fireplace, and the only lamp he'd lit was dim. He moved a chair closer to her and settled in it.

"Where'd you learn to be such a bossy nurse?" She ate a cracker with a square of cheese.

He grabbed a slice of apple.

They were going to have to talk about this, eventually.

"Rosie used to say that." Just speaking his sister's name raised a lump in his throat. "About stubborn patients."

"Your sister?"

"Mm-hm." He braced for the barrage of questions or accusations or...or whatever Brooklynn was going to throw at him.

Her hand slid around his wrist. "I'm sorry, Forbes. I'm so sorry that happened to them. And to you."

The unexpected tenderness had his eyes stinging.

He hadn't shed a tear for his family in decades. And he'd only ever talked about them to his therapist, not even to Grandmother anymore. The subject seemed too painful for her, especially where Rosie was concerned.

He couldn't remember the last time anyone had expressed sympathy for his loss. How could they, when they didn't know who he really was?

Here, in the house where they'd all lived, his family felt so close.

And farther away than ever. He missed them. He longed for

them, tonight, right now, more than since he was a little boy, hiding his damp cheeks from bullies at boarding school.

Brooklynn linked their fingers and held on. She didn't say anything, and she didn't seem to expect anything. She was just there for him.

Grief washed over him like a wave crashing on the beach. And like a wave, it rolled away again. He let it come, and let it go. And held onto Brooklynn like a life preserver.

Just when the silence started to feel awkward, Brooklynn said, "Tell me about her."

"She was..." He swallowed fresh emotion, feeling like a fool. But Brooklynn didn't seem embarrassed by it. "She was ten years older, but somehow she always felt like my best friend. She played with me and read to me and told me stories. She was funny and sweet and happy, and when I was sad, she could always make me smile." He lifted his gaze to find Brooklynn watching him as if he were the most important person in the world. "You remind me of her. She was cheerful and kind, like you."

Though he'd managed to keep his own tears at bay, Brooklynn's trailed down her cheeks. "What a nice thing to say, Forbes. Thank you."

She should be angry that he'd lied, or at least guarded. But Brooklynn was neither. She was too filled with hope to hold a grudge, too good to be anything else.

"That last summer, Rosie was getting ready to go to college. I could already feel her pulling away. I remember thinking how lonely I would be without her."

"Pulling away how?" Brooklynn asked.

"She had this guy she was spending a lot of time with. She didn't tell me much about him—not even his name—only that he was older and very sweet. She confided to me that she didn't want to go to college because she didn't want to leave him. I thought it was stupid that she might give up college for some boy, but, you know, I was eight." He shrugged. "I didn't mind the idea of her staying home, though, even if it was for some stupid guy."

"Did you ever figure out who it was?"

"No. I'd actually forgotten about him until just now."

While she ate her snack, sipped her water, and took pain tablets, he told her about Mom and Dad and their lives at the mansion. He told her about summer days splashing in the waves in their small, private cove and fall hikes through the forests west of town. About skiing and trips to the city to see new construction projects Dad was proud of. He told her about family dinners and Sunday morning breakfasts before church and game nights and so many other memories he'd long forgotten. "We were happy. We had everything we needed. I'll never understand why Dad…" He swallowed emotion that choked off his words.

"What do you think he did?"

"He was involved in all of this." His words came out too harsh. He softened them as he faced the woman who deserved none of his wrath. "We know that."

She bit her lip. "Do we? We know he knew what The Network was doing, but that doesn't prove he was involved. Maybe he was investigating. Maybe—"

"He was involved."

"Tell me why you think that."

He huffed a breath, his gaze catching on the room's only hiding place. It was a tiny cutout beside the fireplace. With the grate covering it, it looked like part of a ventilation system. It wasn't, though, just a tiny boxlike hole. It used to be Forbes's favorite spot when he and Rosie played hide-and-seek because he could see out and, thanks to the mesh between the slats, nobody could see in. It was ingenious.

She followed his gaze, her eyes narrowing. "What?"

"You heard the story about what happened here? That the boy..." He didn't need to lie anymore. "That *I* was at my grandmother's house?"

"Yes."

"That wasn't true." He walked across the room, undid the rusty latch, and swung open the grate. "I was in here."

Tossing the ice pack aside, she used the arm of the sofa to stand and limped close. She bent down to look.

It seemed smaller now than it had back then. It'd fit an eight-year-old boy perfectly, even if the space had become claustrophobic after a few hours.

Nothing had felt safe since that day.

The opening was two feet wide and two feet tall, but inside, it stretched on the side away from the fireplace. Back then, he'd been able to lie down flat. He wouldn't even make it through the opening now.

Brooklynn straightened, her eyes wide with horror. "You were here?"

He glanced toward the hallway. "Dad didn't know. He brought them here. There were two of them, a man and a woman. They accused him of betraying them. Dad swore he didn't, that he'd never told a soul, but they..."

He swallowed all the pain and fury the memories brought.

"Oh, Forbes." Brooklynn slipped her arms around him, pressing her cheek to his chest. "I'm so sorry. I can't imagine... I'm so sorry."

He held onto her, allowing the memories to crash over him. "I did nothing. I just hid and let them die. I did nothing to help."

"That's not true."

"I didn't scream or try to call the police. I did nothing."

She leaned back and lifted her hands to his cheeks. Her fingers were cool, her touch soothing. "It's not true, Forbes. Your life was just as valuable as your father's and mother's and sister's. You weren't able to save them—what little boy could have?—so you did exactly the right thing, exactly what your parents and sister must have prayed you would do. You did exactly what God wanted you to do. You stayed alive."

That couldn't be true. Could it?

All his life, he'd seen himself as a failure and a coward, but maybe...maybe Brooklynn had a point.

He'd never seen his actions like that before. His therapist had always wanted him to see that he couldn't have saved them. It'd never occurred to him that his family wouldn't have wanted him to risk his life.

Even that God hadn't wanted it.

If God had wanted Forbes's family saved, He'd have done it. He was much more capable than an eight-year-old boy.

Moments before Dad and the strangers came in, Rosie had told him to hide, that she was going to do the same thing. He'd done what his sister said because he'd always done what she said. He'd trusted her.

Rosie had closed the grate and left in a rush.

Dad came in a few minutes later, the others following him. They'd argued.

Mom's voice had carried into the room from the open doorway. "Darling? Is everything okay?"

Dad yelled, "Run!"

A gunshot had deafened Forbes as his father's lifeless body crashed to the floor.

His mother's scream seemed to come from miles away. Another gunshot, then silence.

After Forbes helped Brooklynn back to the sofa, he told her the story, every gruesome detail, some he hadn't remembered until that moment. The telling was painful, but somehow it released something inside of him.

He felt lighter afterward.

They were on the sofa together. He'd pulled her injured foot onto his lap. One hand held the ice pack steady on her ankle. His other held her hand, a warm connection he never wanted to break.

The ice had melted by the time he finished the story.

"Grandmother found me the next day." He nodded to his hiding place. "I was still there. I'd never gotten the courage to leave. She took me home and changed my name and protected me, all these years."

"What a strong woman she must be."

They were the first words Brooklynn had uttered since he'd begun the story.

Her cheeks were damp, her eyes rimmed in red. She squeezed his hand. "Thank you for trusting me with the truth."

"Thank you for helping me carry it."

She smiled that sweet, tender smile of hers. "You've done enough carrying me around." But her expression dimmed. "Can I ask a question about...all of that? Do you mind?"

"Ask me anything."

"You didn't recognize the man and woman?"

"I could only see them from the knees down."

"Would you recognize their voices, if you heard them?"

Considering he still heard them in his nightmares... "I think so."

"You didn't hear when your sister was shot?"

"No, but her blood was found in the basement, which was far enough away that I wouldn't have heard. Mom's and Dad's bodies washed in with the tide a few weeks later."

"But Rosie's was never recovered."

It'd probably been eaten by scavengers or snagged on rocks somewhere. He didn't like to think about it. "It's a big ocean."

"One more question?" At his nod, she said, "They accused your dad of betraying them."

"Yeah?"

"What if he did? What if he was working with the authorities?"

"The police said he wasn't. Of course, I've always believed the police were in on it."

"Why?"

"Because they didn't find the killers and because...I don't know why. It's just something I always believed, but I could never say why. There's so much from that day I don't remember. Snippets of conversation. Maybe someone said something, or...I don't know." Frustration had his lips clamping shut. Rather than follow that dead-end road—he'd been there often enough—he added, "In any event, it never seemed like anyone cared enough to find out the truth."

"People cared. Your family was part of the community. Their murders rocked the town. But you weren't here to see that. As far as you knew, everything went on as usual."

"There is one other reason I distrust the police. My grandmother told a Shadow Cove detective that I was at the house, but he kept that information out of the file and told me not to tell anyone else. Though he didn't say so explicitly, I took that to mean not even other police officers."

"He thought someone in the department was involved?"

Forbes shrugged. "He died before I was old enough to start investigating. I never got to question him, so I don't know."

"If we assume Nathan is working for The Network—"

"A safe assumption, I think," Forbes said.

"Agreed." Brooklynn pushed herself higher on the sofa. "What if... what if your dad knew that a local cop was involved? What if he was gathering evidence to tell somebody else, somebody higher up, and The Network found out?"

Forbes had had the same idea many times over the years. "There's no evidence—"

"There's plenty of evidence. It's all in how you look at it. Come on, help me up." She tugged his hand. "We need to go to your dad's office."

After twenty-plus years, Forbes should know better, but against his wishes, hope bubbled up inside.

Maybe Dad hadn't been a criminal. Maybe…maybe Forbes and Brooklynn could finally get to the bottom of this.

CHAPTER TWENTY-NINE

The ice pack and ibuprofen had brought down the swelling in Brooklynn's ankle, and with it, the pain. Forbes had found an old Ace bandage and wrapped her ankle, giving her more stability.

She walked all by herself to the door of the family room. She'd taken her things out of the old-lady purse and, with her backpack slung over her shoulders, turned back to Forbes, who watched from beside the sofa, arms crossed.

"See? I'm fine."

"I see." He stepped forward, stopping just a foot away. "I'm carrying you downstairs."

"I don't need—"

"I know you don't need me." Before she could protest, he lifted her as if she weighed no more than the tray of food he'd brought up earlier. "Maybe I just want to, hmm? Ever think of that?"

She would swear amusement danced in his eyes. Amusement, which was not at all the same as what she was feeling.

Desire warmed her, and she fought the temptation to run

her fingers into his auburn hair. She slid her arms around his neck as if she needed to hold onto him. And maybe she did.

When he'd shared his memories, he'd shared the deepest parts of himself with her. He'd trusted her with the truth, something he hadn't shared with anyone else. She'd never felt closer to a man.

Being in his arms felt perfect, as if she'd been longing for this place all her life without even knowing it.

Maybe God had more for Brooklynn and Forbes.

His eyebrows hiked as if he waited for an answer. Had he asked her a question?

Perhaps sensing her confusion, he bumped his arms, jostling her. "May I carry you?"

"It's a little late for that question now, all things considered."

"Still, it feels rude not to ask."

She laughed. "If you insist."

"I do." Holding her against him, he carried her down the center staircase and into the office, where he lowered her feet to the floor in front of a chair.

She didn't sit, though, not ready to be apart from him. She stood, weight on one foot, only inches from this man she was falling for, enjoying the warmth of him and unwilling to leave it.

He held her eye contact, his arms slipping around her waist.

Inhaling, she picked up the scents of pine and forest and books, mixed with something distinctly Forbes. Every nerve ending vibrated with need. The desire that rose inside her was unlike anything she'd experienced before, almost unbearable.

He lowered his head, pausing centimeters from her. His breath fanned into her hair, but he didn't move closer. Just held there in delicious anticipation.

She couldn't wait another moment. She closed the distance between them, pressing her lips to his.

He seemed surprised at first. Then tentative.

And then he dove in, exploring her mouth, deepening their kiss.

Sliding her hands over his broad shoulders, she pulled him closer. All her fears, all her worries, all her dreams... They faded away until all that was left were Forbes and Brooklynn and this kiss.

She couldn't get enough. Everything inside of her yearned for him. Every moment in her past seemed to lead up to this moment, not a pinnacle but a turning point.

She would never be the same.

His mouth left hers, his kisses trailing down her neck. He brushed her hair back and continued onto her shoulder. Then returned to her mouth for more.

How much time passed? It could have been seconds. It could've been days. She could've stayed like that forever.

His hand slid beneath her shirt, up her back.

Abruptly he stopped and stepped away.

They stared at each other, both breathing heavily.

He rubbed his lips together, and then they parted in a tiny, beautiful smile. "I think..." He blinked a couple of times, swallowed. "I think I love you."

Oh.

Of course that was what this was. She'd never experienced it before, this feeling that was desire and affection and a million other things she'd never dreamed could all exist at the same time.

Brooklynn had never believed in the idea of soulmates. That wasn't how life worked. Marriage was about two people who fell in love and decided to keep loving each other forever. The falling part was a little mystical, maybe, so she'd never really trusted it. But the deciding part, the following-through on loving someone even when they were unlovable—that was hard work. She'd never been one to rely on the mystical—or even trust it.

But this was... Mystical wasn't the word. It was more... spiritual. As if God had known all along, and He'd brought them together at this time for more than just this unsolved murder.

She might not have trusted the falling part, but she'd fallen anyway. Hard.

"I think I love you too."

His tiny smile bloomed, and he was the most handsome man she'd ever seen. She memorized his beautiful features, his kind eyes, his square jaw hidden by whiskers. They weren't long enough to hide a dimple on his right cheek, a dimple she'd never seen before.

She loved that dimple. It was as if it'd been created just for her.

"I want to kiss you again." He stepped back. "I want to do all sorts of things I absolutely will not do. I promise."

"I trust you, Forbes."

His smile broadened. "Okay, then."

Not sure what else to say, she echoed him. "Okay."

They kept staring at each other, both smiling wide.

Finally, he rubbed a hand over his hair, messing it up, making him look boyish and adorable.

"I guess we should..." He looked around.

"Right. The mystery."

His smile disappeared, and his eyes narrowed, fixed on something across the room.

She followed his gaze to the cassette tapes stacked on the desk.

"Are those the ones from upstairs?"

"Yeah. I haven't had a chance to listen to them yet." He gave her a tiny kiss on the cheek. "Sit down and get off that foot."

She did, and he slid the second guest chair closer and angled it so she could prop up her foot.

"I'll be right back." He took off out the door, and his footsteps faded as he jogged down the hall.

Funny how she'd forgotten about the sprain for a little while. Maybe Forbes's kisses had healing properties, like the tears of a phoenix.

She felt a silly grin. She'd share the cultural reference with Forbes, but he'd probably never heard of *Harry Potter* or *The Chamber of Secrets*.

After this was all over, she'd introduce him to her favorite TV shows and movies.

Or...not. She wouldn't need to watch TV to escape her loneliness anymore. She'd have Forbes.

Yet, somehow, with everything happening, that hope felt tenuous. So many things could ruin it, starting with the people who'd come after her that afternoon.

She'd already wanted to survive, of course, but now, she had a new motivation. She wanted to know what would come of this fresh, tender love that had sprouted. She wanted to see the kind of man Forbes would become apart from the mystery that had shaped his life.

She wanted more of him, more of this. She wanted her life to be about more than capturing fleeting moments with her camera.

She wanted long, lingering time with the man she loved.

Father, You are able to... But there was so much to ask, so many moving parts, most of which she didn't know enough about to articulate. "You know, Lord. All of it, every single thing, You know. Just please...work it all out."

"Talking to yourself?"

Forbes stood in the doorway, a crooked smile on his face.

She loved that smile.

"Praying."

"Even better." He stepped in, holding up a box. "I ordered

this after you found the cassettes. It came in earlier, but I haven't had time to listen." Standing beside the desk, he unwrapped a cassette player and plugged it in, then slid the first tape into the slot and pressed Play.

Scratchy sounds filled the room, and then a man's voice.

"May third, ninety-nine. Overheard Stafford talking to OT before the Chamber meeting today. I wasn't seen. She mentioned the March shipment being disappointing. It was less than February by two million. OT blamed troubles in Montreal, said infighting. He must be in contact with MM—"

"Dinner's ready, sweetheart."

If the first voice was Charles, then that second voice had to be Grace.

"Be right..."

His voice cut off abruptly.

Forbes pressed the Pause button.

This was it. Proof! Charles Ballentine had been a confidential informant collecting information on The Network for... somebody.

Brooklynn looked at Forbes, expecting to see the same excitement on his face that she felt inside.

But he'd leaned over the desk, hands gripping the edge. His face was pale, his eyes red.

Realization hit her.

She stood and slid her hand around his arm. "Sit down." She soothed the words, tugging him onto the chair that'd held her foot a moment before.

He didn't even look at her, though his arm, where she touched it, tightened.

"Come on, love. Sit with me." She tugged, and he seemed to come back to himself.

He didn't sit. He didn't speak. He pulled her into his arms

and buried his face in her hair. Though he nearly enveloped her, she felt like she was the one holding him up.

She didn't know what to say, so she just held him while the grief or whatever he was experiencing washed over him.

It was a few minutes before he looked up at the ceiling.

As if she would judge him for his tears.

"Please. Sit down." She tugged on his arm, and he complied, folding over his knees.

She scooted her chair closer and rubbed his back, waiting for him to get his bearings again.

Thinking about how it would feel to hear the voices of loved ones long dead. The room felt heavy with memories, as if his family hovered nearby. They weren't here, but evil had resided in this house a long time, hiding as if waiting to be unleashed.

Lord, fill this place with Yourself, and drive out anything that doesn't glorify You.

Her God was bigger than any dark spirit. Her God was big enough to handle all of this.

And give me words and wisdom to comfort Forbes.

She'd felt extreme emotional highs and lows since she'd run from those men on Monday, and for Forbes, it was all so much more personal. His ride had begun when he was eight years old.

He swiped at his eyes, shook his head as if he could shake off grief and sadness, and looked at her. "Sorry."

"Don't apologize for being authentic. I love that about you. Are you okay?"

"I-I thought maybe he'd recorded something, but thinking it and hearing his voice. And Mom's. It was…"

She gave him time to finish his sentence, but he only looked away.

"Indescribable," she suggested.

"Yeah."

"Do you want me to keep listening? You can do something else."

"No." He sat up straight. "I can do it. Let's do it." He stood to resume the recording, but she stopped him.

"Forbes, did you hear what he said? This recording was intended for somebody else. I think your father was a confidential informant."

∼

BROOKLYNN TRIED to give Forbes his space.

Though he'd insisted he could handle listening to the tapes, after he'd started the recording again, he'd sunk into the chair, propped his elbows on his knees, and held his head in his hands.

Seemed he was just taking in his father's voice, savoring it.

Brooklynn, on the other hand, made copious notes, stopping the recording when necessary, jotting down every name, every place, every date, every detail from the cassettes.

When she wasn't writing, she took everything off the large desk and laid out all her notes and all the handwritten notes Charles had hidden in his files.

His final words on the cassettes weren't significant, only details about a June shipment and when it was due to arrive. There'd been no indication that he knew someone had learned of his duplicity.

The last recording played until, when it reached the end of the tape, it shut itself off, a loud click in the otherwise silent room.

Forbes had hardly moved.

Now, he took a big breath, blew it out, and looked up. His gaze caught on the desktop. "You've been busy." Apparently, he'd been so intent on the voices he'd missed all her activity.

"Trying to get organized." She searched his face for grief or sadness, but those were gone now. His expression was back to the stoic one that was his norm.

He stood and studied the information they'd gathered. "Any insights?"

She'd been standing too long, and her ankle throbbed. She settled on her chair and propped her leg up.

Forbes bent over the desk, his forehead wrinkled in concentration. His jaw was set, his chin strong. He supported his weight on his arms, bulging his muscles. This man was highly intelligent, incredibly kind, and exceedingly beautiful.

"I think we should look for repeated names and initials," she said, "see if we can match them up."

"Good plan." They set to work.

By the time they were finished, they had a list of twenty name-and-initial pairings.

OT had been mentioned a lot. *OT took care of that. OT handled it on his end.*

"I think OT is Leo Taggart," Brooklynn suggested.

"Why?" He didn't seem skeptical, just curious as to her logic. "His name is Leo."

"Your father seemed to believe he had a lot of authority and ability to handle the problems as they arose. What if OT stands for Officer Taggart?"

"Wow. That could be true. It's the best guess we have so far." Still standing, he penciled the man's name beside the initials, then tapped the next pairing. "SD could be the fisherman, Shane Dawson."

"He's Bryce's uncle."

While he wrote that name, she found notes about him in the notebook. "Your father said, 'SD could be an asset.'" She looked up. "So maybe SD—Shane, if it's him—wasn't involved?"

"If Dad really was a confidential informant, then maybe.

But if that's the case, then how did his nephew get involved now?"

"Someone else recruited him."

"Another unknown someone," Forbes muttered. He tapped the name *Stratton,* one of the few people called by name on the cassettes. "Tell me about Maury Stratton."

"It can't be her."

Forbes straightened, his eyebrows high on his forehead.

She knew exactly what that look meant. "I mean, I know it *could* be. I'm just... I can't imagine Maury being involved in something like this."

"She found you in the historical society today. So she could've alerted someone."

Brooklynn's certainty dissolved. "But why would she...?"

"Money, power. Take your pick. Unless there are other Stratton women around? Owen's a Stratton, right? Who's his mother?"

"She was my second-grade teacher."

"That doesn't mean—"

"I know, I'm just saying. She would've been in her twenties at this time. Even if she was involved"—Brooklynn waved toward the cassette tape—"your dad made the Stratton woman sound like a bigger fish than I'd guess a twenty-something woman would be."

Forbes conceded the point with a nod. "Maury, then. Tell me more about her."

"She's a Realtor. She started selling real estate in oh-three, opened her own brokerage house about ten years later, and now has a number of agents who work for her. She's one of the most successful real estate agents on the central coast because she puts her clients' needs first."

Forbes grinned. "You're quite the cheerleader, aren't you?"

"When I asked her for a bio for the Old Home Days

website, she gave me a handwritten copy. I tend to remember what I type."

"So she could've been involved. She'd have been in her forties at the time of my family's murders, and the woman who was here that night sounded about that age."

The thought that Brooklynn's friend, her parents' old friend, would have been involved in a murder made Brooklynn question everything. If she couldn't trust a woman like Maury, who could be trusted? Could anyone?

"What did she do before she was a Realtor?"

"Oh!" Brooklynn remembered something that chased her dark thoughts away. "You're brilliant, Forbes. That's exactly the right question. Maury and her husband—Don or Dirk or something like that—moved to North Carolina. He took a job in the Research Triangle in Raleigh. They got divorced years later, and that's when she moved back."

"That was all in the bio?"

"It was a long bio."

He chuckled, then started to scratch her name out. He stopped, tapping the pencil on the paper. "She was in the photo, though, right?" He looked back at Brooklynn. "The one we looked at the other day?"

She had been, which meant that Maury had been involved in commerce in Shadow Cove even when she was gone. "But why would your father call her *LS*?"

"Maybe L.S. and *Stratton* aren't the same person. Is Stratton her married name?"

"Yeah. In fact..."

Brooklynn's words trailed as a thought moved in like the fog. Or maybe a plague.

But it couldn't be. Of course it couldn't be.

"In fact what?"

"I'm not sure. Let me... Let's move on to something else."

"What are you thinking? Maybe I can help."

"Nothing. Just..." She waved toward the notes they'd made, not wanting to put words to the notion that had just occurred to her.

Forbes studied her for a long moment, then tapped another letter pairing. "What do you think about MM and Bazz? We still haven't..."

Her phone vibrated on the desk, loud in the quiet room.

She checked the screen. "It's a text message from a guy who says he's a friend of Grant's."

"Your cousin?"

"He wants me to call him." She dialed his number and put it on speaker.

"Jon Donley." The man had a deep, commanding voice.

"Hi, Jon. This is Brooklynn Wright."

"Grant forwarded your message to me. He asked me to make sure you're safe."

"Is he okay?"

"Better than. Summer's in labor, so they're at the hospital."

"Oh, that's good news."

"Yup. Explain these photographs you mentioned."

"They might be evidence of a crime. I'm worried the local police are involved in what's going on here, so I wasn't sure what I should do with them—who I should forward them to."

"I'm a private detective, not a cop, but I'd recommend you call the state police or the FBI."

"That could work. We think it's a smuggling ring."

"Okay." His matter-of-fact manner calmed her. This was crazy to her, but for some people, this was another day at the office. "You're in Shadow Cove?"

"Correct."

"I'll make some calls and get you a point person at both state and feds."

"As long as they're people we can trust."

"Of course. Listen, Grant asked me to ensure you're safe. He'd have called you himself, but apparently Summer can't breathe without his coaching, which is…"

In the background a woman said, "Attentive men are the best kind."

"Aren't you the lucky one, then?"

The woman giggled.

"Sorry about that," Jon said. "Denise is very excited about the baby."

From far away, she called, "Don't lie. You are too."

He chuckled. "The point is, Brooklynn, we've got a nice guest house here where you could stay, and it's right on our property. Grant and I used to work together, so—"

"You're a bodyguard?"

"Used to be. Look, I have no idea what's going on, but if you have evidence of a smuggling ring, and you think the local cops are in on it, then you're in danger."

"I'm aware." She glanced at Forbes, who was watching from the other side of the desk. "I'm safe where I am."

"If you ever feel less than safe, call me."

"I will. Thank you. And thank Grant for me."

"Sure thing."

Before he hung up, she said, "Can I ask you a question?"

"Sure."

Forbes leaned in, clearly curious.

She met his eyes and posed her question to Jon. "We're trying to figure out something here, and I think it has to do with drug cartels or organized crime, maybe in Canada?"

"Okay."

"We have this…clue, as it were." She felt stupid using the word. "There've been multiple references to MM and something called Bazz. Or maybe someone? We believe they were involved in smuggling or—"

"The Montreal Mafia." The words were spoken as if there could be no doubt. She did doubt, however, until he added, "One of the arms of the organization is run by the Bazzini family."

Her heart thumped. Bazzini...Bazz.

Forbes straightened. "Jon, this is...a friend of Brooklynn's. How long have the Bazzinis been operating up there?"

"Long time. Decades, as far as I know. The Montreal Mafia controls most of the drugs coming into eastern Canada. I'm pretty sure the Bazzinis are based in Halifax."

Brooklynn sucked in a breath through her teeth.

"I take it that helps," Jon guessed.

"Yes. Yes, it helps very much."

"Good. Let me know what else I can do. More importantly... Look, it sounds like what you're researching is bigger than two people can take on themselves. Why don't you come up to Coventry—both of you—where we can keep you safe until you get this sorted out? I can help you put your clues together."

"I'll bring Brooklynn to you," Forbes said. "I want to get her out of the middle of this. We'll leave here first thing in the morning."

"Perfect. I'll text my address. Let me know if you want me to meet you halfway."

She felt like a child being passed between divorced parents. "I'm not leaving until this is over."

Forbes grunted. "We'll see."

A chuckle sounded over the phone. "Good luck with that, man." Jon sounded amused as he ended the call.

She glared at Forbes. "I'm not leaving."

"This isn't up for debate. This is my fight. It was my family that was killed. I'm not having you here to deal with the Canadian Mafia."

"I'm not... They're not coming. It's not them, it's—"

"People who are hunting you down." His voice was too loud in the small space. He lowered it. "It doesn't matter who they are, small-time or big-time, their bullets will kill either way. It's not safe. It was selfish of me to bring you here just because I crave your company."

She refused to be swayed by his kind words. "Nobody knows where I am."

"For now, but I need to figure out what's going on, and that means I'm going to have to venture into town and start asking questions, ruffling feathers. As soon as I do that, this house will cease to be a safe haven."

"But then you'll be in danger. You can't do that. You should come with me."

"I'm not leaving until I know who killed my parents. I'm closer than I've ever been."

"But Jon could help. He obviously knows what he's doing."

"I'm close now. You go, work with Jon if you want, but I'm not leaving until I've found the murderers."

"Forbes, it's waited all these years. It can wait a little longer."

"No." Gone was his smile. Gone was any trace of the amusement and humor she'd seen since their kiss. The serious, brooding man she'd first met was back. "It has to be now. They could go to ground again. And maybe this time, they'll never come out."

The thought of leaving Forbes to deal with this by himself... The thought that someone might hurt him, or kill him, had adrenaline coursing through her veins as if enemies were closing in that very second.

She tried to come up with an argument that would convince

him to go to Coventry with her. Her memory snagged on something he'd told her a few days before. "What if the anonymous tip that brought you here was intended to get you out into the open? What if...what if that's exactly what they want, so they can take you out?"

"Nobody knows I was in the house that night."

"Your grandmother knew."

"My grandmother would never—"

"That detective knew. Maybe he trusted the wrong person. Maybe that person wants to eliminate you."

The tiny wrinkles around Forbes's eyes deepened as if he were considering her words, but then his stoic look returned. "It doesn't matter."

"It doesn't matter? How can you say that? We're talking about your life!"

"We're talking about justice."

"So you'd put yourself in danger—"

"Yes! Anything to find out who killed them."

The words felt like poison darts. He would get himself killed, and there was nothing she could do to stop him.

She stood to face him, reaching across the desk. "You can't save them, Forbes. They're gone. I think...I think you're still trying to redeem that scared little boy, but he doesn't need redemption. He didn't do anything wrong. He didn't do anything to be ashamed of." When Forbes didn't argue—and his expression gave no indication of what he was thinking—she pressed further. "Let's just take what we've learned to the state police and let them handle it."

He held her eye contact for a long moment, and she braced for an argument, a list of demands.

And then, he blinked. "I'll think about it. But no matter what, you need to go."

"Not without—"

"Please." The word sounded wrenched from deep inside. He moved around the desk and pulled her against his chest, wrapping her in his arms.

She was stunned by the sudden shift in his mood.

"Please, Brooklynn." His breath was warm in her ear. "Please go where you'll be safe. You mean so much to me, and I've already lost…so much. I can't lose you too."

Tears stung her eyes at all this man had gone through. "If you promise to consider my idea—"

"I will. Either way, you'll go to Coventry." He leaned back so he could see into her eyes. "Okay?"

"Okay." She wanted to convince him to come with her, but he'd agreed to think about it. For now, that was the best she would get.

CHAPTER THIRTY

It was nearly ten o'clock, but energy hummed in Forbes's veins.

The truth of what had happened to his family was laid out on his father's desk. He just needed to decode it amid all Brooklynn's notes, Forbes's notes, Dad's notes. All the noise.

The killers were right there.

He stared at the names and initials and dates and numbers. Most were still unidentified. They blurred in his vision.

Brooklynn's hand slid up his back. "I have an idea."

"Good, because I'm fresh out."

"Why don't I make a few calls?"

He faced her. "To whom?"

"Ian Prescott. He owned that charter company with Leo Taggart—the one that used the seagull logo. There's been no indication that he was involved in anything."

"Or Dad didn't know about him." Though Dad had seemed to know a lot.

"Fair enough. But he doesn't know where I am, and maybe he could shed some light on Leo. Maybe he could...I don't know, either confirm what we believe or turn us in a different direction. He's smart, and he's been in Shadow Cove all his life—well, except for college, I guess."

"He's the mayor, right? You said he's ambitious."

"Ambitious, yeah. But also savvy and..." She shrugged. "Ian likes me."

Forbes would bet he did.

Brooklynn smiled. "Not like that. He's married with children. But he thinks I'm talented, and he's always asking my opinion about things—visual stuff, like artwork for the town offices and landscape layouts, as if I have any clue. He's the one who roped me into managing the Old Home Days booths. He thinks I'm more competent than I am."

"I suspect you're the only one who doubts your competency."

Her lips twisted to the side as if she didn't agree. "Well, anyway. It was just an idea. I don't know what else to try."

"It's ten o'clock."

"It's literally a matter of life and death."

Forbes didn't like it. It was possible the smugglers already suspected Brooklynn was researching what had happened to Forbes's family twenty-five years earlier. If she called Prescott and he was involved, then she'd confirm it.

On the other hand, she was already their target. And Forbes didn't know what else to do.

"Don't tell him where you are or who you're with."

She rolled her eyes. "You think?" She found the number, muttering a low "sheesh." The phone rang, then went to voicemail. She tapped a text at top speed.

Seconds later, her phone rang. She connected the call, putting it on speaker so Forbes could listen. "I'm sorry to bother you so late."

"Not a problem, Brooklynn. I assume it's not about Old Home Days."

"It's about what happened at the Haunted Inlet a few days ago."

"I'm sorry they haven't gotten you home yet. I know Taggart's working on it."

Brooklynn shot Forbes a sardonic look.

"I don't want to get into all the details tonight, but I wanted to ask you a question about the charter company you and Chief Taggart used to own."

"That?" He sounded purely surprised. "What about it?"

"Was it very successful?"

He laughed. "No, unfortunately. I think Leo was trying to supplement his income—he was still a uniformed cop back then—but we couldn't get enough business to keep it afloat. Pun intended."

She smiled as if he could see her through the phone. "How involved were you in the day-to-day?"

"Not much. I was just getting my law practice up and running. I invested and managed the legalities. He managed the tours and paid the employees."

"How long was the business open?"

After a pause, Ian asked, "What does this have to do with anything?"

"It's kind of a long story, and I promise I'll fill you in one of these days." She didn't add more, just waited.

Finally, he said, "A few years. The money was good at first, but then it petered out. I think he just got too busy with work and family to manage it. When his father died, he got a decent inheritance."

For some reason, that information had Brooklynn's eyes popping wide.

"He decided the business wasn't worth all the time it was taking," Ian continued. "Between the money his father left him and the proceeds we received for the boat—he'd repaired it and fixed it up—he had a nice nest egg. Bought that big house, and as far as I know, must've invested smartly. He's lived well since then."

"One more question. The logo—the seagull in the circle—was really similar to Arthur Whitmore's. Was that a coincidence?"

"I remember a spat between Arthur and Leo about it. Arthur used the logo first, but after Lois and Arthur married, she talked Arthur into changing his. In retrospect, he should've hung on to it, considering the charter business only lasted a couple of years. Arthur's work will be around a lot longer than that. Like yours, I think."

"Thank you, Ian. I hope you're right."

"Anything else?"

"That's it for now."

"Good, good. You'll tell me everything? I am the mayor, you know. I need to know what's going on in my own town."

"I will, in good time. Do me a favor and don't tell Leo I called?"

Forbes winced, wishing she hadn't said that. It would be better if Leo didn't know they were on to him, but was it a good idea to let this man know? Leo's old friend?

A long silence followed Brooklynn's question. "I need... He's my chief of police, Brooklynn. I trust him."

"I'm not asking you not to trust him. I am asking you to trust me for a few days. That's all."

"A few days." His tone was more serious now, all amusement and solicitousness gone. "And then I expect an update."

"Fair enough. Thanks, and apologize to your wife for my late call." Brooklynn ended the call. "It's Leo," she said. "No question."

Forbes hadn't concluded that at all. "Why?"

"The inheritance. Lenny told me Leo and his father had

had a falling out, and Lenny's grandfather cut his dad out of his will. He put all the money in a trust for his grandchildren."

"Was the man wealthy?"

"Maybe not Ballentine-fortune wealthy, but I got the impression Leo had been expecting a good chunk of cash. The point is, Leo told Ian that he received an inheritance, but according to Lenny, he got nothing."

"So the nest egg Ian mentioned, the nice house—"

"The money had to come from somewhere."

Forbes's pulse raced. They were getting so close.

"I'm convinced," Brooklynn said. "But we can confirm it."

"How?"

"You said you would recognize his voice, right? Assuming he was here that night?"

Forbes swallowed, her suggestion coming clear. He nodded.

"I'm going to call him." She lifted her phone. "Lois sent me his number the morning after the storm."

"Wait." Forbes's anxiety spiked, not wanting Brooklynn anywhere near that man. Not wanting her on his radar at all. "What are you going to say?" They discussed it, and though he didn't like it, he saw the wisdom in her idea.

She put the phone on speaker and dialed.

Two rings in, the man answered. "Chief Taggart."

His voice... Was it familiar? He didn't know, not yet.

Leaning against Dad's desk, Forbes closed his eyes to better focus his hearing. A low hum carried below Taggart's words. An engine, or perhaps road noise?

"Sorry to bother you so late, Chief," Brooklynn said. "I don't know if you've heard, but I witnessed an incident at the Hidden Inlet the other day, and I've been in hiding ever since."

"I'm aware." His voice was gruff. He was older than the man Forbes had heard talking to his father. But twenty-five years had passed. "Len tells me you're out of town."

Her eyes widened, but she didn't miss a beat. "Right. I'm staying with friends in New York."

She was a quick thinker.

Odd that Lenny hadn't told his father the truth, though.

"Is there any update on finding Bryce Dawson?"

"He's still in the wind, but we'll pick him up. Just a matter of time."

"And Shane doesn't know where he is?"

"Claims he hasn't seen his nephew in years."

The background noise made it hard for Forbes to hear.

Brooklynn and Forbes had decided she should ask him everything she could think of about the case, even though neither expected him to tell her the truth. It was what she'd do if she didn't suspect him.

"Any update on the photographs?"

"Nope. Ask Church."

Loquacious, the chief wasn't.

"That's the thing." She briefly explained the incident at the library. "When I was hiding, I reached out to Nathan, but as far as I can tell, he never reported it. He never sent anyone to help me. I'm worried he's involved."

"Huh. You're sure he understood your text?"

"I haven't talked to him." She tapped on her phone and recited to the chief the text she'd written to Nathan.

The engine noise or whatever it was lessened in the background.

"You asked for help, and he didn't send it." The chief paused. "All right. I'll take care of it. If he's dirty, I'll find out, and he'll be held to account."

Forbes sat heavily in Dad's leather chair, the chief's voice resonating in his head.

You've left us no choice.

The words were as clear as they'd been that day.

Then, the gunshot.

His father fell.

The scene replayed in his head on a loop.

It had been Leo Taggart. There was no doubt. The man who'd sworn to protect and defend had murdered Forbes's father. Then he'd turned the gun on Mom.

He'd hunted Rosie, caught up with her in the basement, and killed her too. An innocent teenage girl.

And now, the same man was after Brooklynn, and if he caught up with her, her future would be the same as his family's.

CHAPTER THIRTY-ONE

Brooklynn ended the call and set the phone on the desk. She didn't need to ask what Forbes thought.

The truth had shown in his eyes.

Leo Taggart had murdered his family.

Now, Forbes's fingers were curled over his knees, the knuckles white. His head was bowed.

She settled on the chair beside him and slid her hand over his. "You okay?"

"I knew it." He flipped his hand and gripped hers, holding it solidly as if pulling in strength. "I knew...I don't know how I knew. Maybe I'd heard his voice before and seen him in uniform. But I knew the police were involved." When Forbes looked up, she expected to see sadness or grief or even anger.

But it was steely determination.

"Get your things." He stood and tugged her to her feet. "We're leaving."

"Wait. What? Where are—?"

"You're going to Jon's. We'll call whoever he says we should call. Someone at the state police, someone at the FBI. Both. I don't care. But I'm getting you out of here."

"Forbes, we need to stay together."

"No."

His cold, emotionless answer had her stepping back, wincing at the pain in her ankle.

"Sorry." He squeezed his eyes shut. When he opened them again, a flicker of worry creased the corners. "I can't lose you too. I need to make sure you're safe. Nothing else matters. Get your things, or I'll get them."

"I don't have a choice?"

"No."

She stared at him, trying to figure out what she could say to convince him to change his mind.

But...but all her reasons for staying in Shadow Cove seemed less than relevant now. The gallery. The photography contest. Old Home Days.

Was any of that worth risking her life?

It was time to face facts.

The chief of police was a murderer. And if he knew that she knew his secrets, he'd kill her.

The problem was, her gallery and the contest weren't why she was still at Forbes's house. *He* was why she was still here. She didn't want to leave him. She didn't want to lose him.

"I think—"

"This is not a debate, Brooklynn. We're leaving, and that's that."

"I was going to say, I think you're right. We should go. It's time to turn it all over to the authorities. There's no reason for either of us to risk our lives for this."

His brows lowered. "It's different. They were my family."

"I know that. I also know your parents and Rosie wouldn't want you to sacrifice yourself. I know they would want you to live a full and complete and *long* life. Let's turn all this evidence over and let the professionals handle it."

"I'm not..."

Her phone dinged with a text. She didn't look, just gave him space to finish his sentence. But he didn't.

After a moment, she checked the screen, then pressed the number Jon had texted, putting the call on speaker.

"What are you doing?" The old Forbes was back—demanding tone, suspicious nature. But now she knew the kindhearted man beneath. He didn't scare her.

"I'm calling the state police."

"When we get away from here—"

"Lori Putnam."

Brooklynn had expected a dispatcher or receptionist, but this was the name of the woman Jon had said she should talk to.

"My name is Brooklynn Wright." She ignored Forbes's glare. "I'm here with..." She paused to let him supply whichever name he preferred.

"Ford Baker, legally," he said. "But I'm Forbes Ballentine."

"As in, the Ballentine murders, down in Shadow Cove?"

"Correct," he said. "We're at the mansion now, and we believe we know who killed my family."

"Okay." The word held neither excitement nor disbelief. Seemed she was reserving judgment.

"We've been going through Charles Ballentine's old files," Brooklynn said, "and we also found some recordings—"

"Let's skip to the punch line," Putnam said. "Whodunit?"

"Leonard Taggart." Forbes's Adam's apple bobbed. "He's the police chief in Shadow Cove."

"Leo?"

Brooklynn shrank back from the phone. "You know him?"

"I've met him, yeah. He's a good guy. Or... Well, he seems like a good guy."

"I agree," Brooklynn said. "I dated his son, and Leo was always kind to me. He's been a good police chief in Shadow

Cove. I've lived here all my life. But we have evidence." Even if it was mostly circumstantial.

"He didn't work alone," Forbes added. "The night my family was killed, there was a woman. We have a name—Stratton. Could be Maury Stratton, who's a Realtor here in town. Also, there's a smuggling ring operating out of a remote inlet on the north side of the property. It was operating back then too. We believe drugs are coming in from Halifax, from the Montreal Mafia. Do you want to look at what we've got? Or should we contact the FBI?"

Brooklynn heard the scratch of a pen on paper.

"I'll bring the FBI in," she said.

"We've got a contact," Forbes said, though they didn't yet. "We'll bring them in. No offense, but I'm not great at trusting law enforcement."

"Most of us are—"

"Considering my whole family is dead at the hands of a cop, *most* isn't good enough for me."

There was a protracted silence before the woman said, "I understand. You're at the mansion now?"

"We're about to leave."

"I'm in Portland. I'll send you an address. We'll meet in an hour."

Tonight?

She wanted to meet that soon?

Forbes studied her phone as if he could see through to the woman on the other end. He was suspicious, but he agreed to the meeting.

Brooklynn ended the call.

"Can you be ready in five?"

"Yup." She hobbled toward the door, thankful the ice had brought her swelling down.

Behind her, he said, "Wait. I forgot about... Just sit. I'll take care of it."

The last thing she wanted was Forbes seeing her dirty underwear. "I have...personal things."

"I bought them, remember?"

Not all of them, and they'd been clean then, but she didn't argue. Instead, after he left, she set to work with the little time she had.

CHAPTER THIRTY-TWO

Seven minutes later, Forbes helped Brooklynn into his pickup.

He was going to keep her safe if it killed him. God willing, they'd both make it out of this alive. Now that the police were involved, now that Forbes had names and dates and evidence, the people who'd murdered his family would be brought to justice.

Leo Taggart and Maury Stratton.

A cop and a real estate agent, of all things.

He could hardly fathom it. After a lifetime of wondering, of searching and digging and praying, he'd finally found the truth —thanks to Brooklynn.

He put her backpack, a shopping bag filled with the clothes he'd bought her, and his duffel bag onto the backseat beside the box he'd hastily filled with evidence.

"You're sure there's no tracker on the truck?" Brooklynn asked.

"I left it on the workbench. We're safe." When they were both buckled, Forbes hit the remote attached to his visor, and the garage door lifted. "You got the directions?"

"Yup. Should take us a little over an hour to get there."

An hour.

One hour, and he'd hand all this over to Lori Putnam and the state police. He'd loop in the FBI as soon as he got a name.

It would be out of his hands. No matter what happened next, he could rest in the knowledge that he'd done everything he could.

Brooklynn's phone dinged, and she glanced at the screen. "Jon sent his FBI contact."

"He's johnny-on-the-spot, isn't he?"

She must've clicked the number because her phone was ringing. "We'll send him a gift basket."

Smiling, Forbes shifted and rolled the truck out of the garage into the darkness and around the winding lane to the circular drive in front of the house.

Up ahead, something glinted in the moonlight.

He slammed on the brakes.

She looked up. "What's—?"

A car was parked between the stone pillars, blocking their exit.

A tiny voice was speaking through the phone, but there was no time for that now.

A man stepped out of the hedge that Brooklynn had pushed through a few days earlier. He raised an object that reflected the dim light.

"Watch out!"

Her words were followed by a booming thump.

"Get down." Forbes shifted into reverse and twisted to see the way back to the garage. If they could get inside...

A man dressed all in black jogged from the side of the house.

Forbes cursed.

Brooklynn twisted to see. "What is—?"

Another gunshot. The truck jostled with the hit.

"Stay low!" He jammed the gear into drive, then floored the accelerator. The tires spun on the old, cracked asphalt, kicking up gravel.

The pickup lurched forward.

Forbes turned onto the yard and aimed for the forest.

Men were moving in. He'd counted three in front. When the truck rounded the far corner of the house, a fourth man approached from the back.

Bullets pelted the pickup.

The rear window shattered.

Brooklynn, irrationally, was watching behind them.

He palmed the back of her head and pressed it forward. "Stay. Down." He needed her to be safe so he could focus.

"Sorry sorry sorry." Her words came high-pitched and fast.

He aimed for space between the thick trees. "As soon as I stop, jump out and run for the cave."

"What? I'm not leaving—"

"I'll be right behind you."

"I don't know where it is."

Right. Of course she wouldn't remember. Forbes had ensured it was hidden well.

He'd just have to survive.

He yanked the car to the left to give them cover from the bullets. "Out. Get out."

She did, and he crawled over the console and followed.

The woods were dark and deep, but Brooklynn still wore the pale-blue jogging suit. It would stand out.

He grabbed her hand and ran for the cave entrance.

Shouts followed them, and gunshots.

A bullet hit a tree trunk a foot from his head.

She was moving too slowly. He'd forgotten about her injured ankle. No time to stop and carry her.

Come on, come on!

But he didn't say that. She wanted to live as much as he did.

He usually got to the entrance via the trail, and angling from this direction... Where was it?

Lead me, Lord.

He scanned the woods. His gaze landed on the bent birch that dipped over the entrance like a gateway.

He shifted that way, practically dragging Brooklynn behind him.

They reached the entrance. He pushed the vines aside. "Go, go."

She slid inside, and he followed her down the steep slope into the heavy blackness.

Outside, the gunshots had stopped.

"They went this way," one man shouted. That sounded like Niles.

"No, they were over here," another said. Could be Bryce, but Forbes couldn't be sure.

Had the men passed the cave entrance? Were they moving deeper into the woods?

He hoped so. Prayed so.

He and Brooklynn had gone maybe ten steps when he bumped into her. "Sorry." His voice was barely a whisper. "You okay?"

"I don't know where I'm going."

He should've gone first. Not that he knew every turn and dip, but he was accustomed to this space. He knew what to expect. "Press against the side, and I'll get in front of you."

She did, and he squeezed into the narrow space between her and the wall.

He could feel her fear, her warmth, her so-vulnerable, so-precious flesh.

He should keep moving, get them farther into the cave, though if the men found them here, there would be no escape.

He pressed his hand to the cold stone behind her and leaned in. "I'm sorry."

"None of this is your fault."

That wasn't true.

He should have sent Brooklynn away at the first sign of her snooping. He should have taken her to her cousin's house, or to a friend's house, or...anywhere far from him.

He just hadn't wanted to. He'd wanted her near him. Even before he'd developed feelings for Brooklynn, he'd craved her lightness and optimism and hope. He'd needed her like dry earth needed rain.

Now, he needed her more than ever. Needed her to be safe to live her life and grow old and be happy. He'd make sure Brooklynn had that. No matter what, if it meant never finding his family's killers. If it meant sacrificing himself, he'd do whatever it took to get Brooklynn out of this.

"Brooklynn, I lo—"

"Don't do that." Her fingers covered his mouth. "There'll be plenty of time for that later."

Her palm found his whiskers, her fingers trailing through them to the back of his neck. "You got us here. We're going to be okay."

And there it was, her optimism, her hope.

He held her and whispered a prayer in her ear, asking God for their lives. For justice. For help.

And then he took her hand, and they continued deeper into the cave.

CHAPTER THIRTY-THREE

Following Forbes, Brooklynn unlocked her phone and found the number Jon had sent. Whoever had answered her call to the FBI earlier had ended it. Maybe they'd been able to track the call. Maybe they'd sent help, but she couldn't count on it.

"What are you doing?" Forbes whispered.

"Calling in the cavalry."

"What? How?"

She stopped and tapped a text to the state police detective they'd spoken to earlier.

> We were ambushed leaving the house. Taking cover in the woods. Send help.

"We need to move."

"One second." She watched the screen, but the message hadn't sent yet. Were they too deep in the ground?

Lord, send it. You are bigger than cellphone networks.

Seconds passed. Forbes's impatience was palpable, but she needed to be sure the text was sent. Who knew what they'd find at the cove? They needed help.

Finally, the text was delivered. But it went unread for seconds.

Brooklynn wanted to call, to be sure, but even the low sound of a ringing phone or the woman's answer might be too loud in the rocky corridor.

Forbes sucked in a breath, looking beyond her as if threats were moving in.

She'd done all she could. She shoved her phone back in her pocket and followed Forbes deeper into the darkness.

The path sloped downward, and she moved carefully, using the cave walls to support her when she needed to put weight on her ankle.

Even so, every step with her injured leg sent pain. She gritted her teeth and kept moving. Toward the rocky headland and the beach and the surf and...

"Wait. Stop." Her whisper was vehement.

Forbes twisted. "Are you hurt?"

"No, but... When I was talking to Leo, there was a noise in the background."

"An engine. I assumed he was driving."

"But it was rhythmic. I didn't process it at the time, but I think it was..."

"The surf?"

"He was already here," she guessed. "At the cove."

Forbes turned back and peered at the path they'd just traversed, then ahead. "Okay. Maybe. Stay here. I'm going to check it out."

"No." She grabbed his wrist. "We need to stay together."

"We need to know if it's safe to go on or if we should go back."

"Back? We can't go back."

"We can't stay here for the rest of our lives. We need to get out, one way or the other."

"We can wait until Putnam moves in." She would, wouldn't she?

Except the last time Brooklynn had tried to summon help—had it just been a few hours before?—nobody had come to her rescue.

Nathan hadn't been trustworthy.

Maybe Putnam couldn't be trusted, either.

No. She refused to consider that. There were untrustworthy people in the world, but Forbes wasn't one of them. And neither was Grant. If Grant said Jon was trustworthy, and Jon said Putnam was trustworthy, then Brooklynn would believe them.

"She's going to send help."

"I can manage..." But his words faded. He huffed a breath and blew it out. "No, you're right. We need help. But we can help them too."

"Meaning?"

"If there are men on the beach, Putnam needs to know. I promise, I won't be seen. I'll just listen, learn what I can, and be right back. I'll be safe." He pressed a kiss to her lips, adding, "I promise."

He disappeared into the darkness.

CHAPTER THIRTY-FOUR

As Forbes neared the cave's entrance, he pulled his handgun from the holster at the small of his back and crept forward until dim moonlight brightened the narrow cave opening.

He moved toward it and was about to peek outside when a noise stopped him. Sounded like a rock falling, bouncing off other rocks on the steep slope.

Rocks didn't just randomly hurl themselves down cliffs.

Somebody was out there.

He settled to wait, listening for voices. Hoping one man would speak to another man, maybe go over the entire plan.

That would be too easy, but he'd take it.

Who were they? Locals? Friends of Brooklynn's? Or strangers? Hired thugs?

The surf crashed against the rocks and sand. It sounded louder, more violent, than usual, as if an unseen storm stirred the waters.

Forbes waited for a lull, hoping the man—or men—who guarded the cove would reveal themselves.

And then a lull came.

Forbes didn't hear voices.

He heard breathing.

Someone was *right there*.

On the other side of the rock where Forbes hid.

Waiting for him to emerge.

But why? How?

The truth was pure acid in his insides.

They knew about the cave. *They knew!*

The whole thing had been a trap.

Those gunshots had been close, but the men following had guessed where they were going. They must have found the cave.

He was stepping back silently when a voice came.

"Yeah?" The man's voice was low. "We're here. She was limping, so it'll take..." A long pause, then, "They won't."

Forbes didn't hear another voice, so he must've been on the phone.

Another man whispered, "No chatter. They must not have called..." The rest of his words were drowned by a wave crashing on the headland.

Chatter, as if on a police radio. Leo was reassuring his men that Forbes and Brooklynn hadn't called 911. He didn't realize yet that they knew the chief was in on the smuggling ring.

Small favors.

Forbes backed away silently, gun aimed toward the cave mouth.

His heart thumped so loudly that he feared the men outside would hear.

He and Brooklynn would wait in the cave, and if they had to, they'd make their stand there. In the middle of the pitch-black rocky space.

If anyone tried to hurt Brooklynn, Forbes would kill him. Or *her*, he added, thinking of Maury Stratton.

He'd die before he let harm come to Brooklynn.

He feared it would come to exactly that. And, just like with his father and mother and sister, he'd fail.

And the one he loved would pay the price.

CHAPTER THIRTY-FIVE

The silence and darkness pressed in until Brooklynn could hardly stand it. She'd texted Grant and Jon and Lori Putnam and the number Grant had sent for the FBI.

None of the texts had gone through. She was too deep underground.

With no other options, she prayed, lifting her fears and needs to the Lord who was always close, no matter the dense rocks and soil and roots between her and clean, fresh air.

God was in the cave with her. She knew that, even if she didn't feel His presence.

Help us, Lord. Bring Forbes back. Please, please...

It seemed he'd been gone an hour by the time she heard quiet footsteps on the rocks.

"Is that you?" Her voice was barely a whisper.

"Yes."

She exhaled her terror. He was here. He was safe.

He reached her, still without his flashlight. "You all right?"

"Glad you're back. What'd you learn?"

"They know." His voice was tight with worry. "They're waiting for us at the mouth."

She gasped. "They know we're here?" Turning back the way they'd come, she half expected to see enemies approaching. "What should we do?"

"They think we'll go out by the shore. I'm just lucky I heard them talking. We have no choice. We have to go back to the mansion."

"But...but they'll see us."

"If we wait in here, they'll eventually come after us. They'll have us cornered. Our only hope is to get out and hide in the mansion. They won't be able to find us. We can call Jon's friends again. We can wait for help."

But they had to get there. They'd be exposed.

"We have no choice." Forbes scooted past her and continued up the slope. "Come on. We need to move fast."

The trek back up toward the house was harder than the trek down had been. The closer they got to the forest beside Forbes's house, the more she dreaded the moment they'd reach the entrance to the passage.

This was crazy. But staying in here wasn't a better plan. They couldn't fight enemies who came from both directions. And Leo and his men had no idea they knew he was waiting for them.

Also, if Putnam had gotten the message, she'd have sent police to the house, not the shore.

Maybe they'd survive this.

For all Forbes's confident talk, he didn't turn on his phone's flashlight. He kept his voice at a whisper and moved quietly.

The enemy might be coming toward them right now.

The thought spiked her anxiety.

And then, up ahead, came the tiniest glimmer of light.

Forbes peeked around the final corner, then turned and

whispered, "It's clear. We're going to crawl out, then run to the door. Can you do it on your ankle?"

"I...I guess I have to."

"You remember where it is?"

"Yes."

"Memorize this. One-three-four-six-five-five-pound."

She pictured the numbers on a keypad. The top corners, then the numbers on the outside edges, then the center number twice. "Got it. But you'll be there."

"I need to watch for enemies. You'll have to get us inside. You remember it?"

She repeated the code. "I can do it."

He pressed a kiss to her lips, barely a peck. "I know you can."

She loved his confidence—and wished she shared it.

"Let's go." He continued to the mouth of the cave, stopping in the deep shaft just outside the glow of moonlight.

He didn't move for a long moment, listening.

Leaves rustled nearby. Somebody was right there.

He leaned close and whispered, "Stay here." Then, he inched upward and, gun aimed, peered out the entrance.

She had no idea what he was seeing.

He climbed up and disappeared.

CHAPTER THIRTY-SIX

The thug was five feet away, looking toward the cave. It was Bryce, built as solidly as the oaks that towered all around. This was no skinny Niles. Bryce would be a challenge.

His gaze was too high, and he didn't notice Forbes, who was just enough above the dark bracken-covered ground to survey the surroundings.

Forbes could shoot the guard, but then all his cohorts would come running.

He needed the man to get distracted long enough for Forbes to climb out and attack.

Okay, God. You've gotten us this far. A cracking branch would be really helpful about now.

When had Forbes started praying as if God listened?

But God must've listened. They were still alive, weren't they? It was him and Brooklynn against a gang of killers.

Obviously, God was on Brooklynn's side. That had been clear from that very first day, the way He'd brought Forbes to rescue her.

He'd thought that was all about Brooklynn, that God was using Forbes for her sake.

What an idiot he'd been.

As if Brooklynn wasn't the greatest gift God had ever given him.

He knew now that God was on his side, too, and had been all his life.

Forbes had survived that terrible night. He'd never wanted for anything. He hadn't been sent to foster care but instead had been raised by a loving and devoted grandmother.

Now he had a woman he loved, a woman he thought that he could build a life with. If God granted it and smiled on him. If God loved him.

Which...which of course He did.

He'd proved it in a million ways. It was only Forbes's foolishness that had convinced him otherwise. His bitterness and anger and quest for vengeance.

God had been there all along.

A snap had Bryce's head turning.

Forbes launched himself out of the cave and barreled into the larger man, aiming for his back.

They both went down.

But Forbes had the element of surprise. He braced himself with his knees and one hand, wrapped his other arm around Bryce's neck, and squeezed.

The man tried to buck him off, but Forbes hooked his foot around Bryce's ankle, keeping them connected, never letting up pressure against his carotid artery.

Bryce's strength seeped away. He went limp.

But Forbes stayed on top of him, to be sure.

The man's breathing evened out. He'd wake up soon, though he'd be woozy.

Forbes scrambled off him, found his weapon and pocketed it, then brought his own gun down—hard—on Bryce's head.

He wasn't sorry for the headache the man would suffer. At least he'd still be breathing when this was over.

Forbes returned to the mouth of the cave and peeked down.

Brooklynn's eyes were wide with fear. Seeing him, she climbed the first few steps, and then Forbes gripped her wrist and pulled her out.

They paused for a few seconds, both catching their breath, both peering into the woods.

No more enemies that he could see. Where was everybody?

Hopefully, the rest of them had climbed down the rocky slope to the cove to wait for Forbes and Brooklynn to emerge. But he wouldn't count on it.

"Stay low," he said. "Move as fast as you can. I'll provide cover. When you get the door open, go inside and leave it cracked." He handed her Bryce's gun. "You know how to use that?"

She checked the safety, ensured it wasn't engaged, then gripped it like a pro.

"I'll take that as a yes. Let's move."

They stepped carefully along the path, then paused at the edge of the lawn.

Still, nobody stopped them.

Not that he'd wanted to run into enemies, but where were they? What were they doing?

He had a very bad feeling about this.

So many things could go wrong. Somebody could be watching the yard from a window—he checked, though, and saw none opened or cracked. Somebody could be watching from the forest.

He peered both ways between the trees and saw nothing

worrisome. His truck bed stuck out over the edge of the weedy lawn, the cab hidden behind the trees.

Leo and his fellow thugs had likely found all the evidence.

Forbes couldn't worry about that. Right now, they just needed to survive.

Forbes gripped Brooklynn's hand and leaned in to whisper in her ear. "Straight to the door. You remember the code?"

She repeated it.

"Good. Go inside. If I don't come right behind you, close it, and—"

"I'm not closing you out."

Of course she wouldn't. "Go in and hide where you were the other day."

Her eyes widened, and he couldn't help his smile. "Spiders won't kill you. These people will."

She swallowed, nodded.

He held her against his chest, prayed for her safety, and said, "Go."

She stepped out of the cover of trees, then hurried as quickly as she could on her injured ankle to the door.

No gunshots rang out. No shouts.

She pressed the code and slipped inside, leaving the door cracked for him.

Movement at the front of the house caught Forbes's attention. He peered toward the driveway, where the dark sedan that had blocked the exit earlier was now parked, its trunk open. A man walked toward it from the direction of the front door, carrying...something.

Forbes focused on that object. From the shape of it, it was...

A gas can.

And by the way the man swung it, it was empty.

Fear choked out his breath.

The man put the gas can in the trunk, then pulled out something else. A lighter flamed in his hand. Then something else lit, even brighter.

He hurled the burning object at the house. As it flew, Forbes had a sickening feeling he knew what it was.

The Molotov cocktail shattered a window and then exploded.

Yellow flames spread so fast inside that he saw the glow of them through the window. They flared higher and hotter, igniting the room from floor to ceiling.

Brooklynn!

He sprinted across the grass, not caring if anyone saw him. She was in there. She could be trapped.

He barreled through the open door, flicked on the light, and hurried down the stairs. "Brooklynn!"

"Here!" She was standing beside the compartment where she'd hidden days before. Her eyes were wide. "What was that?"

"Fire! The house is on fire. We have to—"

A loud crack, and the ceiling between them collapsed.

Brooklynn screamed.

The room filled with smoke and flames. How much gasoline had been poured? How fast would the place be reduced to ashes?

"Where are you?" He had to shout over the roar.

"Here!" Her voice was faint.

"Are you hurt?"

"No. I just...I can't...get..."

"What? What is it?"

"I'm... I'm stuck!" Her tone pitched high and panicked. "I can't get out!"

"Okay. It's okay. I'm coming."

Her back had been to the concrete wall. Beside her, the basement stretched the length of the house, but there was no escape that way, even if she weren't stuck. The only way out was behind him.

Soon, the entire first floor would come down. She'd die of smoke inhalation long before the flames took her.

Small favors.

He bent low, assuming she knew to do the same, and looked at the obstacles between himself and her. A rafter, and above it, furniture aflame.

But the rafter was at an angle. If he could get beneath it, maybe...

He searched for something, something...

The laundry.

He turned on the washer, filling the tub, then grabbed all the dirty linens he'd dropped down the chute from the second floor. He dipped them in the water and squeezed them out over his clothes, then wet them again. He covered his head and shoulders with a wet sheet, tucking another in his waistband.

"Hang on," he shouted. "I'm coming."

The rafter smoldered, thick black smoke wafting off it. He covered his mouth with one of the wet garments and climbed over the rubble until he reached it. He ducked low and passed under it, brushing his hand on the burning wood.

He ignored the pain.

On the other side, he caught sight of an expanse of fiery, smoky...junk. An upholstered chair. A table angled onto its side. The whole living room had slid between them.

Brooklynn was on the floor on the far side, a thick piece of wood over her.

She was trapped, her back to the wall, the board over her lap.

He moved toward her, smacking at flames that licked his ankles.

It was so hot. Sweat dripped in his eyes, making it nearly impossible to see past the smoke.

Finally, he reached her, though she was hard to make out in the haze. He bent to lift the board. Its heat scorched his skin. He pulled layers of the wet sheet over his hands and tried again.

He could barely budge it.

It was wedged into the concrete corner, its weight held down by more stuff from above.

"You're going to have to slide out."

"There's nowhere to go." She was yelling over the flames, but to her credit, her panic had passed. She seemed perfectly in control.

"If I lift it enough, can you stand?"

Her eyes widened. "I-I don't know. Maybe."

It was their only option. "Try. You ready?"

She nodded, and he gripped the board tightly. He took a breath. "Now." He lifted with all his might.

She tried. He could see how hard she tried. But she couldn't get enough room to move.

Another rafter fell from above, filling the space with sparks and smoke.

He dropped the board to cover her. This wasn't going to work.

"You need to go." Brooklynn's words were strong, resigned. "Forbes, you need to get out."

"Don't do that."

"I don't want you to die here. Go. Go!"

"Stop talking." His voice was rough and low. Everything was growing darker. He needed air. He needed oxygen.

Once again, he'd failed to protect his loved one.

But this time...this time he wouldn't save himself. This time, if someone he loved was going to die, he'd die with her.

He climbed over the board.

"What are you doing?" Her eyes were wide. Tears tracked down her soot-covered cheeks. "Go! Please, go!" Her voice broke. "You have to, Forbes. You have to leave."

He settled beside her. He couldn't stretch out in the tiny space, so he lowered to a crouch, his knees against the hot wood. "I'm not leaving you."

"Please." She tilted into him. "I can't...I can't let you die here. I can't stand it."

"I know." He wrapped his arm around her and pulled her close. "I know."

"If the situation were reversed—"

"Then you'd leave, and that would be right. But I can't."

They would die here. They would die together.

Lord...

He didn't know what to ask.

Take us home.

That was it. That was all there was left. He wished, oh how he wished he'd left Brooklynn in the cave. Maybe she could've waited it out. Stayed hidden until help arrived.

Better yet, he should never have brought her back here in the first place. His quest for vengeance came down to this. All the evidence would be destroyed. Nobody would pay for his family's murders. Nobody would pay for Brooklynn's.

Everything he'd lived for, and he'd failed.

They were going to die, and there was nothing he could do about it.

CHAPTER THIRTY-SEVEN

Brooklynn could feel Forbes's despair. It matched her own.

"Please." She gripped his T-shirt, hating that he was there and not wanting to let him go. "Please go. Maybe you can get help."

"From the murderers and thugs? I haven't heard any sirens."

Would they, though? With all the noise? From the basement?

Probably.

He shifted, and a spark of hope lit. Maybe he would actually leave.

But no.

He dropped to his bottom right beside her.

"What are you doing?"

"Getting comfortable."

"No! Please..." But he wouldn't leave. Of course he wouldn't.

That wasn't the kind of man he was.

The space was too small for his overlarge body, but he settled beside her, pulling in a deep breath.

"Air's cleaner down here." His voice was gruff with smoke damage.

He shifted to his butt, putting the soles of his shoes on the board.

It shifted.

His eyes widened. "Can you try again? To stand?"

She wouldn't *try*. It was their only chance. "I'll do it."

He shimmied down so his back was pressed against the corner of the wall and the floor, his neck bent at a terrible angle. He pushed with both feet as hard as he could.

The board lifted off her.

She angled and twisted, leaning over him in the cramped space.

He closed his eyes, holding the board away.

Please, God. Help me. Pull me up.

And then she stood. Just like that.

He opened his eyes "Yes!" He let the board drop, scrambling up beside her. "Let's get out of here." He wrapped a wet sheet around her head and shoulders. "Can you walk?"

"I'll figure it out." She'd deal with the stupid ankle later. That was the least of her worries right now.

"Let's go." He took her hand and led the way over the charred remnants of furniture and under the smoking rafter.

At the bottom of the stairs that led to the door, he said, "They might still be out there."

She readied the handgun she'd shoved in the pocket of her tracksuit and disengaged the safety. "Then we'll deal with it."

"The goal is my truck. Hopefully they left the keys in it."

"Okay."

He pulled her in for a quick hug, holding on extra tight. "God, protect us."

"Amen."

Gun in hand, he climbed the stairs, and she followed.

As he pushed open the door, he angled back toward her, just in case. Cool, humid air rushed in, and she filled her lungs, which led to a cough. Though the fire was loud, she feared she'd been heard.

No gunshots came.

Maybe Leo and his band of thugs had left after they started the fire.

Forbes got low and stepped outside.

Still, no sign that anybody was looking for them.

"Come on."

She followed him onto the lawn, and they dashed toward the trees.

A gunshot exploded in the darkness.

Forbes went down.

No!

She fell beside him, looking for the shooter. Where was he? Movement in the trees. A man looked back, and in the glow of the fire, she saw his face.

Owen.

Her sister's boyfriend. Her friend's nephew.

The man whose voice she'd recognized outside the library. Recognized but refused to believe.

Their eyes met, and though he could've shot her, he didn't. He turned and ran.

Another figure bolted from behind the house to the tree line, a woman with a messy bun.

Who in the world...?

Forbes grunted, and Brooklynn turned her focus to him "Are you all right?"

"Yeah, I-I think."

"You have to move." Sirens sounded, distant, but still she looked toward the driveway, hoping someone would come, someone would help.

A figure stood there, silhouetted by the fire.

She blinked. It couldn't be. It couldn't.

The woman raised her weapon, aimed straight at Brooklynn. But Lois wouldn't shoot her. How could she—?

The crack of a rifle, and the woman jerked back, then collapsed.

Brooklynn's head snapped around. What...? Who'd shot her?

She had no idea.

Before Forbes could voice the obvious question, she said, "We need to get out of the open." They might as well have giant targets on their heads, though it seemed they had a guardian angel somewhere looking out for them.

"No, you—"

"Now, Forbes, or we'll both be killed."

He grunted again but rose to a crouch, then started moving toward the cover of the woods. He supported his right arm with his left.

Following, she kept her weapon ready, just in case.

Considering all the threats she'd seen and failed to fire at... A commando she was not.

The screech of tires had her turning as a car careened away, down the driveway and onto the road, turning opposite Shadow Cove and all the emergency vehicles surely on the way.

Not ten feet into the woods, Forbes collapsed on the dirt and fallen leaves.

She kneeled beside him. "You all right?"

"Can't go farther."

"That's okay. That's okay. This is far enough." She prayed it was, anyway. As long as the bad guys were leaving and the good guys were coming.

But Owen?

Lois?

How were they among the bad guys? She couldn't fathom it.

Blood seeped from a bullet hole high on Forbes's shoulder. She set her gun aside, then took off her jacket and pressed it against the wound, trying to staunch the flow.

She knew very little about how to treat injuries. Her polyester clothes weren't exactly absorbent. Maybe her socks would be better?

Gross, but better.

She sat on the cold ground, ripped off a sneaker, then pulled off her cotton sock, which she pressed against the bloody wound.

Forbes sucked in air.

"Sorry. I'm sorry. I'm just—"

"It's okay, sweetheart. You're doing—"

A snap deeper in the woods cut him off.

Brooklynn looked up as a man emerged from behind a tree.

Leo Taggart lifted his gun and aimed at her. "I really wish you'd just minded your own business."

She glanced at her weapon. It was right there, inches from her fingertips.

"Go ahead," he said. "It would be better for me if it was in your hand. Of course, it will be by the time anybody gets here. I'll tell them I didn't recognize you, that you aimed, and I fired, just like I'm trained to do. Nobody will doubt me."

He must've climbed through the cave. He must've been waiting for them, knowing that, if the burned house hadn't taken them, they'd eventually show themselves.

"They know. We told the state police everything."

"The ramblings of two amateur detectives—and no evidence? I won't be charged."

She hated to think it, but he was probably right. "You're going to kill the woman your son loves?"

"You don't love him, though. Never did. Once you're dead

and buried, at least he'll be able to move on. Never could figure out why he was so obsessed with you." A cold glint filled his eyes.

She was going to die.

Forbes lurched up in front of her.

The crack of a gunshot.

"No!" Her scream seemed to come from far away. She wasn't hit, but Forbes...

Leo fell forward, landing face down in the dirt.

What happened?

Who...who'd shot him?

A woman emerged from the darkness behind where the chief of police had stood a moment before.

It was the woman with the bun. She stepped nearer, gun aimed at Leo. She reached down and grabbed his weapon, then lifted her gaze. It fixed on Forbes.

Maybe this was the state police officer Brooklynn had talked to earlier? She couldn't imagine who else it could be. She said, "Lori? It's me. Brooklynn."

But the woman acted as if she hadn't heard.

She never took her eyes off Forbes.

CHAPTER THIRTY-EIGHT

Forbes started at the apparition.

The ghost.

There was no other explanation. Unless he'd bled to death and hovered somewhere between this life and eternity.

He hoped not, considering how his shoulder throbbed.

The woman standing in front of him couldn't be there. She couldn't be real.

She stepped closer, lowering her gun. Her gaze barely flicked to Brooklynn, who'd called her a name that made no sense.

The apparition moved closer and dropped to her knees, staring at him as he was staring at her. Light came from the moon above and the flames behind. A few red and blue flashes penetrated the darkness. It wasn't much, but he didn't need more. He knew this woman.

The teenager.

The girl.

All grown up. Somehow, alive and well and...

"Forbes?" Her voice was the same. Just the same as before.

"What...? How did you...?" His voice was rough from the

smoke and cracked with emotion. He pitched forward into his sister's arms. "Rosie."

Beside him, Brooklynn gasped.

Forbes held onto his big sister, and in an instant he was eight years old. Hearing her voice, feeling her tugging, tugging him to the closest hiding spot in the house.

"In here," she'd said. *"They're coming. Don't come out."*

He hadn't known who *they* were, but somehow, she had. And she'd known they were coming. And she'd escaped.

She'd *escaped*.

He didn't understand.

Now, he gripped her tightly, afraid that if he let go, she'd disappear again. All the bad things would happen again.

Except he wasn't eight years old, and she wasn't eighteen, and the killer lay face down in the dirt behind them.

He looked at the spot, just in case Leo decided to rise from the dead.

Apparently, that was a thing now.

Forbes was confused and elated, and angry and brokenhearted. It was too many emotions for him to deal with.

Brooklynn's hand slipped over his good shoulder an instant before she pressed something to the bleeding wound on his back. It hurt, but he didn't care. She was safe and alive. Rosie was here—

Nothing else mattered.

If he could just keep these two women close, right with him, forever, then all might be well.

CHAPTER THIRTY-NINE

Brooklynn pressed her sock over Forbes's wound.

It seemed he'd all but forgotten he'd been shot. He was fixated on the woman in his arms.

Rosie. His sister, back from the dead.

There was going to be a story there. Brooklynn prayed they'd be around to hear it. She couldn't help scanning the woods, fearing another enemy might pop out to shoot them.

But the cavalry had finally arrived. The lights of emergency vehicles, along with men's shouts, told her they were safe now. Surely, any remaining enemies were hightailing it away.

"Brooklynn!"

The man's shout had Forbes backing away from his sister. He twisted to look behind them. "Who was that?"

"I'm not sure." And she wasn't, but she had a feeling. "Rosie, can you hold onto this? Try to stop his bleeding? I'll go see."

"No, don't." Forbes reached to grab her, then winced. "Stay here where it's safe."

"It's safe, Forbes." Surely the entire Shadow Cove Police Department wasn't crooked. And there were firemen and paramedics and EMTs.

She squeezed his opposite shoulder. "I'll be right back." She pushed to her feet and jogged through the forest to the edge of the yard.

Firemen aimed water at the house, but from where she stood, the old beauty was done for.

Her heart broke just a little to see the amazing structure, in the Ballentine family for over a hundred years, crumble in flames.

"Brookie!"

She turned in time to see Lenny running toward her. Her normal reaction to him was quickly squelched as he approached.

"Are you all right?" He looked her over, head to toe, then swiped a thumb across her cheek. "Is this soot?" His volume rose. "Were you in there?"

She kept herself from shrinking away from his touch and his raised voice. "I'm fine, Lenny."

"What happened? Did he get you into this? Ford Baker? I ran a check, and that's not even his real name, you know. He's really—"

"Forbes Ballentine. I know." She took Lenny's hand and led him back toward the emergency vehicles that now filled the front yard. "He needs a paramedic."

"Oh." Lenny froze, looking behind him.

"Run and get somebody, would you? My ankle—"

"Here, let me—"

"Go, Lenny. He's been shot."

He looked conflicted, finally bolting toward an ambulance. She watched as he grabbed someone and pointed.

One person followed him back at a jog while two others carried a gurney.

A cop must've heard him, because a woman hurried their direction as well.

A coughing fit had Brooklynn wanting to lie down in the damp grass and rest. She hobbled to the edge of the forest to lean against a tree. When the paramedics reached her, she pointed to where she'd left Forbes and Rosie.

Praying Rosie was still there, though she half-expected the woman to disappear as mysteriously as she'd arrived.

The paramedics shouted, and Forbes's sister responded.

Lenny followed the paramedics, but Brooklynn called his name.

He shifted. "I need to go help—"

"Get someone else to do it."

A tiny smile bloomed on his face. "I can stay with you."

She hated, *hated*, that she had to do this. And the fact that he'd misunderstood why she didn't want him to go into the woods only made it worse.

The other cop approached. "Are you Brooklynn Wright?"

"Yes."

The woman moved closer, arm outstretched. "Lori Putnam. I'm sorry we were late to the party. Everybody okay?"

"Forbes and I are, and... Go on into the woods there. You'll see. I'll be here when you get out."

The woman looked between Lenny and Brooklynn, then continued toward the light between the trees.

Lenny watched until she disappeared in the darkness. "Why did you call them? You should've called me."

"I couldn't." She took a deep breath and blew it out. "I'm sorry, Lenny."

"None of this is your fault. It was that Forbes—"

"It wasn't Forbes's fault, either. His family was murdered here twenty-five years ago."

"I know that, but he came back and stirred it all up. I wouldn't care about that, except he got you involved."

"*I got me involved.*" She started hobbling toward an ambulance, sucking in oxygen and needing to get off her feet.

Men were shouting, running. They'd discovered Leo's body, no doubt. But the way the man had fallen, the way he hadn't moved at all...

He was dead.

A fireman ran up to her. "Anybody in the house?"

"Not that I know of. There shouldn't be."

"Thanks." He bolted back toward the melee.

Lenny wrapped an arm around her waist and helped her. Normally, she'd push him away, but she didn't have it in her tonight.

He'd hate her soon enough.

They reached the ambulance, and a paramedic started asking her questions.

"Can you give us a minute, please?" she asked.

He looked from her to Lenny, must've decided the man's police uniform made him safe, and stepped back a few feet.

Lenny lifted her onto the back of the ambulance.

Thank heavens for sweet relief.

"Tell me what happened."

"I'll tell the whole story to Lori and the FBI."

"The FBI? Why would they... What are you talking about?"

"Lenny, your father..." She swallowed. "He was part of this."

"He's a cop. This is what we do."

"No, I mean..." She took his hands. "He tried to kill me."

Lenny yanked back. "You're crazy. Dad would never—"

"He was shot."

"What?" His head whipped back toward the woods. "Dad wasn't... You're wrong."

"I'm sorry."

He took another step back. "Be careful what you say about my father."

"I promise to only tell the truth."

That wasn't going to help Lenny, though.

He spun and bolted toward the forest, where Forbes was being carried out, his sister at his side, holding his good hand.

She half-expected Lenny to say something to Forbes, but he didn't, just raced past him.

She hadn't wanted Lenny to see his father's body. She'd hoped to soften the blow a little, but maybe that was a blow that couldn't be softened.

The EMTs were taking Forbes to a different ambulance. She needed to see him, so despite the pain in her ankle, she pushed herself off the back of the ambulance and hobbled that direction.

Before they slid him into the back, he said, "Wait!"

Thanks to that commanding voice of his, the EMTs stopped.

With Rosie's help, he sat up, looking around.

Their eyes met, and she closed the distance between them. "Hey."

"You okay?"

"I'm alive, thanks to you."

He chuckled. "I was about to say the same thing." His gaze flicked to Rosie. "And thanks to you."

She didn't smile back. "You're here because of me. This is my fault."

Forbes squinted as if he was trying to figure her out.

Brooklynn asked the question. "What do you mean? How is this your fault?"

"Why are you here, Forbes?" Rosie asked.

"I got... Did you send it?"

"Send what?"

"I got an anonymous note, a letter."

Her lips pressed closed a moment as she thought about that. "I told Grandmother the smugglers were operating again. I told her to keep you away from here. I told her—"

"Wait. Grandmother knows you're alive?"

"Don't be angry with her. She was trying to protect me. I was trying to protect you. All these years, though, she wanted... She needed to know who killed them. I think... I was trying to keep you safe, but I think she must've sent the note."

"Gran wouldn't..." But the protest died on his lips. He blinked, looked up at the house. The flames weren't out, but the firemen were winning the battle. "She wanted to know."

Brooklynn couldn't make sense of that. "She wouldn't have sent you into danger, though. Would she?"

"To find out who killed her son? Maybe."

Rosie laughed, though the sound held no amusement, "Yes. She would have. She did. I told her to protect you, and she dangled a carrot instead."

Brooklynn couldn't fathom.

And then Forbes's lips tipped up at the corners. "She trusted me to figure it out and stay alive."

That was giving the old woman more credit than Brooklynn would have.

"She's too much like me," Forbes said. "Desperate for justice, no matter what the cost. She knew she couldn't get it herself, but she thought I could." He stared at the remains of his childhood legacy. "And I did." He squeezed Brooklynn's hand. "We did."

There were still unanswered questions, not the least of which involved the living, breathing woman standing beside them, a woman thought dead for twenty-five years.

The danger was past, but there were still mysteries to solve.

CHAPTER FORTY

At the hospital, Brooklynn's ankle had been X-rayed, confirming the sprain she'd self-diagnosed. She'd been treated for smoke inhalation and given oxygen. Hers wasn't as bad as Forbes's—she'd been on the floor, below the worst of it, whereas he'd been up and moving. She'd only needed oxygen for a short time, but he still had a little tube running below his nose, feeding it to him.

Now, she dozed on a chair, her head resting on the bed where Forbes slept. Half awake, half asleep, memories of the terrifying ordeal morphed into nightmares that had startled her awake every few minutes since the orderlies had finally brought him in from surgery.

The nurses hadn't told her much, only that he'd lost a lot of blood—not exactly news to her—and was out of the woods.

Out of the woods. Ironic, considering how much they'd needed the cover of the woods. But in this case, it was a good thing.

A gentle hand brushed hair away from her face, and she sat up.

"I didn't mean to wake you." Forbes's voice was rough with sleep and fatigue.

"I wasn't sleeping." She yawned. "Just resting a little." She glanced at the window where light peeked around the drawn curtains. It was morning, a whole new day.

Forbes looked pale, highlighting the dark smudges under his eyes. But he was breathing. He was awake.

He studied her. "How do you always look so good?"

"You *did* lose a lot of blood."

His lips tipped up at the corners, the smile small but holding promise. It faded. "Where's Rosie? Did I...? Was she really there?"

"She was there, and she was here most of the night." Brooklynn and Forbes's sister hadn't talked much. She'd introduced herself as Rayne, the false name she'd gone by most of her adult life. Though Brooklynn had been tempted to pepper her with questions, she figured Forbes deserved the answers before she did. And Rayne/Rosie had been too worried about her brother to talk. Rather than chat, they'd sat side by side and watched Forbes sleep.

"Once she was convinced you were going to survive the night," Brooklynn said, "she left to get a shower. I think she's going to see your grandmother."

"And then she'll be back?"

"She said she would. And she left her cell phone number."

That news seemed to startle him. "I can't believe... I don't understand how she's alive. And where she's been, and what happened."

"I'm sure she'll tell you when she gets back."

He considered that, then chuckled, which quickly turned into a violent cough.

Brooklynn gave him a sip from the cup on his bedside table.

"Thanks." He reclined again. "She has a cell phone. It's so weird."

Brooklynn couldn't imagine how strange it must be. "How do you feel?"

"Like I was shot." He pressed the button to lift his head a little more.

"Don't sit up for me. You need your rest."

He left the bed at a slight incline. "I don't remember much after we left the house. Am I gonna make it?"

"According to the nurses, you'll be back to your old self in no time." Well, *no time* was a bit of an exaggeration. "My uncle suggested you'll need physical therapy for that shoulder."

"Your...uncle?"

"Roger. He's a physician—mostly retired now. I called him last night. He knows everything there is to know."

"As long as you're not overselling him."

She grinned. "About medicine, anyway. He offered to come, but you're being well taken care of. My whole family knows what happened. I've been avoiding their calls, but if their texts are any indication, they're peeved at me for not getting out of town."

"I am, too. Very...peeved."

She grinned. "I'm not sorry I didn't leave."

"It's a good thing you didn't. I never would have figured any of it out without your help. I wouldn't be here without you. I thought I could do it all by myself. What an idiot."

"Not an idiot." She kissed his cheek. "A little stubborn, a little too independent, but otherwise very smart."

He pressed his hand to her cheek. "Seriously, thank you. You saved my life."

"You saved mine too."

"But your life was only in danger because of me."

Brooklynn straightened and leaned back. "Listen, we're

done with that. If we're together..." She paused to give him the opportunity to explain that they weren't together. That this was a short-term thing. That he was leaving and wouldn't be coming back, *but gosh, it's been fun.*

She half-expected that. Maybe three-quarters expected it.

"Which we are," Forbes said. "Together," he added, in case she hadn't understood his meaning. "Aren't we?"

"Yes. And that means whatever we face, we face together. So there's no *I dragged you into it.* I wasn't dragged. I walked into it because...because that's what people who care about each other do."

He held her eye contact, then nodded. "You're right. That's what we do." Lifting his good arm, he said, "I need a little closer *together* with you."

She climbed onto the bed and snuggled beside him, settling exactly where she was meant to be.

CHAPTER FORTY-ONE

Forbes slept soundly with Brooklynn by his side, and not because of painkillers and sleep aids.

A nurse wrecked it when she ordered Brooklynn out of his bed so she could check his vitals.

His vitals were a lot better with Brooklynn cuddled beside him, but he figured the nurse didn't need to hear that.

He wanted nothing more than to drift off again after she left, but then the doctor came to tell him he'd be released later that day. He gave all sorts of instructions about antibiotics and treating the wound, followed by a long dissertation on the importance of rest.

As if he was about to run a marathon. All he wanted was to sleep.

Brooklynn made notes on her phone like there might be a test. He loved how seriously she took his health. He loved that concerned expression on her face as she asked questions he hadn't thought to ask.

As soon as the doctor left, the door opened again.

Why even bother to have a door with so many intrusions?

But he didn't complain when Rosie stepped in, Grandmother on her heels.

He pressed the button to sit up, staring at his sister. It'd been dark the night before, and he hadn't gotten a good look at her. Now, he drank her in, this sister he'd adored throughout his childhood.

She'd been eighteen the last time he saw her. Tall and skinny and mostly shapeless. She'd had shoulder-length, layered brown hair—a style from *Friends* that was so popular at the time—and apple cheekbones and a wide, inviting smile.

She looked different, of course. She was no longer skinny, though certainly not fat. She'd grown her hair longer and added reddish-blond highlights. She wore jeans and a T-shirt, a little makeup on those apple cheeks.

Her smile wasn't as wide or as inviting—as if something had dimmed it permanently—but it was there, aimed at him.

They'd been staring at each other for so long that it started to feel awkward.

He grinned. "Speaking of shooting bad guys, way to make an entrance."

"You know how I love the drama." She closed the distance and hugged him, holding on even tighter than he did.

His shoulder ached, but he didn't complain. How could he with his beloved sister back from the grave?

When she released him, she searched his face. "You're so handsome."

He laughed. "You have to say that. I'm your little brother." He felt his wide smile but couldn't seem to tame it. And didn't want to.

"Uh-uh. If you looked like an ogre, I'd tell you."

He tugged a lock of her strawberry-blonde hair. "It's different. I like it."

"Had to hide the gray."

How could she be old enough to have gray hair? How could she be here?

His questions must've shown in his expression because hers darkened. "It's a long story."

He made a show of glancing around the hospital room. His gaze caught on Grandmother, who didn't look away.

He wasn't sure how to feel about her now that he knew she'd been lying to him for years. He focused on Rosie again. "I have nowhere else to be."

Brooklynn stood from her chair. "I'll step outside."

"Stay." Realizing how like a command that sounded, he added, "Please?"

"I don't mind," Rosie said.

Grandmother shrugged. She looked tired this morning, or maybe *worried* was the right word.

"Okay, then." Brooklynn moved to the end of the bed. "Take my seat, Mrs. Ballentine."

"Thank you, dear." Grandmother rounded the bed and settled on the chair beside Forbes.

He fixed his attention to his sister, who perched on the edge of his bed and held his hand.

She took a deep breath and blew it out. "That terrible day, after I got you hidden in the cubby hole by the fireplace, I headed for my bedroom to hide behind my wardrobe. But Dad and the others were coming up the center stairs."

"How did you know they were bad?"

"I knew something was going on down at the dock. I'd asked Dad about it, and he told me to stay away. But I didn't. I watched. I couldn't imagine Dad was involved in anything illegal, so I couldn't reconcile what was happening. That day, I'd been looking out my window when I saw a couple of people drive up. I couldn't see their faces, but... I don't know. I had a feeling something bad was about to happen."

She'd known about the smuggling operation? She'd never said a word. Of course, he'd been eight—not exactly old enough to understand any of it.

"I was afraid they'd see me if I tried to get to my room, so I slipped into the hidden staircase. I listened through the cupboard door. There were so many voices. I decided I'd just hide until they were gone. I should have stayed there."

She should have. If she had, they'd have been together all these years. He couldn't help the harshness in his voice when he demanded, "Why didn't you?"

She didn't shrink from his anger, just lifted one shoulder and let it drop. "I heard the gunshots, and I...I panicked. I ran down the hall toward the door, just wanting out of the house. But the front was being guarded, and through the windows, I could see men in the backyard. There were so many people there, it was..." She took a breath and glanced around the room. "I haven't talked about it much. It feels weird to relive it after trying to forget for so many years."

Forbes understood that. He'd felt the same way when he'd told Brooklynn about that night.

"Where did you go?"

"The living room was empty, so I opened the hidden door and went to the basement. I didn't turn on the lights and sliced my hand on one of Dad's tools."

That explained the blood.

"I escaped out the side and into the woods. I made it to the cave."

"You hid there?"

"I should have, but I was afraid. I thought if I could get to the beach, I could climb the headland and run into town for help. But someone saw me."

Picturing what she described, his heart pounded as if Rosie

were in danger at that moment. "Were you hurt? Did they try to kill you?"

She shook her head and took another deep breath, as if it took courage to relate the story. Which he understood, except she was to the end of it now. What was so scary?

"I think...I realize in retrospect what happened, but I didn't know at the time. I swear I didn't have any idea."

"What are you talking about?"

"He let me go."

Forbes jerked, sending a shot of pain to his shoulder. "Who? Why?"

But even as he voiced the questions, he remembered. She'd had a new boyfriend, a secret older boyfriend.

"I didn't know." Tears filled her eyes, and she lowered her head, hiding her face with her hair. "I swear, Forbes, I didn't know."

Leo had cheated on his wife. He'd been in his mid-twenties. Married too young. Apparently, not ready to be tied down.

The rumors had been that he'd cheated with a younger woman.

"You were having an affair with Leo Taggart."

"I was so stupid. I knew he was married, but he said he wasn't happy, and their marriage wasn't going to last. He said he loved me."

Hot fury had Forbes's heart monitor beeping double-time.

Of course that snake had told Rosie he loved her.

Forbes was ready to hunt him down and kill him. Except...

"You shot him."

"Yes."

"Did you know it was him?"

"Back then? I had no idea. It's only in retrospect that I realize he's probably the one who let me go."

"But last night?"

"I saw him leaving the house, carrying a gas can. I didn't know who it was until the flames lit his face."

It was too much for Forbes to process. He couldn't imagine how she felt.

"I'm sorry you had to shoot him."

"I'm just sorry I didn't figure it out twenty-five years ago."

"Where did you go?"

"I called Gran." She smiled across his bed at their grandmother, who'd listened to the story with her eyes closed.

She didn't open them now.

"She was worried they'd come after me," Rosie said, "and worried that, if they did, they'd harm you. So she arranged for me to meet with a lawyer, who got me set up with a new identity. I moved south. With Gran's help, I got into Duke. Without you and Mom and Dad, I felt totally alone. But midway through my freshman year, I met a friend. She learned my parents had been killed. She and her family took me in and basically became my new family. I call her sister. I call them Mom and Dad. It's not the same, but it's family, you know?"

He nodded, though he didn't know. He'd only ever had Gran. "All these years, you never reached out to me."

Again, Rosie flicked a gaze to Grandmother. "She didn't think it would be safe."

The old woman didn't defend herself. She didn't say a word, though her shoulders shook.

He'd never seen Gran cry.

Brooklynn crouched beside her and wrapped her arm around her shoulders. She didn't say anything, just comforted her with her presence.

Forbes didn't know how to feel. Angry at Gran for lying to him for all those years—that was there.

But he was so grateful that Rosie was alive and well, and

that was because of Gran too. They'd come through it, and now they were together again.

"Tell me about this." Forbes gave his sister's left hand a pointed look, focused on the wedding ring.

She smiled. "His name is Steve. We have three kids. I can't wait for them to meet their Uncle Forbes."

Tears stung his eyes. He was an uncle? His sister was alive and married. If her smile was any indication, she was happy.

"But how were you there last night?"

"I installed my own cameras at the house years ago. Not inside but on the grounds. When I saw you there, I got close. I rented the house just to the north. I've been monitoring everything. Last night, I saw you two get back, and then cars parked on the street. I knew something was going on."

"Why didn't you call the police?"

"I did. I called the state police. They were already on their way."

"You knew Leo was involved."

"I didn't *know*. But...I always suspected. The older I got, the more convinced I became that somebody in authority had to have been in on it. How else could the smuggling have gone on as long as it did?"

She hadn't called the Shadow Cove Police for the same reason he and Brooklynn hadn't. Thank heavens for Jon... He couldn't even remember the man's last name, but his contact at the state police had shown up just in time.

One more reason for Forbes to thank Brooklynn.

From beside his grandmother, she watched him, her expression filled with concern.

He'd spent his entire life longing for justice, but he'd never thought about what life would look like on the other side. And even if he had, he would never in a million years have imagined this.

His sister and a woman he loved.

It was a better ending than any he could have conjured in his wildest dreams.

~

FORBES'S SISTER was telling him about her family when the door pushed open a second before a knock sounded on it.

"Can I come in?"

Forbes expected a nurse, but it was a woman dressed in a smart pantsuit who paused, waiting for an invitation.

She was vaguely familiar.

At his nod, she advanced, her gaze skimming the crowd before it landed on him. She held out her hand to shake. "Lori Putnam, state police. You were a little distracted last night."

His right arm was in a sling, so he grabbed her hand awkwardly with his left.

A man followed her. He had gray hair and, like Lori, wore a business suit. He nodded. "Simon Bergstrom, FBI. We need to ask you some questions." He addressed the others in the room. "You'll need to step out."

Forbes didn't want any of them to leave, but he didn't argue as Rosie, Brooklynn, and Grandmother made their way toward the door.

Grandmother held her back straight, though she didn't glance his way. Was she feeling ashamed for having lied to him all those years? Did she fear his anger?

As he watched her disappear, he tried to name how he felt about what she'd done. He'd been angry at first, but that hadn't lasted. At the moment, the dominant emotion was gratitude.

He was alive, as was Rosie. They'd both survived that terrible night and everything since then, largely because of his grandmother's actions. Did he wish he'd known about Rosie? Of course. But maybe, if they'd had contact sooner, Leo Taggart and his cohorts would have found them and killed them.

It seemed to take forever to relate the events of the previous night to the FBI agent and the police detective. The detective took copious notes. The FBI agent just watched.

Forbes went over all the details chronologically, sharing the facts as dispassionately as he could. When he was finished, they bombarded him with questions, which he answered carefully.

Finally, Putnam snapped her notebook closed. "What you've said lines up with what Ms. Wright and Mrs. Cartwell told us."

"Who's Mrs.—?"

"Your sister," Bergstrom supplied.

Rosie was married, so of course her name wasn't Ballentine anymore.

Bizarre that he hadn't even known her last name. Bizarre that she was still alive.

All this was going to take him a while to process.

"We have some information for you," Putnam said. "I'd rather tell you all at the same time. Shall I bring them back in?"

"Please."

Grandmother led the way. He wasn't sure what the ladies had said or done while he was being questioned, but she met his eyes squarely this time.

He smiled at her, reaching out with his good arm, and a little of the starch went out of her spine as she took his hand.

"I don't understand everything." He kept his words low, just for the woman who'd raised him. "But I know everything you did, you did to protect us. I love you for that."

"Well, of course." Though her words were strong, tears dripped from her eyes. She dabbed them with a tissue in her regal way.

Rosie stood next to Grandmother, and Brooklynn rounded

to the other side of the bed. All of them looked at the two cops who'd summoned them.

Putnam cleared her throat. "Here's what we know. As you two suggested"—she nodded to Forbes and Brooklynn—"we've pulled video footage from the cameras recording the happenings at the inlet on the Ballentine property. We're still putting all the pieces together, but one of the men we arrested last night..." She flipped back in her notebook. "Owen Stratton. He's been really chatty about everything going on. He'd been hired to haul boxes. Though nobody told him what was inside, he peeked once. Saw bags of pills. Fentanyl, probably. They've been pouring into the area, but we didn't know where they were coming from."

"He told you about his grandmother? Maury Stratton?" Forbes asked.

Putnam's eyes narrowed, and she looked at her notes again. "Not his grandmother. It was—"

"Lois Whitmore."

Forbes shot a look at Brooklynn. "Your friend? Your mentor? But...the break-in at her house."

"Was staged, or made up entirely, I assume." Brooklynn shrugged as if it didn't matter. "She would've shot me last night if not for your sister, who shot her first. I'd forgotten until you suggested Stratton could be a married name. I realized it could be Lois. I didn't believe it. I didn't want to believe it."

"I've still got some painkillers running through me," Forbes said. "Stratton was Maury's married name, right? I'm confused."

"Sorry, Whitmore is *Lois's* married name. Maury married Lois's brother, the one who moved them to North Carolina. Before she got married—"

"Oh. L.S." It was coming together now. "Lois *Stratton*."

Brooklynn nodded, and then Forbes realized what else she'd said. "Is she...? Did she survive?"

"She's in critical condition." Brooklynn swiped the sleeve of her sweatshirt beneath her eyes.

Somewhere along the way, she'd changed out of the old-lady jogging suit, though he didn't know when or how she'd gotten clothes.

"Even if she survives... She was going to shoot me. I'm thinking she's no longer my mentor."

He held out his hand for hers, then squeezed it. "I'm sorry."

"I'm glad I know who she really is." Brooklynn faced Putnam. "She got her nephew involved. Owen."

"Owen?" Forbes had heard the name earlier, but now it registered. "Your sister's boyfriend?"

"I haven't told Delaney yet."

"It's all over the internet." Rosie looked apologetic when she added, "Sorry to say, but she probably already knows."

"Right. I hate that. I'll call her when we're done here."

Putnam cleared her throat. "According to Owen, Lois Whitmore and Leo Taggart were in charge. Leo pulled Bryce over a few months back and found drugs in his car. Bryce was on probation and looking at jail time. Leo offered him a deal—he'd let him go if Bryce would come work for him. Bryce didn't think he could refuse. Not sure how Ned Salcito got involved."

Forbes looked from the detective to Brooklynn. "Ned?"

"Niles."

"Ah. Okay."

"There were more men last night, most of whom claim they were recruited for this one job. They didn't know what they were doing at the house. They're just local thugs who were looking to make some extra money."

"Do we know how they knew Brooklynn was at the house? Or did they plan to hit the house anyway, and it was just dumb luck?"

"Good question." Putnam smiled as if at a star student.

"The only things left in the truck were Brooklynn's backpack and a sack of clothes."

That explained how she'd changed, at least.

"We found a tracker in the backpack."

"What?" Brooklynn's eyes popped wide. "How did that happen?"

"Owen admitted he put it there when he saw you in the historical society. He was very chatty. And, honestly"—her lips slipped into a smirk—"filled with regret. He didn't ask for a lawyer or claim innocence, just told us everything. He swears he had no idea they were trying to kill you."

"He's the one who shot Forbes." Brooklynn bit her lip. "He could've shot me, though, and he didn't. He just ran."

Putnam made a note. "That's good to know. He claims he thought they just wanted to get your camera. He said he took the job Bryce offered so he could save money to buy his girlfriend an engagement ring."

Brooklynn cringed at that last bit. Thank heavens he'd been found out before he'd proposed to Delaney.

"He just happened to have a tracker on him?" Forbes asked.

"He said that Lois had given him one in case he ran into you."

"That's probably why he kept offering to help me," Brooklynn said.

"So you've figured out who was involved now, but all the evidence from back then..." Forbes already knew the answer but asked anyway. He needed to prove to Grandmother and Rosie—to himself once again—that Dad hadn't been a criminal. He'd been a confidential informant. "Any chance it was still in the back of my pickup?"

"Nope." Putnam didn't seem at all upset. "We assume it burned with the house."

So his house was destroyed. He'd known that, of course, but it still hurt to hear it.

Even worse, the evidence was gone.

"He doesn't know." Brooklynn spoke to the detective before turning to him. "First, the whole house didn't burn, just the main part. They were able to save most of the new wing and the garage."

That was something, at least. So many of the family's treasures had been moved to the garage, so at least those weren't lost. But the house his ancestor had built, where his parents had lived, was ruined.

Forbes allowed himself to taste that thought, to examine it. That house had been home to wonderful memories, but all of them were tainted by that last terrible day.

The evidence was all that mattered now.

Brooklynn smiled. "Before we left last night, while you were getting my things, I took photographs of all your dad's papers and all our notes. I emailed them to Putnam."

What was she saying? "The evidence was saved?"

Putnam was nodding. "The pictures of it. And we also got the ones Brooklynn took of the men at the inlet last week—which had been sent to the state police lab but were too corrupted to do anything with."

"Does that mean Nathan—?"

"He's in custody. He hasn't said a word, but he'll be charged." Lori stifled a yawn. "Sorry. It's been a long night. From what I saw, you two took good notes about what was on the cassette tapes."

Forbes hadn't taken any notes. That'd been all Brooklynn.

Putnam continued. "That'll give us a running start to nail down the rest of the people involved with your parents' murders. We'll do everything we can to match all those initials and names with people so they answer for what they did."

"It was Leo who shot them."

The woman patted the top of his foot, an awkward gesture at best. "We know. Leo and Lois were working together. Leo's dead, and if Lois survives, she'll face charges."

"Are all of those terrible people in custody now?" The question came from Grandmother, who hadn't spoken before this.

"Everyone we know of, yes ma'am."

She nodded, then backed up to sit in the chair as if the information was more than she could take.

Forbes understood how she felt.

The FBI agent, who'd been quiet since his introduction, cleared his throat. "I have some information I think will be a comfort to you."

All eyes turned to him.

"Charles Ballentine was informing for the FBI. That summer, twenty-five years ago, another agent in the Boston field office was diagnosed with a very aggressive form of cancer. He passed less than six months after his diagnosis. I took over all his cases. There was one I never did understand. We think he was working on it off book, maybe something he planned to take to the higher-ups when he'd proved something. I had a note in the system for years"—he nodded to Brooklynn—"all those initials you wrote down. The information you provided matched what this agent had in the file. The whole thing just slipped through the cracks."

Forbes absorbed that.

Brooklynn had been right.

Dad hadn't been a criminal. Forbes had never understood how his good and decent father could've done something like be involved in smuggling, but the evidence had seemed concrete.

Only because Forbes hadn't had all of it.

Rosie squeezed his hand, tears dripping from her eyes. "I didn't... I didn't know."

He sniffed back a fresh wave of emotion. "Me, either, sis. But it makes sense. Dad would never—"

"But why would he even inform for the FBI?" she snapped. "Why get involved at all?"

"According to the file," Bergstrom said, "they didn't give him any choice. They threatened his family if he reported what they were doing. He felt trapped and thought his only chance to get out was to inform."

Grandmother stood, the motion taking more effort than it ought. "They should have gone in and arrested everyone immediately. They shouldn't have put my son and his family in danger like that."

"You're right." The agent's expression was grim. "I agree entirely."

Gran didn't seem to know what to say to that, just mumbling a "Hmph."

Whatever that FBI agent had been thinking, whatever Dad had been thinking, what happened had happened. Their family had been ripped apart that night.

But as Forbes glanced at the people surrounding his hospital bed, he realized God was putting it back together. Not just Rosie and Grandmother, but now there were Rosie's husband and children, and her husband's family, and the family that had taken her in, all part of the circle.

And Brooklynn, who smiled at him.

He wasn't sure what would happen next. He'd spent his entire life hiding his identity, something he no longer needed to do.

Now, he could be himself. Forbes Ballentine. And he had a real family.

He hardly remembered what that felt like, but he was eager to find out.

CHAPTER FORTY-TWO

Two weeks had passed since that terrible night. As Brooklynn looked out over the cove where her life had nearly ended, she still struggled to make sense of it.

A hundred feet below, waves crashed over the small, pebbly beach and against the granite headlands, as they had since the beginning of time. But the land didn't give way to the powerful sea.

It was strong, sort of like the man who'd seemed so terrifying to Brooklynn at first. Now she knew him, the man she'd come to love. Maybe it was new and fresh and untested—though, the *untested* part didn't feel true, all things considered—but what she had with Forbes felt real and solid.

After he'd been released from the hospital, he'd taken a hotel room in town, where he could be close to his grandmother at the retirement home in Portland, and to Brooklynn. He'd shed his alias and was in the process of taking his real name back legally.

Some of the townspeople acted as if he was some sort of celebrity. Brooklynn had seen more bootlicking in the last two weeks than in her entire life—and that was saying something, considering how wealthy and powerful her own father was.

Forbes Ballentine, aside from being a famous, reclusive billionaire, was a local legend, especially now that the news was out that he'd been at the house when his family died. If anything, Forbes was embarrassed by all the attention.

It was strange what people regarded as important.

To her, he was just Forbes. The man who'd saved her life, over and over.

His shadow in the evening sun announced his approach an instant before his arm slid around her waist.

She looked up at him, studying his face. He looked... pensive. "You okay?"

He nodded, then shrugged. "I'm sad about the house. But also...I don't think I could've kept it. I did, all these years, because I believed it held secrets. Now those secrets are out, and what remained were just...memories."

"Some good memories."

"Some. But the bad memories tainted the good. All of them are stored here." He tapped the side of his head. "I don't need the house to remind me who they were, how much they loved me."

Brooklynn leaned in to him. "Will you sell it?"

"I don't know. Maybe. Or maybe I'll rebuild."

That had her turning to face him. "Here? But you live in Boston."

"*Ford* lived in Boston. *Forbes* is from Maine." He squeezed her closer. "Forbes has a really pretty girlfriend in Shadow Cove. He'd be an idiot to leave her."

Brooklynn's heart did a little jig.

For two weeks, she'd dreaded the moment when he announced he was going home. She figured they'd try long-distance dating, and if it worked, she'd have to move away from her life, her gallery, her beloved town to be near him.

She would have done that, for Forbes.

It seemed he'd do the same for her.

His eyebrows hiked. "You seem surprised."

"I just thought... You have this whole big...enterprise."

"I've run it via conference call for years. Why change that now?"

"I guess because you can."

"Boston isn't that far. If the drive is too long, I'll rent a jet."

"I have a cousin who can help you with that."

His brows lowered, though a smile played at his lips. "I need to meet these cousins of yours."

"You'll like them. And they'll like you."

Forbes had met her parents and sisters, who'd converged the day after the big showdown. Even Kenzie had come up from South Carolina. They'd all been eager to get to know Forbes, and not because he was rich or famous but because they knew he mattered to Brooklynn.

Only Delaney had been reticent with him, even quieter than usual. Brooklynn worried about her second-youngest sister, who seemed to believe that Owen's part in the whole ordeal had somehow been her fault. Delaney had always taken everything to heart, feeling things more deeply than the rest of them.

Brooklynn would keep praying for her.

It was hard for Brooklynn to be sad for Delaney when she was so happy for herself.

"You're okay with it," Forbes asked, "if I stick around?"

She felt a silly grin. "I'm better than okay with it. If you rebuild, can I help design and decorate? It'll give me something to do when I lose my gallery."

"Lose it? Why would you?"

"Oh, you know. It's hard to keep the lights on. But maybe I'll win that contest. The prize money would help."

He laughed. A full-throated, head-back, out-loud laugh.

"What?" She couldn't help joining him, even if she wasn't in on the joke.

"My love," he finally said, "I'm pretty sure we can keep the lights on."

"Oh, but I wouldn't ask you—"

"I know. You didn't." He kissed her on the forehead. "I'm offering. And if you don't accept my help, then I guess you're a little more like me than you thought, hmm?"

"But it's not... I wouldn't want to take your money."

"Why not? I thought you said we were in this together."

"Well, yes, but—"

"Then it's settled." He nodded as if there were nothing else to discuss. Not that she wanted to take Forbes's money, but it was nice to know there was a safety net, if she needed one. And this from a man who respected her, who would share his wealth not out of obligation but out of love.

Forbes flicked his gaze to the burned-out ruins of his family home. "Maybe...maybe I can turn what was horrible into something beautiful."

"It is a lovely spot."

"Whether I do or I don't"—he looked down at Brooklynn—"as long as you're in my life, I'm up for anything."

She tried to come up with some pithy response, but then his lips were on hers, and all rational thought fled.

She had no idea what the future held, but with this man, it would be a beautiful picture.

The End...

FOR NOW, but don't miss the Capturing You Bonus Epilogue, a little glimpse into what happens next for Brooklynn and Forbes. Grab your copy at https://www.subscribepage.com/capturing-you-bonus-epilogue. If you have trouble downloading it, email me at robin@robinpatchen.com, and I'll see if I can help.

~

IF YOU LIKED Forbes and Brooklynn's story, you're going to love Cici and Asher's. While working as a jewelry appraiser, Cici discovers a priceless ruby necklace linked to the murders of Forbes's parents a generation before. Before she can raise the alarm, armed men enter the store where she's working and murder the proprietor. With no choice, Cici grabs the necklace and goes on the run.

Enter bodyguard Asher Rhodes, who's tasked with protecting Cici on her journey back to Maine. Together, they find themselves in a deadly game of cat-and-mouse, protecting the necklace—and each other—from murderers determined to keep them from reaching safety.

Turn the page for a sneak peek of *Defending You*. Keep in mind, this story is still being written, and this chapter hasn't been edited.

~

DON'T WANT TO WAIT? Check out *Vanished in the Darkness*, (previously titled *Glimmer in the Darkness*) book one in the Coventry Saga. This story features a kidnapped little girl, an unsolved mystery, and a second-chance romance. With 2,500 reviews and ratings on Amazon—and 4.6-stars!—readers are loving it.

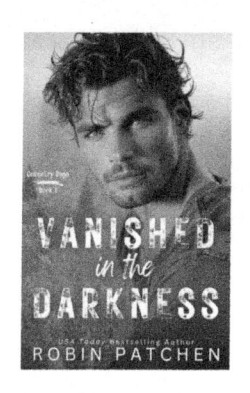

WANT A FREE BOOK? Check out *Escaping with You*, a Wright Heroes of Maine prequel. When Darcy and her aunt are shot at, Logan steps in to save their lives. They escape into the Maine woods to elude the shooter and reach safety. Download it at https://robinpatchen.com/subscribe/.

Now, turn the page for more about *Defending You*.

DEFENDING YOU: COMING THIS FALL.

She stumbled onto a deadly secret. The man she once wronged is the only one who can keep her alive.

Cecilia "Cici" Wright has built a life she loves as a jewelry appraiser. But when her latest find—a priceless ruby necklace—links to decades-old murders in her hometown of Shadow Cove, Cici becomes the target of ruthless killers. Forced to flee for her life, she must rely on the man she humiliated in the most shameful moment of her life.

Asher Rhodes puts his Navy SEAL training to good use as a bodyguard for high-paying clients. Keeping his emotions locked away is the secret to his strength. But Cici Wright isn't just a client—she's the girl who scorned him, the last woman in the world he ever wanted to see again. Having her close churns up all the reasons he once loved her. Protecting her means facing not just the killers chasing them but the wounds she left behind.

Cici and Asher find themselves in a deadly game of cat and mouse, where trust is their only weapon and attraction their greatest vulnerability. With time running out, they must overcome their painful history and work together to defeat their enemies—before it's too late.

Don't miss *Defending You*, book 7 in Robin Patchen's Wright Heroes of Maine series. Packed with heart-pounding suspense, sizzling romance, and unforgettable characters, you won't be able to put this one down.

NOTE TO READER

I love driving up the coastline in my native New Hampshire. Between Hampton and Portland are a number of beautiful homes overlooking the sea. Though none are high on cliffs like the one in this story, many are as grand as the Ballentine Mansion. I've always wondered about the people who built those homes and those who live there now. Those wonderings became a tiny seed that grew into the setting for this story.

One note: Although the Montreal Mafia is real, the Bazzini family is completely fabricated. Also, very few drugs actually come over the northern border into the US, and most of those that do are carried across the border, not smuggled in by boat.

But it's sure fun to consider how it could work.

ACKNOWLEDGMENTS

After thirtyish books, I'm still amazed when the tiny seed of an idea turns into a full-length story. I couldn't make it happen on my own. In fact, without friends on this journey, I'd have quit a long time ago.

My gratitude to my brainstorming and writing friends, Misty Beller, Lacy Williams, Susan May Warren, Hallee Bridgeman, Sharon Srock, and Tracy Higley. Thank you for your help fleshing out this story idea.

Also, thank you to Ray Rhamey for your wonderful developmental editing, Lesley MacDonald for your crazy copyediting skills, and Sara Jo Odom (whom I like to call *Mom*) for proofreading.

Thank you to my husband, Eddie, my partner in this amazing writing and publishing adventure—and everything else. I love doing life with you.

Finally, of course, thank you to my Lord and Savior, Jesus Christ. Without You, none of this would matter at all. You are the strength of my heart and my portion forever.

ALSO BY ROBIN PATCHEN

The Wright Heroes of Maine

Running to You

Rescuing You

Finding You

Sheltering You

Protecting You

Capturing You

Defending You

Fighting for You

The Coventry Saga

Vanished in the Darkness

Redemption for Ransom

Betrayal of Genius

Traces of Virtue

Touch of Innocence

Inheritance of Secrets

Lineage of Corruption

Wreathed in Disgrace

Courage in the Shadows

Vengeance in the Mist

A Mountain Too Steep

The Nutfield Saga

Convenient Lies

Twisted Lies

Generous Lies

Innocent Lies

Beautiful Lies

Legacy Rejected

Legacy Restored

Legacy Reclaimed

Legacy Redeemed

Christmas in Nutfield

Amanda Series

Chasing Amanda

Finding Amanda

Nutfield Saga Boxsets

Nutfield Saga Books 1-3

Nutfield Saga Books 4-6

Nutfield Saga Books 7-9

Coventry Saga Boxsets

Coventry Saga Books 1-3

Coventry Saga books 4-7

Coventry Saga books 8-11

ABOUT ROBIN PATCHEN

Robin Patchen is a *USA Today* bestselling and award-winning author of Christian romantic suspense. She grew up in a small town in New Hampshire, the setting of her Coventry Saga books, and then headed to Boston to earn a journalism degree. After college, working in marketing and public relations, she discovered how much she loathed the nine-to-five ball and chain. She started writing her first novel while she homeschooled her three children. The novel was dreadful, but her passion for storytelling didn't wane. Thankfully, as her children grew, so did her skill. Now that her kids are adults, she has more time to play with the lives of fictional heroes and heroines, wreaking havoc and working magic to give her characters happy endings. When she's not writing, she's editing or reading, proving that most of her life revolves around the twenty-six letters of the alphabet.

Made in the USA
Monee, IL
10 July 2025